The Polarian-Denebian War
War
(Volume 1)

The Polarian-Denebian War

(Volume 1)

The Time Spiral
Operation Aphrodite
The Man from Outer Space

by
Jimmy Guieu

translated by
Michael Shreve

Preface by
Richard D. Nolane

A Black Coat Press Book

ISBN 978-1-61227-516-1. First Printing. July 2016. Published by Black Coat Press, an imprint of Hollywood Comics.com, LLC, P.O. Box 17270, Encino, CA 91416.

TABLE OF CONTENTS

JIMMY GUIEU
la Spirale du temps
ANTICIPATION
Editions
"Fleuve Noir"

Introduction

Henri René "Jimmy" Guieu (1926-2000) made his literary debut in 1952 with his novel *Le Pionnier de l'Atome* [The Pioneer of the Atom], No.5 in the newly-launched *Anticipation* imprint of Editions Fleuve Noir.[1]

Guieu quickly became conspicuous among his generation of new writers of popular SF who began publishing in the 1950s, because his readership reached beyond the confines of the genre.

This happened because Guieu was primarily a man fascinated by all the mysteries of the universe, the paranormal and, especially, "flying saucers." While he averaged four novels a year for *Anticipation*, Guieu also became one of the most notorious pioneers of Ufology in France. His first book on the subject, *Les Soucoupes volantes viennent d'un autre monde* [The Flying Saucers come from Another World] as published with considerable success in 1954, and was soon followed by a "sequel," *Black-out sur les Soucoupes Volantes* [The Flying Saucer Black-out] in 1956.

From the very beginning, therefore, Guieu's two careers intermingled and cohabitated side by side, one feeding the other and vice versa: the "mystery hunter" nourishing the speculations of the SF writer. Thus, right from the start, Guieu struck a very different note in the universe of SF, which he hardly knew, admitting once that he rarely read any genre novels. His contacts with the SF community always remained

---

[1] Black Coat Press has previously discussed Editions Fleuve Noir in its translations of other Fleuve Noir authors such as G.-J. Arnaud, Richard Bessière, André Caroff, P.-J. Herault, Gérard Klein, Maurice Limat, Pierre Pelot and Kurt Steiner. Fleuve Noir, one of the leading publishers of French SF and horror, published over 2000 titles until the 1990s.

virtually non-existent, except with a few other authors of the *Anticipation* imprint who shared his interests in the paranormal and UFOs. For Guieu, SF was "a pretext, an excuse, the sugar pill that makes the medicine palatable." Indeed, he became convinced that the premises of his novels were more or less "suggested" to him by forces from beyond and that his own imagination did not explain everything that found its way into his novels...

There is no doubt that Guieu's SF oeuvre served primarily to promote his ideas about UFOs and other paranormal phenomenon. It is enough to read them in the order in which they were released to see that they soon ceased to be mere SF adventure stories, but reflected their author's concerns. The best illustration of this is the appearance of the character of Jean Kariven in 1953.

This source of inspiration permeated most of Guieu's 100 SF novels, even occasionally finding its way into his pure space opera novels, such as the Blade & Baker series. It is therefore not surprising that Gilles Novak, his signature character, created in 1967 in the novel *Le Retour des Dieux* [Return of the Gods], and whose adventures he chronicled for over twenty years, was himself an investigator of the paranormal, a precursor to *The X-Files'* Fox Mulder. Indeed, Guieu's last great commercial success were two semifictionalized volumes exposing the "truth" behind an alleged "conspiracy" between the US government and aliens: *E.B.E. 1: Alerte rouge* [*Extraterrestrial Biological Entity 1: Red Alert*] (1990) and *E.B.E. 2: L'entité noire d'Andamooka* [*EBE2: The Dark Entity from Andamooka*] (1991).

Beginning in 1979, Guieu had his own paperback imprint which reprinted all his novels, often in revised and updated editions, and that continued for several years after his death as a licensed operation, for which other writers (such as noted French SF authors Roland C. Wagner), continued to pen new stories featuring Gilles Novak and Blade & Baker under the housename "Jimmy Guieu."

8

Surprisingly, compared to the volume of his SF production, Guieu's actual number of non-fiction books is rather small. His first two books on flying saucers had made him a pioneer in the field in France; yet he never seized the opportunity to further mine this rich vein and ignored the booming demand for such works in the 1990s. He did, however, produce a series of documentaries on videocassettes during that period.

Forty of Guieu's books were translated into English, Spanish, Greek, German, Dutch, Portuguese (both Portugal and Brazil), Romanian and Italian, and several were adapted into comics and radio serials. His main best-seller abroad remained *The Flying Saucers Come from Another World* which was published in a hardcover edition in 1956 in England.

Apart from his literary activities, Guieu was a busy public speaker much in demand in France and, occasionally, abroad. He often appeared on television in the late 80s. He had a long-standing column on UFOs syndicated in several daily newspapers in the 50s and produced several radio broadcasts and, as we have seen, video documentaries.

Seen from a strictly SF-centric perspective, Jimmy Guieu was a very atypical author of popular novels; his books have understandably aged—as exemplified by the novels translated here, originally published in the 1950s—but they have retained a nostalgic charm coupled with a unique and singular voice.

Guieu succeeded commercially because his single-minded focus on UFOs and the paranormal enabled him to gain an audience outside the traditional SF niche market, and thus outlast many of his colleagues. At the time of his death, he was one of the best-selling SF writers in France, and his name had become a successful "brand."

However, his adhesion in the late 80s to far-fetched conspiracies about aliens colluding with the American government hurt his reputation, even in the UFO community. It was as if he was at long last relieved to have found an answer to a question that had puzzled him all his life.

Despite believing in the "duplicity" of the US authorities, Guieu never lost his affection for the American people; he had rubbed shoulders with their soldiers sat the time of the liberation of France at the end of World War II when he, himself, had been a young member of the French Resistance in Western France, and never forgot that debt.

It is a safe bet that Guieu would be thrilled to see published today, for the first time in the US, this selection of the early adventures of Jean Kariven, the character who launched his career...

Richard D. Nolane

THE TIME SPIRAL

The connection of Australia with the Indian Peninsula, Madagascar and Africa (the ancient continent of Gondwana) existed, according to most of the respected authors, from the Cambrian Period until the start of the Jurassic Period, when it would have disappeared... The ancient land-bridge between Madagascar and the Deccan (Lemuria) would have disappeared even later, for instance toward the end of the Cretaceous and the beginning of the Tertiary.

-- A. Wegener
Die Entstehung der Kontinente und Ozeane
(The Origin of Continents and Oceans, 1915)

But there are a number of circumstances (especially chronological facts) that suggest that the primeval home of man was a continent now sunk below the surface of the Indian Ocean.

-- Ernst Haeckel,
Natürliche Schöpfungsgeschichte
(The History of Creation, 1868)

CHAPTER ONE

For the *umpteenth* time the dark red Willys-Overland jeep[2] of Professor Red Harrington was stopped by an MP roadblock. Coming out of the small town of Indian Springs on Highway 95 crossing Nevada, a group of six MPs armed with Thompson machine guns checked the few vehicles driving in the area.

Professor Harrington, being used to this kind of formality, took out his pass. The sergeant of the Military Police leaned casually on the door and read the information. He glanced at the photo, looked at the driver and gave him back the document.

The man accompanying Professor Harrington also handed him his pass. When he was satisfied the sergeant stepped away, gave them a little salute and ordered the sentinels to raise the barrier. The car started up and sped off westward.

Professor Harrington at the wheel of his powerful "Canadian" was a man in his fifties. His pearl gray, gabardine suit and colorful tie might have looked a little "showy" at the Academy of Sciences in Paris but in the USA the scientists and engineers are not bothered by useless and outdated prejudices in matters of clothing. With his slightly wavy, graying hair and his rectangular glasses he looked more like a businessman than a scientist.

A distinguished mathematician occupying the chair of applied physics at Caltech[3], Professor Red Harrington was going to the experimental Polygon located "somewhere" in the Nevada desert. His passenger, Jean Kariven, a French paleoan-

---

[2] A big model with a sedan body, like the mixed "Canadian" Jeep. (Author's Note)

[3] California Institute of Technology, the famous American research center. (Author's Note)

thropologist renowned for his various scientific works, was getting impatient to arrive at their destination.

Around 30 years old, tall, brown-haired, looking a little like Clark Gable with his thin black mustache, Dr. Jean Kariven was on academic leave at Caltech. His old friend Professor Harrington had asked him to join in on a rather unusual and top-secret undertaking. In two hours they were going to participate in the strangest experiment ever attempted by man.

The Jeep left the highway. In the blazing sun it veered off to the right and took a side road reserved exclusively for vehicles from the army and the Experimental Center of Las Vegas, which specialized in "special machines," meaning rockets.

The uniformity of the ochre sand stretched out as far as the eye could see. A few Yuccas and other cactus rose up periodically along the chaotic route.

The Willys Overland finally arrived in front of a concrete building, the first outpost of the experimental territory.

Through a narrow, horizontal slot the barrel of a machine gun pointed at the Jeep. The MPs, streaming with sweat, once again went through the process of checking the passengers. Satisfied with the scientists' identification the guard let them through. The barrel of the machine gun went back to watching the long stretch of road.

Soon the massive buildings of the Nevada Center appeared. In the distance stood the polygons of the super-rocket launches with different components. A huge metal hangar, 165 feet high and 300 feet long glimmered in the sun over four miles beyond the observation bunkers.

The car stopped in front of a concrete, rectangular building with bay windows made of quartz. Professor Harrington and Kariven were greeted by Kurt Streiler, a young Austrian scientist, the great specialist of rockets, who in 1938 had fled his country to escape the Nazis. Standing well above average height, his hair cut short, with steel blue eyes, Streiler smiled kindly when he shook the newcomers' hands. Although he spoke very good English, he still had a slight guttural accent, the remains of his native tongue.

While talking about their latest work Professor Harrington and Streiler headed toward the end of the building. Kariven, pretty much a stranger to rocket science and other so-called special machines, followed the two men pensively. Without doubting his friend's good intentions Kariven was still hesitant to accept the whole truth of Harrington's revelations.

Streiler went first into the small room. In the middle stood a metal cage where four rhesus monkeys were continually screaming and jumping from one wall to another. When the scientists entered they stopped their bedlam for an instant to clutch the bars and stare at their visitors. Their tiny eyes contemplated them curiously. One of the monkeys was carefully chewing a spider, spitting out of the hard pieces with great dignity.

"You can see, Professor," Streiler began by addressing Harrington, "these monkeys are in perfect health. They came back the day before yesterday from the experimental voyage and show no negative effects from it. Their electrocardiogram, their reflexes and the control of their vital organs were meticulously studied during the trip, which unquestionable proves that nothing stands in the way of putting us in their place."

At these words Kariven batted an eye. "Do you mean, Dr. Streiler, that humans, without any other preliminary experiments, are going to be able to try this... this journey?"

"This very day, Dr. Kariven. Are you still dubious?"

"I don't want to hide anything, so... yes," the young French scientist admitted. "If you and my friend Harrington think that it's possible, I'll agree to follow you. But I'll be skeptical... until I get more information. The positive reactions of the rhesus monkeys might predict the same for a man, I don't deny. All the same, are you sure that the rocket, the Retro-Timeship, as you call it, really went where you think it did?"

Streiler and Harrington smiled at each other. "But of course, Kariven," Harrington stated. "Otherwise I wouldn't have dragged you away from your Parisian lab."

They left the monkeys to their peanuts and acrobats to enter a huge laboratory equipped with countless machines of strange form and function. On a big, black, plastic board in the middle of all the control panels, all the signal lights, buttons and calibrated knobs, was placed an iridescent screen, two by three feet large.

"You can judge for yourself, Kariven, and then decide whether you'll follow us or sit calmly in *our time*."

Streiler pressed a button. The screen lit up, blinking. The Austrian engineer slowly turned one of the calibrated knobs, all the while keeping an eye on a needle fluttering in a lighted dial. The screen turned dark bluish, then showed the night sky where silvery constellations slowly took shape. In the lower left corner appeared a small, yellow disk, very bright, surrounded by nine, shining points that moved in circles or ellipses around it. The yellow disk and the points of light drifted in a spiral toward the upper right of the screen where a stationary point gleamed.

"This is an animated montage of the solar system moving toward the Apex, meaning the zone of space toward which the sun is heading. In other words, towards the star Vega in the Lyra constellation[4]. This spiral traced on the screen, remaining there in dots, is the route taken by the sun towards Vega at 12 miles per second. Naturally, the sun drags its nine main planets with it, including ours. With respect to the present position

---

[4] This point in space is imaginary. When the sun and its planets have reached the *present* area of Vega, this star will also have moved and be shining in another area of space just as far away. The *Apex* will remain; it is only a direction, a point that a new star will occupy later. The direction diametrically opposed to the *Apex* (called the Antopex) is a "point" next to the stars Phact and Markeb in the Columba constellation. (Author's Note)

of the Earth, the region of space where the solar system is heading is *theoretically in the future*. The sun's course, therefore, tends to the future. But the dots that you see here, falling diagonally into the bottom left corner of the screen, trace a spiral path that is *theoretically in the past*.

"Let's follow the reasoning because for the moment this is just a purely imaginary representation. If we admit that light conveys the images of events that happen at any given moment on Earth, we can infer from this that these images are escaping into space at the speed of light while the Earth continues its route in the opposite direction, dragged away by the sun toward Vega. By 'recapturing' these escaped images we will be watching a film where the visually perceptible sequences would be reversed, the latest past events becoming the first seen as we pass through the vision of this 'film'. Because it would only be a *vision,* just *images* of an episode of the past brought back to life, in a way, but it would have no material support; it wouldn't be showing a concrete reality.

"But let's forget about these mental pictures and face the reality of today. Thanks to the Retro-Timeship that Professor Harrington and I have perfected, we are now able to 'enter' directly into the past! Keep in mind that it's not just to see images but to really live in the materialized past. In other words, we managed to build and test—with the monkeys so far—a machine *capable of traveling into the past.* After months of laborious work we've ended up formulating a provisional theory in which the past time of our planet would follow a huge spiral around itself. We call this hypothesis— *The Time Spiral*. But, I repeat, it's all still only a theory. The researchers who will come after us will put the finishing touches to what is today just a practical hypothesis to summarize a rather complex phenomenon.

"Our ship moves in Space-Time or the Fourth Dimension, at speeds of variable *temporal regression*, all the while keeping its ability to stop at a determined point on the Time Spiral. During these stops we will do research and exploration. And that, Dr. Kariven, is where you come in. The voyage into the distant past of the Earth is going to allow you to verify your theories on the origin of mankind. In spite of your skepticism, will you go with us?"

"Without a second thought!" Kariven declared enthusiastically.

"Bravo!" Professor Harrington rejoiced. "This project plans to 'integrate' us into an era of the past with a reasonable amount of danger. However, we've got an ace up our sleeve. Ideally we would be able to become invisible to move around without problems in the midst of events or among 'people' who might be dangerous. Unfortunately it is absolutely impossible because an invisible man *would necessarily be blind*. The sensing tissues of his eyes would become incapable of absorbing light to transform into sight. The eye has a kind of 'black box' that light rays cross through to be impressed on the retina and that is necessary for the physical mechanism of vision. In an invisible body, purely imaginary of course, this black box would cease to exist and therefore undeniable blindness. An invisible man is just a myth, an entertaining, literary fiction. But if we can't be invisible, at least we can make ourselves partially transparent."

"You're joking," Kariven was stunned by his statement.

Professor Harrington smiled as he turned to the Austrian engineer. "Kurt, you want to show the 'guinea pig' to our friend?"

Streiler nodded with an amused smile on his face and went to open a door with three bolt locks. He cracked it open, leaned through the doorway, made a sign to the locked up guinea pig and then stepped back, throwing the door open all the way.

Kariven shuddered and blinked his eyes several times. Never in his life had he seen such a paradoxical, unsettling "thing."

"This is Bob, our human guinea pig. A volunteer, of course."

In the doorway, casually leaning against the frame, stood a man with a *transparent body*. He was wearing only briefs of some clear gray plastic material. His skeleton was a little more noticeable as a slightly darker shadow in the mass of glassy tissue.

It was necessary to look straight at him to see him. Looking a little to the right or left he disappeared into a hazy, vaporous shape. Only his blue eyes were clearly visible because the transparent serum had no effect on them. The faint cloudiness of his inner organs could barely be seen.

"So, Dr. Kariven, what do you say?" Streiler laughed at his flabbergasted stare. "This GI who accepted the experiment enthusiastically got the shots of transparency as well as those that protect his visual organs. The operation is absolutely painless and safe. The effect of this serum, depending on the dose, varies between one, five and ten hours. Prolonging it beyond ten hours presents certain drawbacks that we still haven't been able to eliminate."

"But how... how is this possible?"

"You've no doubt heard of Dr. Vasiliev?"

"Of course. The physiologist who ran around Russia during that last war in an exhibit car with a horse made somewhat transparent and two or three human corpses you could see through to the ravages of alcoholism[5]."

"Exactly. Our biologists took up the Russian scientist's work and created a serum that makes all the tissues of the human body transparent. The effect of one shot takes 30 or 40 minutes to manifest and depending on the dose it lasts between one and ten hours. The serum gives the body such a weak refraction index that you'd really have to know that a

---

[5] Absolutely correct. Dr. Vasiliev, the Russian physiologist, had got encouraging results on the transparency of bodies (animals and men), bathed in a special liquid. His recent death put an end to his experiments. Similar work is being today in various laboratories in France and abroad. (Author's Note) This refers to L.L. Vasiliev (1891-1966), parapsychologist and professor of physiology at the University of Leningrad, who also conducted dubious experiments in telepathy.

transparent man is in such or such a place to see him in full daylight. At night, in the shadows, he's practically invisible. Of course he has to be naked, or almost, to become transparent because even though we can treat the body effectively, the same can't be said for clothes. If you're wearing pants, shirt, shoes and a hat you'd look like a carnival freak and everybody would stare at you."

Streiler gave the human "guinea pig" a friendly pat on the shoulder and told him, "A little more patience, Bob. In one and half hours you'll be back to normal and you can go on leave. For a harmless experiment that lasts five hours you'll get 15 days leave. Gotta admit that it's worth playing the guinea pig!"

The man lit a Lucky Strike and laughed softly. Then he went back into the room where he lay down on a bunk and started thumbing through a magazine. The smoke that he blew out was enough to sometimes mask his entire body.

"Now we're not talking theory anymore but practical application," Streiler declared. "Departure in two hours. I have to check the insides of the ship and the set-up, the food reserves and the nuclear fuel before... lifting anchor," he ended with a laugh.

The sliding doors of the giant hangar opened as the Willys Overland Jeep that Kariven, Harrington and Streiler had taken went to park in a corner of the vast building. The three scientists talked for a minute with the few official personnel who had come to watch this memorable event that was carefully kept secret.

The Retro-Timeship, a kind of metal cigar, 75 yards long by 25 in its widest diameter, stood in the middle of the hangar. Metalo-plastex portholes ran along its armored hull that could withstand the highest temperatures. A long radar pole stuck out from its "nose" in the middle of the cockpit, also in clear metalo-plastex.

A line of remote-controlled carts was transporting the crates of supplies and material that automatic lifters raised into the holds where uniformed men duly piled them up.

On the side of the machine was an oval hatchway where a man in a US Army uniform stood. On the lapel of his officer's jacket was pinned the sign for *Special Services*: two gold arrows crossed. Over his left breast pocket the blue Wings on a shield under a five-pointed star designating his rank of Command Pilot. This officer of the Air Transport Command, Commander Mark Taylor, along with his team, was going to participate in the expedition into the Time Spiral.

The venture was under the aegis of the American government. There was no way for a private company to build such a ship or pay the enormous amounts for years of research to develop it. A group of financial backers would probably not be interested in "traveling into the past" but the government saw the problem in a different light. It was not without good reason nor without specific expectations that it had subsidized the research at the Nevada Center for this incredible project carried out in absolute secrecy. The future and the peace of the world might depend on it someday.

Commander Taylor gave a friendly salute to the newcomers. "Everything's ready, Dr. Streiler. My men have brought in the bags of Professor Harrington and Dr. Kariven. Yours have been here since this morning. The crew is at their posts."

"OK, Mark! Let's climb on board," Streiler announced as he stepped onto the telescopic stairs leading up to the hatchway.

Kariven walked around with a fascinated look in his eyes. He was in a metal corridor on the lower deck. Huge rivets held the plates of the double-layered inner hull. A luminescent tube ran along the ceiling sprinkling the corridor with bright light.

They followed Commander Taylor to the cockpit, which also served as the observation post. In front of the dome lit up by electroluminescence with a soft, blue light, the control panel console glimmered from all its dials and luminous buttons. To the right of the pilot's chair had been added another control panel, smaller but complex enough to activate the "time retrograde" device: a kind of temporal accelerator.

Two seats for the observers were lined up on either side of the pilot. Streiler sat to the left of the commander while Harrington and Kariven took their places to the right.

Standing in front of the control panel, Commander Taylor made a sign with his hand to the mechanics on the ground. A powerful tractor came slowly out of the ship, which rolled on its four-train, detachable landing gear until it was 100 yards from the hangar. The tractor stopped. Its driver jumped to the ground and waved his arms over his head.

All the technicians, researchers and the "officials"—namely two high-ranking officers from the Pentagon—gathered in front of the hangar and watched with some nervousness as the giant cigar prepared for its flight.

The Commander answered the signal and activated a breaker with his right hand while his left worked the control of the anti-gravitational repeller. A faint rumbling filled the room and the metallic monster rose up slowly, leaving the tow-train on the ground.

Everyone gradually tensed up for the take off. The Retro-Timeship sped up its vertical ascent... then it disappeared from sight, vanishing like a puff of smoke being blown away by the wind.

"We've entered the Time Spiral!" Streiler announced, so full of emotion that his voice was flat.

Indeed, Commander Taylor had just activated the *retrograde system* and was carefully watching a big, light blue screen on his console where three needles were quivering over different colored and calibrated triangles. The officer turned on the automatic pilot and waited...

Suddenly a red light blinked on the top of the screen. The needles came to a stop, one over another. Right away a weird, dusky light filtered through the cockpit and the portholes of the extraordinary vehicle.

Kariven, Streiler and Harrington struggled in vain to see something through the portholes. Only this gloomy gray hue was visible.

"What's happening?" Kariven asked.

"We're traveling through the Time Spiral," Harrington answered, turning on a visual periscope screen. The lighted rectangle showed an oscillating ball of indistinct color floating in the perpetual gray abstraction.

"This special visual process, which captures colored views in relief every *millionth of a second*, lets us see what our eyes can't make out because the space/time movement of the Retro-Timeship is too fast. Thus, the hazy images on the screen right now are already in the past with respect to our present position, even though they're taken at a millionth of a second. By the time they hit our retina their source is buried in the past that we're leaving 'behind us'."

"So what does this strangely colored, oscillating sphere represent?"

"That's Earth! Or rather the ghost of Earth, meaning *what it was at some point in the past.* The grayish, dusky glow surrounding us comes partly from the rapid succession of days and nights on the one hand and partly from passing through a dark and light hemisphere."

In a split second the screen showed a series of very bright but brief flashes, then three blinding flashes in quick succession that attracted the attention of the observers.

Responding to Kariven's unspoken question, Streiler gave the answer to the enigma. "What we've just glimpsed are the flashes from the nuclear experiments performed since 1945. We're seeing them in reverse. The latest ones, in Montebello, Nevada, Eniwetok and Bikini, we're the first ones we saw. The three other explosions that came afterward were the older ones from Hiroshima, Nagasaki and Los Alamos. We saw them in reverse chronological order; the last became the first."

"We're already in 1945?" Kariven expressed his surprise almost naïvely.

"You mean *we were*. The speed of the Retro-Timeship is constantly increasing since it is based on an acceleration. We're diving deeper into the past every second."

Streiler looked at a control panel and focused the screen onto starry space, at least such as was visible in a period of the past. The others followed his eyes and quickly saw an interesting phenomenon.

Like a ball of lightning, impossibly bright, a sphere exploded in space and vanished as quickly as it had appeared, leaving the screen open onto the abyss of the past.

"Right now we're in the Middle Ages and what we just saw was none other than the Nova discovered by Tycho Brahe, the famous Danish astronomer, in 1572 in the constellation Cassiopeia... We can see these extraordinary phenomena again on our way back because there are cameras on all sides of the Retro-Timeship. They work automatically and are recording our whole expedition that we only catch a few, random glimpses of."

"I'm getting used to not being surprised at anything," Kariven said, "but I have to admit that this voyage is far beyond anything I've ever seen or lived through before. Where exactly are we going?"

"You should say... *when* are we going?" Streiler joked. "We're going past the so-called prehistoric ages. The historic period stretches back from the 20th century to the first Egyptian dynasties and farther even into the Paleolithic, which doesn't interest us for the moment. When our mutual friend, Professor Harrington, informed me that he wanted to bring you on this voyage into the past, he told me what you work on. I knew nothing about your remarkable work and your bold anthropological theories. You've come up with some stunning hypotheses about the origin of humanity. That persuaded me to bring you with us because this exploration of the Time Spiral will either confirm or deny your theories and it won't be the least or last service the Retro-Timeship renders to Science."

Commander Taylor turned away from his control panel and said, "We're in the 45th millionth year before the atomic age. Should I stop?"

"45 million years before the atomic age!" Kariven exclaimed. "But that's almost the beginning of the Tertiary period!"

"Exactly right," Streiler confirmed with a smile. "We'll stop here before going any farther back into the past. In your opinion, Kariven, what should we find on Earth in this epoch?"

"The geology shows that the continents were different and the fauna was monstrous."

"And men?" Harrington asked.

"Science doesn't give them such an ancient origin. Legend, however, says differently and upholds that 40 or 50 million years ago the Earth and its main continent, Lemuria, was inhabited."

"OK, Mark!" Streiler rubbed his hands together. "You can stop at this time. Turn off the magneto-cosmotron generator. Everyone grab your suits and get ready to leave the Retro-Timeship."

CHAPTER II

When Commander Taylor stopped the magneto-cosmotron that powered the Retro-Timeship along the Time Spiral, the gray dusk changed to night.

The stars in space showed up perfectly clear not only on the screen but through the portholes as well. The hazy, vibrating sphere lost its blurriness and looked like our planet, as it was 45 million years ago.

The planetary ghost transformed into a tangible world: the Earth of the past materialized at the point in space that it occupied at the start of the Tertiary period. Seeing the globe whose continents were completely different, the Time explorers felt something indefinable. They had the impression of flying over a totally unknown world at a very high altitude.

Nothing in this strange geography led them to believe that they were looking at the planet Earth. The two American continents did not yet exist. The South, a long, irregular mass, was "biting" what would later become Tierra del Fuego. Instead of present day Australia and Micronesia a huge continent took up a good part of the Pacific.

"Lemuria!" Kariven uttered. "What wouldn't a geologist sacrifice to see such a sight! Look, right by the jagged sides of what will become Europe and Africa, there's that huge island... That's Atlantis or rather the island mountain that will give birth to it in the future... I mean in the past... Anyway, after this current Tertiary and before the Quaternary period in which we live in the atomic age," the young French scientist stammered.

"Before landing, let's fly over Lemuria and take a few pictures," Professor Harrington proposed.

Commander Taylor reduced the strength of the anti-gravitational repeller and the ship lost altitude. The continental landmass of Lemuria seemed to shoot up, its coasts and terrain becoming clearer. Towards the interior a mountain range stretched from east to west.

The anti-gravitational counter showed the descent speed at 300 feet/second. The commander reduced it even more and watched the altimeter decreasing its reading: 30,000 feet... 25,000 feet... 20,000 feet... At 3,000 feet from the ground Commander Taylor abruptly stopped the descent and brought the ship to a standstill thanks to the lift reactors.

The occupants of the cockpit bellowed in surprise. Their faces glued to the portholes, stupefied, they stood speechless.

Before their eyes, in the gulf of a bay that gently lapped at the ocean, was a dazzling white city, an extraordinary city, with majestic palaces, towers, dwellings and a port with huge cranes and weird, thin ships without masts or funnels. To the northwest of the white city, a glimmering oval indicated the position of an aerodrome! Several machines of strange shapes—metal spheres mounted on tripods—were lined up in front of hemispherical hangars.

Fearing they might be spotted too soon, Commander Taylor activated the breaker of the device that absorbed—*without sending them back*—the electromagnetic waves capable of revealing them. Silent and motionless the Retro-Timeship would be very hard to spot now.

Kariven looked at his companions one by one and read the same surprise on their faces as was on his. He murmured, "Are you sure that we're on Earth?"

"Absolutely. The Retro-Timeship never left the Time Spiral," Commander Taylor confirmed.

"One of the metal spheres is taking off!" Kariven exclaimed.

Indeed, with a spray of pinkish flames, one of the spherical machines rose up slowly, sparkling in the bright sunlight, and retracting its tripod landing gear. The ship accelerated faster and faster and in a few seconds faded off into the horizon. Meanwhile three other spherical airships had taken off in three different directions.

"I hate to admit that 45 million years *before* the atomic age the earthlings had reached such a stage of development," Kariven confessed dreamily.

"We would never admit it either," Professor Harrington spread his hands out in resignation, "if we didn't see this undeniable proof with our own eyes. A people living on the continent in the past as developed—if not more so—as us."

"It fits with your theories, Dr. Kariven, on the origins of humanity," Streiler said. "Despite all opposition you were right to believe that remarkable civilizations could have existed in the Tertiary period."

"Yes, I said that, but still putting them at a more recent epoch, towards the end of the Tertiary or start of the Quaternary around 500,000 years ago to one million maximum."

"The impossibility of finding remains or traces of this civilization, as you maintained, Kariven," Professor Harrington expounded, "is explained by the cataclysms that buried Lemuria and made Atlantis rise up. The cities and buildings, everything that the Lemurians had built was sunk to the bottom of the ocean, covered by hundreds of feet of sediment or even transformed through recrystallization into metamorphic rocks that we know very little about."

Professor Harrington turned to Commander Taylor. "Let's ascend into the atmosphere to stay out of sight and we can have a snack before visiting this ghostly white city of the past. We'll give ourselves a dose of the transparency serum and when night falls we can operate in complete safety."

The commander pressed the button for his interior video and called Rudy Clark, the specialist lieutenant assigned to the magneto-cosmotron, with his five-man team. His kindly face appeared on the screen.

"We're climbing into the ionosphere, lieutenant. Get a meal ready that we can have when we reach maximum height. Over and out."

"OK, Commander!" The Lieutenant saluted and the screen went dark.

The Retro-Timeship leaped into the sky, crossed the dense atmospheric layer in a blink of an eye and came to a halt at 60 miles altitude. At this height a purplish twilight replaced the daylight produced by the sun's rays illuminating air molecules.

The four men left the cockpit and went down to the lower deck. In the mess room with riveted walls, Lieutenant Clark and his men were waiting for them, at attention, in front of a table that was already set.

All the occupants of the Time ship ate very democratically at the same table, served by one of the crew members. Commander Taylor chatted as freely with the three scientists as he did with his subordinates, Lieutenant Clark and the GI technicians assigned to the Special Service of the Air Material Command.

The time explorers looked at one another with a strange feeling. The transparency serum had taken effect.

Their bodies—except for the eyes—were now see-through. The only thing they wore was tight-fitting shorts of a gray, plastic material and a wide belt whose buckle contained a small two-way radio no bigger than a pack of cigarettes. The microphone, the size of an aspirin, worked like a laryngophone, a throat mic, and simply had to be pressed to the larynx. A thin ribbon of transparent *plastic* around the neck kept it in place. The wire connecting it to the transmitter was no more than 1 mm thick.

The Retro-Timeship stopped silently at the edge of the strange airfield, that is three or four miles from the first buildings that could only be seen by their lighted windows since the terrain had no signal lights.

One GI was assigned to guard the ship. His duty was to receive and carry out to the letter whatever orders came in over the radio from the pioneer visitors of this epoch.

The transparent men, the commander following the scientists, stepped onto the ground and in close formation marched bravely forward. They crossed the huge, deserted airfield until they came to a corner of a building with wide bay windows. A gigantic, square metal tower was built on top of its roof. As curious as could be imagined they stuck their faces to the bluish windows.

It was a spacious room with desks and metal furniture—file cabinets undoubtedly?—in front if which some very tall men and women were consulting documents made of shiny material. Complex machines—electronic brains?—fitted with blinking screens sat in the corners of the room.

On the left wall a big relief map was being examined by three men, real giants at seven feet tall, give or take a couple of inches. Dressed in a blue jacket, narrow at the waist, and tights that hugged their muscular legs, they were watching four points of light that were moving in different directions across the relief map. The heads of these strange people were covered by a round helmet that, in shape, looked like a swimming cap but very thick and with a peculiar mechanism with a flexible stem sticking out of the top.

In front of a tilted control panel next to the mural map—only six feet away from the window through which the explorers were spying—a round screen lit up, framing the face of a young, blonde woman, marvelously pure and charming.

The three giants looked down at the convex glass displaying the ravishing girl and in perfect unison they brought their right hands up to their left shoulders. The girl answered the salute with the same gesture and started talking excitedly. Her deep blue eyes sparkled with intelligence. Her dark red lips poured out a flood of words that our friends could not hear.

"Except for being much taller than us and their weird clothes these Earthlings are like us," Streiler observed.

Without taking his eyes off the radiant blonde beauty Kariven looked puzzled. "Earthlings? Hmm… I don't know about that."

"What do you mean?"

"We'll have time later to discuss our origins, Streiler," he hinted at something ambiguously. "Let's call them

'Lemurians' until we know more. If we can crack open the door maybe we can hear their language?"

"Why not," Professor Harrington agreed. "If we stay quiet we won't be noticed. At least I hope so."

Kariven felt around for a moment looking for the knob or the lock of the oval door. At last he noticed a twinkling point in the frame to the right that hid a photoelectric cell. He waved his hand in front of what he believed to be the beam but the door did not open. Defeated and weary he simply pressed the lighted button... and the door opened silently.

The new men struggled in vain to understand the conversation of the giant Earthlings—our ancestors!

None of the "Lemurians" had noticed the quiet movement of the door. Kariven preferred to go back to the window. He pressed up close to it again in order to watch the screen where the pretty blonde could be seen, helmeted like her three comrades.

The time explorers expressed their astonishment by nodding their heads and whispering in each other's ears. All of a sudden some of the Lemurians, particularly the three giants talking with the girl, furrowed their brows in interest. They looked around as if they were searching for something or someone.

"These creatures look suspicious of something unusual," Kariven whispered almost inaudibly.

When he finished saying this, even though he was sure the Lemurians could not hear him, Kariven saw their faces turn to utter surprise. The blonde girl was irritated and called her comrades who responded to her looking both anxious and embarrassed. The Lemurian girl then raised her eyebrows and shook her pretty head while saying something that the 20th century Earthlings heard but could not understand. She brought her hand up to her helmet and her fingers pressed different points of the device wrapped in a transparent material with the flexible stem sticking out.

"What are they doing?" Professor Harrington whispered. "They can't see us or hear us so I can't understand why they…"

"Thoughts!" Kariven pointed to his forehead. "They're reading our minds with an ability that we don't have: telepathy!"

"That's possible," Streiler admitted. "But how can they understand our thoughts when we're thinking in *English*? We can't understand a single word of their language, just like they surely can't understand ours."

"That's a logical conclusion but false," Kariven whispered. "These beings don't translate the words but the 'ideographic' images of our thoughts. For example if I say 'spaceship' I *see mentally* a ship able to move in space. This psychic image is then interpreted and translated immediately by these beings endowed with a telepathic sense. An abstract concept like the theory of relativity, the fourth dimension or the philosophy of nirvana would be a lot harder for them to interpret by reading minds."

The giants looked at one another, completely astounded. They had, indeed, heard and understood the thoughts that were put into words by the transparent Earthlings. Once again the giants talked with the girl before giving an order to the other Lemurians and pointing at the two doors of the room.

"They're obviously going to search the buildings," Kariven said. "Let's get out of here!"

Putting his words into action they bolted toward a strip of tall grass bordering the airfield, ready to dive down in case the giants decided to light up the terrain. The Lemurians shouted other orders and along with five giants went to hunt for the "invisible" *thought transmitters*.

Suddenly a series of multi-colored lights near the buildings lit up. The Earthlings dove into the tall grass less than 10 yards away from the farthest signal light. Thank God the refraction index of their transparent bodies was so small… as long as nobody looked at them too closely.

Face down in the grass, on the lookout, the Earthlings were panting hard. The Lemurians had stopped and were scanning all around. After half an hour, having found nothing, they went back, as puzzled as they were overexcited.

The Earthlings did not wait for them to reconsider—they ran full speed back to the Retro-Timeship. "I don't think we have any reason to be scared," Taylor huffed as he, like his companions, put pants and a khaki shirt on his still transparent body. "Nothing proves that these guys mean us any harm. Let's put ourselves in their place. What would we have done if we heard voices nearby and couldn't explain where they came from?"

"That's right," Kariven agreed. "But when in doubt, refrain, as the sage said. I figure it'd be better to know a little more about Lemuria and its inhabitants before making contact with them."

"I think so too," Professor Harrington agreed. "So let's explore the continent. There should be other cities where we might be able to get to know the natives and without them knowing."

"I wonder what those three Lemurians were doing in front of that relief map and why they were getting upset before our 'psychic intrusion'? Because they looked as worried and preoccupied as that pretty blonde."

"You might be able to ask that pretty blonde soon enough," Commander Taylor joked. "She knocked you out, didn't she?"

"Bah," Kariven smiled. "She's been dead for 45 million years. I'm not some romantic smitten by a ghostly muse."

All four of them broke out laughing and sat in their seats while the Retro-Timeship shot up into the sky. The ship soared away from the white city toward the west at only 1,000 feet altitude. It was flying over a dense forest when Commander Taylor slowed it down and hovered at a fixed point.

"There's a round spaceship in this jungle... Look, to the east, between those bushy trees by that chain of rocks."

"It must have crash landed," the Austrian engineer remarked. "Its landing tripod is off to the left instead of being underneath. It probably tumbled onto its side. There was an accident."

"So that's why the Lemurians and the young pin-up doll were worried."

"The four round spaceships that took off right after we flew over the city must have gone out looking for us. They didn't find anything. But we have to do something for the survivors. They might be wounded and need help inside the damaged spaceship. Let's land," Kariven advised.

Commander Taylor frowned, "Land? Easier said than done. The jungle's too thick. I don't see an inch of open space. The only solution is to hover over the trees and go down on the elektron ladder.[6]"

"OK," Streiler seconded. "Let's go!"

The Retro-Timeship vibrated slightly as it floated six feet above the treetops that reached over 150 feet tall.

"Here we go," Streiler said, watching his hands turn from transparent gray to murky pink. "We're soon going to be perfectly visible to the Lemurians. I hope they aren't aggressive... or xenophobic!"

Lieutenant Clark opened the hold and let down the extensible elektron ladder. The end of the ladder almost touched the crashed spaceship.

The sun was starting to set on the horizon and the sunlight was rapidly declining behind the equatorial latitude. Commander Taylor, as the government attaché, had demanded that everyone carry a Thomson machine gun and a Colt 45 with two extra rounds. This precaution, although fitting for a soldier, made Professor Harrington smile, being the pacifist he was.

---

[6] The French explorer Robert de Joly pioneered the use of ever-lighter rope ladders until developing the *Elektron Ladder*, a light wire ladder with aluminum rungs.

"Don't you know that according to international agreements tourists should not carry weapons of war?" he said sarcastically.

"Yeah," the officer grumbled. "You built this marvelous ship, that's a fact, but when it comes to prudence and military discipline in unknown territory you're under my jurisdiction. Hold on to the guns and don't forget that we're *not* tourists."

Realizing that he was taking it a little too seriously Commander Taylor laughed raucously and went first down the ladder swinging in the open air. Two crew members kept watch at the edge of hold. Kariven grabbed the narrow bars and followed the officer, just before the other members of the space/time expedition.

He moved aside a leafy branch where the Commander had been entangled and joined him on the green soil that blanketed the feet of the tall trees. The day was gloomy in the thick of the jungle. The rays of the setting sun barely scraped the horizon.

"It took a weird fall," Commander Taylor pointed to the spaceship and its twisted landing gear. Under the ship an airtight hatchway had been half torn off and was hanging on one hinge.

When the members of this improvised rescue mission were all on solid ground Taylor and Kariven got down on their hands and knees and climbed into the spaceship. Their Thomson machine guns were too unwieldy so they had to sling them over their shoulders to slip through the opening.

Standing up in the cabin that was dimly lit by an electric light the two men remained motionless and wary. They gestured to their friends to keep silent. Cautiously they approached the interior hatch that led to another cabin. An unexpected noise, like lapping water or a clicking tongue mixed with fast, heavy breathing attracted their attention.

Taylor and Kariven stood on tiptoes to see over the hatch. What they found in the cockpit froze them with horror.

Their puzzled comrades saw them climb over the rectangular opening and quick as lightning rain a hail of bullets at a target that was hidden by the broken wall. An awful, inhuman scream rang through the air in the dreary metal chamber.

Taylor and Kariven, gritting their teeth, sneering with disgust and gripping their Thomsons tightly, shot off a second round that emptied their guns. Another croaky grunt cried out, broken off by muffled panting.

The petrified explorers in the first cabin of the mysterious spaceship suddenly got goose bumps!

CHAPTER THREE

At first baffled by the behavior of Kariven and Taylor, Streiler and Professor Harrington ran to the circular door that their two partners had just entered. Walking on the wall that was now the floor of the crashed spaceship lying on its side, they stepped through the doorway and were in turn riveted by the emotional scene.

In the center of the tilted cabin a monstrous being was dying—covered in red fur, with a huge, shiny head and an enormous, single eye in the middle of its bulging forehead. Sharp fangs stuck out of the upper lip of its disgusting mouth full of red drool. It must have been over eight feet tall and for the most part looked like a gorilla with a vaguely *hominoid* face. Its muscular chest showed the bloody traces of the machine gun fire.

Next to it lay the corpse of a young, white girl, torn up by fangs. Savagely torn up. The body of the poor girl had been fodder for the monster hungry for human flesh.

"Could this girl have been flying the spaceship alone?" Commander Taylor wondered aloud.

"She wasn't alone," Kariven remarked. "These shreds of clothing lying on the floor—or rather the wall of the cabin— don't belong to the victim. They come from the clothes of the other Lemurians who were with her. And this girl was obviously conscious when this monster attacked her. Her hands are still clutching the red fur that she ripped off her attacker before being eaten."

"What a disgusting animal!" Commander Taylor said with a sickened grimace.

"It's not an animal," Kariven corrected, "but a primitive being, maybe the *Missing Link*[7] in the evolutionary chain of

---

[7] According to Darwinism, a creature who served as the intermediate step between money and man, since both man and the

the terrestrial species... It's got a crude loincloth made of plant fiber around its waist and on its left arm is a bracelet of twined cane. These are not ornaments found in the animal kingdom. Except for its cyclops eye this primitive may not be so different from the Telanthropus that lived in the south of Africa 800,000 years ago. Unfortunately since no bones from these monsters have survived from this sunken continent it'll never be discovered. My paleontologist friends have no chance at all of finding their remains."

"For a Lemurian it's a lot different from the ones we saw at the airfield," Streiler said.

"Let's not stay here," Kariven suggested. "We can't do anything for this poor girl. Let's go looking for her companions instead... if we're not too late."

They climbed back up the ladder into the Retro-Timeship as night started falling on the jungle. The space/time ship rose up and zigzagged low over the forest. After 15 minutes the time explorers spotted a big fire burning in the middle of a clearing. Commander Taylor brought the ship down to hover silently just 100 feet off the ground. Several dozens of cyclop monsters were waving their arms and grunting around a campfire.

"It's ghastly," Professor Harrington gasped, nervously clenching his fists.

A Lemurian, captured by the hairy cyclops, had been tied to a long spit that was turning slowly in the flames. Devoured by the fire the unfortunate thing was no longer alive.

Nearby three Lemurian males and two females of the white race in their torn clothes were being held tightly by the cyclops. Apparently they were going to roast them one by one.

The prisoners struggled, but in vain because their executioners had a strong grip. One captive girl managed to wriggled free from her guard by slipping out of the remains of her

---

anthropoids share common ancestors. The monkey is, therefore, not our "father," but rather a "cousin." (Author's Note)

clothes but the monster caught her by the hair and dragged her roughly back to her friends.

"Open the hold!" Commander Taylor barked into the microphone. "Grab your weapons, Clark, and get your men."

Like a battleship at arms the Retro-Timeship was soon echoing with frantic footsteps. The occupants ran down the walkways of the lower deck and in no time were in the holds that opened by remote control. Kneeling at the edge of the opening Kariven and his friends were anxiously watching the cannibal horde howling 100 feet below. The monsters had eyes only for their living food or for the girl being roasted so that they did not seem to have noticed the presence of the Retro-Timeship.

"Shoot at the group huddled around the spit," Kariven ordered. "In the meantime I'll take care of the cyclop slave drivers."

Commander Taylor nodded and on his signal he sprayed bullets over 60 monsters jumping around in front of the fire. The other machine guns joined in and blasted furiously.

Kariven shouldered his gun, aimed carefully and shot one by one. The six monsters guarding the captives collapsed, fatally wounded. Five others came to the rescue to seize the two young women but Kariven, thumbing over to automatic, spat a rain of bullets at the newcomers who straightaway bit the dust.

"Land!" Commander Taylor shouted.

The background microphones transmitted his order to Lieutenant Clark who had stayed in the cockpit. Next to him a GI was calmly filming the battle while chewing gum.

Giving up all thought of getting their prey back the surviving monsters ran off into the jungle, leaving a great many corpses scattered around the clearing.

Disoriented and not really believing their eyes, the captives looked up at the strange, heaven-sent spaceship. Still carrying their weapons Kariven and his friends jumped to the ground and rushed over to the prisoners.

"Follow us!" Kariven enjoined, guessing that he would be understood by telepathy.

The Austrian engineer helped the girl who had been roughed up by the cyclops while Commander Taylor assisted the other Lemurians to climb through the hatchway. Kariven and Professor Harrington, with their machine guns ready at the hip, watched the surrounding area and guarded the boarding of the survivors. They got in last and immediately went to the cockpit where Commander Taylor was already at the controls and taking off.

The Lemurian girl whose clothes had been torn off got a short cape from her comrade. She wrapped it around her waist to pull herself together. Combing one hand through her hair she tried to smooth out her blonde waves. Her transparent helmet must have been torn off when she fell into the hands of the cyclops. Her comrade and the three men had kept theirs.

Kariven stared hard at her before exclaiming, "But this is the young blonde woman we saw on the screen talking with the giants!"

Streiler and the others scrutinized her and had to agree.

The young woman seemed to be listening to their thoughts and she smiled. She said a few words to one of the Lemurians who took off his helmet and handed it to her. She adjusted it on her head, closed the chinstrap and played her fingers over the transparent material. The mechanism immediately gave off a weird bluish light and the flexible stem vibrated silently.

The young woman stared at Kariven straight in the eyes. He felt a strange, almost unpleasant sensation. At first hazily, then more and more clearly he felt that an alien force was doing something to his brain, *in his brain*. Inexplicable impulses seemed to collide with his own thoughts, which he could no longer formulate properly.

Relax. Clear your mind. Relax.

Kariven shuddered. He did not think this! He tried to figure out how his brain could have thought up these commands.

Why would he order this young woman to relax and clear her…

He understood right away and was amazed. These thoughts had been suggested to him by the Lemurian! There was no way they were coming from his subconscious.

He forced himself to think of nothing and relax as he looked calmly at the mysterious survivor. She gently pressed something in the complex mechanism on her transparent helmet.

There now, that's better.

This thought, clear and precise, wormed its way into the young French scientist's brain.

Speak slowly or just "think" to talk to me.

Kariven was wildly excited by this parapsychological phenomenon. The girl's thoughts came to him with extraordinary clearness. The mechanism on her helmet must have been a thought amplifier to project mental messages onto someone lacking the sixth sense. But since the Lemurians were telepathic, why did they need this device to communicate among themselves? Besides their ability to read thoughts they could also speak. Maybe they were in contact with people who, like the Earthlings from the Atomic Age, did not have this sixth sense?

Your train of thought is too muddled. Think about only one thing at a time.

Kariven plunged into his thought process and looked calmly at the silent young woman.

I am not Leyla, the young woman whom you saw on the screen at the astrodome of Shâlami. I am Glanya, her twin sister.

Although intrigued by Kariven's silence as he just stared at Glanya, the explorers grew impatient.

"You want to burn this pin-up doll's face into your memory, Kariven?" Streiler joked. "Why are you two staring at each other like statues?"

"We're talking," Kariven replied without taking his eyes off the Lemurian.

41

"You're… You're talking," Professor Harrington raised an eyebrow.

"Yes, mentally," Kariven droned. His reply left them dazed.

"And what is she saying that's so interesting?" Commander Taylor asked skeptically.

"If you leave me alone for a minute maybe I can tell you," the young Frenchman grumbled, getting annoyed.

Explain to your brothers that we are exchanging thoughts in a pure state, Glanya advised.

Kariven did so succinctly.

Flabbergasted, they let him continue his psychic conversation, hoping to know more very soon.

My brothers and I thank you for saving us, Kariven.

The paleoanthropologist was not especially surprised to hear his name psychically. Glanya had easily read it in his subconscious.

"We only did our duty. But who are you? Are you really Lemurians?"

Glanya telepathically read the meaning of this question.

Only by adoption. I can't understand very well your train of subconscious thoughts. I perceive latent images of cities and beings like you but I can't locate your place on Earth. Do you come from another solar system?

"No, Glanya. We travel in Time and come from the Atomic Age."

Glanya gazed at him without hiding her surprise.

I don't believe it, Kariven. Our archives from the past contain no trace of an invention made in the Atomic Age capable of sending Earthlings forward in Time…

"But… but we don't come from the Past! We come from the Future. It's you, Glanya, who are in Earth's Past. A distance of 45 million years separates your epoch from ours."

Glanya looked completely flustered. She stammered to her companions who abruptly shared her bewilderment.

Think slowly, Kariven. I fear I won't be understood very well. The Atomic Age on Earth began on this continent that

*you call Lemuria 9,000 years ago when the races of Earth
after being taught by our Instructors without their knowing,
reached this stage of their evolution. If, as I have suggested, a
time machine had been built at this time, we would have kept a
record of it in our archives. Now, neither on Earth, which we
educated in peace, nor on Bimkam, the capital planet of our
own solar system, is there any evidence of such an invention.*

Kariven felt his mind reeling. How was he going to sort
out this mess?

"Listen, Glanya, We're both victims of a misunderstanding. You Lemurians or whoever you are had peopled the Earth
around the middle of the geological period called Tertiary.
And we Earthlings peopled the Earth in the Quaternary period,
that is more than 45 million years *after you!* We come from
the Atomic Age of the Quaternary period. For us you are the
Past. Your continent was swallowed up by the Pacific Ocean
around 40 million years ago."

Glanya, whose astonishment was growing, translated
these stunning words to her friends, before resuming her conversation with Kariven.

*I'm beginning to understand but it's really incredible.
The Lemurian Atomic Age belongs to the Past of Lemuria. And
the Atomic Age you're talking about belongs to your cycle, to
your period situated in the Future for us, the Dragons of Wisdom...*

"Hold on," Kariven broke in. "Now it's me who doesn't
understand very well. What do you mean by Bimkam and the
Dragons of Wisdom?"

Glanya smiled and looked up to examine the sky through
the cockpit of the Retro-Timeship. She searched for a few
seconds, then taking Kariven's arm spoke to him mentally
while pointing at the stars.

*Do you see that star shining red next to the two smaller
stars? The three of them form a tilted triangle.*

Kariven scanned the starry night but he did not recognize
the constellations. The sky was obviously not the same as he
could gaze upon in Paris or Las Vegas but the one visible on

Earth 450,000 centuries before! At this fantastically remote time the constellations were in a clearly different position from their current disposition. He also had to give up all hope of finding stars that were absolutely unidentifiable to a human of the Atomic Age.

This star, Glanya told him, *is Katong, our sun. The giant star, which is 483 times bigger than the sun shining on Earth—but infinitely less dense—has a train of 17 planets, of which Bimkam is ours. A very old civilization is there and has spread over the whole Galaxy for millions of years. When we reach a new planet with intelligent beings less developed than us, we establish a base on the planet and educate the "natives."*

This base is placed under the authority of a Grand Instructor who guides and manages the technicians whose mission it is to mingle with the people to civilize or improve them. For generations, even millennia, these "Dragons of Wisdom" run around the world to lead the population toward the beautiful and good. Certain particularly learned instructors, gifted with powerful, personal magnetism, are even deified by the masses to whom they have given their guidance and knowledge.

These Grand Bimkamian Instructors—men and women— travel on spaceships whose nature the native Earthlings cannot explain. That's why the Masters, and by extension we the technicians, are called Dragons of Wisdom. In the mind of the primitives every flying machine is a dragon and its occupants, since they come from the sky, are Gods... Gods among men!

When the races that we teach are on the good path of evolution, we leave them to their own free will and come back to our solar system. Our stay on the planet varies from several years to generations, depending on its evolutionary stage. Sometimes, when these races are morphologically like us— such is the case with Earth—we can even end up joining with the natives and creating a branch by crossbreeding the two types.

There automatically follows a more rapid evolution and we can thus leave the "stopover" planet after a shorter period. However, in an educational category like this, we keep a permanent base for a long time before abandoning our students forever. The mixed race, therefore, stays on the planet and over generations becomes its natives.

The countless interbreeding of races that take place in the Galaxy has provided powerful civilizing currents. Unfortunately, sometimes we leave a planet to its fate, believing that its inhabitants will keep on the path towards good and perfection, but the opposite happens. Earth is a woeful example.

10,000 years ago when we landed on Earth the beings here were primitive. They barely knew how to work metals. We had to leave a Grand Instructor who, through his vast wisdom and the means at his disposal, was able to start a revolutionary movement among the Earthlings. His successor and those who came after managed to make the people progress to the point where they reached the "Atomic Age" after ten centuries. This all happened 9,000 years ago, she smiled mentally.

Kariven also smiled on remembering the confusion caused by this Atomic Age situated in the Past for Glanya and the Future for himself.

At this period the Grand Instructor and his disciples summoned a squadron of spaceships and left the Earthlings to the benefits that they could get from the nuclear power plants providing energy for all kinds of use. Obviously they could have stayed to teach the Earthlings the astronautical science so they could travel in space to other planets, but this was not their intention. For all worlds the Atomic Age is a transition period between the ancestral type and the supra-evolved type. Therefore, they left the Earthlings to improve themselves.

It was the wrong move.

A few scientists, starting from the industrial use of nuclear energy came to modify the principle of slow disintegration into instantaneous disintegration. The Atomic Bomb was born.

We were very careful not to teach this method to men, hoping that if they discovered it they would not use it for harmful ends.

A generation passed during which time this dangerous invention was used only as a controlled explosive for building dams, destroying mountains to divert the flow of rivers, etc. But one day a scientist drunk on power built A-bombs with the agreement of his government, which appointed him War Minister, he started a dreadful conflict. The conquered, under the supervision of the conquerors, pursued their own research no less secretly. We do not know exactly how it happened, but the fact is that 20 years later a new atomic war broke out. This time the two antagonists each had their A bombs and even hydrogen bombs. It was a cataclysm of unheard of violence.

80 out of 100 Earthlings were exterminated on both sides and the centers of habitation were reduced to dust. The few surviving citizens and the Earthlings from remote villages escaped when they could and deserted these countries that became fatally radioactive. Many of them died from the radiation, others became sterile or gave birth to blind, defective offspring, unfit to perpetuate the race.

Those who escaped the cataclysm fell back into the state of barbarism that their ancestors had risen out of. They wandered in groups through the forests and jungles and ended up living in grottoes and big trees. The primitive life resumed but the births, paradoxically, produced only cyclop monsters! A sudden mutation had been caused by the frightful atomic conflict. The Earthlings had been exposed to the radiation and their genes[8] were changed; they could engender only half-human, half-animal beings of gigantic size, with red hair and an abnormally large eye in the middle of their forehead.

This new race soon took possession of much of Lemuria, hunting in packs that howled after the few Earthlings who

---

[8] Hereditary elements contained in the nucleus of a cell that determine the morphological and physiological characteristics transmitted to the progeny. (Author's Note)

were miraculously spared by the war and radiation. These last survivors lived desperately in the mountains, fearing the cyclops like death, which inevitably accompanied them.

This lasted for thousands of years, seven to be precise. One of our interplanetary groups crossing this solar system passed by Earth for a quick look without dreaming of landing because the Earthlings, they thought, must have forgotten about their original evolution. Imagine the surprise of the "Space Controllers": there were no more cities and chaos reigned everywhere! They came back later to help the normal descendants on Earth and to chase away the cyclops. This has lasted around 900 years.

I belong to the instructor group on Earth, Glanya concluded, *and I think we've stopped the danger. The Earthlings have evolved again and they will soon be able to stand on their own two feet. But from now on, so that the atrocious carnage doesn't happen again, we will watch over Earth and its people who are too prone to kill each other.*

"Your surveillance, unfortunately, will end," Kariven sighed. "Lemuria will be... or rather was swallowed up millions of years ago by a cosmic cataclysm and you don't know about it because it will happen 40 million years after your own existence, Glanya."

The young Bimkamian reflected on this and then said:

Without this landing accident I never would have met you.

"How did it happen?" Kariven asked.

We were doing a reconnaissance flight to locate the cyclops tribe when our lifters broke down and we dropped over 300 feet out of the sky. We only had time to get our individual lifters working to give us air in the cockpit. Although we were saved from the crash we were still knocked unconscious by the shock. The screams of our companions being eaten alive by the cyclops snapped us out of it.

During the crash landing the exterior hatch was opened and a bunch of cyclops got into our ship. The first jumped on our friend who was just waking up, and tore her to pieces with

47

his fangs. The other monsters grabbed us and brought us to their camp where you saved us.

"We're coming up on the astrodome," Commander Taylor announced. "I can see the runway lights. What should we do?"

CHAPTER FOUR

Kariven consulted Glanya and replied, "Land, Commander. Glanya is going to send a message and vouch for our good intentions."

Commander Taylor pulled the lever to reverse the anti-gravitational boosters and lowered his head. "OK, doc, we'll get our feet back on the ground."

While the Retro-timeship lost altitude, Streiler observed the young Bimkamian women and their three companions with great interest. The divinely beautiful girls must have been almost six feet tall and the men well over six and a half. With their muscular chests, broad shoulders and imposing bearing they would have fit right in among the purest masterpieces of classical sculpture.

Watching Glanya the Austrian smiled, thinking that he and his friends had mistaken these beings for Earthlings whereas they came from a solar system located 217 light years from the Earth, according to what Kariven had just translated.

217 light years, he thought, *that means around 1,275,000 billion miles!*

And continuing his monologue:

Good old Shakespeare was barking up the wrong tree when he wrote "Fragility, thy name is woman." *Is it possible that these "fragile" and remarkably beautiful creatures had accomplished this fantastic voyage to resolve interplanetary conflicts and devote their lives to educating barbarians and savages?*

Glanya, who was watching him lost in contemplation, could not help but smile. Naturally, she had picked up his thoughts. Pressing the contacts on her helmet once again to amplify the psychic waves, she answered him by mental suggestion and interpreting the Shakespeare quote in her own way.

"We are not 'fragile,' Kurt Streiler, but the representatives, male and female, of a highly evolved race whose mission is to watch over the development of backward planets."

On perceiving these thoughts the Austrian engineer felt something he could not explain. To know that his brain was open to this being endowed with a sixth sense was not a particularly pleasant feeling.

He managed a little smile to put up a front and turned away, pretending to watch the landing of the Retro-timeship in the astrodome... all the while thinking this woman had her share of charm and he would not have to be asked twice to take her in his arms.

Interrupting his private thoughts here he turned back, instinctively, to peek at Glanya.

She had stopped examining the machines on board. Having expected to be gazed at by the young engineer she looked deep into his eyes. Shaking her head slowly, pretending to be stern, she whispered a reproach.

"Tsk, tsk, tsk..." Then in thought language she added, "You're a real lecher, Kurt."

The Austrian turned red on being caught thinking so freely and did not know what to do in his confusion. He coughed, leaned casually against the transparent cockpit and, forcing a smile, he concentrated on the countryside.

When Commander Taylor feinted a maneuver before landing, he shouted, "Good God! They're going to think we're attacking."

Indeed, a troop of giant Bimkamians came running out. Armed with a kind of machine gun with a long barrel, they encircled the Retro-timeship and pointed their weapons at the hatches.

At the head of the troop our friends recognized three of the people from the control room who had spoken with the young blonde on the viewer. They must have detected the approaching ship, which the explorers had forgotten to cloak, and were approaching it ready for any eventuality.

The hatches opened slowly.

The Bimkamians turned their machine guns turned on the "strangers." But soon they lowered them on seeing Glanya, the other young woman and the three men, the missing crew.

The Bimkamians welcomed their comrades with shouts of joy, but their enthusiasm died when they saw the Earthling time explorers step out in their khaki uniforms with all the pockets and their tiny stature (despite Kariven and Streiler being over six feet tall); they were startled and wary.

What outlandish outfits! they must have thought. *And what backward beings!*

One of the leaders from the control room spoke to Glanya while casting furtive glances at the Earthlings from the future. He and Glanya talked for ten minutes. The Bimkamiam's bewilderment turned to comical shock. His eyebrows arched and his mouth dropped open, a little like a clown.

Glanya introduced him to the time explorers to whom he declared psychically, "So you're the ones we detected in control room when you were invisible."

"We weren't invisible, just transparent and we were hiding behind the control room window. Your sixth sense picked up our thoughts. That's why you were so upset, sensing our thoughts without being able to see us..."

Kariven broke off. He had been distracted by a faint whistle coming from the sky. Everyone looked up with him.

A strange object was quickly taking shape over the aerodrome. Elongated, with delta wingtips, the metallic object glowed bright orange in the night before dropping toward the ground as its whistling grew louder.

The little rocket ship, 15 feet long and barely 5 feet in diameter, made a hairpin pin to set down alongside the formidable Retro-timeship. They heard a clicking sound, then a metal panel, curved like the ship, slid open into its housing.

In the "one-seater" rocket a young blonde girl was lying on her stomach, her arms stretched out in reach of a circular control instrument panel. She released the commands and started climbing out. When she got her feet on the ground Kariven stared at her agape.

Lit by the beams of polychrome landing lights, *this girl was absolutely identical*—a spitting image—*of Glanya.* Therefore, she was Leyla, her twin sister, the Grand Instructor of Earth, Queen of the Dragons of Wisdom assigned to this planet.

A kind of opalescent pink sweater hugged her faultless bust. A wide black belt and shiny short pants completed her stunning uniform. On her chest a green sun glowed, strongly phosphorescent, the symbol of the Grand Galactic Instructors.

In the face of Kariven's astonished and marveling gaze, Leyla smiled. She had read his inner thoughts...

The two twin sisters hugged each other in an open show of joy and affection. Their resemblance was so striking that it was like one single woman and her image in a mirror. The only thing that differentiated them was their clothes: Leyla's phosphorescence and Glanya's semi-nudity. The short cape wrapped around her waist made no error possible in telling them apart.

The two young women, flanked by the Earthlings being escorted by the Bimkamians, crossed the vast aerodrome and headed for the control room.

Shâmali, the capital of the extraterrestrial Instructors, cast its multi-colored rays of light into the night sky. The white buildings, swept by the variegated beams of spotlights, looked surprisingly beautiful in its kaleidoscopic hues. Reds, greens, yellows, blues and garnets mingled in a moving tapestry that was a delight for the eyes.

The armed troop reached the station. Torka, the Chief of Military Operations, stayed with his two subordinates in the control room while Leyla and Glanya took the Earthlings with them.

Kariven, Streiler, Professor Harrington and Commander Taylor followed them to a site next to the aerodrome that looked like the grandstands of a sports stadium. But instead of being filled with seats, under this stadium's slanted roof were a multitude of rectangular plates, a foot thick and piled on top of one another.

Leyla and Glanya reached for a control panel at the entrance and each of them pressed two different buttons. Straightaway two different, huge plates left the top of a pile and swayed through the air until they landed gently on the ground. Their edges lit up and a row of telescopic rods popped up from their sides to form a two-foot high barrier.

Leyla climbed onto one of these unusual plates and invited Kariven and Taylor to do the same. Glanya jumped on the other taking Streiler by the hand to stay by her side. Harrington looked curiously at these slabs. Undecidedly he stepped in behind the girl and the Austrian.

Commander Taylor, seeing Leyla casually grab Kariven's hand, decided just to plop down cross-legged and lean back against the telescopic railing. Kariven remarked that the metal they were sitting on was unbelievably soft and sank comfortably under his bottom.

"Hold onto me, Kariven, and don't worry about anything."

Kariven answered this "thought-advice" with a smile. But when the plates rose up and soared off into the night at 300 miles per hour, he felt his stomach turn in spite of his experience in airplanes and... the Retro-timeship!

The flat speeding bullets, propelled by magneto-cosmic energy, leapt up toward the sky. They flew over the city being flooded with colored lights and headed for a marvelous, completely transparent building.

Kariven and Commander Taylor clung nervously onto the thin guardrail encircling the aerocar.

By what miracle did they not plunge to the ground?

They cautiously turned their heads and noticed, with relief and a hint of irony, that Streiler and Harrington were as scared as they were. The Austrian even had his arms around Glanya but, Kariven saw, he did not look really terrorized. His face betrayed a little satisfaction.

He stole a furtive glance at Leyla and saw her right hand holding onto the soft metal right next to his. He hesitated to do what Streiler did but watched her with admiration in his eyes, and not a little respect.

What a lovely creature, he told himself privately. *Thank God that being over six feet tall I won't look like a dwarf if I take her in my arms! Is our weird situation a good excuse for such... intimacy?*

Leyla suddenly turned to him. A mischievous glimmer sparkled in her eyes. "Are you all like this on the future Earth? Do you think so much before doing anything at all?" she asked in thought while the aerocar set down gently on an elevated spiral road leading to the building.

Kariven looked at her in surprise. Once again his thoughts had betrayed him. The young French scientist asked, "Are you criticizing, Leyla?"

Leyla shook her blonde locks, amused. "No, Kariven, just an observation... and not an unpleasant one at that." On saying this she took his hand and helped him to his feet. She graced him with a friendly smile and put her arm around him casually.

The two of them preceded the others down the suspended, spiral path that led to a majestic, green portal opening onto the entrance hall of the strange palace that seemed built out of one solid piece of crystal.

"This is my home, Kariven. To you and your friends, welcome to Shâlmali."

They walked through the arched portal, crossed the hall and entered an impressive, circular room under a dome diffusing a bluish light.

"I'll show you to your rooms where you can take the rest that you must sorely need."

When he opened his eyes, Kariven tried to organize his thoughts still clouded with sleep.

The walls of his spacious room were white. After climbing out of bed he walked around the room until he found the bathroom. A cold shower woke him up completely.

While the refreshing water streamed over his body Kariven suddenly stopped washing himself so he could listen to the inner voice that he was starting to get used to.

He looked around, vaguely disturbed, but did not see anyone. However, in his mind the same psychic question echoed again: "Did you sleep well, Kariven?"

Kariven abruptly turned off the shower, jumped out and wrapped himself clumsily in a towel.

Could Leyla make herself invisible?

The paleoanthropologist got dressed in a hurry and was about to leave when the walls of his room suddenly lit up, brighter and brighter, until they turned crystalline. Behind the now transparent walls Leyla was smiling, amused by the Earthling's baffled look. Her bolero and short, gold spangled skirt were a ravishing fit.

"Excuse me for being indiscreet, Kariven."

Kariven waved it off to hide his discomfort and marveling at the girl he said, "I guess that for you these psychic reflections in the brains of your colleagues is not indiscreet at all. For me, however, they're still startling."

"Don't be upset," she apologized, regretting her indiscretion toward a guest. "This ability is so common and natural to us that we sometimes abuse it without wanting to. I'm sorry for upsetting you, Kariven."

"It's nothing, really," Kariven admitted, seeing that Leyla had meant no harm in what he had seen as plain rudeness.

Reading the sincerity in his mind Leyla pressed a button on a rolling control panel and to Kariven's utter surprise the wall puckered, then stretched out and an oblong opening grew in the wall that looked doughy.

"Please enter."

Slightly disconcerted he obeyed and went through the malleable wall that closed up behind him. The two young people sat comfortably on a block of soft, spongy metal balanced in the air by a repelling field emanated by the shiny floor.

"How much time do you have to stay with us?" Leyla asked.

"A few days, maybe a week."

Leyla remained quiet, thoughtful. She stared at an imaginary point on the tips of her red boots with silky fringes. *Too bad... Why does this handsome guy...*

Kariven, startled at having caught this abruptly interrupted inner thought, stared at her.

Looking embarrassed she fumbled with her helmet to press the contact that created a protective field around her thoughts.

Kariven received no more psychic input.

He could only dream that Leyla had let slip out something that she wanted to keep secret. She stood up and by conscious telepathy this time declared, "I would be glad to show you around Shâmali, Kariven, and the Lemurian continent before you leave."

Kariven stood up as well. Looking into her big, blue eyes, so as not to drop what he had just overheard, he whispered, "Why can't this girl understand that she's not the only one who's sorry about the upcoming departure."

Leyla shot him a reproachful look, but when he took her in his arms she laid her head gently on his shoulder and closed her eyes.

"I'm not angry that I heard your thoughts, Leyla. You obviously know mine, right?"

Seeing that she did not answer Kariven held her shoulders and scrutinized her face. She was crying silently.

He wanted to kiss her but she turned her head away slowly.

"It's impossible... Dear," he perceived in his head where the most conflicting ideas were battling.

"My feelings have to come after my duty. I'm the Supreme Wisdom, the Grand Instructor of Earth and I don't belong to myself."

"But that's ridiculous!" Kariven was indignant. "Didn't Glanya tell me that Bimkamians frequently mate with the natives they're supposed to educate and they establish a mixed race?"

"That's right, Kariven, but not for this planet. The Earthlings abused their power by starting a fratricidal war that decimated their race. We have orders to educate them but no longer to mix the two kinds of humanity. Later, when the Lemurians have reached a favorable level of evolution, the ban will probably be lifted."

"I'm not a Lemurian, Leyla. You know it as well as I do. I come from the future."

"And you will return there. What's the point of making crazy, futile plans. You do, in fact, come from the future whereas I am... I was from the past. I've been dead to you, my darling, for 45 million years! A man can't think about sharing his life with a dead girl."

Kariven shrugged his shoulders, holding Leyla close to his chest. Then he kissed her tenderly. The young woman struggled for an instant before giving in.

"Our love will last only eight days, Kariven. Is it wise to be happy for so short a time when we will be unhappy in the future after you leave, separated forever, each of us on a different point in the Time Spiral?"

"Fate works in mysterious ways, we say in our time. Let's live for today without worrying about tomorrow... which might be full of surprises for us."

Leyla sighed, "If our Supreme Ruler, the Eternal Wisdom residing on Bimkam, learned of my transgression, I would be banished from Earth and sent to an inferior planet where I'd have to educate beings who are so different from us that we would never even think of falling in love with them."

"Ha!" Kariven snorted. "How would the Eternal Wisdom ever found out about our love?"

Leyla shrugged. "Nothing's impossible."

Leyla and Glanya led their guests into a room on an upper floor cluttered with machines that looked like giant cameras pointing down through a rectangular opening in the metallic wall. The explorers peered through this window and were rather surprised to see that it overlooked a huge, semi-circular room with rows of seats like an amphitheater. Sitting there in a half circle in front of a raised desk were a hundred women, all young and remarkably beautiful, waiting patiently while chatting *in silence...* quite an unexpected sight for an assembly of women!

"This is the base of our Center for Gynecocratic Instructors," Leyla explained. "Because Earth is being not only being educated by Bimkamian men but also by Bimkamian women. I have the honor of presiding over this high council that sends the orders to the men and women in charge of instructing the masses. You'll be watching one of our sessions. This booth houses, as you see, the cameras that record our debates and send them to the Collection Center on the planet Bimkam in the Katong solar system. Special frequencies for *instant diffusion* allow the Galactic Government to capture the transmissions live."

The twin sisters left their friends in the recording booth and went down to the amphitheater by a tubular elevator.

Glanya sat behind a command console next to the raised desk to control the cameras. Her sister, the Grand Instructor of the Dragons of Wisdom come from space, sat at the desk and listened to the oral reports of the young ladies in the seats.

Once in a while Leyla spoke up to ask for details or to give advice and she pressed a lit button embedded in her desk. An electronic brain recorded the conversation and set off a network of transmissions that would immediately implement the orders or modifications.

All of a sudden a siren filled the room with its mournful howl.

A 3-D color screen turned on showing Torka, the Military Operations Chief. The officer saluted Leyla by bringing his right hand up to his left shoulder and then he reeled off a hurried speech.

The Grand Instructor jumped out of her seat and called a halt to the session. Rushing up to the booth where they had left the Earthlings, Leyla and her twin sister explained the reason for the sudden interruption.

"A horde of 10,000 cyclops just attacked Balkum, a city in the west! The inhabitants can't defend themselves alone so we have to fly out to help them..."

CHAPTER FIVE

The astrodome in Shâmali was full of commotion. 100 combat spaceships—slim, shiny metal needles—had been brought out from the huge hangars. 20 spherical spaceships were also lined up in formation for takeoff.

From all quarters of the city groups of giant Bimkamians arrived, alerted by the sirens and loudspeakers. In 15 minutes the ships were fully crewed.

In the control room the chief of the astrodome sat before a massive, chrome control panel pressing buttons on a black keyboard. In every ship a red light turned on, indicating to the pilots that they were clear for departure

The spaceships took off in waves, 20 at a time.

Not wanting to be useless and act like tourists while their "ancestors" went into combat, the time explorers boarded the Retro-timeship and followed the Bimkamians.

Leyla had gone on board the ship with Torka, Chief of Military Operations. She would have preferred to be with the Earthlings from the future but her duty compelled her to stay by the side of her immediate subordinate.

Glanya, on the other hand, was free. And she did not hesitate to join the Earthlings... particularly Streiler who was not blind to her charms.

"How could the cyclops, those primitive beasts, barely at the tribal stage, gather enough of them to attack a city?" Kariven asked.

"This city," Glanya explained, projecting her thoughts into their listening minds, "is located at edge of the forest where you saved us. In this area of the west there are countless tribes of cyclops. The whole jungle we're flying over right now harbors around 3,000 tribes, each made up of 200 hairy monsters. So, we're lucky that that their sense of camaraderie is not very developed, otherwise there wouldn't be 10,000 cyclops attacking the city but hundreds of thousands! An attack like this already happened, nine years ago, but by fewer assailants. Today a hungry tribe must have asked for something from a bigger tribe that in turn went to another tribe for food, each as needy as the last.

"From one clan to the next the cyclops apparently agreed to attack Balkum. Usually when a tribe is threatened with starvation because it can't find enough to hunt, it fights its neighbors, captures them and eats them. Even so, I think that in their slow evolution the cyclops are starting to understand the futility of such wars. Killing their own kind will lead to a quicker extinction than a long-lasting shortage of food. They somehow managed to stir up a whole region to kidnap the isolated Lemurians, who are choice prey for them.

"In every city on Earth we have an Instructor whose duty is to make sure that social life runs smoothly. Mingling with the inhabitants, he's like a friendly giant always ready to be at their service. The citizens are unaware of his power and extraterrestrial origins. As you'll see, after the horrible atomic war 9,000 years ago, the present evolution on Earth is still pretty primitive compared with your future civilization. On Lemuria the Earthlings have not yet reached the Atomic Age, very far from it. They've barely discovered electricity!"

"But haven't these Earthlings ever gone to Shâmali?" Streiler asked in surprise. "Haven't they seen your ultramodern, super-evolved base set up on the continent where they live? Such an anachronism must be astonishing to them!"

"Don't kid yourself, Kurt," Glanya clarified. "These Lemurians have explored several times up to the edge of the lagoon where Shâmali lies, but they couldn't see our base because it's protected by an invisibility field. They ran into an invisible wall that stopped their progress. If you were able to enter our city it's because Time and Space mean nothing to your ship. Otherwise you never would have found us. Being blocked by an invisible obstacle threw the Lemurians into utter confusion, especially since they couldn't explain the strange phenomenon."

Through the cockpit window Kariven observed the precision with which the Bimkamian spaceships flew in triangular formation.

At the edge of the thick jungle, on a plain bordered by high mountains to the west, he saw a city come quickly into clear view. Two or three-story houses stood with their chimneys and their "attics" like our ancestors had built. The narrow streets of the poor areas contrasted starkly with the wide boulevards and the open courts of the so-called "bourgeois" neighborhoods.

A weird building formed of three giant obelisks supporting a platform that served as a base for a red sphere, rose up in the middle of the city. Glanya explained to her friends that it was a temple dedicated to the Lemurians' deity, the Kosmos-God, symbolized by a sphere.

In a panic, men, women and children with light brown skin were running all over the place and tumbling into the main street. Riders mounted on animals that looked like a cross between a pony and a bovid were spurring on their animals and driving through the crowd to flee even faster. Carriages and carts attached to these creatures, and even vehicles being drawn by quadrupeds no bigger than a wolf-dog, were blocking the street in an indescribable traffic jam.

In the widespread panic very few people had noticed the weird balls flying over the city. But all of a sudden the mob cried out in a single voice of horror.

Cyclops had just appeared at the other end of the boulevard. Their massive bodies, covered with red hair, and their huge, bulging eye made them look unreal, terrifying. They moved forward, roaring like raging wild beasts.

On seeing the Lemurians they grunted inarticulately and took off after them. Some still held onto bloody limbs—arms or legs—that they had ripped off their victims.

When the prey heard the croaking grunts they fled all the faster, in mad hysteria, stampeding each other in their attempt to escape the monsters.

Torka's spaceship started dropping straight down. Only 30 feet from the ground he bore down the street and from the disintegrator cannon in the nose of the forward cabin shot a ray of bright light, as blinding as a camera flash.

The cyclops horde looked petrified. The ray swept through them, from the front ranks to the rear. All of a sudden the monsters lit up and in a few seconds the street was illuminated by a million spotlights before the blinding glare disappeared, in a heartbeat, and the regular light came back.

The street was deserted. The only thing left of the horrifying cyclops was a blackish stain on the asphalt. They had been evaporated by the disintegrator ray.

Seized by a superstitious fear before these "flying dragons that spit lethal fire," still hesitating to accept their miraculous salvation, the inhabitants of Balkum did not know what to do.

Not lingering on this spot in the city the ships split up to clear out the other districts invaded by the monsters. Once in a while gunshots echoed through the streets. A few citizens were defending their families with what rudimentary weapons they had. But these sporadic attempts were of little use. For every cyclops shot down, ten more rose up or a hundred, to slaughter everything in their path in a minute.

After disintegrating a few more thousand monsters teeming at intersections Leyla and Torka decided to land in order to finish off the cyclops for good. In small groups the monsters were breaking into the houses and pitilessly butchering the terrorized, powerless inhabitants.

The spaceships and the Retro-timeship set down on a wide-open space to the south. The Bimkamians, under Torka's orders, ran into the embattled city through the boulevards around it. In companies of 100 men armed with big disintegrator guns they advanced, shooting all cyclops they came across.

Kariven and his friends, wielding their Thomson machine guns, joined Leyla. At Torka's side the Grand Instructor was firing away like a rebel at the barricades!

The city echoed with gunfire and the crackle of the disintegrator rifles. The battle for the streets was in full swing.

The Bimkamians crept down the alleys, slipped into the buildings, one after another, and came out only after making sure all monsters were down for the count.

Leyla, Kariven and Torka, working together, witnessed a scene that was abominable from the human point of view but natural for the "struggle for life"[9] in the animal world. All three of them had just entered the second floor of a house and automatically leaned over a spiral staircase in the corner. That was when they saw the despicable scene: in a courtyard a 10-foot tall female cyclops and her two "children," as big as full-grown men, were greedily devouring a brown-skinned girl. The poor thing was still groaning in agony while the "baby" cyclops tore at her bloody legs. The female pounced on the victim, but just as she was about to sink her fangs into the throat, Leyla's rifle shot its ray at the same time as Kariven gunned down the monsters. The man-eaters were riddled with bullets and instantly evaporated. The dying young girl finally saw an end to her suffering. The awful wounds in her belly, unfortunately, left her no chance of survival.

Only the shadows of the vanished bodies remained on the ground. Leyla wiped her forehead with a shaky hand. The disgusting scene had shaken her up. Kariven put his arm around her as they searched the rest of the house, which turned up empty. Its occupants, luckier than the poor girl, had time to escape.

In spite of their great number the Bimkamians had to run through the city all night long. The monsters had taken refuge on the roofs, sometimes carrying some of their prey with them. Often enough the Earthlings and Bimkamians came across gruesome remains: feet, hands, arms or legs, and other bits and pieces of humans left behind by the cyclops.

[9] Expression summing up one of the principles of Darwinism. (Author's Note)

When the Lemurians were brave enough to come out of their cellars they saw—with such relief!—that the monsters had gone. The weird flying dragons, whose timely arrival they could not explain, had mysteriously evaporated them into thin air along with their no less mysterious rifles.

The Bimkamian squadron and the Retro-timeship made one last tour over newly freed Balkum before making their way back home. This time Leyla left the command to Torka so she could be with her friends from the Future.

"This fight won't be over for months," she sighed in her psychic voice. "And we won't be sure to finish off all the monsters. We'll have to skim over their lairs and spray them with disintegrators…"

"There will always be some families who will hide away in the mountains and breed a new threat for some time later," Streiler remarked.

"There is a way," Kariven intervened, "a radical way you haven't thought of: an epidemic! Spread a deadly epidemic among the cyclops to decimate them without a fight."

Leyla thought about it and saw her lover's cleverness. "I have to admit that we never thought the problem like that. However, if this is the only way we have, we'll have to learn about the monsters' physiology to make it work. We'll be forced to capture one of them and when we know what virus they can't produce anti-bodies for, we can cultivate the micro-organisms and spread them all over their territory. But we'll also have to make sure that the virus does no harm to the Lemurians or to ourselves. Only the cyclops must be affected by the epidemic."

"We're ready to help you if you want," Professor Harrington offered. "Our ship is at your service. But allow me to make a suggestion. Instead of capturing one cyclops to study its physiology, capture a dozen or more whom you could inject with the lethal virus you find. These infected monsters could be sent back to their fellows and contaminate them in no time."

"Bravo!" Commander Taylor cheered. "Original germ warfare, and it'll take place millions of years before our old H bomb and its ancestor the A bomb!"

"I'll call the council of biologists together tomorrow," Leyla declared, "and tell them about the idea. The chemists and physiologists will also be present, as well as the cosmobiologists specialized in the study of endemic illnesses and their distribution zone in different solar systems occupied by our race. These scientists will soon have to make a ruling on the plan and after dissecting a cyclops they'll head up the research in a well defined direction."

Kariven asked point blank, "Do you know what happened to the Bimkamian who was watching over Balkum? He's the one who alerted the Shâmali base when the cyclops attacked, right?"

"He was," Leyla answered telepathically. In the event of this kind of problem or of social troubles that are always possible, the building he lives in is equipped with a basement that leads to a well where a rocket is waiting to evacuate him automatically to our base. He locked himself into the basement but did not deem it necessary to flee, trusting in his refuge. He just warned us over the viewer. Torka, the Military Operations Chief, got in touch with him after our battle with the cyclops. Since he wasn't found out by the Lemurians in Balkum, he continued his secret surveillance mission among them for the benefit of all."

When our friends woke up, late in the morning, and after they had showered, the viewer on the wall lit up in each of their rooms and Leyla was on the screen. A tight-fitting bodysuit, lilac with gold and silver sequin, hugged her delicate form perfectly. The emblem of Grand Instructor sparkled on her breast, sculpted by the strange metallic tissue.

Presently the viewers perceived that her thoughts were being broadcast by the viewer, a marvelous machine that transmitted them directly to their brains.

"I met with the different scientists concerning your plan of the germ war. They said they were ready to study the details of breeding microorganisms when we get them a cyclops for dissection. Torka and I have decided to leave today in search of the monsters."

Before she had finished explaining, Kariven and Streiler, at the same time, completely spontaneously, asked, "What time are you leaving?"

They looked at each other and started laughing, quickly joined by Leyla who agreed to meet them after lunch.

The Retro-timeship took off with Leyla, her twin sister and the Earthlings on board, heading for the cyclops territory. A Bimkamian ship piloted by Torka with a group of giants on board, accompanied the timeship.

Half an hour later, cruising comfortably at 1,000 miles per hour, the two ships reached the jungle. They slowed down to 30 miles per hour, lowered their altitude and watched the forest through the trees.

"There they are!" Commander Taylor shouted, pointing at a clearing on the bank of a river.

A few crude cabins of intertwined branches made up the village of the small cyclops tribe. 20 monsters and their 6-foot tall "babies" were squatting in a circle, staring at a fire where a long-eared mammal, the size of a pony, was being grilled.

"When they feel safe," Leyla explained, "these filthy creatures take the time to cook their prey, but during the tribal wars or the raids on the cities they'd rather eat devour their victims on the spot, raw."

"Very charming," Kariven smirked.

Leyla touched her clear plastic helmet and sent a message to Torka. A minute later her meditative face woke up and she informed her friends psychically, "We're going to drop an anesthetic mist. When the monsters are knocked out we'll land and bring them on board. The operation will take less than an hour. Look there…"

The Earthlings gathered round the dome and eagerly watched what was happening.

The hatch in the Bimkamian spaceship opened and Torka appeared, holding a transparent sphere that he tossed into the air. The ball dropped like a stone and crashed barely 30 feet from the fire that the monsters huddled around. It did not make a loud noise but the gas, suddenly freed, whistled out.

The cyclops jumped up, growling, probably expecting an attack from a hungry tribe tempted by the smell of the "well done" prey. The red hair bristled on their square skulls and on their spines; their eyes spun furiously in their sockets; their claws were ready to tear at the enemy; their nostrils quivered. They bumped into each other looking for the attackers.

Gradually their movements became slower and their growling less ferocious. A few baby cyclops wobbled and fell to the ground, their eyes closed. The males and females approached their offspring cautiously before they, too, collapsed unconsciously. The anesthetic gas had done its job.

The two spaceships descended slowly and landed 40 feet from the village. The giant Bimkamians, armed with disintegrator rifles and the earthlings with their Thomsons, all faces protected by gas masks, stepped forward. The robust Bimkamians split into groups of four and carried the sleeping cyclops straight to the ten armored cages in the ship's hull. 25 minutes later the 20 adults and nine babies were shackled in their special cages brought for the occasion. 10 feet high and wide, 15 feet long, with 4-inch thick bars of steel hardened by ultrasound, they would stand up to the most violent efforts of the captives.

For three days the big laboratories in Shâmali echoed with the cries and roars of the maddened cyclops. Their cages were lined up in a metal hangar that vibrated from their constant violence. The frantic monsters, in fits of rage, shook the bars and howled hideously. They only calmed down when a Bimkamian at the wheel of an electric tractor brought them fresh meat that they pounced on, groaning in pleasure.

Physiologists, biologists and cosmobiologists had submitted the results of their research. The dissected cyclops and the one that had been tested for vulnerability to possible microorganisms had proved to them that the bacillus NZ 14 was lethal without being communicable to humans. The germ war to decimate this monstrous race was about to begin.

In front of the cyclops' cages Leyla, Glanya and the Earthlings avidly followed the telepathic report of the envoy from the research center. The Bimkamian who was responsible for taking care of the monsters was getting ready to leave on his electric tractor when they heard him cry out in terror. Everyone turned around but they were too late.

One of the cyclops, a particularly fierce male, had managed to grab the steel lance that the guardian carried and had stuck it into Leyla's back. Her eyes dilated by the unbearable pain, she wheezed out a death rattle as the bloody point of the lance came out the middle of her chest. After skewering her through, the raging cyclops pulled her to him and gripping her panting body he crushed it against the bars of his cage and sunk his fangs into the blood-streaming corpse.

The harrowing scene lasted only a few seconds. Petrified by horror, wild-eyed and mad, Kariven drew his Colt and pulled the trigger. One bullet struck the monster in the heart and two others exploded his skull. The filthy creature let go of his victim and slid down between the bars of his cage.

Kariven dropped the smoking gun and with his eyes filled with tears he fell sobbing over Leyla's body.

The woman whom he adored would no longer answer to his love.

Through the guardian's carelessness, getting too close to the monsters, she had died, casting one last look on the man she loved.

Her body, pierced by the steel lance and crushed by the strong arms of the cyclops, lay on the floor of the hangar where the explorers stood motionless, tortured by sorrow. In the face of this horrible death Glanya had fainted in Streiler's arms.

CHAPTER SIX

Overwhelmed with grief, Kariven decided to devote himself to the extermination of the hairy monsters, the nightmarish creatures who threatened the Lemurians and who had killed the woman whom he held dearest in the world. He and his friends offered themselves to Torka, the Chief of Military Operations, to actively participate in the germ war.

Two days after the tragic death of Leyla, the vials of NZ 14 were ready in abundance and the bombs containing them were loaded on the Bimkamian spaceships as well as the Retro-timeship.

In their armored cages placed around the hatch openings the contaminated cyclops were making an infernal racket.

While the ships got ready for takeoff the viewer on board informed them that Myln'ha, the Grand Instructor who would succeed Leyla, had just left the distant planet Bimkam and was heading toward Earth. In 48 hours her interstellar spaceship would land at Shâmali where she would start her functions right away. On her arrival the inauguration ceremony would take place in the huge amphitheater reserved for the assemblies of the "Dragons of Wisdom."

The message aggravated Dr. Kariven's grief. Glanya, the twin sister who could have been Leyla's double, had no less effect on him. Kariven felt a shock every time he looked at her. He lied to himself sometimes, saying that this gorgeous blonde was Leyla, the girl he had held in his arms and whose lips he had tasted passionately. But when this "copy" of Leyla put her head on Streiler's shoulder, he looked away so that he would not become unjustly jealous by the deceiving appearances.

Torka finally gave orders to take off.

The squadron of elliptical ships shining brightly in the sun soared off to the vast jungle that covered the interior of Lemuria. When they sped over the riverbanks and were in sight of the place where the empty cabins of the captured cyclops stood, Kariven raged inside; this was the place that held the roots of his affliction.

In the lush vegetation, among the high branches and intertwined vines, huge insects puttered out of the way of the ships skimming over the tops of the tall trees. Groups of monkeys with reddish fur leaped from branch to branch, screeching loudly.

Soon the spaceships reached another camp, not empty this time but inhabited by a tribe of around 150 monsters. The oldest ones, in a hut built after a fashion (a very crude fashion) with rectangular sheets of dried liana resembling hemp.

Most of the males were dozing, lying on the ground, heedless of the raucous cries of their offspring who were hopping around them. A few females were nursing babies the size of chimpanzees. When not on the hunt the hardy males rested while the older beasts and the females did all the work around the camp.

The ships' hatches opened silently. One cyclops fitted with a parachute dropped into the tribe. On seeing one of their own falling out of the sky like this under a white crown, the monsters bowed down to the ground. Quite terrified, the red monster tumbled to the ground, got tangled in the parachute and struggled to get free. It did not know how to unfasten the straps and bindings but with herculean strength it ripped them apart, one after another, like a child ripping up a piece of paper.

Out of its shackles now it left the parachute behind and went roaring into the camp of its unknown brothers. Its arrival from the skies, totally unique in the annals of the cyclops, made a splash. This magical way of entering would earn it the respect of the other cyclops who had no trouble accepting it. Unfortunately for them this monster was a carrier of the NZ 14 germ that would, after three days of incubation, strike them down in 24 hours. Indeed, this contaminated creature would have time to spread his incurable, lethal, secret illness to the whole tribe in no time.

To be absolutely sure, the ships dropped microbe bombs all over the territory, from one tribe to the next. At the end of the day 27 cyclops had been parachuted into as many camps covering an area of around 8,000 square miles. The huge center of infection would be more than enough to spread the epidemic that would sound the death knell of all cyclops in Lemuria. The continent had been literally infested with germ bombs. Harmless to the Lemurians the NZ 14 germ would wreak deadly havoc among the monsters and exterminate their race in a few days.

Thus the Bimkamians, as real "Guardian Angels" of the not yet evolved planet, took control of the situation following the advice of Dr. Kariven and Professor Harrington. The Earth would soon be free of the perpetual threat posed by the cyclops, the monstrous product of a degenerate humanity.

When the incubation period was over the anticipated results passed all expectations.

The ground inhabited by the cyclops in the wild regions was turned into a ghastly mass grave. Hundreds of thousands of monsters died, struck down by the epidemic.

For two days the Bimkamian spaceships had to fly over the slaughter and disintegrate the rotting corpses that might have polluted the lakes and rivers from which the forest animals drank. Hundreds of tons of disinfectant were sprayed over the jungle, the swamps, the mountains and plains. Not an inch of land escaped their preventative actions.

The cyclops had had their day. At least if any rare survivors remained they would present no serious danger to men. Thus the deformed and phenomenal brood of one of Earth's earliest human races disappeared.

Together in the cockpit of the Retro-timeship, Kariven and his friends were taking leave of Torka who had come to say goodbye. The Chief of Military Operations shook the hands of his Earthling friends and to Glanya, who had decided to go with them, he wished luck and happiness:

"I understand your desire to leave Shâmali where everything reminds you of your sister, whom you venerated so profoundly. You will be happy with Kurt Streiler and forget the pain and sorrow you lived through."

The young Austrian engineer, with his arm around Glanya's shoulder, respected her emotions.

Kariven communicated telepathically. "Goodbye, Torka. We're continuing our voyage in Time and will visit epochs even earlier than yours. Then we'll go back to the Present... I mean the Future according to you."

Torka was sorry to leave his friends as he closed the hatch to their ship. He stopped in the middle of the astrodome and waved his arms, forcing a feeble smile for the Earthlings in the forward cockpit of the Space/Time machine. The Chief of Military Operations also sorely regretted the absence of Leyla. If this tragedy had not happened, she would be present at this farewell that might not be joyful but at least would be without this dread that gripped his throat.

The Retro-timeship rose slowly into the clouds.

In the center of the terrain Torka's figure grew smaller and smaller.

Shâmali, the splendid Bimkamian city established on Earth, soon disappeared, abruptly, melting into a chaotic whirlwind. A gray void swept over the ship, which had just made another leap into the Time Spiral, even father back in the past of Earth.

Commander Taylor kept his eyes riveted on the illuminated screens of the chrome control panel, scrutinizing the movements of the needle marking their regression in Time.

Professor Harrington and Streiler were examining the rotation of a calibrated drum that rolled out a plastic ribbon on which were printed different numbers with the symbols plus and minus sometimes separated by vertical red stripes.

"This is the *Physiotempograph* showing a schematic of our travel," Professor Harrington explained to Glanya. "The numbers represent millions of years *before* our Atomic Age, the divisions are hundreds of thousands and the subdivisions thousands. The part of the ribbon appearing now in light blue shows the chronological information of our stay in Shâmali, meaning the start of the Tertiary Period. The dark blue numbers are the days and in this case the 24 orange subdivisions represent the hours we spent with our Bimkamian friends…"

Kariven, lost in his dark thoughts, was not listening. The professor's eyes shifted from him to Glanya, then settled on Streiler. The two scientists shook their heads sadly.

Wanting to pull him out of his grief, Professor Harrington tried to appeal to his scientific knowledge in anthropology and geology. "Tell me, Kariven, would you advise us to make a stopover in the Secondary or Primary?"

"Excuse me?" the young scientists was startled out of his ruminations.

The physicist obediently repeated his question.

"I suggest holding off on exploring the Secondary, though it's terribly important, until later," Kariven answered. "So we can 'skip over' this period and reach the very dawn of the Universe."

Everyone supported his bold proposition. Without a moment's hesitation Professor Harrington gave the necessary instructions to Commander Taylor. The American officer fiddled with his controls and adjusted the Physiotempograph. He engaged the retrogrador and then turned on the Space/Time viewer.

The Retro-timeship shuddered. The starry space visible on the screen transformed instantly into a gray twilight brighter than the usual gloom that accompanied the ship's progress along the Time Spiral.

"This brightness of space around Earth," Professor Harrington explained, "is due to our incredible speed on the one hand and to the increased light of the sun on the other. You know, I'm sure, that our sun, in its infancy, shined infinitely brighter than it does today. We're flying back in time at a billion years per hour!"

"So, we'll witness the birth of the Earth in around three hours," Kariven remarked. "Most geologists and geophysicians believe our planet is around three billion years old. This estimate comes from the study of the oldest uranium deposits in the world, discovered in South Africa. Now, we know for sure that uranium takes five billion years to lose all of its radioactivity and transform into lead. In our universe, the Galaxy—or the Milky Way—was born at the same time" all its suns were born at the same minute! It's agreed today that the other Galaxies—those astounding star clusters like the Milky Way—*are moving away from a common, original center*. The latest scientific discoveries have proven that these huge stellar archipelagos also started on the move three billion years ago[10]."

Professor Harrington supported Kariven's views and a passionate discussion followed, constantly fueled by questions from Glanya and Commander Taylor who were not so familiar with these rather complex theories. Thus the three-hour voyage passed without the passengers realizing, being so caught up in the fascinating conversation.

It was Commander Taylor, always with an eye on the Physiotempograph's feed, who finally announced, "Already? The temporal regressor is registering the programmed number. We've reached three billion years before our Age!"

"Stop!"

The American officer pressed various buttons and flipped some switches on the control panel, then he pulled a lever down on the Physiotempograph and the Retro-timeship

---

[10] This is, in fact, the latest theory proposed by geophysicists. What follows about the origin of the world is likewise based on this hypothesis. (Author's Note) The age of the Earth is now estimated at 4.5 billion years. Rocks returned from the Moon have been dated at a maximum of around 4.4 and 4.5 billion years old. Martian meteorites that have landed upon Earth have also been dated to around 4.5 billion years old by lead-lead dating.

immediately dragged to a halt. It vibrated quietly, rocked lightly backed and forth but gradually regained its stability.

The light gray of space had disappeared.

Through the dome of the cockpit the time explorers struggled to see something but to no avail. The Universe was invisible *because it was not yet born!*

Outside the ship was nothing but inky dark, a frightening blackness, a total void beyond imagination.

Nothing, absolutely nothing, to be used as a point of reference, a system of reference.

The first lines of the Bible came to Kariven's mind: *In the beginning darkness was upon the face of the deep.*

The Earthlings had reached Zero Age, the absolute void, the Non-Time that preceded the World.

Choked up, panting, full of indescribable emotions, the explorers looked at one another. A shiver of dread ran down their spines. Facing this void, this blackness, or rather this absence of Everything, their reason failed.

Is man made to know the secrets of the Universe? Can he probe with impunity the inner workings of Time, Space and the Great Mystery that precedes the ages?

Commander Taylor nervously wiped his sweaty forehead and gulped loudly. "What do we do, Professor?" he asked awkwardly.

Without answering, Professor Harrington reached hesitatingly for the Physiotempograph and slowly turned a calibrated knob. The Retro-timeship vibrated again, lightly, and hummed softly.

All of a sudden on the screen that visualized the images that were unseen by the naked eye, a faint glimmer, a tiny point showed up in the dreadful dark of empty space. Professor Harrington's fingers gently turned the knob of the Physiotempograph to speed up a little the voyage through the void. The hazy spot grew clear, a pale halo on the flat black background.

"Time is beginning," the physicist panted, his eyes riveted on the mysterious point, becoming visible to the eye now that it was acclimated to the darkness.

Gradually the eerie glimmer became a perfectly round ball, hardly brighter than a very distant beacon light softened by a thick fog. In a few minutes this ball changed into a puffed up globe filling up more and more space, although no brighter in its pale phosphorescence. Its mysterious mass took the form of a nebulous sphere on its axis. The gaseous but compact cluster, with its unimaginable density, could have contained the volume of the solar system such as the Earthlings knew.

"That's the Initial Atom! The Egg of the Universe! Its temperature was 20 billion degrees!"[11] Kariven gasped as his eyes scanned the space that was starting to illuminate, very faintly, the extraordinary star.

The expanding mass started turning on itself, slowly at first, then faster and faster. A kind of radio luminosity grew out of the center of the "ball" as if coming from its core. Little by little the globe swelled up, its poles flattened out as it turned into a kind of nebulous circle, a monstrous pancake with a phosphorescent core, measuring billions of miles across.

All of a sudden the Initial Atom burst. It exploded with such violence that the H-bomb looked like a harmless little firecracker in comparison. The cosmic explosion was awful, unthinkable, beyond the wildest imagination.

In a few minutes the gigantic Initial Atom, relatively murky, fragmented into billions of incandescent clouds that spun off from one another. It was like a fantastic downfall of snowflakes glimmering in the rays of an invisible sun and soaring off over the black background.

---

[11] According to current scientific understanding, at 10^{-43} seconds, the Universe's temperature was 10^{32} K. At one second after the Big Bang, its temperature had already cooled to 10^{10} K.

"These rotating masses that are flying off in all directions," Kariven commented, "will become the nebulae that make up the whole Universe."

"But how are we going to recognize our Galaxy in this impossible chaos, in this flood of cosmic clouds from which the other galaxies are born?" Glanya asked, overwhelmed by the grandeur of the sight.

"Patience," Professor Harrington advised as he increased the speed of the Physiotempograph.

Kariven continued, "Everything we just saw is the very image of creation. *And creation lasted only one hour.*[12] From the explosion of the Initial Atom, the Egg of the Universe, up to the distribution of the masses of matter before forming the nebulae later on, barely 60 minutes went by."

Out of the huge swarm in the center of the chaos of billions of budding nebulae a shapeless cloud drifted toward the Retro-timeship.

"There's the answer to your question, Glanya," Professor Harrington said. "Our ship stopped at the farthest edge of the Time Spiral. The Earth, therefore, wasn't visible because it was still one with the Initial Atom. But when it's born, *it will materialize in the exact spot where the ship is now.* The creation of the Earth can't happen anywhere else but 'under' this spot where we are. My deductions are strictly logical and mathematical. Therefore, we can't get lost in the chaos. It's not the ship that's moving now but the Earth—or rather the solar system—that's coming to us by starting its spiral path toward the Apex."

"You mean... you mean to say that this spinning mass heading for us will become the Milky Way? So, from a fragment of this cosmic 'ball' our solar system will be born?"

---

[12] Hardly! In Linde's chaotic inflation model, inflation starts at the Planck time (10^{-43} seconds) and truly begins at 10^{-35} seconds after the Big Bang.

"Exactly. Just keep your eye on the screen," he continued watching and accelerating the Retro-timeship's forward motion through Time.

The ship leaped into the Time Spiral and the surrounding darkness suddenly changed into a lighter shade, embellished with milky white and some red spots that danced on their viewer.

"The nebulae are still moving away and the Universe is taking shape. The cloud of cosmic matter that was heading toward us is now our Galaxy. Without realizing it we are already in the Milky Way at the start of its creation. The bright ball you saw earlier has finally condensed, then exploded into the Galaxy to give birth to new spinning clusters that are roughly spherical—the future planets of the solar system. And there's Earth at its birth…"

One of the shining, spinning stars was oscillating in space in front of the astounded eyes of the spectators. Professor Harrington carefully turned the Physiotempograph's knob once again. The terrestrial globe diminished. Its reddish surface darkened and the embryonic continents started floating on a sea of viscous matter that was, in parts, on fire.

Our planet was semi-liquid then and was cooling down while spinning faster and faster. The acceleration of its rotation along with the attraction of the sun deformed its mass, which under the opposing forces became slightly oval. By a similar effect of the tides a "suction" of seas and continents rose up as a star passed by.

Thanks to the exceptional possibilities of the Retro-timeship traveling through the course of ages, the evolution of our planet looked like it was on fast-forward. The small end of the terrestrial "egg" stretched out, became spindle-shaped, then suddenly broke off from the Earth in a flaming apocalypse. Shreds of fusing matter fell back into the fiery gulf left on the surface of the forming planet while the detached part of the Earth's crust flew off into space.

After several days—a few seconds for the explorers—this fragment of Earth slowly started spinning around and became... the Moon![13]

Our friends stood agape. This fantastic evolution was as delightful as it was frightening.

Lost in contemplation of the dawn of the World, Kariven finally broke the silence, "See there on the surface of the Earth that's still cooling down that hollow part left by the Moon casting off into space? By changing slowly this gulf will become the Pacific Ocean. In fact, the Pacific is surrounded by high mountains including a bunch of volcanoes—the ring of fire of geophysicists. They are the splinters left by the Moon when it broke away from the Earth[14].

"Our globe will continue to cool down; the continents will stop temporarily on their geological foundations; the meteor storms and floods that rained down on the nascent world will lose their magnitude and one day, after the atmosphere forms, which will filter the harsh rays of the sun, life will be born at the bottom of the oceans. The first signs of life will begin in the seas with the Lymph and protoplasm. These two entities, after a slow evolution made up of mutations and transformations, will end up as man, the king of creation, the crowning achievement of hundreds of millions, maybe billions

---

[13] The current leading theory of the origins of the Moon is that, at the time Earth was formed, 4.5 billion years ago, other smaller planetary bodies were also growing. One of these hit the Earth late in its growth process, blowing out rocky debris. A fraction of that debris went into orbit around the Earth and aggregated into the Moon.

[14] Hypothesis recently put forward and well supported by American Professor Georges Gamow. (Author's Note) Gamow (18904-1968) was interested in the early history of the Solar System. In 1945, he co-authored a paper supporting work by German theoretical physicist Carl Friedrich von Weizsäcker on planetary formation in the early Solar System.

of years since the cosmobiologists and paleontologists think that life was born at this distant epoch."

"This 'film' of the birth of the World was really impressive," Glanya acknowledged. "It makes me want to see it end up with all its various animal and vegetal life forms closer to us…"

"I'm anxious too," Streiler seconded. "The vision of the initial chaos left a mark on us and I think it'd be good to visit a later age… An age when we won't feel like such 'intruders'…"

"That would be good," Kariven agreed. "Let's leave behind the Primary and its infancy. This calls for exploring the Secondary Period… and it might surprise us because this age was marked by the famous Gondwana continent. After a cataclysm, the continent produced part of Lemuria, which we just visited. Gondwana and Lemuria have common geological foundations. The cataclysm dates back to around 100 million years ago. Therefore, we have to go into Time at a point after this to get in contact with the future Gondwanian civilization that we really know nothing about. Science even categorically denies its existence. And we can't blame it because we have, in fact, no trace, not the slightest material vestige of this hypothetical civilization except for some animal and plant fossils that have nothing to do with a thinking species.

"Some informal researchers base themselves on the beliefs or traditions passed down from initiate to initiate and adept to adept in order to establish the chronology of these vanished races. Of course, not everyone agrees with the dates or the duration of the periods ascribed to these possible humans, just as there are various schools at present[15]. It is unquestionable that in their ramblings the truth must lie beneath many layers of legends and beliefs that still exist among the peoples of the Earth today. Some scholars who study legends

---

[15] These "occult" beliefs and traditions are not accepted by offivcial science, which refuses to admit—for current lack of proof—the existence of said vanished races. (Author's Note)

and folklore have concluded that it was very possible that civilizations long before ours really existed. Legendary characters, such as dwarves, gnomes, giants, fairies and all powerful genies are, perhaps, the disguised forms of our distant ancestors or of beings come to Earth from another world... The Dragons of Wisdom—the Bimkamians—natives of the Katong solar system, are proof of this. In essence, humankind on Earth, or rather the different humans who had come after one another, had instructors—at the very least Masters—who were replaced over the course of the geological periods... Masters or Instructors who came from another planet."

"Where are we now, in fact?" Glanya inquired.

Commander Taylor looked at the screens on the control panel and answered, "We've come to a point on the Time Spiral that corresponds to 39 million years before our Atomic Age."

"Let's stop the Retro-timeship," Professor Harrington decided. "We should be at the dawn of Gondwanian civilization."

The American officer threw the breaker. The ship started shaking violently, then everything fell silent. The grayish light outside was replaced by a darkness full of shining stars. The majestic orb of the planet Earth—of the *full Earth* because in direct sunlight—sat in empty space. A geographer, even a regular graduate student, would have been astonished to be told that this planet lost in the heart of the cosmos, surrounded by unknown stars, was *his* planet.

The Retro-timeship was set over a vast, elongated continent, including what is today South America, Africa, part of South Asia and a large portion of Oceania (e.g. Australia).

"So, there's the famous Gondwana continent!" Professor Harrington got excited as he looked out upon the hemisphere flooded by sunlight.

A thin, dark crescent covered the edge of the planet. The Moon hung like a white disc with marbled continents and bluish zones of small seas that in this tremendously ancient age existed on our satellite. A thin atmosphere haloed the Moon.

The cosmic cataclysms[16] had not yet wounded its surface. Craters, chasms and gigantic pits were still not blemishing the face of our night star.

"Get closer to the land, Commander," Professor Harrington said. "We'll take a sightseeing tour and find a good place to land."

The Retro-timeship wobbled gently before diving down on a slight curve. The view was clouded through the dense atmosphere but daylight soon replaced the empty, interplanetary night.

The ship flew over the eastern rivers of Gondwana where Australia would be in the future. Huge forests of leafy ferns formed green patches contrasting with the ochre of the open spaces. The sea, a darker bluish-green, battered the coastal reefs with raging waves. Giant swells crested with white foam broke against the coral formations whose red-orange ridges stood out in the shallow lagoons, like strange, tangled, twisted byways.

On the banks of a sheltered cove a great number of glittering domes were lined up in rows of a hundred. One in particular, right in the middle, rose up higher than the others.

"Weird," Kariven observed, "those don't look like natural formations."

"Let's land," Professor Harrington suggested, as intrigued as his friends.

The ship set down around 150 feet from the bizarre constructions. Before opening the hatch the time explorers inspected their surroundings meticulously but they saw no living being.

"Now that we're a little more familiar with time travel and vanished countries, do you think we should still use the transparency serum?" Streiler questioned.

---

[16] See *Nous, les Martiens* [*We, Martians*] by the same author. (Author's Note) A 1954 novel in which Kariven discovers that Humanity is descended from Ancient Martian colonists, whose homeworld was threatened by a comet.

"We can always take the first dose that doesn't last for more than an hour," Commander Taylor proposed, a believer in the politics of prudence. "We'll leave like that and if we run into something too dangerous we can come back to the 'bus' to get a second or third dose to last longer. What do you think?"

The proposition was accepted unanimously and Kariven used his expertise on his friends: he injected them with the transparency serum as well as the antidote to protect their vision. The harmless shot had more than its usual effect on Glanya who looked in the mirror every five minutes to watch herself undergo the strange process of her tissues *fading* into transparency.

Half an hour passed and our transparent friends took off their clothes and put on the plastic underwear. They each grabbed a weapon and prepared for the expedition into the mysterious city. Glanya picked up the disintegrator rifle that she had carried away from Shâmali and her time.

When they were on the ground a crushing silence pressed down on them. No sound, no animal cries disturbed the tranquility. The silence, so intense on the edge of so many buildings, utterly astonished Kariven and his friends. They were overcome by an indefinable feeling that added to the weirdness of the phenomenon.

"Could it be a dead city?" Streiler scratched his head thoughtfully, puzzled.

They walked slowly, almost afraid to make a sound in the extraordinary solitude, until they reached the first spherical constructions.

The sun cast its rays through the transparent men making them even less visible.

The explorers paced around the first dome they came across and found a narrow door around six and half feet high. Kariven pushed it open and squinted, intrigued. Inside the "house" was a bluish light. Hazy forms in motion flitted about furtively and then, all of a sudden, the sourceless light turned yellow-gold.

The ghostly forms melted away in the light that, after examination, seemed to be coming from the concave ceiling, which had turned golden.

"Did you see what I saw, Kariven?" Professor Harrington asked, adjusting the rectangular glasses on his nose... his invisible nose.

"I was just going to ask you the same thing."

"What do you think it is?" Glanya inquired, inching timidly closer to Streiler.

Kariven frowned. "Apparently there's nothing in here. But we all saw or think we saw something moving. I suppose..."

He broke off and suddenly stretched his hands out in front of him. He looked completely stunned. *His hands felt like they were kneading the empty space.*

"Good God!" he exclaimed. "Touch this! Could we have 'rivals' who can make themselves invisible?"

Commander Taylor raised his eyebrows and gawked as he said, "Touch what? I don't see what you're fiddling with here..."

In spite of the unease caused by Kariven's cryptic words, everyone reached out toward what he was feeling. Taylor, Harrington, Streiler and Glanya all turned pale and stood speechless, astounded, troubled.

Some light obstacle had stopped their hands in the apparently empty space!

"And it's like... what is it like, do you think?" Commander Taylor muttered, fumbling and skeptical.

"I have no idea! But *it* is moving..."

"Hey, it's leaving," Streiler shouted, waving his open hands around the empty space.

Indeed, the form they had touched had slipped away and disappeared, if you can say that for something that cannot be seen...

"Let's get out of here," Kariven suggested, "and visit the city, which I think we can call this collection of shiny domes."

They walked down an avenue lined with these weird buildings, made of an unidentifiable material, until they reached a relatively open space. In the middle stood the grand dome seen during their flyover.

A row of oval openings ran along the base of the dome that sparkled in emerald green. The time explorers risked a glance inside the first arch. What they saw froze them on the spot.

Under the great dome, which also gave off a bluish light, there were haunting figures milling around, ghosts of a sort that had a vaguely human but quasi-fluidic appearance.

In the blue light they looked brown and floated jerkily through the air, a little like seahorses, those strange "horse-fish" that swim vertically by undulating their bodies. The "phantoms" had lumpy heads, huge, pale eyes, two legs and a slender body without a well-defined outline or surface. They spun around, moved forward, then backward, and sometimes intermingled to become one, bigger, phantom form. And all this in deathly silence.

"This is the most extraordinary ballet I've ever seen," Commander Taylor whispered. "But what's the point of mixing together like that?"

Deep in thought, Professor Harrington hazarded an explanation, "Don't think me a doddering old fool, Commander, but I have the feeling that this is a building meant for procreation. Look at how those things fuse together in pairs…"

"Of course! They come together as two but they separate as three…"

"Exactly. These curious creatures are joining to give birth to other complete creatures, *in an adult state*, if I may say so. Unlike the human race and the animal species, they don't have a period of gestation, an actual birth, growth and gradual development. Among them two complete creatures fuse and instantly give birth to a third complete creature."

"I think the ceremony is over," Commander Taylor remarked on seeing all the ghosts head for the oval openings.

The blue concave dome slowly grew dark and only the light of day lit the building.

When one of these strange beings left through a door and went outside its color faded. It became nothing but a vaporous body with a weird, very pale yellow *aura*, hardly visible in the natural light. Crossing the sunny plaza they disappeared, melting in the sunrays, leaving only a spectral trembling in the air, like those little mirages on hot roads during a heat wave—fluttering, shimmering puddles on the road gave an impression of these extraordinary beings.

"This form of life is so different from ours," Kariven observed, "that it seems to me really hard, if not impossible, to communicate with them."

"I'm probably going to sound dull as dishwater to you," Commander Taylor smiled, "but what do you say to some breakfast?"

The explorers immediately approved his wise invitation and left the "City of Ghosts."

When they reached their improvised landing strip Kariven opened his mouth and raised his arm to stop his companions. 100 yards from them and passing close by the ship, apparently unnoticed, were ten men and women, *bright yellow*, as if endowed with bodies of malleable gold.

CHAPTER SEVEN

The time explorers watched these strange humans with understandable surprise. Although transparent Kariven and his friends moved away and hid safely behind some bushes to let the weird group pass by.

"Are they painted or are they...?" Commander Taylor whispered without finishing his thought.

"Certainly not," Kariven whispered back. "That pigmentation is natural."

They snuck after them and soon stopped behind one of the domes that was used as a house for the ghostly forms. When the golden men had gone inside, the explorers approached the narrow door and peeked inside.

In the concave dome the bluish light showed the rippling, brownish, spectral forms fluttering around their golden visitors and sometimes touching them with their wispy aura. The ghostly, ectoplasmic beings went from one golden man to another, darting like a fish in water.

"What could they be doing?" Glanya whispered, fascinated.

Kariven made a guess. "Wouldn't this be their way of communicating? Couldn't they be exchanging telepathic waves like the Bimkamians of your race, Glanya?"

After half an hour of this strange affair the visitors left their ephemeral hosts. Passing by the explorers again the strange humans surprised them in the most singular, most astonishing way.

Kariven scrutinized them minutely and whispered, "But... they're not men and women. They're asexual or rather bisexual... they're androgynous!"

In fact, being totally nude, nothing of their peculiar anatomy was hidden. All of them had the same intersexualization characteristics: their structure was derived from that of man and woman.

Reflecting on this unusual observation the time explorers followed the androgynes. Unaware of their presence, they led the explorers to a cove where the green waves of the ocean came to die peacefully. They jumped into a strange boat—a kind of wide, pink metal dinghy—and headed out to sea. An engine huffed noisily under the back as it dug a deep wake through the liquid.

"A jet turbine!" the engineer Streiler remarked. "Or something like it. Obviously our ancestors are still full of surprises for us."

"We're not going to swim after them," Commander Taylor said. "Let's take the bus. Besides," he noted looking at the others, "we're starting to become visible again."

They ran through the city of ectoplasmic beings and reached the Retro-timeship that, very soon, was taking off. Only at an altitude of 1,000 feet did the American officer turn the ship toward the coast.

The sea, colored by thousands of little waves, glimmered like an emerald basking in the sun. A pink spot slicing through the water around 50 miles from the coast appeared on the screen showing how fast the androgynes' dinghy was. 50 miles in 10 minutes was a worthy performance for any boat... from 1,390,000 centuries in the past.

15 minutes later the super-fast dinghy made a wide circle and slowed down into an artificial channel that led to a port.

"Wow," Glanya's eyes widened with surprise, "that white city is identical to... Shâmali!"

Through the cockpit the Earthlings from the future recognized that except for some minor details the city was an exact replica of Shâmali, the Bimkamian base established on Earth over 9 million years later.

An astrodome with oval spaceships—whereas the Bimkamian ships were spherical—was located to the north of the city. To the west, at the foot of a mountain around 20 miles away as the crow flies, stood another cluster of buildings that was nothing like the big port city. Its houses were low, two or three floors apparently; its streets seen on the viewer were more like those in small cities of the Atomic Age. One main road linked the Shâmali look-alike to this place.

On Professor Harrington's order Commander Taylor landed his ship close to the astrodome. Glanya did not let her eyes feast on the magnificent white city that reminded her of Shâmali. She snuck a peek at Kariven and saw the deep sadness written on his face. Like her, he was thinking of Leyla.

From a tall, rectangular, metal building on top of a huge cement structure two giants over nine feet tall came out! They took a moving escalator that brought them down to the runway. There they stopped in front of the first oval spaceship and had a conversation, pointing to the spaceship but apparently not seeing the Retro-timeship parked at the end of the site. Dressed in long, white coats and tight fitting, purple pants, their heads protected by a big, round helmet that reflected the sunlight.

Glanya examined them, astonished and speechless. Streiler put his arm affectionately around her waist and asked the reason for her astonishment: "Seeing these giants is really so disturbing to you, Glanya? Don't they look like your brothers? Of course, they're taller but…"

"*These are my ancestors*, Kurt," she ended up muttering. "Our archives in the artificial astro-base that is floating a million miles from Bimkam tell the complete history of our humanity. I studied a compilation about our expansion in the Galaxy. For 200 million years our race flew all over intra-galactic space trying to peacefully colonize the solar systems with planets inhabited by thinking beings. Colonization is not the right word because we're happy just to educate the peoples without exploiting them. I clearly remember having learned that from the start of our Astronautical Age our mother race sent subjects to thousands of different worlds. The Bimkamian Instructors, therefore, educated countless races. They came to Earth several times where the civilization had been ravaged by one disaster after another. When the new humanity on Earth, after these cataclysms, started becoming civilized the Instructors came to this planet to teach them the good and develop

90

their knowledge. My ancestors didn't always live on Bimkam, needless to say. Because they also experienced disasters. But their vast empire in space spared them the ruin suffered by the ancient races on Earth. When a planet occupied by Bimkamians suffers one of these cosmic disasters the colonists can flee to other planetary refuges. Even if they were totally engulfed in the end of the world, their brothers in other systems would continue their civilizing mission. By sheer number and power the Bimkamians will never die out.

"Obviously our race changes and develops over the years. That's why these giants, almost ten feel tall, my ancestors, are bigger than us, the Bimkamians of Shâmali. And you Earthlings from the Atomic Age are smaller than us but the human race survives and will always survive. Even if in a million years—*after the Age you come from*—your Earthling race changes and gives birth to dwarves... the representatives of the Mother Race will keep pretty much the same morphology. We occupied two planets of this solar system: first Mars, then Earth. Later our descendants will occupy Venus, which is not yet inhabitable."

"So, they're also our ancestors," the young French scientist observed. "In a talk at the Academy of Sciences I proposed a hypothesis in which Earthlings would have a Martian origin. In an expedition in Antarctica, some American technicians and myself discovered a bronze-skinned race that descended directly from Atlanteans and that lived in a sheltered valley in the polar ice. These beings were Martian offspring that had come to colonize the Earth after a cataclysm had ruined their mother planet[17]."

---

[17] See *Nous les Martiens* (q.v.) and *Le Monde oublié* [*The Forgotten World*]. (Author's Note) *The Forgotten World* is another 1954 novel in which Kariven discovers a lost valley in Antarctica, which is inhabited by descendents from Atlantis. Bizarrely, *The Forgotten World* was published just after *The Time Spiral*, which must have confused readers.

Glanya thought for a minute before saying, "The Bimkamians, therefore, would have mixed with the Martians and their cross-breed would have colonized Earth because our race is white."

"In this case, by going back farther to reach the roots of common genealogical tree, who were… or rather who are these immaterial beings, the transparent, fluidic creatures we saw in the houses?" Professor Harrington asked.

"I didn't want to believe it," Glanya started, "but I have to admit it now that they can't be anything else but *Plakshians*, the ancestors of the Earthling androgynes with golden skin. These translucent beings are the first form of thinking life that appeared on Earth. From their race was born, by mutation, the yellow-gold Earthlings like the ones who visited them a little while ago."

"I understand," Kariven mused. "When the territory of Gondwana became buried under the sea and only Lemuria was left—with the other islands that emerged from the depths—the survivors from the Earthling androgynes in turn gave birth to the Lemurians, the Earthlings with light brown skin whom we saved from the cyclops."

"Exactly," Glanya confirmed. "As long as these giants are my ancestors, we have nothing to fear from them. Let's go talk to them. You're starting to get used to our telepathic communication now. Thanks to their helmets that amplify psychic waves you'll be able to hear our thought-talk."

"Great!" Streiler rubbed his hands together by habit. "Commander, you can open the hatch."

"OK," Commander Taylor answered simply, pressing a button with his right hand and turning a knob with his left.

The time explorers left the ship and crossed the astrodome, talking casually. On hearing strange voices getting closer the two pre-Bimkamian looked around. They were stunned to see a huge, shiny metal rocket ship (that should not have been there!) in their astrodome. And likewise on seeing the weird dwarves walking toward them.

Instinctively their hands went to their belts and promptly unholstered long-barreled guns. With an agile bound they leapt behind the ship's landing gear and waited, on guard, for the strangers who had come out of the mysterious machine.

Glanya was marching at the head her friends and stopped three feet from the giants. With impeccable style she saluted them by bringing her right hand up to her left shoulder. The two men in their spotless white coats hesitated, looked at each other and then automatically answered the salute after switching the gun into the other hand.

Glanya pressed the button in her transparent helmet so that her friends could hear the thought conversation. Unsure, the pre-Bimkamians wondered at her helmet. All of a sudden their faces showed an intense surprise. They had just received the thoughts from this pretty, young blonde.

"We'd like to be brought to the Grand Instructor," Glanya said mentally.

"I *am* the Grand Instructor," one of them responded. "My name is Hornuk and this is Inshtug, my chief aide. You seem familiar with our customs…"

She introduced herself and her friends and continued, "Contrary to what you believe, we don't come from another solar system but from the Future."

Hornuk and his aide raised their eyebrows. "What do you mean?" the Grand Instructor gaped.

"My friends come from an Age on Earth placed in the future, 130 million years from your time. I, too, come from a future era… 94 million years. However, although my friends are native Earthlings, I myself belong to your extraterrestrial race. My twin sister was the Grand Instructor of my generation with the Bio Galactic Code 733 100 91 KLP."

Hornuk furrowed his brow. "You talk about this so-called Instructor from the future in the past tense. Moreover, I'm afraid my aide and I don't take your story seriously…"

A cloud of sadness shadowed Glanya's face. "My sister is dead…"

"We can furnish you with irrefutable proof that we come from the Future," Kariven confirmed through telepathic speech. "The ship that brought us into these different epochs is at your disposal. Come with us and see for yourselves if we speak the truth. We will take you into the Time Spiral to an era of your choice."

Hornuk abruptly brought out his gun, which he had put back in his holster, and taking a step back shouted, "You think we're stupid! It's you who are coming with us. And you can be sure that we won't bring you into the Future or the Past but into a good and solid prison of the present time. Come on, march!" and he waved his gun to back up his order.

"But you can clearly see that we're not armed," Kariven tried to protest. "If our intentions were hostile as you seem to think, why would we be coming to you in full daylight and without weapons?"

"You will explain that later. Now get going!" the Grand Instructor barked, obviously unwilling to take them on their word.

Kariven looked at his companions and shrugged his shoulders. He decided to obey.

The explorers were taken into the cement building surmounted by the metal tower. The least that could be said was that their entrance made a splash.

20 men and women stopped their work to watch them pass by. Every pre-Bimkamian was sitting before a metal panel full of buttons, knobs and multi-colored blinking lights. The muscular women, beaming with health, were between six and eight feet tall. They were, therefore, smaller than the other sex. A simple "two-piece" was all they wore.

The prisoners crossed the huge room and before the threatening guns they entered the next room. Inshtug put them in individual *boxes* with one seat in each and closed a thick, transparent door behind them.

"Sit down," Hornuk ordered. "I'll give you one minute to tell me in what zone your squadrons are hiding and the real purpose of your being here."

"But since I've already said that…" Glanya risked.

Pointing at Kariven in the first box Hornuk ignored the girl and said, "I'm interrogating you!'

As Hornuk had not turned on his psychic amplifying helmet, Kariven could not hear his thoughts.

"I'm warning you," the Grand Instructor growled. "When the time's up, we'll put you under the psychic probe and I can tell you that your brain will not like it."

"You're idiots!" Glanya lost patience. "I'm the only one here who can hear your thoughts without needing the wave amplifier. I'm telepathic because you and I are of the same race. My friends talk but they can't hear your thoughts without the help of your psychic-amplifiers. So, go up to them and probe their brains—you have no need of a machine."

Her animated rant, although telepathic, made an impression on Hornuk and his aide. The Grand Instructor thought about this for a second, then decided to approach Kariven. With his big hand he pressed the button on his helmet. Right away the young French scientist received the thought message:

"Relax and empty your mind."

Kariven obeyed and forced himself, without too much difficulty, to think of nothing. After a few minutes of drifting, during which Hornuk concentrated hard, the barrier that guarded the unconscious thoughts was broken through. The two of them stayed like that, facing each other, for more than half an hour. The giant had to squat down so that he could look into the eyes of his prisoner.

For his part, Inshtug tried the same thing on Streiler. Then came the turn of Professor Harrington and Commander Taylor to undergo this psychic inspection that they played along with willingly.

The probing ended two long hours later after which the Grand Instructor and his aide withdrew into an adjoining room. They were gone for a long time and when they came back, looking worried, they turned on their helmets. Inshtug opened the individual cages and led out the captives who noticed that the guns remained in the holsters hanging from the giants' belts.

Hornuk took Glanya's hand and looking down into her eyes, which barely reached his stomach, he smiled kindly, "I'm sorry, Glanya. We treated you and your friends a little… rudely. I apologize. My aide and I got indisputable confirmation of your intentions in the subconscious of these… humans from the Future. It's incredible, but I believe it!"

"You're forgiven, Hornuk," Glanya smiled back and looking up to stare the giant in the eyes. "But why did you treat us like thieves?"

"Not thieves," Hornuk corrected, "but spies. We were sure that you belonged to the League of Independent Worlds."

"Spies!" Kariven gasped as he could now hear the Grand Instructor's thoughts being amplified through the system in his helmet.

"We're in more or less open conflict with a group of seven solar systems totaling 23 evolved planets," Hornuk explained. "Instructed and perfected by our care, the civilizations on these worlds joined forces in a 'League of Independent Worlds.' After taking from our Empire the benefits that we grant to all inferior worlds, these beings are constantly led astray by the false promises of a powerful chief who is trying to get total power by any means possible. For Siomak—that's his name—the most vile tricks are common practice. Three times already he's tried to corrupt the population on Earth to recruit them into his revolutionary league, although in the end the planetary races we educated and perfected never had any complaints about our presence. Our methods are basically pacifist and no act of violence was ever committed against these peoples. The fault, therefore, is not ours. Siomak is just a jealous creature with no scruples, ready to sacrifice more than one world to quench his thirst for power."

"So, get rid of him, put him in prison or make him disappear," Commander Taylor spoke out, thinking of the Euro-Asians who, while shouting out their desire for "Peace," were only fighting to enslave their neighboring states. Because though the times change, the customs stay the same!

Hornuk sighed, "I'm afraid we'll be forced to do just that when this chain reaction of takeovers threatens us directly..."

"Don't kid yourself," Glanya broke in. "I studied our history that you don't know about. Even though I can't remember the dates, I can guarantee you that Siomak will have the last word... at least in a small portion of the Galaxy. After taking over 51 planets, the schemer will start a huge war in which hundreds of millions of human beings will die. Using a secret weapon invented by a research group affiliated with the League of Independent Worlds, he will just miss conquering out Galactic Empire."

"What secret weapon?" Inshtug asked, who was particularly interested in new weapons.

"An absolute-speed missile *capable of instantly crossing the 100,000 light years of our universe!*[18] This extraordinary device was built after an invention no less extraordinary of a device that could 'launch' into space solid objects *transmuted instantly into waves*. A 'receiving unit' was therefore sent by traditional means, but secretly, to the planet to be destroyed and when it landed in a deserted zone the absolute-speed missile was placed in the 'transmitting unit'. It created a kind of radio transmission of matter, not on the principle of hertzian waves, whose speed at almost 200 miles per second is insufficient, but on a new formula imprinted for the mass of the missile—a mass that the 'transmitter' renders unchangeable—at absolute speed. The device, therefore, disappears from the 'transmitting unit' in which it had been placed and appears instantly in the 'receiving unit' located at any distance whatsoever. Its disintegrator cone could pulverize an entire planet! The secret of this phenomenal weapon was lost in the cataclysm and it just might be for the best..."

---

[18] Guieu means our Milky Way Galaxy, not the Universe itself, which is estimated at 93 billion light years in diameter.

"That's terrifying!" Hornuk groaned. "Are you sure about all this?"

"It's not me who said it, it's history," Glanya emphasized logically. "Coming from a future age, I'm in a better position to talk about the past than you are to talk about the future."

"Of course, of course," the Grand Instructor conceded, being battered by a storm of alarming thoughts. "But I hesitate to admit that Siomak could have succeeded... hmm... that he *will succeed* in conquering so many planets and sow death on such a large scale. This absolute-speed missile should, therefore—if what you say is true—be perfected in a few years? Don't you know when he'll attack and *where* it'll happen?"

Glanya thought hard, searching, racking her brains but in vain. "I can't remember the date but I think the first target world has a weird name, something like Tekla-na or Katlaka... Names change, you know, over millions of years and maybe even..."

"Katlounka!" Hornuk said with fear in his eyes, clenching his big belt.

"That's the name, I think..."

"I'm sure of it," he raged. "A planet in the Lit'Rak solar system, the site of our research center for experimental spaceship prototypes. It's also where new weapons and intergalactic vehicles are tested, where we can work in secret. If this planet were destroyed, it would delay generations of thinking beings in their planned evolution... Not to mention finding ourselves in dire straits to defend against a heavy attack in that isolated corner of the universe."

"Siomak, I can assure you, destroyed this important research center," Glanya repeated firmly, "and the treachery allowed him to destroy any planet that tried to resist while waiting for reinforcements and weapons that never came. Our race had to endure Siomak and his crimes for 92 Bimkamian years. The Galactic Empire itself was under threat. But my ancestors were finally able to overthrow him and free the peoples whom he had so wickedly deceived and almost completely enslaved."

"We have to fight this tyrant and *make history lie!*" Commander Taylor shouted angrily.

CHAPTER EIGHT

While the Earthlings were having a friendly chat with Hornuk and Inshtug, Lieutenant Clark and four men were giving each other the transparency serum. They had, in fact, watched on worriedly as their superiors were arrested by the two giants and they were ready to help.

Made almost invisible they snuck around the control tower cautiously. After peeking through the windows they went up to a door in the back of the building. On guard, arms at the ready, Clark and his men opened the door ever so slowly. The lieutenant looked through the partially open door and almost dropped his machine gun at the unimaginable sight before him.

In a huge room, a kind of office with a lighted ceiling, Commander Taylor and the members of the expedition were sitting comfortably in green *plastic* chairs, talking casually with the two giants!

They obviously had no idea that the team from the Retro-timeship was standing so close to them.

Since Inshtug and Hornuk were using their psychic amplifiers to "converse" with the Earthlings, Clark and his GIs could clearly perceive their telepathic exchange. Relieved by the peaceful nature of the thought-conversation, they concluded that their companions were no longer in danger. It must have been considered a wrongful arrest caused by a misunderstanding that was all cleared up now.

Fully reassured about their superiors' security, the GIs went quietly back to the ship without being noticed.

As the door closed silently behind dutiful Lieutenant Clark and his team, Hornuk declared after careful consideration, "I'm ready to try the impossible to put Siomak out of commission. But by killing him before he has started this war, we'll be committing a willful murder."

"Not a murder," Kariven corrected him, "an absolutely justified, preventative execution!"

"I'm afraid I must refer it to the Eternal Wisdom, the Supreme Chief of the Galactic Empire... and I highly doubt that he'll believe your story right away. He won't be satisfied, like I was, with probing your subconscious and he'll probably demand irrefutable proof. He might ask you to take a group of scientists into your future age before making up his mind."

"But," Glanya objected, "the fact that I don't remember the date of Siomak's attack could mean we'll lose valuable, perhaps crucial time for your era."

Hornuk looked at his aide, Inshtug, and saw the same worry in his eyes. "Would you suggest that I forget about the need to refer the matter to the Eternal Wisdom?"

"Undertake a pre-emptive expedition against Siomak, today if possible," Glanya advised.

"Where is Siomak's headquarters?" Professor Harrington asked.

"On Nysmi, the main planet of the Choïko solar system, 27 light years from Earth. With our reconnaissance ships we can make the trip in around three hours." After a short pause he added, "If you're not afraid of being exposed to danger, I'll accept you on board my ship."

A smile lit up Professor Harrington's face. In the eyes of his companions he could read the pleasure they took in the offer.

"We're at your disposal, Hornuk."

The Grand Instructor sat before the powerful viewer that linked the various bases of the vast Galactic Empire. He pushed three black buttons on the chrome panel, slowly spun a selector knob and the rectangular screen lit up, showing the most impressive man in colored relief.

In general appearance he could have been a "wonderman" or a mutant. His skin was green and scaly like a reptile. His red eyes and thick lips had something clearly inhuman about them. His slightly pointy ears and his hooked nose made him look like a faun. His head was bald and covered with a brown, horny shell.

Hornuk saluted him. The Nysmian—the green man from the planet Nysmi—responded in kind, raising his right hand with three bony, webbed fingers.

"Peace be with you, N'xok," the Grand Instructor bowed.

"Peace is always with us and our dependents, Hornuk," the green-skinned Nysmian replied.

Our friends were not sure if this thought striking their brains was ironic or if was simply a polite expression.

"Our planet," Hornuk began, "has just received a delegation from Bitnak, the last star landed on only one *K'tag* ago. The representatives have expressed a desire to visit your Independent worlds. They've got authorization from the Eternal Wisdom to make a survey trip in the Empire. I would appreciate if you would submit to His Majesty Siomak their wish to get to know the worlds of your League. If His Majesty does them the honor of granting their wish, I will take them to Nysmi."

N'xok the green Nysmian nodded his head. "I will transmit your request to His Majesty Siomak. You will have your answer within a *N'btog.*"

The screen went dark and Hornuk turned to his friends. "This Nysmian, N'xok, is the Plenipotentiary Minister, the emissary to the Galactic Empire. He's kind of like Siomak's ambassador, his right-hand man."

"His accomplice, then!" Commander Taylor spoke up, not mincing words.

"So, it's these pseudo-men, these abortive crocodiles, these sideshow freaks who want to conquer the Universe!" Kariven was indignant. "Have you got a plan, Hornuk, for attacking Siomak without committing suicide?"

The Grand Instructor thought for a minute and then said, "We'll go to Nysmi on board the galactic fighter ship *Okan.* It's just come out of our testing center and is able to reach amazing speeds. Plus, it's equipped with formidable weapons system, including a disintegrator cannon, which is so new that even the Nysmians don't know about it."

Glanya smiled. "Right now... I mean in our future age even simple handguns are disintegrators."

"We're not there yet," Inshtug said, "but I figure it'd be better not to use the weapon. There's a better way to beat Siomak: Put in his capital one or more *Z'nabag* bombs. The bombs can explode after our visit and spread the gas that affects the brain's nerve center. The chemical compound drives them crazy by combining with the blood's oxygen. All the capital's inhabitants will become homicidal and kill each other like savages. Siomak and his cronies won't escape."

"Bravo!" Hornuk congratulated. "The gas will get rid of the tyrant without exposing us. Revamp the weapons on the Okan, Inshtug, and wait for us on the runway."

"I'll go with Inshtug," Commander Taylor offered. "You can show me a hangar where I can park the Retro-timeship during our trip."

As the American officer and the pre-Bimkamian were leaving, the long-range viewer screen lit up. N'xok's hideous face was framed in the rectangle.

"His Majesty Siomak is honored to welcome the delegation from Bitnak to Nysmi. The League of Independent Worlds is always ready to open its doors to new members from the Galactic Empire." Addressing the Grand Instructor personally N'xok added, "If you leave immediately you will arrive in M'zom, our capital, by the end of the day... of *our* day, of course. You can take a rest and tomorrow visit whatever you'd like."

"Thank you, N'xok. We recognize the infinite kindness of His Majesty Siomak. Peace be with you."

When the screen turned off Hornuk muttered thoughtfully, "We're lucky to arrive at night on this hemisphere of the planet Nysmi. It'll make our job easier..."

Hornuk and his friends met up with Inshtug in the astrodome along with Commander Taylor.

"Lieutenant Clark and his men complained because we left them here instead of taking them with us into the fight," Taylor said. "Since the Retro-timeship is closed up safely in the hangar, I gave them free time until we get back. Inshtug set them up with one of his friends to be their tour guide."

"He'll have his work cut out for him," Streiler snorted. "Rudy Clark and his five GIs are great guys but there's no one better at chasing skirts."

In fact, leaving the huge, metal hangar Lieutenant Clark and his team, accompanied by a well-built giant, were heading for the city. Hands in pockets, smoking a Lucky or chewing gum, the Americans were strolling casually, glad to abandon their "bus" and inactivity for a while.

The galactic fighter Okan, with its slender form, its nose pointed like a needle, its fuselage lined with windows and its tripod landing gear, looked like a supersonic jet from the Atomic Age, but its sensational capabilities naturally put it far above those snail-paced jets.

Before entering the cockpit, Inshtug opened a hidden recess in the wall and showed the bombs with Z'nabag gas. These powerful weapons were composed of a cylinder about 20 inches long and 6 inches in diameter. Their upper cap enclosed the time delay mechanism. When it went off, the gas would stream out silently and in less than 15 minutes would cover over half a square mile.

According to the Grand Instructor's calculations, 20 to 30 bombs would be enough to contaminate the atmosphere of M'zom, Siomak's capital. But in case of any hitch they were carrying 40.

The hatch closed with a click and the Okan took off without a sound. With its anti-gravitational thrusters working at full power it shot off like an arrow and passed the atmospheric layer in a split second. Without the anti-g system counteracting the effects of acceleration in the cabin, the passengers felt like mush. The speedometer spun off higher and higher numbers on the indicator.

The galactic fighter reacted magnificently to the toughest demands. Using the inexhaustible energy of the cosmic rays that filled the Universe, like the Retro-timeship did, it would touch down on Nysmi in the Choïko solar system in a little less than three hours.

From time to time a meteor detected on the radar exploded and for a brief time lit up the eternal night of space. The sensors that had spotted it had instantly shot the disintegrator cannon. The celestial rock was thus transformed into radiation before it presented any danger to the ship.

Streiler, who was a specialist in super-rockets, sat in amazement of the space jet. The windows made of *Baxlin*, an indestructible and incombustible alloy fabricated in a magnetic field (the elements to be fused floating in the air and bombarded with special rays), were transparent but the outrageous speed of the ship kept the passengers from admiring the endless constellations of the cosmos or the dazzling disintegration of the meteors.

The interstellar viewer screen used special frequencies that allowed for brief communication: a green-scaled Nysmian popped up. Hornuk was surprised but being a good diplomat he saluted and greeted him kindly. The Nysmians loved showing off with flashy protocol.

"This is space control," the green thing announced. "You're about to enter the cosmic zone of the Independent Worlds. Please adjust your radars' wavelengths targeting meteorites and break the connection with your disintegrator cannons."

The Nysmian waited for Hornuk to do this. When he saw him flip a switch and turn a calibrated dial, he nodded and after pressing a button on the control panel in front of him said, "A security patrol is coming to you. You will stop your ship so they can board and inspect you. They will then escort you to the M'zom astrodome where you are expected. Over and out."

Hornuk signed out. He gradually reversed the direction of the magneto-cosmic thrusters and quickly stopped the ship, as safely in decelerating as in accelerating.

"They're suspicious by nature," he smiled. "If you've got weapons, I advise you to hide them in the secret compartment in the cabin. They'll be safe with the gas bombs because the door is made of an ultra-thick element. Even if they pound on the wall the Nysmians won't be able to detect the hole."

Regretfully the time explorers put their Colts in the secret compartment and returned to the cockpit. Through the Baxlin windows they saw the bright, blinking light of the anticipated patrol. It grew bigger as it got closer and after a minute it eased up alongside the Okan, motionless in space.

An articulated, circular tube came out of the patrol, a small, elliptical spaceship, and magnetically attached to the fighter's hatch, fitting the curve perfectly. Hornuk verified the seal before ordering the hatch to be opened. The Grand Instructor and his friends watched the operation through the viewer that was now switched over to the cabin.

Four scaly Nysmians came into focus on the screen. They had just entered the airlock of the Okan and were carefully closing the hatch of the pressurized chamber that was connected by a tube to their own spaceship.

The cameras installed along the passageways and corridors broadcast the image of the four lizard men walking to the cockpit. The group stopped in front of the sealed door and the chief banged on the reinforced armor with the butt of his paralyzing pistol. Hornuk ordered the door to be opened immediately.

"Our ship is open to you," he greeted. "You can search it from the upper deck to the bottom hold. Would you like me to go with you?"

The chief of the patrol thanked him and accepted his offer.

The search lasted two hours and was conducted as meticulously as possible. The machine room, the supply holds, the observation equipment, the radar cases, everything was checked carefully, felt physically and probed by ultrasound.

Hornuk wondered if the Nysmians wouldn't go so far as to dismantle the huge cosmic ray generator piece by piece!

Satisfied with their examination, which confirmed the delegation's good intentions, they went back to their patrol ship to escort the foreigners.

Once again Streiler rubbed his hands together and put on a radiant smile. "Now we're safe and probably considered harmless."

"We can only hope so, although this... friendly visit could have ulterior motives. Either the Nysmians are convinced that we've come to spy on them or they really believe that since you've only recently come under the Galactic Empire's protection you're thinking of joining the League of Independent Worlds. If that's the case, the Nysmians will be forced to make a good impression on you by any means possible. Maybe they'll even make you an offer, thinking you're official representatives from your... imaginary government."

Everyone smiled, thinking of the comical outcome.

The patrol flew at the same reduced speed as the fighter and escorted it roughly 10,000 yards. Little by little a star grew bigger: an enormous green sun. It shined in space without lighting it up but with the intensity of a blinding, electric arc.

"Choïko!" Hornuk announced, pointing at the sun that drifted away to the right as the galactic fighter changed direction. "We're heading for the planet Nysmi, which you can see now off the radar."

The time explorers looked out the windows and saw a pale sphere crossed by a dark crescent.

The Grand Instructor informed them, "This planet is a little bigger than earth. Therefore, the gravity is heavier although totally supportable. Its atmosphere, which we can breath, contains more ozone than on Earth, but for a short stay it won't have any serious effects on your lungs."

The globe gradually filled up the horizon.

Hornuk reduced the speed even more and dove into the atmosphere at only 1,000 miles an hour. The effects of acceleration, just like those of deceleration, were offset by a single reverse mechanism. The spaceship came almost immediately out of the zone lit by the green sun into the hemisphere darkened by night.

The Grand Instructor asked for his position and received it instantly from the observation post that had tracked them since they entered the planet's attraction field. Guided by the radar signals sent from the ground the fighter soon came in sight of M'zom, an immense metropolis, headquarters of Siomak, the tyrant of the so-called Independent Worlds.

The brightly lit city formed a rectangle of around 12 by 5 miles. The astrodome with its red and blue beacons formed another rectangle to the north of the city. The control tower authorized their landing and gave the necessary signals to the pilots of the two ships. The Okan and the escort patrol made a complete circle before losing altitude and setting down on the runway that was marked out for them with lights.

As they got out of the ship they were welcomed by N'xok in person. The Nysmians from the patrol, since their mission was accomplished, saluted and went back on board their ship, which shot off immediately into the starry heavens.

N'xok show respect to the members of the delegation. "Welcome to M'zom. His majesty greets you. Please accept his hospitality. Rooms will be prepared for you in the Royal Palace. His Majesty is sorry that he cannot see you tonight. An important meeting with high dignitaries of the realm is keeping him from this pleasure. Nonetheless, tomorrow you will be greeted and welcomed as is proper."

"You really show us too much honor, N'xok," Hornuk bowed his head. "The infinite kindness of His Majesty puzzles us. We didn't expect to be received by him…"

"Would you like to rest in your rooms or do you prefer to visit our capital?" N'xok asked submissively.

"We don't want to put you out but… since you offered I think we'd like to walk around a little."

"With pleasure," the scaly Nysmian bowed. "I'll be glad to show you some attractions in M'zom. Tonight there happens to be an excellent historical show at the *teleorama*. Would you like to go?"

"Well what a coincidence! This delegation with me is very interested in history," Hornuk accepted casually.

N'xok could obviously not understand the irony of this little joke.

A car with a turbine drove them through the streets illuminated by green spheres. The strange streetlights were floating in the air by electromagnetism, the side walls producing a strong enough field to keep them in the air.

The *teleorama*, crowded with male and female Nysmians, was a giant parallelepiped rectangle. One end served as a screen. The Plenipotentiary Minister and his guests sat in one of the box seats that hung like magic from the wall on the right.

The lights went out and after the short credits, courteously translated by N'xok, the actors appeared. They were in an apparently real scene: a mountain that really looked like a mountain, a real spaceship, everything in three dimensions, nothing like film, television or stereorama. The process was obviously original but our friends understood absolutely nothing of the story!

Kariven thought for a minute and then asked Hornuk to translate this question to N'xok: "After the show can we take a tour in the ship and fly over the area before heading to His Majesty's palace? N'xok could maybe come with us?"

When he got an answer Hornuk translated, "N'xok will be delighted to join us."

"Good," Kariven nodded. "So, we can all go together on a little tour…"

Hornuk pretended to concentrate on the giant teleorama screen but in truth he was wondering what Kariven was cooking up. Starting a thought-conversation with him would have raised the Nysmian's suspicions if he were paying any attention to their body language or the expressions on their faces.

Coming out of the show N'xok and his guests took the road back to the astrodome while chatting about the charms of M'zom, the capital. Since the delegation was accompanied by Siomak's Plenipotentiary Minister the guards gave them no trouble. N'xok sat next to Hornuk at the commands and the fighter took off. It rose slowly at cruising speed.

While the Grand Instructor was describing his ship to the Nysmian, Kariven took Inshtug aside and whispered, "Quietly open the secret compartment and give me a Colt. Do it quick!"

Glanya and Streiler stood behind the giant to screen the action as best they could. Two minutes later, Kariven, Colt in hand, stuck the barrel of his weapon against the neck of the captured Nysmian. "Tell this filthy creature not to move," he ordered Hornuk.

N'xok, feeling the cold steel against his neck, swung around. Kariven pushed the gun harder into the scaly skin. Stunned, the Plenipotentiary Minister could not understand the change in attitude.

Although they did not know the details of Kariven's plans, his friends quickly surrounded him. Each of them held a Colt, finger on the trigger, aimed at the prisoner.

"If you make a wrong move, we'll shoot you down mercilessly," Hornuk growled. "Our sudden change intrigues you, doesn't it? Well, now you can know that we've come to M'zom to kill Siomak."

Furious at being deceived, N'xok lunged at Kariven, who stepped aside and hammered the Nysmian's skull with his Colt. He hit him hard, hard enough to kill a man, but on the scaly, green carapace it only clinked and bounced back.

N'xok swung back and tried to grab Glanya. Three shots fired abruptly.

Hit in the stomach and chest N'xok howled out but did not give up. He staggered and reached out his webbed fingers toward the fighter's control panel, hoping, no doubt, to sabotage some vital system.

Kariven's Colt spit out more 11.25mm bullets. The Nysmian's head exploded and its lizard body dropped to the metal floor at the feet of the pilot.

"Drop the bombs!" Kariven ordered as he reholstered his smoking gun.

While the Grand Instructor kept the fighter flying in circles, Inshtug slipped the bombs one by one into a slanted cylinder with airtight valves. The Okan then crossed over M'zom in two diagonal, intersecting flights to make sure the bombs would fall inside the city.

"It's done, let's get out of here!" Inshtug shouted. "The 40 bombs dropped will release the gas on impact. We didn't have time to set any timers."

The galactic fighter soared into the sky at an incredible speed. It disappeared in an instant, flying across space at maximum speed.

When the spaceship with Hornuk at the helm finally slowed its crazy pace to enter the local cluster of stars that formed the heart of our solar system, the people of M'zom, in the throes of collective madness caused by the Z'nabag gas, had finished killing one another.

During the meeting of the high dignitaries of the Independent Worlds, Siomak and his cohorts had a weird, inexplicable feeling. Little by little, as the gas-laden air filled their lungs, they felt a silent rage swell inside them, a kind of hatred toward their fellows. All of a sudden, in their troubled minds, the madness exploded, lunatic murder that pitted one against another, brother against brother, friend against friend.

Siomak's eyes turned red, rolled upwards and looked like they shot lightning. He drew his paralyzing pistol and shot straight in front of him, freezing a dozen Nysmians in the most ridiculous postures. Eight of his scaly cohorts rushed him and in no time at all pummeled his body, bit it, trampled it and left it twitching on the corpse-ridden floor.

When this was done the maniacs beat each other in an all-out brawl. All night long the city rang out with the clamor of this violent battle. The next morning the majestic orb of the fantastic green sun rose over the metropolis transformed into a massacre. Only a few Nysmians were spared, with a crazed look in their eyes, their fingers stained red with the blood of their victims, searching among the corpses for the rare survivors who could put up one last fight.

That evening a squadron left the space station alerted by the General Staff of a nearby city. They were supposed to get control over the last inhabitants of M'zom who had been affected by the raging madness. Siomak and his leaders of the League of Independent Worlds had survived. The terrible war of planetary conquests told by history would not take place. Hundreds of millions of innocent beings would not die at the murderous hands of Siomak's hordes. The enslaved planets would soon be liberated.

Thanks to the Earthlings from the Future an entire chapter in the history of unknown civilizations had been unwritten.

CHAPTER NINE

After spending the night as the Grand Instructor's guests, Kariven and his three companions met their host for breakfast. After sacrificing themselves to this pleasant necessity, our friends went to the astrodome where the Retro-timeship was waiting in the giant hangar.

Just when they felt puzzled at not finding Lieutenant Rudy Clark and his men, the latter came back from the white city. Commander Taylor looked at them with an amused smile. But when he saw the six ravishing young women accompanying them his smile disappeared.

"What is this?" he growled at Lieutenant Clark, nodding at the pre-Bimkamians holding onto their arms.

Each of the women was holding a small case.

Lieutenant Clark gulped awkwardly, gently pulled his arm away from his brown companion and coughed before muttering, "This, Commander Taylor, is… These are our… wives."

Commander Taylor scowled, the veins popped out on his neck like he was about to have a stroke, and he barked, "What? Your… *Your wives?*"

Lieutenant Clark looked embarrassed and did not know how to react. As for his GIs, they did not look confident. Kariven, Harrington, Streiler and Glanya looked at each other with great surprise at this revelation.

Hornuk stared at the young pre-Bimkamians, obviously trying to capture their thoughts. It did not take long for him to understand and he smiled, shaking his head good-naturedly. With the hope of putting an end to this precarious situation, very embarrassing for Lieutenant Clark, he put his hand on Commander Taylor's shoulder and transmitted this thought telepathically:

"During our absence and taking legal advantage of the free time you gave them, Commander, your men met these young women…"

The American officer raised his eyes and looked askance at the smiling face of the giant Hornuk.

"As often happens the natives of the planet, identical to us—proportionally—take wives from members of our race. That's what your men did last night, Commander."

"You… You're married, Lieutenant?" Taylor sputtered, wide-eyed.

"Listen, Commander… I… I'm not the only one… My men are also…"

"That's rich!" the superior officer shouted. "And didn't you know that your marriage needed my consent? Military regulations of the…"

"Military regulations of the USA are not applicable in the Secondary Period," Professor Harrington remarked judiciously, not without a smirk. "Making a nun…"

"One reason! One reason! You're funny, Prof! I'm going to look great when I tell them that my GIs left their wives back in the Secondary Period! My superiors will tell me to open a dating service."

Lieutenant Clark, who was fiddling nervously with the buttons of his pea coat, took the liberty to explain, "It's that… Commander, with your permission, we… we'd like to bring our wives with us."

That was too much!

While the three scientists and Hornuk burst out laughing, Taylor loosened his tie and unbuttoned his shirt. He was almost choking on his outrage. Before exploding, as he was about to do, Professor Harrington intervened again.

"Come on, Commander. Calm down and give them your consent. I'm sure that Lieutenant Clark and his men thought long and hard before tying the knot. You're the superior officer on our mission, but it belongs to Streiler and me. We're asking you to forget about regulations and authorize the immigration of these six charming ladies who will soon become citizens of the USA."

Commander Taylor opened his mouth, hesitated, held back the flood of cursing he was about to let loose, shrugged his shoulders and in a gruff voice said, "OK, OK, I'm just a little soldier and you're the President of the USA! Do whatever you want and you take responsibility for it."

"About time," Professor Harrington beamed, turning right away to Clark and his men. "Congratulations, Lieutenant and you, too, my friends. Your wives are gorgeous! Now get on board and prepare for takeoff."

He thought quickly and with a twinkle in his eye asked, "At least do they know how to cook?"

Everyone said goodbye to the Grand Instructor, who did not hide his emotions. He was able to appreciate the real virtue and noble sentiments of the Earthlings from the future.

"Goodbye, Hornuk," Kariven shook his hand. "May you live in peace and pursue your important civilizing work for the great benefit of humanity."

He climbed the steps into the hatch and gave one final wave to the giant. A few seconds later the Retro-timeship took off.

Sitting between Commander Taylor and Professor Harrington, in front of the control panel, Kariven was simply staring at the Physiotempograph. The yellow, plastic ribbon was starting to come out of the spinning drum. The 1,000-year periods were reeling off at breakneck speed as the flexible ribbon wound around a second drum.

"We're going to be crossing the Tertiary Period again very soon," Professor Harrington noted, as he scrutinized the red marks indicating tens of millions of years.

Kariven suddenly looked up, his entire being filled with an intense emotion. "You... I'm such an idiot! Harrington, my friend, my old friend," he babbled with tears in his eyes. "How was I so blind not to have thought of it before? We're going to save Leyla! Yes, save her from being killed by the cyclops."

"How's that, Kariven? Explain…"

"The Physiotempograph and this ribbon unrolling the fractions of Time visited by us have opened my eyes. If we go back to the Tertiary Period and stop the Retro-timeship when we went out chasing the cyclops, *won't we be living there before Leyla was killed*?"

"Without a doubt," Harrington confirmed with great interest.

"So, we just have to relive the events up to that fateful moment and jump in at the right time to save Leyla…"

"I get it!" Harrington exclaimed. "Commander," he ordered, "look very carefully at the ribbon and stop the ship when you see the *end of the blue part* that represents our trip to Shâmali. I'm saying the end because the start of the blue part we see now—our trip being made in reverse—must logically represent our final days in the Tertiary."

"OK," the officer answered curtly.

The two rotating drums, one feeding the ribbon into the other, relentlessly spun out the time. Kariven and Glanya kept their eyes riveted on the yellow ribbon, not uttering a sound. It was like their life was hanging on this narrow strip of plastic crowded with lines and numbers.

All of a sudden they heard a click. The ribbon had switched from yellow to blue.

Commander Taylor pulled a lever on the panel and pressed a button. The Retro-timeship vibrated for a second. The hazy glow outside the ship turned into the black of space. Stars twinkled motionlessly and the blurry, shaky ball that the ship flew over formed into a huge globe with strange reliefs, different than what we know today.

The Retro-timeship plunged directly toward the planet.

While Commander Taylor leveled out the ship in the terrestrial atmosphere to follow the curve of the planet, Professor Harrington leaned over the blue ribbon and nodded his head, "We've stopped at the 98th hour of our previous visit."

After a quick calculation he was able to add, "If my memory serves me correctly, this should correspond to the moment when we left with our Bimkamian friends to help the Lemurians attacked by the cyclops. OK, stay at a high altitude, Commander, and turn on the anti-detection shield. We shouldn't be seen by Leyla or Torka, the Military Operations Chief. We'll just be silent, invisible witnesses to scenes from our first visit until the right moment."

Commander Taylor slowed the ship down. Shâmali was soon beneath them. The sight of the impressive Bimkamian base where they had spent so many lovely hours—but also painful moments—brought back strong emotions.

On Professor Harrington's orders the ship hovered high over the white city bathed in the sweltering heat. Thanks to the viewer the buildings were crisp and clear, as if the observers were only 50 yards above them.

"Look," Glanya's voice was flat as she pointed at the astrodome.

Stunned, Streiler unconsciously heard this word. Everyone gathered around them on the right side of the transparent cockpit and held their breath when they saw *their own ship on the runway* next to the sphere.

"Well, well," Professor Harrington smiled, "that's really the Retro-timeship we see, but the Retro-timeship of the past or its ghost if you prefer."

"Leyla!" Kariven shouted out of his daze.

"And that's me!" Commander Taylor was completely befuddled.

Indeed, Leyla and Kariven, followed by Torka, Commander Taylor, Harrington, Streiler and Glanya had just appeared on the airstrip. They were going to their respective ships in order to rescue the city being besieged by the monsters.

"This is crazy," Streiler whispered.

"I wonder what'd we do… or what our *ghosts* would do if we suddenly showed up in front of them," Commander Taylor mused.

"We don't have time to experiment," Harrington noted. "Let's stick to following them, to following *us* I should say and we'll figure it out."

The doubles from the Past boarded the Retro-timeship while Leyla and Torka headed toward the first sphere. On the runway the squadron of Bimkamian spaceships was ready to take off. The Retro-timeship went first, followed by Torka at the head of his formation.

Very high up in the sky the ship watching its own ghost flew off behind the squadron.

"So, we're going to follow them like this until the fateful moment?" Kariven was losing patience.

"Not necessarily. We can speed up Time and choose whatever moment we want."

"Then I propose we stop when we left with Leyla on board to capture the cyclops in order to study their physiology."

"We can do that," Professor Harrington approved.

Once again he studied the blue ribbon on the Physiotempograph, adjusted the sliders for the day and hour and them ordered Commander Taylor to lift into space. The Retro-timeship shuddered and the needles on the different colored control screens swung back and forth. The day finally disappeared and gave way to the dull gray of the Time Spiral.

When the ship came back to Earth and hovered over the city its occupants saw the phantom Retro-timeship on the ground again and their doubles crossing the astrodome. Kariven's heart throbbed when he saw himself offering his arm to Leyla to help her into the ship. When the hatch closed behind Streiler and Glanya, the ship took off.

"Good. Now it's up to us," Kariven said. "Speed up, Commander. We're going to get ahead of our ship from the past and bombard the tribe of cyclops that we captured before. If they're slaughtered, Leyla and our doubles will go capture different ones. *And the cyclops that killed Leyla won't be among them since we'll wipe out the whole tribe!*"

"OK."

Commander Taylor sped up and left the ship from the Past far behind. They soon found the cyclops' camp on the banks of the river. As expected the hairy monsters were staring at the fire where their fame was cooking.

"Drop a bunch of TNT bombs!" Kariven ordered. "No need to use the atomic warheads—these should be more than enough."

Taylor pressed a black button on edge of a wheel atop the control panel. Ten big bombs fell upon the jungle. A series of terrifying explosions blasted the land, throwing huge chunks of dirt in the air, pulverizing the monsters' camp and from the red blaze spreading thick smoke over the deadly forest.

When the brown cloud had dissipated a little, the landscape was unrecognizable. A crater, 250 yards in diameter, had replaced the small clearing. The river was pouring into the chasm, covering the remains of the cyclops tribe with a swirling, liquid shroud. The 20 or 30 red-haired monsters had been literally shredded by the bombs. One part of the jungle was still on fire.

Half an hour later the phantom Retro-timeship showed up, circled the water-filled crater a few times and then flew off.

"Hooray!" Kariven shouted. "Once again we've changed the course of Time!"

Still at a respectable distance they followed the Retro-timeship Number 1 and saw it drop a sleeping bomb on a tribe encamped at the foot of a rocky cliff. The monsters collapsed soon afterward, anesthetized by the gas. Leyla and Kariven and their ghost friends stepped out in masks after the ship landed and loaded the sleeping hideous creatures in their steel cages.

The Retro-timeship Number 2 was hovering high above Shâmali. Night blanketed the city with a dark veil. The Milky Way, surrounded by glimmering constellations, crawled across the sky from one horizon to the other. The explorers, under the effect of the transparency serum, were preparing to act.

"I think we were sleeping at this time? Remember, Harrington…"

"I think so too, Kariven," he agreed.

"We can go now."

The Retro-timeship descended silently on the northern edge of the astrodome and landed barely 30 feet away from the phantom timeship. Huddled around their ship our friends were whispering together.

Kariven stepped over to Glanya and whispered, "Do you think that your disintegrator rifle is powerful enough for what we have to do?"

"Have no fear. Its energy charge will hold up without a problem… and we'll be able to use it for a long time to come."

Kariven got in front of his friends and pointing the weapon at the Retro-timeship Number 1 pressed the trigger. A bright ray swept across the mammoth that became a blinding bulk for five seconds, like a heap of molten metal… then disappeared.

The magnificent ship had been turned into thermal and light energy!

All that was left of the ghost ship was its memory.

The explorers rushed back into their ship—the *real* one—and waited. They were sure that the blinding flash from the disintegration would alert the guards in the control tower. Holed up in the cabin they left Lieutenant Clark—who had not been given the transparency serum—in charge of meeting the giants who were already running toward them.

Rudy Clark explained to the head guard that he had accidentally shot off a flare while making his rounds. For proof he showed the bulky flare gun that was lying on the ground at his feet.

"I was so surprised," the American lied telepathically, "that I dropped the thing."

The giant looked puzzled, hesitated, but finally had to accept this unlikely story. He shrugged his shoulders and went away with his men.

"Ooh," Kariven let out his breath when Clark came back into the cabin where his superiors were hiding. "He swallowed that pretty easily."

"Don't you feel anything after disintegrating your own ship *and the GIs who were inside?*" Glanya asked nervously.

"Yes," Kariven admitted, "but why worry about this 'attack' when Lieutenant Clark and his men are alive here in our Retro-timeship, the original, the one we're in right now in the past?"

"Don't think about it anymore," Commander Taylor advised. "That's only the first stage of our plan. Come on."

They left their hiding place and walked cautiously to Shâmali, ready to hit the ground at the first sign of trouble. Glanya was squeezing Streiler's arm convulsively. In her right hand she held the disintegrator gun that had just destroyed the phantom timeship.

They got to the wide streets of the white city that was flooded with light and took a long detour around the central square. The palace of Leyla, the Grand Instructor of Earth, shimmered like a jewel under the beams of the pivoting spotlights.

The two guards posted at the main entrance had no clue that in the nocturnal silence there were transparent people entering the palace through a hidden door known only to Leyla and her twin sister. Guided by Glanya the Earthlings hurried through the deserted rooms until they came to the hallway with bedrooms where they slept not very long ago.

Kariven took Glanya's weapon and opened the first door, whispering, "Charity begins at home…"

Despite his cheerful smile, nobody was fooled. They all felt as fearfully anxious as he did. Kariven entered *his* room, followed by his friends, and stopped a few feet from the bed in which *another Jean Kariven was sleeping peacefully.*

Professor Harrington swallowed hard before approaching the sleeper and shaking him gently. Then he stepped back into a dark corner with the others. Kariven's double opened his eyes and looked around. He saw nothing but his dark, empty room.

Harrington snuck across the floor, crawled out onto the balcony and slammed the window shut. Kariven's double rubbed his eyes and then jumped out of bed, lured by the unusual noise. Professor Harrington plastered himself against the wall on the balcony.

Almost at point blank range, Kariven fired on his double with the disintegrator gun. A bright flash lit up the balcony. When the time explorers' eyes recovered from the burst of light, they saw that once again their experiment had succeeded. Only the real Kariven, with the rifle at his side, remained. *He would be able to take the place of his ghost.*

Quickly they played out the same macabre scene in the other bedrooms before each of them went quietly back to their rooms that had been so strangely "hijacked" from their dead doubles.

Streiler and Glanya stood in the empty hallway of the palace looking at other passionately. Glanya's double, actually belonging to this time, could not be disintegrated at any price. It was the one who had left Shâmali with Streiler who had to be...

Holding out her rifle Glanya stepped closer to the Austrian engineer. "We have to be strong enough to separate, Kurt. My present body is actually just an illusion. My double's body and mind form another Glanya, the real one, the one sleeping in the next room this very minute... and who loves you like I love you."

Streiler held her in his arms. Their lips joined in a tender kiss and they stayed a long time like that, embracing each other. Glanya shook free, swiftly wiping away a tear. She took three steps back and with one final sob pleaded psychically, "Now Kurt, please..."

Streiler slowly lifted the disintegrator rifle. In his teary-eyed vision he saw his love's slender form dancing. Bracing himself with courage he gritted his teeth, closed his eyes and fired. When he dared to open them again he saw nothing but the bare wall and the dark, empty hallway.

With his nerves shot, Streiler could not get to sleep after the busy night. He left his room and went to smoke a cigarette in the hallway lined with doors. His friends must have been sleeping in their beds... which their ghosts had been in an hour before.

And Glanya? The real one, *she whom he had not killed?* She was sleeping or...

He had to see her!

Leaning on the frame of the bay window Glanya was contemplating the starry sky. Overwhelmed by his emotions, Streiler went straight to her, a little like a robot but trembling and full of anxiety. When she noticed him she threw herself in his arms and wept.

"Oh, Kurt! It was awful! I had a nightmare... we were forced to separate and *you killed me.*"

"It was just a nightmare, dear. We'll never separate. I'll take you with me to the Atomic Age."

When he woke up after the night bursting with emotions, Kariven rushed to Leyla's room.

The Grand Instructor welcomed him with pleasure but was surprised by his excitement. He covered her face with kisses before he left, singing, overflowing with joy at having found *her whom the monster had killed!*

The light of his life was born again from the Past.

Bewildered, Leyla shook her blonde hair wondering why Kariven seemed so happy. Wasn't this a day like any other?

The Bimkamian giant had just handed out the fresh meat to the cyclops in their cages. Commander Taylor, Harrington and Streiler were watching on, wary and worried, as Kariven held Leyla around the waist 15 feet away from the cages where the one-eyed monsters were growling.

Torka, the Military Operations Chief, was surprised to notice that all the Earthlings were nervously fingering the grips of their Colts, ready to unholster them. He saw that their eyes were all focused on the cyclops.

At the moment when the guard passed by in reach, one of the red-haired monsters suddenly shot out its arm trying to steal the metal lance. The Bimkamian giant jumped to the side, barely dodging the monster's claws.

The four Colts fired simultaneously. The monster collapsed, shot dead.

Torka was taken aback by this action that he considered unnecessary. "Why did you kill this monster?" he criticized the Earthlings. "He certainly tried to get the guard's lance but... *he didn't get it.*"

"I know," Kariven replied calmly, discretely caressing Leyla's hand, "*but another would have and killed one of us.* Now let's get away from these cages."

Torka shook his head, pondering and puzzled. "These Earthlings must have some sixth sense for the future," he mused.

The time explorers got ready to board the Retro-timeship. Torka shook their hands warmly and wished great happiness to Glanya and Streiler. Leyla, with tears in her eyes, was troubled to see that he whom she loved was smiling cheerfully at this moment when he was about to leave her.

He walked up, wrapped his arms around her and kissed her passionately. Then, still smiling, he looked at Leyla and asked, "Why are you crying my dear Leyla, *since you're coming with me?*"

Leyla stopped crying, stared at Kariven and then looked at her twin sister, who was hugging Streiler tenderly. She almost choked saying, "You know very well that I can't come with you, Kariven. My duty lies here with my subjects..."

"The Lemurians and the Bimkamians stationed on Earth are not your subjects."

A giant Bimkamian ran up and interrupted this conversation that was particularly amusing to Kariven's friends. They who knew the future also knew that the young French scientist had the right to speak like this.

The giant saluted Torka and Leyla before declaring by telepathy, "The Eternal Wisdom that reigns over the Galactic Empire just appointed a new Grand Instructor by the name of Myln'ha to preside over the evolution of Earth. The ship is expected. There's one thing I don't understand at all in this odd situation: the operator of the intragalactic viewer said that this nomination had been made *after the announcement of Leyla's death!* But here she is."

The news, as weird as it was wonderful, threw Leyla in the greatest confusion. "But... I'm dead!" she was outraged.

"Thank God!" Kariven replied, hugging her. "Now you're free, my dear Leyla. Nothing is holding you back in Shâmali anymore. Do you want to go with me and be my wife... in 45 million years?"

As an answer she put her cheek against his and let tears of happiness flow without even trying to understand the fabric of all these mysterious events.

The Retro-timeship took off.

Torka faded away into the astrodome of Shâmali. The white city, which was the base of the Dragons of Wisdom, who came from infinity to educate the Earthlings, disappeared.

In the heart of the fourth dimension the planet Earth started to oscillate. The grayness of the Time Spiral took the place of the daylight in the Tertiary Period and the return voyage started.

"Head for the Atomic Age!" Professor Harrington called out cheerfully.

"OK," Commander Taylor sighed, imagining all the wedding presents he would have to buy for his friends and GIs, the time explorers.

Kariven and Streiler were watching Leyla and Glanya. The two, gorgeous twins, strangely identical, cast their gentle eyes upon their Knights from the Future.

Kariven held Leyla's hands and winked at Streiler, joking, "I hope that we don't get our wives mixed up, brother-in-law."

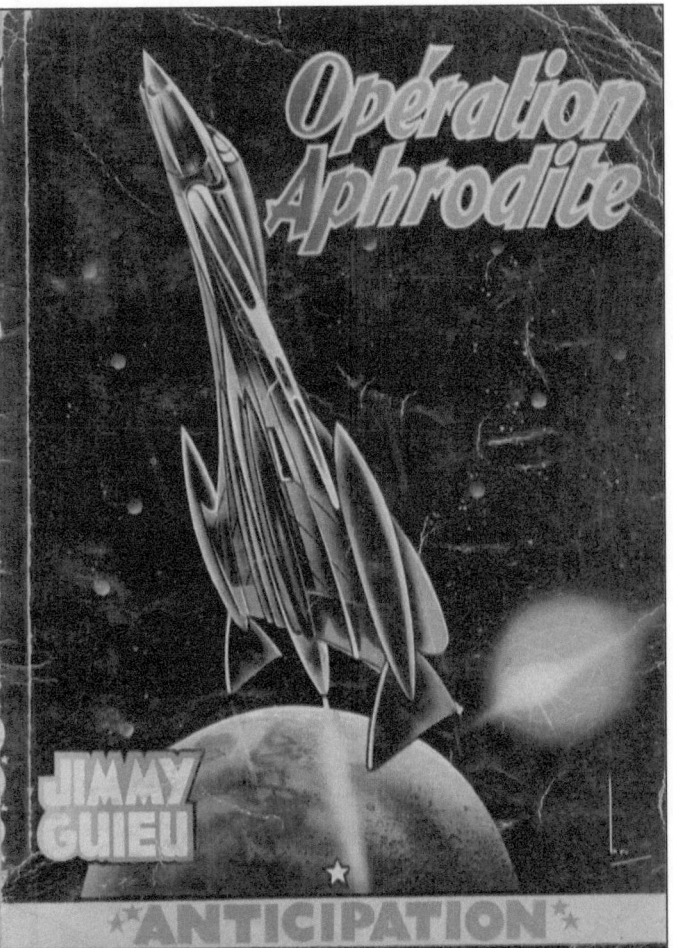

Opération
Aphrodite

JIMMY
GUIEU

★ANTICIPATION★

Editions
"Fleuve Noir"

OPERATION APHRODITE

There is need for the people to stay ignorant about a lot of truths and to believe in a lot of falsehoods.

-- Adapted from Montaigne

"I-just-can't-believe-it" is all one word to highbrows and dimwits alike.

-- Robert Heinlein
The Puppet Masters

CHAPTER ONE

In spite of the early morning hour, a blazing sun shot its blinding rays on the white sand of the New Mexico desert. In the secret base of White Sands Proving Ground, the Rocketeers[19] and other technicians, most of them in shorts, bare-chested and wearing safari helmets or a kind of jockey's cap with a long bill, were dragging around their sweaty bodies. On a gigantic, cement launch pad a huge rocket, 300 feet long and 25 feet wide at the base, was standing like a metal spike.

"Good," the general sighed, slumping back in his chair. "Let's recommend a Test Shot without the 'Rats and Mice' and delay the countdown until tomorrow morning if weather conditions are favorable. Keep me up-to-date frequently."

The chief of the White Sands base crushed out his cigarette shakily, lit another and muttered, "I'm as nervous as a new father right before the happy delivery."

Doctor Howland smiled, tapped his pipe on the ashtray and said, "It'll be OK, General. I have confidence in *Daisy*[20]. The countless launches of experimental rockets before Operation Aphrodite are model enough. You can also put full trust in the... Rats and Mice in our labs."

"You can call them *the team*, Dr. Howland," General Miller said. "Neither the interphone nor the transmission network is turned on."

"These long months of secret preparation have made us too careful," Howland admitted. "We're so used to calling the future astronauts Rats and Mice that we end up really thinking they're rodents."

---

[19] Technicians and scientists specialized in rockets, guided missiles and other "specialized crafts." (Author's Note)

[20] Rocketeers have the habit of calling rockets by a feminine first name. (Author's Note)

The three men exploded in laughter, but nervous, broken laughter. The fantastic Operation Aphrodite was not, in fact, just a simple test run of a guided missile but actually the launch of a spaceship, *Daisy*, to our nearest neighbor, the Moon.

General Miller absent-mindedly picked up one of the many newspaper clippings that cluttered the desk. Three years old, dated December 29, 1953.

January 1, 1962, the article revealed in substance, *an interplanetary ship will leave Earth to go to the Moon. The news, as astounding as it sounds, cannot be taken as pure fantasy. It comes, in fact, from one of the preeminent figures in the world of science, Dr. Kaplan, physics professor at the University of Los Angeles, who announced it in a statement made on December 9 in Geneva before a gathering of scientists, all specialists in aerospace... The government of the USA appears very interested in Dr. Kaplan's atomic rocket project, which it is fully supporting. A Wall Street group has raised the enormous capital needed for such a vast undertaking: four billion dollars. As of today engineers are assembled in the Pacific on the small Johnston Atoll where they are studying the construction of a launch pad*[21] ...

Many other articles dating from 1953 and 1954 announced the construction and the launch, in 1960-1965, of an artificial satellite designed by the inventor of the V2, Werner von Braun, a first before allowing, *at a later date*, the voyage to the Moon first and then to other planets in the solar system.

Naturally, even today, for many people these "projects" sounded more like a utopia than a rational expectation. A little more open minds, however, admitted that "someday" man would walk on the Moon, but to state even the year of departure was considered by them to be a very reckless prophecy. These newspaper articles predicting the Earth-Moon voyage

---

[21] True; see my comments in *Les Soucoupes volantes viennent d'un autre monde* [*The Flying Saucers come from Another World*] (1954) by the same author. (Author's Note)

for 1962, i.e. nine years later, seemed to express a greatly exaggerated optimism.

All these considerations, which came up while reading the papers, General Miller and Drs. Howland and Hutton rightfully imagined to be firmly implanted in the public mind.

Well, in 1953, when Dr. Kaplan announced the first voyage to the Moon for 1962, the Pentagon and a few specialists at White Sands already and quite rightly knew that the departure of the spaceship would take place *well before this date!*

The news concerning the construction project of the artificial satellite (the first phase on the road to interplanetary travel) and the preparation of Dr. Kaplan's rocket were given to the press only to fool the public about the real date. The "average Earthling"—whether or not he believed these projects would be completed—considered them something for the far-off future.

The first stage to build an artificial satellite around 1960-1965 made it clear that man would not go to the Moon before some years after this, around 1970 according to the most optimistic estimations.[22] As for the pessimists, the backward and narrow-minded, they purely and simple denied the possibility of interplanetary travel.

The reality, however, was completely different. While the man on the street was thinking, "We won't be visiting the Lunatics, the Moon people anytime soon", the renowned technicians of the Strategic Air Command in particular and of the Air Force in general were busy on Operation Aphrodite[23], a

---

[22] Not a bad prediction for a novel written in 1953, since Apollo 11 landed Neil Armstrong and Buzz Aldrin on the Moon on July 20, 1969.

[23] Operation Aphrodite is one of the most mysterious "operations" conducted by the USA. In truth, we know nothing about its exact nature. (Author's Note) Now we do. Aphrodite and Anvil were the World War II code names for US Air Force and Navy operations planning to use B-17 and PB4Y bombers as precision-guided munitions against bunkers and other hard-

project surrounded by secrecy comparable to the Manhattan Project which built the atomic bomb in 1945.

Extraordinary precautions had been taken since 1953 (the year in which Operation Aphrodite became reality) to keep the development and the very nature of the work top secret. At no price could they let an agent of the MVD (Russian secret police) get hold of the outlines, plans or documents that would allow the construction of *Daisy*, the first interplanetary rocket ship of the US Air Force.

The regrettable "leaks," a few years earlier in the atomic centers, had to be avoided at all costs for Operation Aphrodite. And this time—the general staff was almost certain—there had been no leaks.

Daisy's team was ready in the cabins in the middle of the night while the base, strongly guarded on a 100-mile radius, was totally deserted on the launch pad. The technicians who were now busy with the final preparations, did not know that by "Rats and Mice" the general staff meant a human team. The specialists who built the rocket, who obviously could not

---

ened/reinforced enemy facilities, such as those targeted during Operation Crossbow. The plan called for B-17 aircraft that had been taken out of operational service (with nicknames such as "robot," "baby," "drone" or "Weary Willy") to be loaded to capacity with explosives, and flown by radio control into bomb-resistant fortifications such as German U-boat pens and V-weapon sites, but it proved dangerous, expensive and unsuccessful. Of 14 missions flown, none resulted in the successful destruction of a target. Many aircraft lost control and crashed or were shot down by flak, and many pilots were killed. However, a handful of aircraft scored near misses. One notable pilot death was Joseph P. Kennedy, Jr., the elder brother of US President John F. Kennedy. Operation Aphrodite effectively ceased on January 27, 1945 when General Spaatz sent an urgent message to Major General James H. Doolittle: "Aphrodite babies must not be launched against the enemy until further orders."

be kept in the dark, were confined to the secret base (somewhere in the USA) and cut off from all contact with the outside world. They could only leave in three months, whatever the outcome of Operation Aphrodite.

"Attention, T minus 25 minutes," the speakers announced.

Lost in their thoughts, General Miller and the two laboratory chiefs jumped.

The commander in chief of White Sands looked at his stopwatch for the umpteenth time. "I wish I were three months older!" he fidgeted in his metal chair, trying to get comfortable. "We're attempting a critical experiment for the US and maybe for world peace."

"Attention, T minus 10 Minutes."

General Miller pressed a button and the television wall screen turned on. The launch pad appeared with the tall, slender behemoth of super-resistant metal with one side white and the other black. The chemical coloring had been incorporated with the alloy that made up the rocket's outer shell. There was no question of using paint to mark the two sides of the machine; the friction of the air molecules in our atmosphere on the metal would liquefy any type of paint. The contrasting colors protected the rocket, with a slight rotational spin, from solar rays in space as well as on the surface of our planet.

The last trucks and Jeeps were driving away from the massive scaffolding that giant tractors had hauled off so that the rocket could take flight. Straight and rigid on its cement platform the rocket looked like it was resting between the jaws of a titan made by the two rolling blocks used as support frames until the moment of launch.

"Attention, T minus one minute."

In the blockhouse occupied by the general and chiefs as well as in the Tracking Stations[24], they no longer heard the

---

[24] Laboratory trucks used as mobile observation stations. (Author's Note)

tick tock of the electronic clocks or the heavy breathing of the observers.

"Attention, T minus 30 seconds... minus 20 seconds... minus five, four, three, two, one... IGNITION!"

On the screen a blinding corolla formed at the base of the rocket. As if it wanted to stay on the ground, it vibrated. A weird rumbling, like a low whistle, almost like thunder, filled the air. The rocket vibrated more. Slowly at first, then faster and faster, it lifted off on a huge column of scarlet flames with oranges flashes veiled by the black steam. The rumbling grew louder, soon reached its peak and became deafening—howling supersonic jets sounded like kazoos compared to the frightening din, the infernal racket that tore through the eardrums.

Little by little the column of flames lost its blinding intensity. *Daisy* was tilting on its axis in flight. The smoke on the ground was dissipating. Only the reddening bottom of the rocket appeared now like a burning ember mysteriously sucked into the sky.

In a few seconds the terrifying rumbling became a waning mumbling that was soon no longer audible. The blue sky, dazzling bright and clear, finally resumed its ordinary condition.

General Miller lit another cigarette, wiped his forehead and turned on the radar. The fluorescent screen lit up. The sweeping line, with every full circle, made a blip appear: *Daisy*, the first interplanetary rocket built by man. The blip displayed by the moving line traveled slowly away from the center of the screen.

Outside, on board the Tracking Stations, the radar men arranged their detector trucks along a line crossing the White Sands desert from east to west. Thus the rocket would be followed by radar until it reached the Moon but not only thanks to the Tracking Stations whose radius of detection was limited by the rotation of our planet. Relays had been set up.

In other parts of the USA and on board special ships and planes patrolling all over Earth, radars were given the mission to observe the trajectory of a "top secret experimental missile" transporting cameras to our satellite. All exchange of information was done in code and no press releases would be given. If by chance a foreign radar picked up the rocket, it would be very easy to make a spokesman of the ATIC[25] say that for some time the radars have spotted the movements of "unidentified flying objects," meaning a Flying Saucer! Once again the narrow minds denying the existence of these machines would gobble up the statement and straightaway put it down as an erroneous interpretation of a natural phenomenon.

General Miller turned off the radar and pulled himself wearily to his feet. "Let's go make a toast to the Rats and Mice of good old *Daisy*."

Dr. Hutton choked back a yawn. "After this all-nighter I think that's a must!"

Daisy, the 8,500 ton rocket, after 80 seconds, had reached "escape velocity" at seven miles per second and burned almost 6,000 tons of fuel and liquid combustive: hydrazine, methanol and oxygen.

The curve of the Earth grew rapidly more pronounced until it soon revealed the roundness of the planet that filled the whole screen onboard the spaceship.

In the cockpit, Dr. Jean Kariven and the other members of the crew, lying on their anti-g sleeping seats, were slowly coming to. The takeoff had subjected them to an acceleration that quickly reached 13 g! Even with their body protected by a special, pressurized spacesuit compressing their chest and abdomen especially, they had still suffered the brutal increase in gravity. And in spite of their helmets, made of a transparent plastic material, their faces were still stretched out, their eyes still painful and their breathing hard and fast.

---

[25] Air Technical Intelligence Center, headquartered at Wright Patterson Air Force Base in Dayton, Ohio, specialized in the study of UFOs, otherwise called "flying saucers." (Author's Note)

A click resounded in the cabin; a red light lit up on the instrument panel and the automatic pilot went to work triggering the ignition of the atomic reactors after stopping the giant pumps of the normal jet propulsion. For more than 28 hours the rocket would be powered through space by atomic energy, the liquid combustion engines held in reserve for takeoffs and landings on the Moon and Earth[26].

Dr. Kariven, tall, well-built, with brown hair and a thin moustache, unfastened his straps and sat up, feeling light, very light, because of the absence of gravity in the ship now free of Earth's pull and traveling at a steady speed. He swung slowly onto the edge of the anti-g bunk and prepared to put his feet on the floor. The big, magnetic soles of his spacesuit stuck fast to the metal floor. In space, "up" and "down" mean nothing; you could just as easily walk on the walls or ceiling!

One by one his companions, bundled up in their greenish-gray spacesuits, got up. In the pit of their stomach they again felt the awful nausea like during the dreadful acceleration. With slow and steady steps, a little awkwardly, sliding their magnetic soles over the metal floor, they gathered in the middle of the cabin and laughed as they shook hands warmly. They laughed but did not hide their intense fear. For the first time human beings had escaped Earth's gravity and were heading to the Moon at 28,000 miles an hour.

Commander Mark Taylor of the Air Strategic Command, Professor Harrington, the celebrated physicist from Caltech[27], Dr. Kurt Streiler, rocket scientist, Lieutenant Rudy Clark and Dr. Jean Kariven, anthropaleontologist and doctor on this expedition, congratulated each other.

---

[26] The takeoff and landing of future spaceships will happen with the help of traditional jet propulsion. Atomic reactors, whose radioactive waste would pollute the atmosphere of Earth (or any other planet), won't be used except in outer space. (Author's Note)

[27] California Institute of Technology. (Author's Note)

The five friends, on account of their "service record"—hadn't they successfully accomplished an astounding voyage into the Past?[28]—had been chosen by General Miller (with the agreement of the Pentagon) to make the first interplanetary flight in the history of mankind.

Daisy, the spaceship with mixed propulsion due to the prodigious work of Dr. Kaplan, had been designed by Professor Harrington and Dr. Streiler, the same ones who a few years earlier had built the Retro-timeship capable of time travel.

In addition to these five engineers and officers *Daisy* carried five handpicked men out of the thousand pilots in astronaut training at Randolph Field[29]. For the moment the five men, all with a different specialization were in a cabin next to the cockpit.

Professor Harrington was in charge of guiding the spaceship. Streiler, the young American engineer originally from Austria, was his second-in-command. Commander Taylor, the military attaché, was head of the expedition.

Harrington and Streiler got set up in the cockpit and examined the information given by all the control dials and screens on the instrument panel, which took up a large part of the circular wall of the cabin. The swiveling anti-g bunks had been folded up to become simple seats. A neon tube ran along the ceiling, lighting the cabin with a bright but not blinding light. The chrome metal walls reflected this light so harmoniously that no part of the room was in shadow. Some movable spotlights also helped so that every instrument and device in the room was clearly lit.

Above the main panel, a big screen was connected to ten periscope cameras stationed all over the surface of the rocket

_____

[28] See *The Time Spiral.* (Author's Note)

[29] Training base in Texas of future interplanetary rocket pilots. By the very existence of this base and the training which the pilots are put through, we can infer that astronautical voyages will be made before too long; see *The Flying Saucers come from Another World*, q.v. (Author's Note)

so that at any given time they could see outer space and the Moon from different directions.

"You can take off your helmets," Professor Harrington declared, throwing back the transparent globe that was protecting his head. "But keep your spacesuits in. We have to be ready to get them back on in a hurry if an accident occurs in the artificial air system or... in case the hull of the ship is pierced by a meteor."

Commander Taylor smiled with satisfaction and said, "This time, my friends, we're not going in search of civilizations buried in the past. We're off to conquer a dead star. In fact, Professor," he turned to Harrington, "is there any chance we'll encounter a life form on the Moon?"

The skeptical physicist shrugged his shoulders. "Practically none, Commander. Anyway, it would be impossible to imagine a 'lunar' life based like 'terrestrial life' on carbon. We ourselves couldn't live on this rock without our spacesuits and Bubble Base."

After 25 hours on the peaceful "astral road," the spaceship started slowing down. The gradual deceleration gave back to the astronauts, little by little, the feeling of weight. The closer the ship got to the lunar surface, the more difficult it got for them to move their magnetic soles.

The periscope cameras encircling the rocket sent back incredible images of the lunar surface to the screens inside the cockpit. Gnawed away by innumerable craters of all sizes, split by deep fissures and "seas" more or less connected, our satellite looked like a monstrous pale lump, grayish with shades of yellow, corroded by a mysterious, lethal pox.

Imperceptibly, as the surface seemed to "rise up" to the cameras, zones of bright green with yellow splotches appeared. From the commands of the spaceship Professor Harrington and Dr. Streiler watched the screen and the instrument panel. From time to time they pulled a lever or slowly turned a big, red, calibrated dial to correct the minute deviations in the trajectory.

With a slow and careful movement, Streiler pushed up a black handle and with his other hand flipped a switch. The nuclear reactor stopped working to bring back the landing rockets... more precisely, the moon-landing rockets. The giant pumps spit out fuel and liquid combustive that instantly flowed into the ignition system of the traditional jets.

Now only a small portion of the Moon was visible on the screen. The rocket decelerated at a constant speed toward the NNE of the satellite. To the east the huge Copernicus crater, a 55-mile diameter circle, displayed its many rays surrounded by countless crater-like formations of smaller size. To the south of this gigantic basin stood a chain of mountains in a rough S—the Montes Carpatus—whose altitude varied from around 6,500 to 13,000 feet high.

On this lifeless, airless star the shadow of these rugged mountains with ragged edges looked extraordinarily clear in the white sunlight. No semi-darkness, no half-tone, no detail blurred by elongation was perceptible on the tortured crust of the Moon. Everything here was either clearly visible or completely black.

At the moment when the spaceship was flying over a crater radiating a series of fissures and crevasses like so many others, Lieutenant Clark shouted out in a real exclamation of surprise, "A light! I just saw a light, some shade of purple, blinking inside that crater there to our left..."

Professor Harrington and the others scrutinized the screen where he was pointing but saw nothing out of the ordinary. Their flight, moreover, had already carried them beyond the bulging ring.

"You were dreaming, Lieutenant. That crater, called Aristarchus, looks absolutely normal just like all the others."

"But I'm sure I..."

"Tiny motes in the eye sometimes play strange tricks, Lieutenant Clark," Streiler added.

Rudy Clark frowned skeptically and shrugged his shoulders. Then he turned and went to join his men to tell them the latest orders. "Motes in the eye!" he mocked under his breath.

With its bottom toward the surface, the rocket descended on a column of burning but invisible gas in the absence of an atmosphere. It set down gently just beyond the Kepler crater whose serrated edges stood just over half a mile from the ship.

Harrington and Streiler shut off the distributor pumps. The screen showed a gloomy moonscape outside, whitish, half-veiled by a cloud of chalky dust (kicked up by the gas emissions of the jets), a dust that slowly floated straight back down without swirling around like it does in our atmosphere.

Seeing this corpse of a star, desolate, arid and plunged in eternal silence, the astronauts felt a kind of oppression in their spacesuits, like an almost superstitious dread.

Harrington, also feeling uncomfortable cleared his throat as if he was afraid to speaking without this polite warning and all he could stammer out was, "Well, uh... We... We're here on the 'poetic' Phoebe."

CHAPTER TWO

With Professor Harrington's nod of agreement, Kariven sat in front of the powerful two-way radio specially built to communicate with Earth on a precise wavelength. He turned it on, adjusted a dial very slowly, manipulated some other controls and waited. After a few seconds a red light started blinking, casting a rhythmical purplish flash.

"Rats and Mice here," he announced in code. "We're in the cheese..."

Around three seconds later—the delay it took the hertzian waves from the Moon to reach Earth and return—the response came back, weak but audible. Gathered around Kariven, silent and attentive, the astronauts listened to the voice coming nearly 240,000 miles through the abyss of space.

"Message received. Cat number 17 here. Turn up your power, Rats and Mice... I'm barely hearing you..."

Kariven delicately adjusted two calibrated dials and tried again, "Rats and Mice to Cat 17, can you connect us to the Big Tomcat?"

Streiler turned on a wall screen showing, in rear projection, an earth map with numbered red circles at different points. "Cat 17," he explained, "is a mobile station set up on a US Navy destroyer off the coast of Dakar."

The speaker crackled and the mobile station answered, "Cat 17 to Rats and Mice. Big Tomcat is informed. Stay on this frequency and wait for his call. We'll put him through. Over and out."

In the vast underground headquarters of White Sands, General Miller—i.e. Big Tomcat in the code—had just received the message relayed by the destroyer off the African coast. The terrestrial hemisphere presently visible from the Moon covered Africa and part of Europe surrounded by fog. Direct radio transmission between the Moon and the USA, therefore, would not be possible until the Earth turned its

143

lighted hemisphere of the Americas to the Moon. They would have to wait at least five hours for the Earth's rotation to bring the American continent in the right conjunction with the Moon, making direct communication possible between the rocket and White Sands.

In the huge underground HQ cluttered with seven rows of giant, electronic, computing machines, General Miller sat in front of a two-way radio. After tuning the controls to the correct wavelength, he plugged in the relay and sent his message to the American destroyer that would in turn send it on to the astronauts waiting near the Kepler crater.

"Big Tomcat to Rats and Mice," General Miller began slowly, "I'm glad to hear that you've reached the cheese without a hitch. Congratulations."

A few seconds later Kariven's voice echoed in the HQ speakers, "Rats and Mice to Big Tomcat. We're going to start nibbling the cheese right away. We'll transmit in two hours, unless there's an emergency. The tape recorder will stay on in case you have orders to give us in the meantime. You can 'pet Mickey' anytime. Over and out."

"Big Tomcat to Rats and Mice. Message received. We'll pet *Mickey* at the appointed time. Good luck. Over and out."

Kariven turned on the tape recorder, which would automatically record a message if a call came in from Earth.

"I believe we can leave now, my friends. *Mickey*, the cargo rocket with our supplies, will take off from White Sands tomorrow morning. We'll get it in 53 hours."

Ivanovitch stood in front of the armored door, hesitant and very worried. He held two sheets of paper typed in the Russian alphabet. Finally he decided to press the metal button embedded in the doorframe. A plate next to it slid open, revealing a camera lens at the same time as a spotlight shined on the visitor from head to toe.

A minute later the armored door slid silently into the wall. Ivanovitch entered the office of General Gorochenko, Commander in Chief of the Soviet Armed Forces, and he stopped six feet away from the desk, clicked his heels together and stood stiffly at attention.

Curious, the general looked up and grumbled, "What is it, Ivanovitch? I don't like to be disturbed."

"Excuse me, General, but considering the importance of the documents…"

"Don't waste time with empty words. Get to the point."

Ivanovitch took two steps forward, put the papers on the general's desk and after stepping back clicked his heels again and went back to his steel pole position. "The cipher office just sent me this message captured by one of our radio-detection ships disguised as an Arab fishing boat in the Red Sea."

The general glanced at the text, reread it, and looked up. "Well? Is this the first time that American agents have infiltrated us? This is a matter for the counter-espionage unit. You don't want me, by God, to track them myself!"

"It's that, General… uh… the responses of these two individuals are all coming at three second intervals between each other."

General Gorochenko flinched and furrowed his brow. "How did you come to notice this… apparently insignificant detail?"

Ivanovitch's face turned red, "It's not me who noticed it, General. At the same time as this message we received a telephone call from the Ziolkowski Institute… The research center for long range radio transmissions also intercepted this message and the interval in question intrigued Professor Fritz Meyer… who alerted us immediately."

The general snatched up the telephone and called the Ziolkowski Institute. "General Gorochenko here. Get me Professor Fritz Meyer. Hello… Herr Professor Fritz Meyer? What's this story about an intercepted message and why are you so interested in the pauses between responses? Are you doing counter-espionage work now?"

"Nein, Herr General. It's only by chance that we intercepted this message on a very unusual wavelength… The message by itself," explained the German scientist who had been "retrieved" by the Russian after the defeat of the Third Reich, "doesn't interest us at all and there's doesn't seem to be any spying scheme in it. I simply wanted to draw your attention to these intervals—unique since the invention of the radio—recorded during this strange conversation."

"Have you been able to locate the two transmissions? And what's so important about these intervals?"

"One of the transmissions is apparently coming from a ship in the Atlantic. In the text its code name is Big Tomcat. As for the other, we have no idea about its location because…"

"And the intervals, Herr Professor?" General Gorochenko barked. "What's so unusual? Do you always just babble on endlessly on the telephone? No. Why would it be any different on the radio?"

"The intervals, Herr General," Professor Fritz Meyer answered calmly, "simply prove that the code name Rats and Mice was not transmitting *from Earth*… where the transmission of hertzian waves is, so to speak, instantaneous."

With their helmets hermetically sealed on the big, airtight collars, the American astronauts were huddled together at the foot of their rocket. Standing 20 yards away from a tiny crater only 40 feet in diameter, the rocket cast a huge shadow on the white lunar soil. As far as the eye could see were craters and mounds, lined up in the blinding light.

A strange spectacle and a terribly impressive one of this dead star flooded with the rays of the sun, that fiery orb shining brightly in the black, starry sky. The absence of atmosphere did, in fact, make it possible to see clearly both the sun—the fantastic blinding globe—and the countless constellations. Mars almost reaching its perigee[30], glowing red, looked like a disc the size of a gold coin. The Earth, on the

---

[30] The point in Mars' orbit where it is closest the Earth. (Author's Note)

other hand, a huge, greenish ball suspended in the black of space, had a diameter four times bigger than that of the sun.

Professor Harrington's voice echoed in the helmets linked together by tiny two-way radios. "We'll examine this dwarf crater. It might be perfect for the temporary installation of the Bubble Base."

While some of the team unloaded the equipment, the others started off. Their big strides on this star whose gravity was only one sixth of the Earth's made them jump 10 or 12 feet high. That was why our astronauts were forced to walk slowly. Their boots sank up to their ankles, sometimes up to their calves, in the thick layer of powdery soil. The chalky dust, white or yellow depending on the spot, drizzled back down in their wake, into the depressions left by their heavy boots.

Climbing up the 10-foot high crater required no effort. They stopped for a moment to contemplate the basin, then jumped with their feet together. Slowly tracing a 15-foot arc, they dropped onto another thick layer of the chalky dust or ash, the "earth" of the Moon.

Streiler, who had miscalculated his leap, fooled by the difference in gravity, somersaulted and bounced (no injuries sustained) onto a small hump in the middle of the crater. Having hit the ground twice, once with his helmet and then with a foot, two clouds of dust were kicked up. Now they were falling back down in weird slow motion like a floating feather and, as always, without swirling.

When he rejoined his friends, Kariven joked, "So, Kurt, you're playing the clown?"

The engineer laughed and gave him a friendly little poke in the side of his spacesuit, which sent the doctor into the dust.

Professor Harrington was squatting down and digging his gloves into the layer of dust. He did the same all around the perimeter of the crater, stopping every six feet to probe the ashy bed.

"This layer of 'seleno-cosmic' dust is around eight inches thick on average," he stated. "The powdery material is like volcanic ash. It's basically a bunch of fine, meteorite grains rained down from space for millions of years. We'll have to empty this crater of all the dust to be able to dig the foundation for our base."

"A long and tedious work that will make us lose precious time," Commander Taylor remarked. "Coming over the crest of the crater I noticed a long crevasse, 10 to 25 feet wide in places but it didn't look too deep. Maybe we could take a look before starting this grunt work."

"OK," Streiler agreed after discussing the possible usefulness of the crevasse with Professor Harrington. "We obviously have little chance of finding a cave in this dead world that suffers no erosion. Let's go."

The crevasse spotted by Commander Taylor stretch out as far as the eye could see, winding out from the base of the half-mile wide crater. It was not, strictly speaking, a crevasse but rather a "fissure," an extension of a crack opening onto the edge of the crater and widening out in the distance with angular twists and turns.

Indeed, the fissure was no more than 15 feet deep where it met the outer wall of the crater. Around 300 feet away it already dropped to 35 feet and widened out to 40 feet.

"That's what I was hoping to find!" Commander Taylor pointed to the bottom of the fissure.

At the base of the wall to the right was a 12-foot high hollow that dug into the rock at least 20 or 25 feet deep and formed a kind of natural cove.

"We'll bring the material for our Bubble Base down here and set up in this sub-lunarian hole. Like that we'll be protected from any eventual rock slide."

When they got back to the spaceship the five men who had just opened an outside panel of the ship on which a winch was attached, were bringing down, one by one, the reinforced Plexiglas parts wrapped in metal strips.

When everything was unloaded, they all headed for the site chosen by Commander Taylor, each carrying one of the parts—a bulky assemblage of curved plates, 10 inches thick and weighing 250 pounds on Earth but only 50 pounds on the Moon.[31]

Professor Harrington hooked together the three parts of a metal ladder, slid it into the fissure and was the first to climb down. While the parts of the "bubble" base were lined up along the edge of the crevasse, he approached the small cave and turned on his Geiger-Muller counter. Holding the tube out he ran it over the natural excavation, 15 feet high by 35 feet long and 30 feet deep, but the typical blinking light did not flash on. No radioactive element, therefore, was present in the rock. If there were uranium on the Moon it was not in this area. Consequently, the base could be set up without fear of harmful radiation.

Except for one man left in the rocket whose mission was to stay in contact with the Earth, all the astronauts started working. The metal strips wrapping the Plexiglas pieces were cut and the pieces put together into a kind of elongated "ball", hence its descriptive name Bubble Base or "Ball Base."

Just under 15 feet high, 20 feet wide and almost 30 feet long, it took six hours of relatively easy work, thanks to the weak lunar gravity, to construct the transparent base. But it was still not finished...

Carrying a big metal tank of compressed air and armed with a spray gun, a specialist shot a sealant over the seams to reinforce the airtight plasto-mastic joints of the different pieces. With his finger on the trigger, he sprayed a thick, colorless film over the joints. This special film, in the lunar air, solidified instantly in a strong bond for the walls of the base.

They could get to the Bubble Base through two tubes, also made of reinforced Plexiglas, one at each end, around 13 feet long and 3 feet in diameter. The astronauts, therefore, had to crawl in on their bellies or at best on hands and knees. A decompression valve separated the middle of the tube from the hatch opening onto the base itself.

---

[31] Actually, more like 41 pounds.

In order to get the equipment and limited furnishings for the expedition into the "ball", four convex panels had been left open. When all the material was brought in, these four pieces were put back and sealed up.

By building their base in this hole the astronauts saved at least 24 hours because they did not need to dig out foundations to install it. The base was built on flooring that was also made of adjustable, super resistance material. The whole was, therefore, put on the flat ground of the cave and anchored down by steel "wedges". After a quick snack—consisting mainly of paste or mash—the astronauts finished the most delicate part of their job: setting up the air distribution system of the sublunarian base.

The chemical generator producing oxygen and helium[32] of the artificial atmosphere measured six feet long by five feet on each side. It also included a system of pumps that expelled the air from the "dome" where the space explorers would be living. Another machine, thankfully less bulky, would be attached to the inside of the base. Its purpose was to catch the bad air and transform it into breathable air. The two machines would function automatically by electronic adjustment either speeding up or slowing down the input and output. Finally, a third machine contained the climate control for cooling the base during the lunar day and heating it up at night[33].

The technicians worked through a good part of night... or rather a period of time that, given the time of their arrival on the Moon, would have represented a part of the night on Earth. When they got back to the rocket, the base was ready for a test to check its sealing, resistance and hence its livability.

---

[32] The nitrogen in airtight bases as well as in spaceships will be replaced by helium that is less prone to cause embolisms. (Author's Note)

[33] The "night" taken here in the same sense as on Earth because on our satellite the lunar night (or day) lasts 14 earth days. (Author's Note)

After a "night" of well deserved rest, the astronauts woke up to the sound of a siren inside the ship, which rang automatically every eight hours (earth hours) as programmed by Commander Taylor.

Without any water at all—according to all information—on our satellite, what was used by the members of the expedition for showers was collected and purified to be used again.

Daisy, the first interplanetary rocket from Earth, was, therefore, a truly automated laboratory. Even the leftovers from the meals were saved. An automatic waste disposal reduced them to a pretty unappetizing mush to be used as fertilizer for the future installation of a permanent American base on the Moon. This "syrup" would be boosted with chemicals before transforming it into the real fertilizer needed for an experimental botany lab. For, such a lab would be built in order to grow, under huge Plexiglas bell jars, the necessary vegetables for future "colonists." Hydroponic fields[34] would also be built under the jar when everything was ready.

The team of technicians headed for the Bubble Base to carry out the necessary trials. Within two hours the various tests were compete: air distribution, sealing, functioning of the electric generator for lights and machines, everything was tested, re-examined, supervised and experimented on to their complete satisfaction.

"We can live in the base now," the physicist lieutenant MacDonald said, crawling out of the decompression tube.

"Bravo!" Streiler cheered, rubbing his gloved hands together. "We'll be able to sleep without our spacesuits tonight and not in that damned old *Daisy*!" Smiling under the transparent globe of his helmet he went on cheerfully, "Now we can start the real exploration of our new territory."

---

[34] Farming without soil for many crops thanks to huge vats where the different vegetables and plants rest on a bed of gravel fed by a nutritive liquid. (Author's Note)

"Good grief!" Commander Taylor cried out. "When we got here I completely forgot to plant the 'Earthling' flag in the lunar ground!"

All the astronauts burst out laughing. Professor Harrington remarked, "Frankly, I'm glad you didn't plant it when we arrived, Commander. The ceremony would have been pretty pompous and overblown."

Commander Taylor, a soldier above all else and trying to hold onto his flame of patriotism, shot a dirty look at the physicist, then after thinking about it, he finally smiled, "Hmm… you may be right, professor. I can see the picture now: very 'cliché.'"

Meanwhile, Lieutenant Clark came leaping in and pulled up at the edge of the crevasse, waving a long, plastic cylinder and calling out to his chief through his microphone, "The flags, Commander… You… We forgot to…"

"Yeah, I know," the superior officer growled, climbing up the ladder, followed by the other astronauts.

The plastic tube that Lieutenant Clark was holding contained the Stars and Stripes and the flag of the United Nations. Grabbing the tube Commander Taylor panned around the dreary, desolate moonscape. His eyes stopped on the crest of a crater, 100 yards away, with a circular wall almost 200 yards high.

"We'll plant our 'standards' on the top of that crater. They'll be clearly visible from all around."

"I'm sure they'll attract all kinds of tourists."

"Lieutenant Clark!" Commander Taylor barked into his helmet. "Your jokes on the matter…"

"Come now, come now," Professor Harrington broke in. "After the extraordinary work we just accomplished, after the most fantastic voyage of all time and the nervous tension we all suffered, don't you think a little humor will do us good?"

The Commander frowned, sticking his lower lip out, stood speechless for a moment, and then realized the virtue of this sage advice. He finally loosened up. "OK, OK, I'm nervous too and as always, Professor, you're right. Let's go play mountain climber!"

He took the lead and bounced lightly, despite looking like a Michelin Man, carrying the long tube holding the emblems of the United Earthlings.

By radio the man on guard in the rocket was called out to participate in the ceremony. Climbing up the slope of the crater was no easy job. The walls had very few footholds and the "moontaineers" often stumbled, almost falling back down the steep wall. Even with their heavy spacesuits and "lightened" by the weak gravity, such a fall would not have been without danger.

After half an hour of slow climbing the ten men reached the summit, 740-foot high as indicated by the special altimeters on the chest of their spacesuits. The crater was somewhere between 5,000 and 5,000 feet in diameter. In the middle was a kind of rocky spike standing almost 600 feet high. Its top looked like a jagged mushroom folding up on itself.

Such craters with central spikes are common on our satellite, but this was the first one that the Earthlings were seeing up close.

Kariven, scanning the inside of the crater through prismatic binoculars, interrupted his examination. He moved his face closer to the transparent cover of his helmet, pressed the binoculars hard against the Plexiglas and refocused.

"No doubt about it," he spoke into his mic. "I clearly see a bunch of round holes at the base of the crater wall… Look for yourselves."

Intrigued, the astronauts took out their prismatic binoculars, did as told and in the face of the evidence had to admit that these weird holes, barely a foot in diameter, really were there.

"What do you think it is?" the Commander asked, laying the tube at his feet. He, too, looked through the binoculars and saw the mysterious holes.

"I have no idea. I see at least a hundred of them on the opposite wall and that's only on the arc running 50 yards beyond the shadow cast by the top of the crater."

The Commander, in order to see the eastern part of the crater better, stepped to the side without taking his eyes off the binoculars. His right boot kicked the tube, which teetered on the wall before rolling off and bouncing gently down. It took three or four slow bounds and settled at the foot of the rocky slope.

"The flags!" Lieutenant Clark cried out. "The tube fell over the edge!"

The Commander cursed at his clumsiness. Lieutenant Clark and Kariven were already helping each other scramble down the steep wall. Johnny Talbert, the cameraman of the expedition, was filming the two men making their way to the bottom of the crater.

The plastic tube had fallen alongside the wall and rolled into a small ditch in the flat surface of the crater. Obviously there was a slight slope at this spot, tilting toward the wall, because from the top they could see part of the light brown tube.

"Darn!" the cameraman blurted out, putting down his camera and grabbing his prismatic binoculars. "I can't see the tube anymore…"

Kariven and Clark, hearing this echo in their helmets, stopped for an instant to glance at the base of the crater 50 yards below them. It did indeed seem to them that the tube was not exactly in the same place.

"Maybe it rolled?" the Lieutenant guessed.

"Rolled? After stopping for minutes at the bottom of a slope?" Kariven disagreed. "That would surprise me. We probably didn't get a good look at its position or else Johnny's hallucinating."

"You scientists are funny," Clark grinned. "If a good guy sees something weird either he's hallucinating or he's dreaming!"

"Are you referring to the 'light' you think you saw?"

"That I *did see*," he corrected.

"That you *say you saw*?" Kariven corrected in turn.

"Absolutely. I saw a bright, purple beam shoot out of the Aristarchus crater after the rocket flew over the area."

Starting back down the wall Kariven asked, "And you think it's normal for a metal tube to change positions all by itself? Come on, pal, you're believing in ghosts!"

All of a sudden eight shouts of surprise rang inside their helmets.

"But… *it's moving!* Good God! The flags are taking off!"

It was Commander Taylor who had just yelled this. Once again Clark and Kariven stopped to examine the basin.

"Billions of blistering booster rockets!" Kariven swore in astronaut jargon.

With their eyes bulging out the two men watched, 30 feet below them, the still visible part of the tube. Slowly, with little jerks, the tube seemed to be sinking into the base of the crater still hidden by a tiny overhanging ledge.

Throwing all caution to the wind and devoured by curiosity, in three bounds they jumped onto the floor of the crater. They barrel-rolled on the ground and stopped after leaving a deep groove in the seleno-cosmic ash. The voices of the astronauts left on top buzzed in their ears in a muddled confusion.

Lieutenant Clark and Kariven took a few steps toward the foot of the crater wall, then suddenly stood still and speechless. On the ground, in the wall of the crater, was a series of holes identical to those they had seen from the summit through the binoculars. And into one of these holes the long plastic tube holding the flags *was disappearing!*

Kariven jumped and threw himself flat on the ground, grabbing the end of the tube, which was squirming into the dark hole. He finally got up and yanked the tube back, causing it to shoot out of the hole and go rolling to the feet of Lieutenant Clark.

The horrified officer swore out loud and jumped to the side. Stuck to the end of the tube was *a brown, throbbing mass!*

CHAPTER THREE

Kariven moved closer to Lieutenant Clark and followed his gaze riveted to the ground.

"But… but…," he stammered, "it's… it's ALIVE!"

In rhythmical spasms a weird, brown creature like a kind of flat jellyfish around eight inches in diameter, detached from the tube and slowly went back to the holes. The "thing" moved through the dust by vibrations, making its body ripple in the shape of disc.

"What's wrong?" Professor Harrington asked.

"We… we found an animal… a living being!"

"Living?" Commander Taylor and Streiler echoed together, unbelieving.

"Very alive. This 'thing' is moving, crawling toward the holes in the base of the rocky wall."

"Capture it, by God! Capture it!" the professor screamed. "But don't kill it whatever you do! I want to study it alive!"

Kariven emptied the contents of a plastic bag containing his rations, maps and a miniature sextant. He hurried over to the "moon beast" and squatted down, blocking its path to capture it. With one knee in the dust he opened the 10-inch wide mouth of the bag.

The creature with a brown shell, twitching forward, stopped 20 inches away from the bag. It spun around slowly and even more slowly moved closer. It stopped exactly at the edge of the of the bag that Kariven kept open, then very cautiously touched the plastic with a kind of greenish fringe that stuck out from the edge of its disc-shaped body. Feeling the plastic material, the fringe tremble a little and then retracted quickly. From the top of the body six little, amber stalks squirmed up and bent forward toward the opening of the bag.

"What are you doing, Kariven?" Harrington asked. "Get it in the bag and come back up!"

"The... the 'thing'," he replied, "is busy touching the edge of the bag. Six ringed, flexible stems just came out of its rounded back. They're stretched out over 12 inches long and are now swaying slowly inside the bag. I have the feeling that they're eyes or maybe fingers... We'll have to examine them."

He stopped talking. The "thing" had just pulled back the six swaying stalks and was cautiously moving backward. With a nimble sweep of his hand Kariven slid the bag along the ground and picked the thing up. He closed the bag, pulled the cord tight and hung it from his belt. The moon beast was caught in the trap.

"Watch out!" Clark suddenly shouted, pointing at the wall.

From every hole a great number of "jellyfish" were pouring out, all headed in their direction. How could such creatures that were apparently so slow be rolling now so quickly, as fast as a man jogging?

The flat beasts were already flowing over the sextant and maps and rations and heading straight for the two Earthlings. More creatures kept coming out of their caves and joining the first ones, forming a moving carpet of brown beasts rippling and pulsating over the ground.

"Quick, Clark! Take the flags and maps. I'll get the rations and sextant. Kick these things off and kill them but try not to touch them with your gloves."

"But look, Kariven!" Clark protested. "They're everywhere. We'll never get the stuff free and get to the wall without squashing a whole bunch of them."

"Oh well, but try just the same to move them away with your boots. I don't think they'll bite." He tried to joke.

Digging in the dust with their boots, they kicked away the moon beasts, freed the flag, sextant, maps and rations and then picked it all up, ready to climb up the slope of the crater.

The disc-shaped creatures stopped their weird spasms for a moment. After this brief freeze, as if obeying some kind of signal, they moved as a group and encircled the two astronauts. Thousands of stalks shot out of the carapaces and swayed together toward the space explorers.

Kariven and Clark leaped 15 feet and landed behind the circle of brown creatures. Another leap, this time upward, landed them on an outcrop on the wall. From there they looked back to see the reaction of the mysterious inhabitants of our satellite. They looked surprised and started spinning around, feeling in the dust at the spot trampled by the Earthlings a few seconds before. Finding nothing there the "jellyfish" disbanded and hurried back into their rocky holes.

Professor Harrington, sitting on a metal crate with one elbow on a folding table at the foot of the rocket, was examining the imprisoned "animal" very carefully. It was closed up in a Plexiglas box, 15 inches square, rippling gently. All the astronauts surrounded the physicist, watching the rhythmical movements of the creature.

"It's absolutely amazing!" babbled Terry Brown, the biologist of the expedition, setting down another crate in front of the table to sit on. "Living beings on the Moon, this dried up star with no atmosphere. Who would've believed it?"

Kariven commented, "A number of times astronomers have observed inexplicable changes in the hues and tints in the center of certain lunar craters[35]. We might think that these astronomers were watching the vast movement of these creatures on the surface of the observed craters."

"Could be. In fact, it's very likely," the young biologist surmised. "But how could life sustain itself in a place lacking water and air and bombarded by the unfiltered rays of the sun? it seems inconceivable… and yet, here we have it before our eyes, irrefutable proof: beings—certainly very rudimentary but living beings just the same—existing on the Moon."

"It looks kind of like a jellyfish, a dark, drab jellyfish, with a brown shell, almost metallic."

---

[35] True; observations reported on several occasions notably by Williams Herschel and Pickering. (Author's Note)

Using a duralinox rod, Brown turned the beast onto its back. Its underside was a flat disc with a multitude of rippling grooves, the organs of locomotion. In the narrow spaces between the grooves were a countless number of greenish lumps of the same consistency as the vibrating, retractable crown around the rim of the carapace.

"The sextant!" Clark cried out. "Look at the arm of the sextant! What happened to it?"

One whole side of the arc of the blue metal instrument showed pinkish traces like rust or more like corrosion cause by a potent acid.

"Even though it's plastic the tube holding the flags is also 'rusted,'" Commander Taylor said.

Kariven rifled through the maps and rations—also contained in plastic—and the bag in which he had carried the "beast". His face turned into a model of stupefaction. Through the transparent globe of his helmet they could see tiny beads of sweat forming on his forehead.

"Everything that touched these lunar creatures bears traces of intense corrosion! The maps, sextant, rations, the tube were all swarmed over on the floor of the crater by these brown 'jellyfish'. It was on contact with them that these objects got covered in this pinkish rust. They attacked and even deeper if it was metal."

"Metallophages!" the biologist's eyes were round as saucers. "The greenish bumps we saw between the locomotion-grooves must serve as the animals' mouths."

Brown grabbed the duralinox rod and for a few minutes stroked the flat underbelly of the jellyfish. The tiny bumps started throbbing. In addition, miniscule, microscopic, pink crystals appeared on the tips of the bumps seen under a very strong magnifying glass.

During the examination the duralinox rod ended up being seriously damaged. A series of pink, jagged spots on its surface formed a layer of "rust," sinking in, replacing the layer of duralinox absorbed by the metal-eating monster.

"Should we deduce that this being feeds off the energy in the molecules of whatever it touches?" the biologist wondered out loud, pensively. "Is it really an animal or... animal/mineral being?"

With the rod Brown turned the creature back over and absent-mindedly tapped the shell. The six stalk-organs sprang out of their cells and swayed gently. Their tips were covered with a bundle of shiny needles like polished steel, which were constantly vibrating, maybe 0.2 inches long and as thin as a hair.

Still with his rod the biologist tickled one of these stalks with its bundle of seven needles. The shiny points abruptly started vibrating faster, then suddenly retracted. The five other stalks crept forward cautiously, like snakes slithering vertically, and touched the metal rod warily.

Brown pulled back the rod and tapped three times on the brown shell. The stalks spread apart and five of them disappeared into the body of the lunar creature while one remained swaying. He leaned closer and closer to the rod, hesitantly, then brushed over the glimmering metal with its seven needles. After a momentary freeze, it hit the rod three times.

The biologist and the astronauts were stunned. The most surprised of them all, without a doubt, was the biologist. He tried another experiment and gave five taps on the shell. Four stalks came out of their cells and joined the first. They each hit the rod once with their needles. Brown yelped and dropped the rod in the plastic box.

"It thinks! It's not just an animal but... a *thinking being*. A Selenite!"

An unpleasant shiver ran down the Earthlings' spines.

"Don't get worked up," Professor Harrington began, whose rational, Cartesian mind did not accept things at face value. "What you think is a *response* to your tapping, Brown, might be just a kind of unconscious reflex. If you tap a crystal glass, for example, you'll hear a melodic vibration. But that doesn't mean that the glass is responding *intentionally* to your action. I think that we're seeing a similar phenomenon here."

"Hold on," Kariven intervened, pulling out the rod that the creature had crawled over. It was more corroded and had pink scars that were clearer and deeper than before.

Like Brown, he tapped five times on the brown jellyfish. Right away a green stalk sprung out of the shell and hit the duralinox rod five times.

"Uh-um," Professor Harrington coughed, a little unnerved. "That doesn't prove that it thinks."

Kariven started over by striking the captive "animal" two times lightly on its back. The stalk with seven needles swayed a little and then hit the rod five times. A few seconds went by and then the stalk once again hit the rod five times.

Kariven dropped the rod for the creature, which crawled on top of it right away. "Are you convinced?" he asked the professor.

Stupefied, Harrington nodded several times. "Brown was right. This 'Selenite' is a thinking being. A simple auto-response would not have answered five times to the two taps, but only twice."

"Exactly," the biologist agreed. "When Dr. Kariven hit the Selenite two times, it didn't try to understand the meaning but simply repeated the five taps. Because for this Selenite *five taps means the possibility of absorbing the metal!* We've just witnessed a kind of reverse Conditioned Reflex or Pavlov Reflex. The question was: if, for example, you get in the habit of ringing a bell every time you give a piece of meat to a dog or cat, after a few days if you ring the bell will the cat or dog come to get its snack. The sound of the bell will condition the animal's instinctive reflex.

"Here we're dealing with a more evolved being than a dog or cat. Having associated the five taps with the fact that it'll get its metal food, the Selenite, on its own, hit the rod to ask for said food. Moreover, if a dog or cat gifted with the Pavlov Reflex was able or knew how to act intelligently following this reflex, there's no doubt that at the first signs of hunger it would go—if it could—and ring the bell to call its master for some steak."

Turning to Commander Taylor, fascinated, he concluded, "I have to study these creatures' physiology, Commander. Could you organize a little hunting party? I'll need living Selenites. I'm going to start to dissect this one right now."

"OK, Brown. My men will fish you up three or four of these filthy beasts."

As he was walking away, Kariven started thinking aloud. "It may be stupid, Brown, but I feel a little bad about the idea that you want to kill this Selenite. Even though fundamentally different from us *homo sapiens*, doesn't it represent the thinking form of life on this star? Would you find it normal, for example, if some monstrous (in our eyes), alien being kidnapped Earthlings to study their physiology in some crazy laboratory from some distant planet of the Galaxy?"

The biologist barely shrugged. "This Selenite, unquestionably, has some intelligence. But if we want to establish a permanent base on the Moon, isn't it indispensable that we know about our 'neighbors'? I really don't think I'm committing a crime by killing this creature. Besides, it's necessary. The lives of future colonists might depend on it."

"Certainly," Kariven gave in. "It's necessary. *Man is a wolf to man*," he quoted, "but also to all other forms of life."

Brown stood up, smiling, and put the box containing the Selenite under his arm. "Forget you scruples, Kariven. I wouldn't act like this if we landed on a planet full of intelligent beings showing a semblance of technological evolution. There's nothing of the sort here. At best we could compare these Selenites to troglodytes able to reason in an elementary fashion."

"Anthropomorphism, Brown," Kariven shook his head. "A pity for the Selenite. Science sometimes has very unpleasant demands." He gave him a friendly pat on his air tanks and added, "Don't worry, I won't think of you as a murderer."

The two men separated with smiles. While the biologist headed for the rocket to shut himself into the lab, Kariven and the other astronauts went in the direction of the crater to help hunt down three or four Selenites with Taylor's men.

When they got up on the summit they took out their binoculars and watched the three American technicians laying out as bait a chrome steel ax at the entrance of one of the Selenite "dwellings".

From all the holes at the same time a constant flood of brown shells poured into the crater and circled the astronauts in no time. They deftly swung their bags and imprisoned two Selenites each. But this time the circle of lunar creatures closed in fast on them. Some even tried to crawl up their boots.

The three men started kicking right and left to shake off the Selenites that were already glued to their boots made of a special hybrid of plastic, rubber and metal. The astronauts, now on the defense because of this attack—maybe it was just the Selenites' simple curiosity?—started jumping around without trying to avoid stomping the brown shells. In three bounds they were safe, 30 feet up on the slope of the crater. Down below, under the chalky dust, the Selenites they had trampled did not seem to be affected at all by the punishment. They were twisting around, thrusting out their stalks in all directions and (probably) not sensing any unusual presence. They all went squirming back to their sub-lunar dwellings.

At the top of the summit the three astronauts were examined carefully by Kariven and Professor Harrington. The soles and the legs of their spacesuits showed the pink blotches.

Commander Taylor furrowed his brow and whistled softly. "From now on there has to be at least three of us together down in the crater and armed with a fluoride torch! If one of you gets dizzy down there with the Selenites, the nasty creatures will eat through your spacesuits in no time. You can see here what happened to the poor guy who passed out when attacked by these monsters." Then he called out, "Lieutenant Clark!"

The lieutenant came running and held out the tube containing the flags of the USA and the United Nations.

The Commander took the tube and radioed the biologist in the ship's lab. "Dr. Brown, we're going to proceed with taking possession of this rock. I don't want to drag you away from your urgent work. You can watch the ceremony through the camera set up on the crater. If you zoom in, it'll be just like you were there with us."

"Got it, Commander. I'll put the Selenite under lock and key for the moment and turn on the camera."

Commander Taylor unscrewed the lid of the plastic tube and took out the two flags. All the astronauts, bundled up in the spacesuits, lined up at attention. The superior officer unrolled the two rectangles made up special cloth (one the stars and stripes and the other the emblem of the UN) and then turning to face the space explorers, his voice betraying his emotion, he declared:

"By virtue of the powers invested in me, in the name of the United States of America and of the United Nations, I declare the Moon under control of the United Nations of Earth. This ceremony is not intended for exclusive possession. Earth's satellite belongs to no single nation. The problem of legal ownership comes under the jurisdiction of the United Nations, who will decide what laws and government will rule it. When the day comes, which I hope will be soon, when all peoples of Earth will be united and look upon each other as brothers, every country will be able to contribute to the construction of one or more giant, international bases on the Moon. The representatives of the unified Terrestrial Nations will sit in perfect equality in these permanent bases."

The Commander planted the two flags in a fissure in the crater, filled it in with rocks and moon dust, then stepped back. Standing stiffly he raised his gloved hand up to his globular helmet and saluted.

The emblems of Earth, in the absence of an atmosphere, stood still, frozen, as if petrified in their folds until the end of time. No breeze would ever flutter them. They would stay there, motionless, mute witnesses to the invincible courage of a handful of Earthly heroes.

Commander Taylor lowered his arm and turned back to his men, "Tonight, my friends, we'll use the capsules of concentrated champagne for the first time on the Moon."

Suddenly, the big smiles that had just started to form on the astronauts' faces were turned into looks of astonishment. Inside their helmets the stuttering voice of Dr. Brown, the biologist, was fading in and out.

"Commander! Commander... The Selenite... can live in our atmosphere. It... it attacked me... when I tried to close the box...I... I thought it would die breathing the air inside the ship..."

"Dr. Brown!" the Commander snapped. "What's happening? What's wrong? Dr. Brown!"

The biologist's voice was fading out. Without waiting for orders Kariven, Lieutenant Clark and some other men scrambled down the outer side of the crater, leaping dangerously high and landing hard.

"The Selenite," Brown panted, "has absorbed the plastic box. It's..."

A muffled groan reached the worried astronauts and then the voice resumed, barely audible, "The mineral salts... it feeds on them... and the ones... *in humans!* Be careful... para..."

"Dr. Brown! Dr. Brown!" the Commander howled into his mic. "What's going on?"

No response came back.

The Commander, Professor Harrington and Dr. Streiler ran after the others toward the rocket. When they reached it and entered the decompression chamber, they were sweating bullets. But when they stormed into the ship's laboratory, they froze in horror.

Kariven was holding a smoking torch in his right hand. Brown was lying on the metal floor, his mouth twisted in pain, his eyes bulging, already empty. He was dead. In his right hand he was still holding the microphone up to his lips.

The Selenite was no longer the small, 8-inch creature they had seen before. Now it was over five feet in diameter and covered the legs, belly and part of the biologist's chest. Kariven's fluoride torch had carved a deep groove in the monster's shell. The bitter smell of quicklime floating in the cabin tickled their throats.

Seeing the Commander's look of dismay Kariven explained, "The Selenite is dead. The flame from the torch was no match for it."

"How could it get so big in so short a time?"

"I believe it first fed by absorbing the bottom of the plastic box. Then it must have sucked in the molecules of oxygen, hydrogen and helium in the artificial air after escaping through the corroded box. While Brown was talking with the Commander over the radio or else turning on the camera, the Selenite must have been growing and growing until it attacked him."

"But Brown was a big guy," the superior officer objected. "He could have defended himself, pushed it back, run away…"

Kariven shook his head sadly, "No, Commander. Remember our poor friend's last words. He didn't finish, only uttered a couple of syllables. *Para.* That's what explains why he couldn't defend himself. *Para…* he was trying to say *paralyzed!* In some way that we don't know, probably electrochemical, the monster paralyzed Teddy Brown. The paralysis must have worked fast, not instantaneous since he had time to call us. He fell backwards and sent his warning as the first symptoms of catatonia were taking effect.

"His scientific mind and admirable energy compelled him to give us useful information about the dangers of these Selenites rather than just calling out for help. Thus, he revealed that not only can these creatures live in our atmosphere but they can attack a man and feed off his mineral salts… just look at his corpse."

The Selenite had indeed partly destroyed (by absorption) the biologist's clothes and was stuck to his skin.

Kariven kicked the monster off and it fell to the side of the corpse. Brown's legs, belly and chest were veined with weird marks, not bleeding but pinkish, almost shiny. The skin looked saggy on the skeleton, which looked like it had been squeezed hard. The Selenite had absorbed a good portion of the body's mineral salts through some capillary suction.

Professor Harrington and Streiler were squatting down to examine the corpse of their friend. The skin felt like leather under their fingers.

Streiler grabbed a pyrex stir from the wall of the lab above a table cluttered with instruments and chemical equipment. With this foot-long rod he prodded the monster's body and dug it into the wound caused by the burning tongue of flame. "Wound" is not the right word because it was more of a groove like a flame would make on a steel plate. Its edges were jagged. Through the gash the inside of the Selenite's body looked like a bunch of thin metal leaves, shimmering from steel-blue to dark red and all the colors and hues of the spectrum.

"The Selenite," Streiler observed, "seems to go into rigor mortis like earth bodies. But here rigidity isn't a relative expression. I'm sure that in a very short time this metallophage monster will turn into a block of metal, composed of many different elements no doubt but mostly this shiny white element we can see in the gash. The Selenite's body is a kind of collection of different metallic zones separated from one another by these leaves or layers of silvery metal."

Using some wire cutters he struggled to snap off a piece of the strange, shiny, white metal but it took a while.

"Damn! This stuff is hard. It's like nickel-chrome."

He put it in a petri dish, mixed it with different chemicals and dropped some acids on it, all to no effect. Astounded by this, he plunged it into a nitric-hydrochloric solution and the metal bubbled. Kariven, after watching Streiler's analysis very carefully, cried out, "Why, it's platinum!"

The engineer nodded and waved it off, "Theoretically and until we've done a thorough analysis to evaluate its specific weight, we can consider the Selenites as made of 70% pure platinum."

CHAPTER FOUR

"Platinum," Professor Harrington echoed while Streiler and Kariven performed a more detailed study of the Selenite. "It's fantastic! If the lunar craters are full of these metallophage creatures chiefly made up of platinum, this satellite will be of keen interest from the industrial point of view. The troglodyte holes should be overflowing with incalculable riches."

Commander Taylor, with his helmet tilted onto his back, pinched the bridge of his nose and massaged it. Looking puzzled he said, "This discovery, when it's made public, will cause a real panic on Wall Street and with all the brokers on Earth. Just imagine the drop in platinum prices and the subsequent crash of mining company stocks. What a mess! And yet, the mining industry will have to exploit these lunar deposits to the full... if we can really call these creatures 'minerals'!

"On the other hand, this discovery will make the executives of the Corporation for the Exploitation of Minerals and Metals from the Moon[36] jump with joy, along with the other

---

[36] True. This corporation was created at the beginning of 1953 by Richard de Touche-Skadding, a former Latvian diplomat turned archeologist and mineralogist. A similar company even required membership dues of $200! (Author's Note) Baron Richard J. H. de Touche-Skadding was an eccentric mineralogist and the author of an entertaining book, *Agni Mani: Magic Gem from the Moon* (Ballantine, 1966; Mayflower 1968) about the fabled Javan tektites (*Agni Mani* is a Sanskrit term that translates as "Fire Pearls"). While the book purports to be a non-fiction account of his 30-year search for the stones, it is clearly highly embellished. Touche-Skadding was a true believer and presented specimens to then-Princess Elizabeth, Winston Churchill, and Lord Louis Mountbatten in the 1940s

private organizations created recently in view of a future mineral exploitation of our satellite."

"Provided that the relevant nations let private companies do the research and work for their own profit," Professor Harrington noted quite rightly. "Besides, we're far from science fiction stories where the first astronauts go wandering off to Phoebe on board rocket ships built secretly on private property thanks to the fabulous wealth of a balding, rich professor. Reality—as we all know—is completely different.

"Building *Daisy* and *Mickey*, the remote-controlled ship that we're expecting tomorrow, cost the trifling sum of ten billion dollars![37] Astronautics is the exclusive responsibility of governments and not some fat cat, genius or not."

Streiler and Kariven stopped their examination. Kariven informed them, "I believe we've found some particularities of these creatures. Alive they're semi-rigid, their metallic structure being malleable thanks to the instability of their molecular make-up. Their metallic elements in a paste-like state allows them to interact between the different layers of their body, which gives them life. But in a dead Selenite, these interactions stop and hence the solidification. Its constitutive elements stop combining and in a way are purified by the suppression of the interactions."

"Exactly," Streiler confirmed. "When dead, these creatures become a kind of mass formed, it seems, of palladium, rhodium, osmium, copper, gold and iron with faint traces of uranium to act as the natural cement. Every layer of these various elements is separated by a thick layer of platinum. All together, as Kariven just said, it's malleable, semi-rigid, thanks to a continual molecular motion that we have to admit is rather baffling. All their internal elements are, after death, chemically pure. While alive there's a constant exchange of

---

with the hope of blessing them with the legendary good luck of the Agni Mani.

[37] Not a bad estimate. The Apollo space programme cost was given as $25.4 billion at the time of Apollo 11.

energy between the layers of metal by a kind of endosmosis, the very foundation of their life."

"I hope these creatures don't leave their crater," Kariven said. "In any case, just to be careful, we should never let any useful material off the base or the ship. These monsters can corrode and digest them in no time."

"From now on," Commander Taylor added, "the ship and the base will be guarded by men armed with torches. And when we go out exploring we'll have to be armed as well."

Really for the first time the astronauts felt the dread of their total isolation. Alone almost 240,000 miles from their planetary fatherland, they had to struggle not to fall into what the psychologist and psychotechnicians at Randolph Field called "Space Fever" or "the astronauts' blues." They all looked from the Earth, apparently motionless in the lunar sky, to the two flags that no gust of wind was stirring at the top of the nearby crater.

While they were lost in their dark thoughts, staring at the star and stripes and the emblem of the UN, a strange phenomenon occurred. In the distance, on the dark side of the Moon, beyond the terminator line, a bright light flashed, quick as lightning.

This time Lieutenant Clark was not the only one to see a light on the Moon. The Commander and Kariven had also witnessed the brief illumination.

"What can that be?"

"You saw it, too, Kariven?" Clark asked excitedly, staring at the horizon.

"Maybe you were right, Clark, and you really did see a light in the Aristarchus crater. But the one we just saw didn't come from the crater; it came from the area that's veiled in eternal darkness."

"Do you think the Selenites are able to send light signals?" Clark suggested.

"I don't think these beings are so evolved. Their stage of evolution is much more primitive than ours. Maybe in the troglodyte dwellings they have some 'great minds' capable of organizing them into social groups, nations as it were, but to credit them with technological progress is going a long way."

"What we just saw," Clark explained, "is different from what I saw before. In the Aristarchus crater it looked more like a ray of purple light. Oh, it was brief, like a vision, but a rough image that I can't forget. However, just now it was more of a flash, an explosion. Should we imagine another form of intelligent life on the Moon, higher than what we've discovered here?"

Professor Harrington advised, "Let's not fall into anthropomorphism in speaking about life evolving on the Moon. The two bright lights could, after all, be just natural effects from a volcano, maybe still active on our satellite, or simply a big meteor crashing, which could have kicked up a bunch of chalky dust that looked to us like bright flashes in the sunrays."

"That's OK for what Clark saw in the Aristarchus crater," Kariven admitted, "but for what we just saw it doesn't hold water because it happened beyond the terminator line and therefore on the side of the Moon not lit by the Sun."

"Yes, of course, what you say is logical," Harrington gave in. "The best thing would be to go and check it out after *Mickey* gets here."

If our friends had decided to go to the dark side of the Moon—where Kariven, Clark and the Commander had seen a bright flash—no doubt they would have been dumbstruck by the sight to be seen.

Three miles inside the shadow zone of the Moon a huge interplanetary rocket—not so different from *Daisy*—had just landed and spit out a last blast of ignition fuel that had kicked up a cloud of chalky dust. Everyone knows that without an atmosphere ordinary combustion is impossible. However, for spaceships combustion is entirely possible in empty space because a combustive is mixed with the liquid fuel to allow it to burn. A quick thrust of the reactors while braking increases the exhaust coming out of the rear pipes and makes the glow inside the reactors partially visible. That was what was seen, briefly, 70 miles away by the terrestrial astronauts.

The mysterious rocket, over 300 feet tall and 80 feet wide at the base, had barely set down when a hatch opened in the hull, almost 230 feet high. A metal ladder came out of the side and from the decompression chamber eleven figures wearing spacesuits descended the ladder one by one.

The first of these figures was holding a long, gray tube in its glove that looked like three steel claws. On each of the spacesuits' chests was a small projector that shot a beam of light 25 feet in front of them.

The man—because these figures did resemble human beings—who was clutching the tube in his claw-glove spoke to his companions who formed a circle around him.

"In spite of the unfortunate accident to our astronavigraph, which made us land almost 200 miles from the chosen crater, this day…"

He paused to look around and realized that instead of day they were in darkness lit only by the twinkling stars. He cleared his throat and continued.

"This day, perhaps not the appropriate word but still, is a great day for our country."

He popped open the metal tube and pulled out a flag that had in the center the red star of the USSR!

"In the name of the free people of the Soviet Union and by virtue of the powers thereby, I take possession of the Moon, the satellite of Earth and a new republic for our Union! I am full of emotion and pride in planting our flag in the lunar ground. Let's be thankful to our comrade Professor Obyktchev, the wise astronomer, member of the Moscow Academy, who pronounced these admirable words two years ago: *The planets in the immense universe are burning with impatience for a Russian Christopher Columbus to be the first to come and conquer them.*[38]

---

[38] True quote. (Author's Note) A google search has failed to produce any information under that name or close variants.

"Let's also keep in mind the memorable speech of the President of the Soviet Academy of Sciences that pretty much at the same time declared: *The Russians are almost ready to undertake the liberation of the Moon in case it might be occupied by some fascist regime of unknown origin.*[39]

"Luckily this issue won't arise because we now have the rights of *Primo Occupanti* and we will assert it if necessary."

Zavkom, a colonel in the soviet army and Chief of the expedition, after this short speech ordered, "We'll build a temporary base at the foot of the rocket and when the astronavigraph is fixed we'll go set up in a crater on the bright side of the Moon. We should only have to stay here a few days…"

At 8 o'clock the alarm echoed through the Bubble Base. Commander Taylor had been ready since seven in the morning. The first night in the airtight, reinforced plastic base had been hell for him and his mood showed it!

Moreover, the tragic death of biologist Teddy Brown had affected all the members of the expedition. After washing in the tiny shower and having breakfast, the nine men drew up the work schedule for the day.

Professor Harrington portioned out the most urgent tasks to his team of handpicked technicians. "We're going to devote this day to the study of the Moon's geology and then some astronomical observations that can't be done at the same time because we'll be using explosives to create shock waves through the ground to determine the underlying components. In the meantime four men will make a reconnaissance trip in a radius of six miles and will stay in constant radio contact with the base. You won't split up under any circumstances and… you won't go inside those craters inhabited by Selenites. Your mission will be to pinpoint the craters with troglodytes and

---

[39] True quote from a speech delivered on Radio Moscow in January 1954. (Author's Note)

mark them on the selenographic map[40]. The reconnaissance team will carry individual rations of food and probably won't be back for at least 12 hours."

With the schedule set, the different specialists put on their spacesuits, prepared their instruments and one by one left the Bubble Base through the decompression tube after arming themselves with fluoride torches in case they met any Selenites.

Just when they were ready climb up the ladder to leave the gulch that sheltered the base, a shout of surprise made them turn around.

"Who left the base last night?" Commander Taylor looked at each of them.

The astronauts also looked at one another but in bewilderment.

"Come on, fess up!" the Commander barked, furious at seeing his formal orders broken. "Look at the moon dust. Don't you see those footprints that aren't the same as the faded ones we left last night before entering the base? Two men walked around the Bubble Base and their boots left prints

---

[40] Drawn up by Percy Wilkins, Director of the Lunar Section of the British Astronomical Assiociation, a 300″-diameter map of the Moon divided into quadrants. It took him 14 years to produce. (Author's Note) Hugh Percy Wilkins (1896-1960) was a Welsh-born engineer and amateur astronomer. By profession, he was a mechanical engineer and civil servant, but his reputation rests on his achievements as an amateur astronomer, particularly as a selenographer. He was elected to the British Astronomical Association in 1918 and was Director of its Lunar Section from 1946 to 1956. In 1951 he published a 300"-diameter map of the Moon, considered by some as the culmination of the art of selenography prior to the space age. However his maps were dense with detail, some of which was fictitious, making them less useful. The crater Wilkins on the Moon is named after him.

leading to the ladder. Obviously, after making a tour of the base they climbed back out of the crevasse."

"But, Commander," Professor Harrington spoke up, "Look at your men! Do they look like they're lying? Why would they 'sneak out', I ask you! Do you think they've got any chance of chasing skirts here? Furthermore, the Selenites don't wear boots as far as I know."

"Yeah," the Commander said arrogantly. "If you're seeing the same prints as I do in the dust, it's because we're victims of a hallucination."

Kariven bent down to examine the footprints more carefully. Fine grains of chalky dust had trickled over the edges, obscuring and deforming them in part.

"The wisest recourse, instead of suspecting the members of the expedition," Kariven proposed, "would be to climb up the ladder. We'll see whether or not these prints belong to us."

The Commander grumbled something inaudible into his mic and was the first to grab the rungs. Climbing out of the crevasse one by one they saw the footprints in the ground leading away from the ladder.

"Don't mess up the prints," the Commander barked, "and follow me. I give you my word that if I find out who snuck out last night they'll be in my report!"

Behind him Clark and Kariven looked at each other and shrugged. Obviously the Commander was making a reckless judgment.

In the white dust that no atmospheric flurry had disturbed, the footprints went in two directions: one marking the path followed by two men leading up to the crevasse and the other leading away. The prints left around the rocket were mixed with the astronauts who had trampled the ground the night before and dug a grave for the biologist. But between these groups of superimposed prints there were clearly places where the mysterious lunar visitors had strolled.

"Come and see this!" Lieutenant Clark shouted. "The prints are going off behind the rocket."

Everyone joined him and followed the trail that ended abruptly 50 yards away.

"Well, well! This is... unbelievable," Commander Taylor said. "Where'd they go? They couldn't just disappear! Footprints don't disappear like that on flat ground covered with a thick layer of dust!"

The three or four last footprints were literally swept away as if a strong fan had blown over the dust in which they had formed.

"Unless we're victims of another collective hallucination," Kariven remarked ironically, "we have to admit that these prints end here. Our two men evaporated mysteriously."

"If we were in a desert on Earth," Streiler said, "even though mysterious it wouldn't be so crazy because a helicopter could very well have picked them up by throwing down a rope ladder. But here on this dead planet inhabited only by little round creatures, the deed is truly inexplicable."

"I'll go back to my first idea," Lieutenant Clark offered, "We've got no proof that another life form doesn't exist on the..."

"A life form wearing spacesuits whose boots leave footprints?" the Commander broke in, sounding grumpier and grumpier. "You're crazy, Lieutenant. If there is another life form on the Moon, I can't believe that it would need spacesuits to survive here. They would have adapted, like the Selenites, to this airless, waterless wasteland. The Selenites we've seen are probably the last representatives of a species that once had an atmosphere and stretches of water and even some kind of vegetation to live with. The last surviving species underwent a transformation, either a slow adaptation or a sudden mutation to absorb the mineral elements of the lunar soil in order to hold out... I see where I went wrong. These prints do not belong to two members of our group, but they don't belong to any pseudo-evolved Moonmen either. Therefore, they will remain unexplained for the time being."

"Unless," Kariven thought aloud, "we're not the only foreigners on the Moon."

Commander Taylor scowled inside his helmet. "You mean... The Russians? You really think they've reached the same level as us in astronautics?"

Kariven shrugged and looked like he was hiding something. "It's just a simple hypothesis without naming any specific people or nation..."

"I'm aware," Taylor recognized, "that dangerous leaks have come out of our atomic physics labs over the past six years. Information about the A-bomb and H-bomb have slipped through the Iron Curtain but concerning Operation Aphrodite I'm sure that it's the most protected secret that's ever been."

"Don't underestimate the technical abilities of Russian scientists," Professor Harrington warned. "For at least a decade they've worked hard on an artificial satellite, the Red Star, and on plans for an atomic spaceship able to reach astounding speeds[41]. How can we say that their work hasn't been accomplished?"

"So, you think they might have already set up on the Moon before we got here?"

"Not at all. How would I know? Maybe they flew over this area while we were sleeping. Seeing no sign of life they would have figured that we were holed up inside the rocket and so come to make an inspection of our camp. Following in our footsteps to find the location of our sub-lunar base was easy as pie."

"Sure, that sounds logical," Streiler admitted. "But then we'd have to suppose, to explain the sudden disappearance of their footprints, that the... Russians were waiting, hovering a

---

[41] See the journal *Inter Avia*, No. 2982, June 9, 1954: "A Soviet Motor Rocket?"; excerpt: "...that weighs only 2,720 kg and would have the power equivalent to more than 2,000,000 hp and reach speeds up 5,000,000 mph." See also the same source, No. 2997, June 30, 1954: "Airplanes with Atomic Propulsion": "...according to General A. Ponomarev." (Author's Note)

few feet off the ground, in some sort of miniature rocket that took them away when their visit was over. We'd also have to admit that this miniature rocket could hover in place *without any exhaust waste from its reactors*, which would have wiped away not three or four prints but a whole stretch of lunar dust for 25 to 30 feet around. Our own reconnaissance rockets, called Space Taxis, are incapable of such a feat. Only a gravito-magnetic booster could explain the absence of exhaust gas. And it would surprise me tremendously that a nation on Earth today could perfect such propulsion!"

"I agree with Streiler," Professor Harrington said. "If the Russians have set up a base on the Moon and if they're the ones who came last night to... visit' us, we have to admit that we can't explain how they disappeared..."

Around the same time, Colonel Zavkom, Chief of the Russian astronauts, was spitting out a string of curses through the microphone in his spacesuit. The ten members of the expedition around him, 50 yards from their rocket, were staring at the ground in angry confusion. In the chalky dust lit by the beams from their chests, footprints had disappeared inexplicably on the flat surface.

"Damnation!" Zavkom thundered, lifting the two, heavy, ringed arms of his spacesuit to the sky. "Whoever came spying on us during the night certainly can't levitate!"

A tall, burly guy whose round helmet stood above his comrades, risked, "Couldn't it be... uh... tracks left by... lunar creatures... beings adapted to this dreadful place?"

"Come on, Dr. Petrov, you're a great physicist and an excellent rocket pilot but in cosmobiology allow me to doubt your competence. No, there is no life form possible on the Moon. Our spectrum analyses are clear, and we've had proof since we got here: no trace of water or atmosphere. Therefore, no life form can exist.

"The only logical theory is to admit that the Americans," Colonel Zavkom scowled in rage, "have reached the Moon! I, however, am sure that there was no leak in our Kaluga plants[42] where our spaceship was built. American agents could not have stolen or micro-filmed our plans…"

The pilot/physicist Petrov was about to say something about the fast, parallel development of American technology, but he changed his mind, preferring not to express an opinion that the Colonel might judge "deviant."

"The wisest course," Zavkom concluded, "since we've been spied on, is to finish up the repairs to the astronavigraph quickly and go set up in the crater on the bright side as soon as possible. We'll put an observation post on the nose of the rocket and should be ready to retaliate for any attack." He mumbled some curses before continuing, "What audacity! To come and spy on us on our own territory! We should have been more serious about the radio message intercepted just before we left Earth. The pauses in the communication really did come from the fact that one of the two transmitters was on the Moon."

Kariven and Streiler stood speechless at the door of the rocket's laboratory, not daring to step up through the airtight hatch. They called the other astronauts right away.

"What's happening?" Commander Taylor asked, raising his helmet at the lab entrance.

"The mysterious visitors who left their footprints behind have entered the rocket," Kariven said. "All of us, when we come out of the airlock to enter the decompression chamber, are in the habit of carefully wiping our boots against the rolling suction brushes. The dust on our boots is sucked up and destroyed or neutralized by the hard x-rays so they don't carry God-knows-what micro-organisms or dangerous spores into the ship.

---

[42] Experimental factory and base of "special ships" located southwest of Moscow. The Ziolkowski Institute is also located in Kaluga. (Author's Note)

"Now, look at these tracks on the floor of the lab. You'll find the same ones in every room of the ship. Kurt and I just checked. The tail section of the rocket holding the pumps and atomic generator was particularly interesting to our careless visitors. *They* examined all the machines very carefully, seeing that traces of dust were also on the generator's protective plates... *one of which they took off* to get a good look at the insides. The plate was put back on but the bolts aren't in the same holes as before. Everything's in order and nothing's missing but the 'strangers' have inspected our ship from nose to tailpipe. And I have to admit that they did so with unusual mastery and extraordinary skill. We're not dealing with novices here, if I may say so."

"This is disturbing," Professor Harrington mumbled.

"Disturbing? You mean infuriating!" Commander Taylor railed. "To know that we're being watched, spied on, visited, every nook and cranny inspected and we can't discover who's doing this... this act deserving a court martial... it's more than disturbing... it's an omen of terrible danger!"

Professor Harrington tried to calm him down, "It's all very mysterious but it doesn't mean we're in 'terrible danger', Commander."

"Maybe. Still, everyone arm yourself with a Colt and six clips. The four men going on reconnaissance will also be taking two Thomson machine guns. The Colts and machine guns have been specially designed to function at extreme temperatures, from absolute zero to 200°C, and all parts have been tested for the temperature differences on the Moon. Moreover, we're setting up a guard tower and installing a heavy machine gun at the top of *Daisy*. I'll put the watchtower platform up there."

"Come now, Commander," the pacifist Professor exclaimed, "aren't you going a little overboard?"

"Yeah!" Taylor growled. "If I listened to you, Professor, during our voyage in time and our stay in Shâmali, I wouldn't have given anyone weapons... and we would've ended up in some cyclops monster's belly."[43]

---

[43] See *The Time Spiral*. (Author's Note)

CHAPTER FIVE

Around 7:30 a.m. (Earth time) the four men who had gone on reconnaissance returned to the American base and brought back from their exploration a wealth of mineral samples, three reels of film and a number of highly important observations.

"We visited seven craters," Haller, the mineralogist, summed up, "and we did some quick digs on the plains or 'seas' of the Moon, which produced some weird fossils."

"Fossils?" Kariven was very interested. "Plant or animal?"

"Both. Apparently when the Moon had an atmosphere—hundreds of thousands, maybe millions of years ago—it had only rudimentary fauna and flora. Few trees, mostly shrubs, and some lakes and swamps rather than great oceans. As for the 'superior' fauna, it was mainly a kind of monster with tentacles, the size of sheep, resembling lizard, frog and jellyfish or maybe coral all at the same time. We found huge piles of these gruesome creatures fossilized into gray slabs. No doubt they lived in colonies like coral or sea anemones.

"In all likelihood these tentacled animals evolved over the ages or mutated into the metallophage Selenites. And as for them, we've become convinced that they inhabit all the big and medium-sized craters. If you figure that the only visible side of the Moon has at least 30,000 craters, you can imagine the average 'population'! We counted around 10 to 15 thousand creatures in each crater less than a mile in diameter. It's completely relative and without any scientific value but we made the estimation by launching a little vibrating rocket. As we figured the vibrations on the crater floor attracted the Selenites who came rushing out of their lairs to check it out... So, the Selenite population for this side of the Moon is in the hundreds of millions."

"At only 1,000 francs for a gram for platinum, that would be worth billions!" Kariven observed.

"We also used the Geiger counter and detected a rich vein of uranium at the bottom of a crevasse seven miles NNW of our base toward the Aristarchus crater."

"A few days from now we'll go explore that area with the taxis," Commander Taylor said. "Then Lieutenant Clark can see for himself about the nature and origin of the light he saw in the Aristarchus crater. Plus, we'll have to uncover the mystery of those footprints... and find their base or at least who made them."

In the Bubble Base, the astronauts were sleeping, simply stretched out on the comfortable air mattresses. Rudy Clark was tossing and turning in his restless sleep, snapping awake often. Exhausted and exasperated he finally sat up on his rubbery mattress and dreamed... fully awake!

But at the bottom of the crevasse the hard rays of the sun beat down on a narrow area outside the protected cave and bounced off the end of the oblong base sheltering the Americans. Apparently their "nights" passed in full lunar daylight. On our satellite the days and nights lasted 14 Earth days each. In exactly seven days the lunar "night" would come to stay for 14 days measuring from Earth.

Such as it was, therefore, in the back of the cave, the base was only relatively dark. But the north tube was the only part sticking out in the rays of the sun.

Lieutenant Clark listened to the gentle hum of the generators producing energy for the various machines to circulate and purify the air. In the surrounding half-light his sleepy eyes stared across the base into the bright sunrays. After a while, Clark felt drowsy again. The round end of the base made him feel like he was sitting in a train speeding through a tunnel whose exit could be seen in the distance. The generator's hum added to the illusion, making him sleepy. His eyelids felt heavier and heavier, started to close. He opened them again, yawned and stretched, then lay down, glancing one last time at the bright area. Again his eyelids drooped and his head fell back on the pillow, still turned toward the light.

Was he dreaming now? A shadow passed three times across the light fading under his half-closed eyes. Clark sat up again, cursing his insomnia. All of a sudden he stopped grumbling. His eyes popped open, stunned; he was sure he was not dreaming.

"Commander! Commander!" he shouted as he rushed in pajamas toward the spacesuits.

All at once the astronauts were on their feet, looking at where Clark was pointing.

"Don't turn on the light!" Commander Taylor ordered. "Just leave the auxiliary lights on."

At the front of the base, the curved line of sunlight was being briefly masked at intervals. At the same time a long shadow slid quickly over the floor of the crevasse.

When every man was in his spacesuit, they snuck out of the base through the decompression tube. Soon they were standing, Colts drawn, in a shadow zone under a sloping wall of the crevasse. Kariven and Clark crawled over to the ladder that sat in full light against the opposite wall and moved it 50 feet further down to a shaded curve. Followed by the others they climbed up the ladder, came out of the crevasse and crawled through the chalky ash to hide behind a small hill.

"I don't see anything," Kariven spoke into his mic. "Stay here. Clark and I will go scout it out."

The two men crept from low hill to shallow depression to get to the rocket. Crawling in dust under the blazing sun—the special thermometer on their pressurized spacesuit protected from the cosmic rays registered 177°C or 350°F!—made them nervous.

"Good God!" Commander Taylor thundered. "Look at the rocket, Kariven! Look at the nose! *The thing* is right there!"

Indeed, on the ringed platform they had improvised around the cone of the rocket a shadow was overlapping the darker shadow of the heavy, space machine gun.

"Get back, Clark! Get back, Kariven!" Taylor screamed into his mic. "You're in the open, damn it! The... *the thing* can swoop down on you like an eagle on a field mouse!"

"If *the thing* in question has the nature of an eagle," Kariven said, not moving. "Don't worry about me, Commander, I'll get to safety. You and Clark cover me..."

"No, Kariven! You... I forbid you to..." the officer was fuming with anger against this "civilian" who dared to disobey his orders.

Kariven stood up and in a giant leap sprang 20 feet high, landing softly 30 feet away. Another extraordinary leap brought him exactly to the foot of the spaceship. Now he was safe under the rear tubes and feared no traitorous act by *the thing* that was hiding behind the nose of the rocket and whose presence was betrayed by the shifting shadow. Was *it* examining the machine gun?

The Commander hesitated, torn between the desire to rush forward and the prudent will to retreat into the crevasse. The former won the day and all together the astronauts jumped after Kariven, whom Clark had joined immediately. The nine men were crouched under *Daisy*'s huge bottom now.

"We were smart to close up the airlocks," the Commander remarked. "If a... one of those *things* got into the cockpit and started the ignition when we got under here, the engines would have annihilated us."

Automatically everyone looked up. Under the multitude of reactors staring down at them they felt a cold shiver run down their spines.

"We're not going to just sit here," Lieutenant Clark looked questioningly at Kariven who agreed wholeheartedly.

"Clark and I will crawl along..."

He broke off, stupefied. Between the fins that acted as landing gear, on the white ash, a long shadow was speeding away from the rocket. It looked like the shadow of a low flying object. Everyone scrambled out of the hiding place and stared up in awe.

In the dark sky dotted with bright stars something gray-ish-green, oblong, with a shiny front end, was disappearing into the horizon, heading toward the sun.

"I... I don't know what it is," Commander Taylor admitted, "but it's alive or mechanical... and damn intelligent! That 'thing' took off straight into the sun that would be hard, if not impossible for a pilot to see anything. In fact, we should have seen if it had turned around but even with the blinding sunlight it disappeared smooth as silk."

Kariven, after a long, thoughtful silence, believed he could offer a partial explanation of the phenomenon: "The being or *thing* that examined our machine gun and just disappeared is, for sure, one of the things that left footprints around our base and our rocket. The way that it or he vanished without the spaceship landing and its disappearance into space proves beyond doubt that the *thing* flies. In my opinion it must be fitted with a jet pack to account for all its movements in a place with no atmosphere—as well as in an atmosphere identical to ours for example. I'm saying that only a jet pack or more precisely its retro-jets could have swept away the footprints that vanished in the middle of an empty space. Rocket jets would have literally plowed the soil over a wide surface whereas the effects of a jet pack are obviously much more limited."

"What you say makes sense," the Commander agreed. "But who'd be using such a device on the Moon? Let's suppose that the Russians got here before us and have got some base somewhere, I can't see them with an invention like that. I know there are helicopter jet packs[44] but they're still not able to do the things that the gray-green *thing* just did. As for our jet shooters they can't be used efficiently except in outer space to move outside the spaceships in case of an accident. They're

_____

[44] True: an elite corps of the US Army is training today in the use of these mini helicopters with belts, weighing 100 lbs and able to reach 60 mph. (Author's Note)

not powerful enough to fight the lunar gravity, however weak it is compared to Earth's."

Professor Harrington was puzzled. He reached up to scratch his head absent-mindedly but banged into his isothermal plastic helmet. Smiling at himself he shrugged and proposed, "Let's not rack out brains trying to solve a problem with too many unknowns. Let's go back to bed instead. During our stay here, which has only begun, other factors will arise that may shed some light on this."

While they went back down the metal ladder to go back into the Bubble Base, on the horizon, hidden from them now by the crevasse walls, the repaired Russian rocket was rising into the sky. It shot straight up, then at 30,000 feet tilted and slowed down in order to locate a good site for a research base.

The ship was flying at only 220 mph and its passengers, leaning over the video-periscope, were scrutinizing the ground scrolling by under their eyes. They had just crossed the terminator line[45] to enter the sun-bathed side of the Moon. Their flight path took them a little farther away from the Kepler crater where the American astronauts had established their base.

The soviet pilot suddenly cried out in surprise, "Colonel Zavkom! There in that crater... on the horizon..."

"Damnation!" the Colonel swore. "A spotlight's sweeping the sky. Land quickly! Those damn Americans are already in the Aristarchus crater. So, it's true: they're on the Moon!"

"The beam of light is gone," Petrov, the pilot/physicist, observed. "It was weird, that light ray, dazzlingly and almost purple..."

Zavkom shrugged, "Some stupid experiment on certain wavelengths in outer space probably. Or searching for variations of the light spectrum without an atmosphere."

---

[45] The line of shadow that covers part of the lunar disc. (Author's Note)

Secretly, Petrov frowned in disappointment. He was tired of hearing his chief go on about scientific questions that he only pretended to know about.

Fearing that their presence would be signaled by those whom they believed were Americans set up in Aristarchus, the Russians landed their spaceship in the middle of a crater with a central spike, over a mile and half in diameter and hundreds of miles away from the so-called "Americans".

On landing, the rear rockets kicked up a wave of chalky dust. A crown-shaped cloud rose up slowly from the ground. Although the ship had set down roughly, it was not damaged. Its tail fins, only needed to make it easier to glide on Earth, were buried three feet deep in the ash and flaky rock. In the middle of the crater stood a huge "spike" of rock or some matter that solidified after the formation of the crater. Its mushroom-shaped "head" was almost 600 feet off the ground.

Just to be careful, Zavkom had asked Petrov to land as close as possible to the central spike. Standing only 200 feet away from the rocky column the spaceship was "camouflaged" in a way. In fact, the ship was lined up perfectly with the spike, which buried it in its dark shadow. No one could see it if they came over the crater from a certain direction. Moreover, the sloping walls, almost 1,000 feet high, acted as screens.

"Let's set up our mobile base right away between the rocket and the central spike," Colonel Zavkom ordered.

Said base, composed of three plastic domes reinforced with steel frames, had been "assembled" while the astronavigraph was being repaired on the dark side of the Moon. It was simply a matter of taking the 13-foot wide domes down to the ground and connecting them with tubes, one of which would be the decompression chamber. The inner walls and floor were already installed. Anchoring the "bubbles" to the flat ground with super-metal cables only took a couple of hours. When the work was done the Russians went ahead with the checks and found all the equipment in working order. Then the men received orders from Zavkom to rest for six hours.

With the numbered spacesuits hanging above their bunks made of synthetic foam the astronauts stretched our gratefully in their respective places in the three domes. Everything was calm and quiet around them. The blazing heat of the sun did not bother them a bit in their air-conditioned base. Beyond the shadow of the central spike, the unbearable light of the day star flooded the white surface of the crater.

Confident in their "camouflage," all the Russians fell asleep, figuring that there would be time enough "tomorrow" to set up a lookout on the top of the crater. Besides, even if a lookout was posted immediately on the wall or on the spike, it was unlikely that he could have spotted an enemy *inside the crater*. He would have been looking over the plain beyond the walls.

In the yellowish dust of the surface, he probably would not even have seen those deeper, brownish, disc-shaped spots that were slowly converging on the central spike... or on the rocket! He would have taken the changing color as an effect of the moving sun, probably a physico-chemical (or photo-chemical) reaction.

At the moment, the first rows of Selenites, like waves of a slow tide, had reached the tail fins of the spaceship. Their six ringed stalks topped by seven shiny little needles were sway-ing, cautiously feeling the smooth surface of the fin.

There was something like a ripple that ran through the front rows, then all of a sudden all the Selenites rushed at the spaceship. In a kind of vertical slithering the brown monsters in front crawled slowly up the long fins... leaving behind them thousands of pinkish stings that were in turn wiped away by the following rows that bit more deeply into the metal of the fins keeping the rocket balanced on the ground.

The stampede took place in total calm. In spite of some pushing and shoving the Selenites, obsessed by the metal mass, did not squabble. The last comers, naturally, had trouble finding free space. Moreover, sometimes one or more Sele-nites fell off the flanks of the spaceship. They were not very adept at climbing vertically. Those who fell searched quickly for a gap in the swarming throng so they could assuage their unquenchable hunger for metal. Not finding a place they crawled straight over their fellows from one shell to another until they found an area of open metal.

100 feet away under the three domes of their base, the Russians were sleeping soundly, completely ignorant of the tragedy unfolding so close to them.

Commander Taylor checked the (clearly visible) number on his helmet and started fitting the transparent globe onto the collar ring of his spacesuit. After verifying the seal, he swallowed a yawn and was the first to crawl out of the decompression chamber. Their sleep had been spoiled by the "flying phantom" hunt.

"Today," Taylor decided, "we start with the second geophysical test. Then, when the terrain is cleared away, Kariven, Clark and Streiler will go out on reconnaissance up to the libration zone, the area of sporadic light[46]. Some interesting observations can probably be made there. The rest at the base will continue the necessary tasks: mineral analyses, examination and autopsy of Selenites, locating the exact position of the uranium found yesterday by Dr. Haller and his team. Let's get to work."

Everyone headed to a kind of vertical, metal box full of switches and buttons set on top of four telescopic legs.

Professor Harrington smiled, "Good old Taylor thinks he's still with the military staff. I'm surprised he's not giving the traditional orders: Fall out!"

While the three men appointed to leave on expedition were gathering the necessary equipment, Gordon, the geo-

---

[46] Area of the Moon separating the hemisphere perpetually lit from the dark hemisphere. In addition to its rotation and revolution the Moon also wobbles, which changes the line between the two hemispheres. It varies slightly because of this movement called *libration*, which allows us to see 59/100° of the surface. (Author's Note)

physicist, was walking toward a small hill about 300 yards away from the ship. On this rocky knoll with cracks full of chalky dust, a rocket launcher had been built, formed of five big launch tubes and tilted on its vibration dampeners. The blue cone of a 20-foot long rocket stuck out of one of them.

Equipped with a powerful load of TNT[47], the rocket was going to be launched on a carefully studied trajectory. At the point of impact the TNT explosion would cause a localized "moonquake." The vibrations from this seismic activity would be recorded by various machines that Professor Harrington dealt with.

The professor checked one last time the seismograph, the magnetometer and all the buttons and switches on the chrome panel of the "block" on the telescopic legs. Certain waves or vibrations natural to earthquakes (or moonquakes) passed through solids. Others, however, were stopped by bodies in pasty and even liquid states. The graphics produced by the seismograph and magnetometer, therefore, revealed whether the underlying layers are solid or gluey thereby making it relatively easy to figure out the internal composition of the Earth... or Moon.

It was an experiment of this kind that the astronauts were tackling. With the armed missile ready to go, the geophysicist Gordon joined Professor Harrington who was making the final adjustments to the machines.

"Ready?"

"Ready, Gordon," he simply replied, pulling the metal lever for ignition.

On the plain, the TNT missile ripped out of its launch pad, accelerated quickly and curved through the sky. Shimmering in the sunlight the missile descended toward the horizon at incredible speed at the end of its trajectory. For a second it disappeared, then abruptly a blinding flash rose out of a crater around 100 miles away. The shockwave proliferated

---

[47] Trinitrotoluene, a powerful explosive used especially in torpedoes and aircraft bombs. (Author's Note)

and while shaking up the astronauts produced angular lines on the rotating drum of the seismograph. The needles of the three dials went crazy for a few seconds before the vibrations gradually spaced out and then stopped completely.

From the crater where—in sepulchral silence due to the lack of atmosphere—the rocket had exploded, a cloud of dust rose up, soon falling back down without spreading out or swirling around.

"The missile was not supposed to land in a crater," Professor Harrington was surprised. "Its electronic system must have been affected. Maybe it was the lunar magnetic field? The electronic circuits are so delicate that a simple opposite pulse can mean a large discrepancy in the aim."

"Ahh," the geophysicist said, "at least it'll make a few less Selenites to worry about! We'll make another launch tomorrow but toward the big plain. Anyway, the error in trajectory isn't so serious in itself."

Such was not the opinion of Colonel Zavkom. By the worst luck imaginable the TNT rocket had fallen in the very crater occupied by the Russians!

The soviet astronauts had just been startled awake by the frightening shock of the explosion in the walls of the crater. Before they could realize what was happening, a second, less violent shock shook the ground.

The thick carpet of white dust covering the surface had been kicked up all over the crater. The Russian base was buried in the powder drizzling over the three plastic domes.

"What happened?"

"I don't see a thing outside!"

"It's... maybe it's a... moonquake?"

"Or a sudden landslide of the crater wall..."

"Get your spacesuits on instead of wasting time!" Zavkom ordered, having turned pale.

When they were installed in their suits the astronauts got ready to leave but a howl of rage paralyzed them.

"The rocket! The ro..."

The worlds choked Zavkom's throat. His eyes bulging, his face scarred with unutterable anguish, he was looking through the dust that was finally settling on the ground. The Russian spaceship, whose fins had been eaten away by the Selenites, had toppled over in the explosion. Its nose had hit the top of the rocky spike that had stopped its fall. Leaning at a 45° angle, with its tail fins gnawed away, corroded, the rocket lay like a broken toy, its twisted conic nose on top of the column of rock.

In the violent shock the nose had been shattered and a 10-foot long crack gaped in the upper fuselage. The soviet astronauts fought to hold back their emotional reaction. Faced with this disaster Zavkom's anger vanished in a flush of panic.

"I... I think it'd be better to leave... to see what happened..." the usually decisive officer stammered.

Outside, as the last grains of dusts settled, the sight before their eyes was even more tragic. The spike had been weakened and split down the middle, so the nose of the rocket lay stuck between the jaws on top.

Stunned by what he was seeing Zavkom closed his eyes for a few seconds, hoping that the hellish image was just a hallucination. But when he opened them again, the nightmare was still there.

In its fall the rocket had stopped 20 feet from their base! By a miracle the astronauts had escaped a horrible death. If the rocket had only crashed into one of the domes, the occupants would have suffocated to death. With the artificial air instantly escaping, they would not have had time to put on their spacesuits. Maybe they would have been crushed? The outcome would have been no better.

Crazed and panic-stricken, the eleven men wandered around the base. Grim thoughts ran through their minds. Would they manage to repair the terrible gash in the hull? For sure, but how could they replace the four fins that were so mysteriously corroded, eaten away up to the pipe openings?

"Colonel Zavkom! Colonel Zavkom!" boomed the voice of Boris Ilyine, bent over the ground. "Come here, everyone come here!"

Shaken up and jolted by this call in the middle of the chaos, the astronauts temporarily abandoned their despair and leaped over to their comrade.

"Look at this!" the physicist said, handing the Colonel a piece of blue metal, swollen up as if attacked by a strong flame. "And this!" he held in his articulated claws a metallic fragment as big as a dinner plate and with a distinct curvature.

"It's debris from a rocket, a V2 charged with explosives. We weren't victims of seismic activity but of a bombardment!"

"The Americans!" Colonel Zavkom thundered, clenching his jaws and fists. "They dared to attack us!"

"Just a minute, Colonel," Petrov intervened. "I fell the same as all of you here, maybe even worse since this rocket was a little like... *my* rocket. I watched it being built, I contribute to its technology, I tested it on a secret base and finally I brought it here where..."

"What are trying to say, Petrov?" the Colonel growled.

"This," the pilot replied. "I love this rocket as much as anyone can... but I can't let my feelings blind my reasoning. There's no proof that we were attacked. This V2 might have been just a missile fired to cause a shock wave for the Americans to study..."

"NO!" Zavkom raged. "We, too, have identical missiles to study the structure of the Moon through vibrations. But we'd never launch it into a crater! The walls would absorb part of the shock wave and distort the results of our research. No. We've been attacked, savagely attacked, traitorously attacked by the Americans. And I guarantee you that they'll pay dearly for it! Maybe they're thinking we're destroyed, killed, buried under the wreckage of our ship? Let them believe it and we'll go set up our base on a ledge at the top of the crater. We'll camouflage it well and wait no matter what for the toads[48] to come! We'll welcome them with all the weapons we've got left. No one will be spared. Then it'll be in their rocket that we'll get back to Earth!"

---

[48] A particularly nasty Russian insult. (Author's Note)

CHAPTER SIX

Petrov reflected. He walked up to the rocket and examined the gnawed away base, as if corroded by a strong acid that left a weird, pink, solidified "drool" on the stumps.

"Excuse me, Colonel," the pilot piped up again, "but our spaceship did not fall because of the explosion of a V2. At least the explosion was not the only cause of its fall. How could an explosion, however strong, produce this kind of corrosion? A corrosion capable of transforming the ship's metal into dust?"

Colonel Zavkom and the other specialists, dazed among the wreckage, had to accept his evidence. Petrov's reasoning was correct. This corrosion could not be explained.

"Could they have discovered a process of corrosion that works without an atmosphere?" someone asked. "Maybe…"

He did not finish his thought but suddenly shot his arm out to grab onto somebody or something. Before his astonished comrades he steadied himself by holding onto a tear in a tail pipe.

"Are you feeling dizzy?" Zavkom asked.

With his eyes focused on the ground the man explained, "I felt like the ground was moving… Hey! Look!"

Under a thin layer of dust a Selenite was wriggling feebly. The Russian must have stepped on it and the creature trying to get free had upset his balance.

"Damnation! What's that?"

"It's… it's moving," Ilyine the physicist muttered. "It's… alive!"

One by one or together in small groups, the Selenites that had survived the explosion were slithering out of their ashy death shrouds. Their brown shells, spotted with chalky dust, still bore traces of their burial. Most of them coiled off toward their lairs in the foot of the crater walls, but some headed straight for the bottom of the rocket.

Faced with this tidal wave of living "things" advancing on their spaceship, the astronauts backed away, horrified and not knowing what to do. Some Selenites were already stuck to the fuselage, climbing very slowly they absorbed every inch of metal. It was not a very thick layer of metal, true, but one after another they would end up gradually eating it all, leaving behind only a disgusting, pinkish substance, very thin and glimmering with shifting colors.

"Metal-eating monsters," Colonel Zavkom murmured.

"Metallophage Selenites," Petrov corrected him, his face twisted in fear and almost hypnotized by the progress of the awful creatures.

Commander Taylor was keeping a close eye on the winches lowering the three "space taxis" out of the hold. These machines, 16 feet long and 4 feet wide could hold one man with his arms along his sides lying down on a reinforced rubber-foam "mattress." In spite of the discomfort these space taxis could save an astronaut's life if a space ship crashed or if in the astronomical neighborhood of Earth it started into free fall. By carrying these individual rockets the members of the spacecraft team could abandon their mother ship and escape to Earth. In the terrestrial atmosphere, thanks to the deployable wings, a long, gliding flight would reduce their speed and at a reasonable altitude, 70,000-100,000 feet, a super-resistant metallo-plastex parachute would be automatically ejected. Moreover, every space taxi was *submersible!*

Unfortunately, in case of an "astral shipwreck" millions of miles away from Earth, these space taxis would only be good for coffins!

On the Moon these mini-ships were going to be used as reconnaissance rockets. The Moon's weak gravity would make landing relatively easy.

Dressed in their heavy spacesuits Kariven, Streiler and Lieutenant Clark were each stretched out in their "capsules," on their space taxi beds. They closed up the hatches that were carefully sealed and with their pads on a tilted frame equipped with directional cells, they shot up at high speed. The three ships were soon only three dots shining in the sunlight and heading toward the dark side of our satellite.

In formation 100 feet from each other, the three space taxis crossed to the north of the Marius crater, then flew over the huge Helvetius crater and headed due west. Now they were starting to slow down. The dazzling whiteness of the sun on the lunar horizon stopped rather suddenly to give way to perpetual night on the dark side. The three space taxis took a tight turn and headed due south. At 16,000 feet altitude they flew along the border separating the zone of eternal shadows, which no human eye had ever seen, from the zone of brightness, the only side visible from the Earth.

The automatic cameras with telephoto lens had just turned on, filming the stretch of turbulent terrain, while the magnetometer recorded the variations in the lunar magnetic field.

In spite of their uncomfortable position, the pilots could see a large stretch of ground thanks to a periscopic sight with zoom. In theory the "zone of intermittent visibility" or the "libration zone" was no different than the bright area. Assumedly, the same should be said for the dark side. Craters of all sizes with or without central spikes, vast plains called "seas," mountains and fissures ought to be found on the opposite side with a similar distribution as observed on the visible side. On the other hand, if the temperature on the bright side could reach up to 185°C during the lunar "day" and when the sun was at its zenith, on the dark side it could get as low as -200°C!

The three space taxis just passed by Montes Doerfel and Leibniz at the lunar South Pole and were heading east. They had already made one quarter of their trip and were continuing on a straight line along the libration line. In less than three hours they will have made a complete trip around the Moon and could then pursue a few reconnaissance points on the unknown hemisphere.

Streiler, flying to the left of Kariven, called through his transmitter, "Did you see that, Kariven? On the sides of some of the craters and on the plains we flew over, those dark zones different than the chalky color of the ground?"

"Yes. Some of those huge brown 'stains' stop right at the edge of a canyon."

Lieutenant Clark, flying on Kariven's right, joined in the conversation, "I saw the same marks on the dark side at certain points being swept by our spotlights. They weren't brown, though, but kind of purple. They... There's one to my right!"

"Let's get a closer look," Kariven said as he started descending toward the spot indicated.

The three cylindrical ships entered the shadows with their spotlights on and started circling above the strangely colored area. By moving their spotlights the Earthlings could see that the part of the purple zone unlit was emitting a faint, mauve-tinted phosphorescence.

Adjusting the focus of their periscopic sights the pilots examined their screens to detect some details of the ground. After a moment of careful observation, Kariven was speechless. On the long libration band hundreds of thousands of giant Selenites were moving in close ranks. They each measured from one and a half to two feet in diameter. Their purple shells were flashing that same weird, mauve phosphorescence.

"Giant Selenites!"

"Look to the west!" Streiler cried out. "That brown stain moving fast over the Hannon crater is a bunch of dwarf Selenites... Let's call them brown Selenites since they look the same as the ones we've already seen."

"It's like they're running away from big, purple Selenites," Kariven remarked. "Both of them are heading west or northwest."

The pilots pointed their cameras to film the movements of the two huge "stains," one brown and the other purple.

"Let's land in the zone that the giant Selenites just left," Kariven decided. "We'll take a sample of the soil and take off again to finish our round-the-moon flight."

A minute later the three space taxis set down gently, their pads sinking in the dust. Seen from the libration zone the sun on the horizon gave off a frugal light, partly hidden behind the mountains and the distant craters. In their spacesuits the astronauts left the individual rockets. Without going too far they examined the terrain using a light fixed to their belts.

On one side was the gray plain, dimly lit by the upper part of the sun emerging timidly from the mountain ridge. In the other direction, on the dark side, perpetual night and the cold of outer space reigned. The only difference between the sky and the black ground was the twinkling constellations.

Kicking the dust off his boots, Kariven loosened a rock on the surface. Using a mineralogist hammer he cut off a few shards to examine them. Streiler and Clark, with a plastic bags hanging from their belts, did the same.

"The libration zone appears to be rich in surface minerals," Streiler observed. "I just found a chink of galena or at least it looks like lead sulfide."

"I've got some pieces of the same mineral but I think it's silver sulfide."

"Every vein of this surface mineral," Lieutenant Clark noted, "has deep traces of corrosion caused by the giant Selenites."

"These monsters are luckier than their brothers on the bright side. They've got a rich hunting ground here," Streiler joked.

"Maybe that explains why the brown Selenites are here. The giants are defending their hunting grounds, chasing away any dwarves who set their sights on their territory."

When they had filled their sample bags, they got back in their rockets and took off. All along the libration line the three astronauts witnessed the same counter-attacks pitting the giant Selenites against the dwarf Selenites who scampered away as fast as their belly rolls allowed. There was one strange fact Kariven could not shake off: not only was the general flow of these creatures from one end to the other of the border zone between the two hemispheres, but now, after almost completing their round-the-Moon flight, they noted that the massive movement were into areas far removed from the libration line. It was more like a vast migration on a lunar scale than a flight from the giant Selenites. Brown or purple, the disc-shaped monsters were advancing quickly in a direction that appeared to lead to the Ptolemaeus crater in the center of the bright side. The direction was only vaguely indicated. The Earthlings had, in fact, observed only a general movement away from the border separating the two hemispheres. Logically, if all the Selenites were heading away from the libration zone then it only followed that at the same time they were getting closer to the center of the bright side of the Moon.

Just before veering east to go back to base the three astronauts were witness to an absolutely incomprehensible phenomenon. Beyond the zone of intermittent light, thus in the heart of shadows invisible from Earth, an extraordinary purple flare lit up a big crater. The explorers thought they were seeing a huge globe of bright red fire rise up. The blinding flash went out as suddenly as it appeared.

"Hey... did you see that?" Clark stammered.

"You'd have to be blind not to have seen that!"

Far beyond the crater where this fantastic phenomenon occurred a bright dot disappeared into starry space at incredible speed, its trajectory carrying it behind the horizon.

"And did you see that too?"

"Yes. Do you have any idea what it could be?" Streiler asked.

"No idea," Kariven murmured thoughtfully. "In any case, it could not be a meteor. The rocks from the heavens, near the lunar surface lacking an atmosphere, just like in outer space, don't light up like that."

"What if we fly over the crater where that ball of light showed up? It's not too far."

"OK. Follow me two taxi lengths behind."

At only 125 mph they neared their goal, a crater over a mile in diameter that they were soon flying over at low speed. They were the first Earthlings to see this "dark side" of the

Moon, hidden forever from their fellow men. They circled around the apparently common crater. With their powerful spotlights turned on, the astronauts adjusted the angle of their periscopic sights to get a close-up of the moonscape under their rockets.

"Good God!" Streiler exclaimed. "What happened in that ringed formation?"

In the middle of the flat crater surface a gulf around 2,000 feet wide had opened up, perfectly round and over 150 feet deep. Under the three bright beams of light the walls of the gulf glimmered, studded with crystals that the spotlights made sparkle like sunlight on rock crystal.

"It looks like the walls of the hole were vitrified," Clark observed. "It would take intense heat to melt the rock and dust like this. But what for? And *what...* or *who* could have produced such heat?"

In a worried voice Kariven answered, "How would I know? Right now let's turn around. When we get back to base we'll make out report. If Commander Taylor authorizes it, we'll come back tomorrow to inspect the crater up close."

In triangular formation the three rockets soared away from the darkened crater. On entering the bright side a few minutes later the pilots blinked their eyes in the sudden light that invaded their periscopic sights. Following the signals constantly emitted by the base's directional transmitter, the space taxis approached the Kepler crater where *Daisy* and the Bubble Base were stationed.

Past the Montes Hercynii they were flying over the vast plain that would lead them to camp, but in the gloomy moonscape an unpleasant surprise was awaiting them.

An unthinkable gathering of Selenites was moving SSE. As far as the eye could see on every side the plain was covered. It was like a huge, brown carpet, rippling over the hills and sinking into the craters and fissures to come out on the other side and flow relentlessly to the south without anything stopping it.

"They're… they're marching south," Clark stammered with a hint of anguish in his voice.

"At the speed they're going," Kariven observed, "it'll take them 15 or 20 hours at most to reach the Kepler crater. Let's not kid ourselves, the Selenites, both small and big, are not heading to the center of this hemisphere… *but toward our base!* When we saw this kind of migration from an area around the South Pole first and then all along the libration line that circles the Moon, we were too hasty to conclude that the monsters were heading for the center. In truth all of them are converging on our camp!"

"That's impossible! We'd have to admit that these nightmarish creatures could… communicate with one another… and do so from one pole of the Moon to the other."

"And why not? Isn't this siege proof enough? Follow me here: A group of Selenites has found a rich source of metal and other matter—our spaceship and Bubble Base—a source that some of them have drawn from. The five Selenites we captured died but not before that had tasted our metals, our artificial atmosphere… and unfortunately Teddy Brown. And they had time to send a message out, sounding the alarm and giving the location of this precious food. That, I believe, is how it happened."

Streiler's throat went dry. "We have to alert the base right away."

"Without waiting for this advice Kariven had already tuned his transmitter to centimetric waves. "Patrol K calling base… Patrol K calling base…"

A few seconds passed before he heard, "Base here, go ahead Patrol K."

"Warning! From every direction the Selenites are converging on the base. They'll reach it in less than 20 hours. Cordon off the area and organize a defense. We're heading back and should be there in ten minutes. Over and out."

"Message received. General alert is on. Over and out."

In the crater where the Russian astronauts had unwisely set up their base before knowing about the Selenites, the situation was getting worse.

When they became aware of these mysterious metallophage creatures on the bottom of the crater, the Russians armed themselves with steel bars and in a rage started hitting the monsters stuck to the bottom of their spaceship. They had to whack the brown shells hard to pry them loose and yet most of them were not killed but simply dazed. When a Selenite let go of the metal and dropped into the dust, ten others popped up from the other side and tried to crawl up the metal rocket leaning over the base.

Dripping with sweat inside their spacesuits, muscles flexed, nerves on edge, Colonel Zavkom and his comrades fought fiercely against the mounting tide of lunar creatures.

"We'll never be done with them!" Petrov griped, swinging his steel bar at the monsters.

"We have to!" Zavkom grumbled through clenched teeth, panting as he bashed the filthy shells. "If we let them overwhelm us we're f…"

The physicist Boris Ilyine, being more accustomed to the delicate instruments in a laboratory than to an axe used for slaughter, took a break from the exhausting effort. In spite of his healthy physique (he and his comrades had undergone serious physical training before leaving the secret base in Kaluga) he felt his strength failing rapidly. Suddenly, during this pause, an idea popped up in his mind.

"Colonel Zavkom! These metallophage creatures must be partly made of metal. So, we should be fighting them with fire. Let's try a blowtorch!"

The Colonel grabbed onto this idea like a shipwrecked sailor latches onto a plank. He gave orders right away. Ten minutes later six men came back from the base. Three of them held in their claws big fluoride torches connected by a flexible tube to metal tanks that the other three were carrying.

Three long, bright flames were quickly aimed at the monsters glued to the bottom of the spaceship. The result was immediate. The Selenites hit by the flame fell like flies! Shouts of joy filled the soviet astronauts' helmets. After 15 minutes, the tail pipes and what remained of the fins were freed up.

"The base! They're attacking the base now!"

The man leaped up, carried away by this new alarm. The torch carriers rushed to the three transparent domes of the base. When they got there they froze, mouths agape. Not a single square inch of the surface was visible. Everything was covered by the monsters huddled side by side and even on top of one another. The torches started spitting flames again but handling them here was a more delicate operation since the material could not last long under flames reaching 3,000°C!

Spraying little jets of flame aimed only at the center of the brown shells, it took them more than an hour to clear off the three airtight cabins of the base. When they had finished their cleaning operation, the men with the big metal tanks—despite the weak gravity—sat down, or rather dropped down, on the ground exhausted.

One of them pointed a weary hand at the gauge, "The pressure is 300 grams! They're almost empty. We'll have to get the other ones out of the hold."

At these words, all of them turned their heads to the leaning spaceship, its nose embedded in the split spike rising out of the middle of the crater. Petrov and two men went to the crashed ship. The metal ladder was sticking up toward the sky. Petrov adeptly threw a cable around it and pulled it down. Crawling on all fours he was able to climb slowly into the decompression chamber. Once inside the cockpit, although much was damaged—lights broken in the fall, the short-wave transmitter on the blink, compasses and sextants beyond repair—the walls had stood up. But it was not the same higher up. A 10-foot gash was opened 30 feet from the nose of the rocket. The nose and its radar mast were completely crushed. The rip was in the cabin with the fragile astronavigation equipment. No repair was possible here. Some shrapnel from the American missile had smashed the electronic counter and a piece of rock from the spike had mangled some of the vital instruments. With their rocket rendered useless the Russian astronauts were henceforth condemned to rest on the Moon!

Petrov had to stiffen up in order not to faint at the extent of this horrible disaster. He knew that the spare parts that the rocket had in storage were not enough to replace the front section of the ship and all the electronic devices it contained.

Exiled! They were forever exiled to the Moon! Forever? Certainly not. Forever meant an eternity. But for the members of an astronautical expedition with a limited amount of supplies and artificial air, this "eternity" meant… three months! Maybe four with severe rationing but no more.

Petrov felt exhausted and hopeless. He lumbered up to the gaping tear through which he could see part of the black sky spanned by the Milky Way. He grabbed the twisted metal and poked his head out.

Down below his comrades, like toy soldiers seen from this height, were sitting in a circle with their backs against the base. Petrov shook his head sadly and was about to go back down to get the metal bottles with the other men but an unbelievable sight froze him in place.

From the summit of the crater in which they were set up, a tidal wave of Selenites was slowly flowing toward the center, meaning *toward their base!*

CHAPTER SEVEN

After receiving Kariven's message the American base went into feverish action.

"You're sure that the Selenites from the *whole* planet are heading for us?" Commander Taylor asked anxiously.

"Absolutely certain, Commander. We flew over a strip of land over 60 miles wide making the complete tour of the Moon. All across this line, millions and millions of metallophage monsters, big and small, were moving continually in the same direction: apparently toward the center of this hemisphere. I say 'apparently' because, in fact, they're heading for our camp."

After listening to the three pilots' succinct report the head of the expedition assigned them to organize the southern wing of the camp. Every 30 feet they placed fluoride torches. Each of them was provided with an extra supply of reinforced tanks[49] containing the fluoride mixture that produced a 3,900°C flame.

When the base on the crater floor and the spaceship were well protected, Kariven, Streiler and Lieutenant Clark rejoined their friends who were finishing the installation of the six huge parabolic reflectors begun during their absence. These adjustable "mirrors", 30 feet in diameter, would capture the solar rays and convert them into pure heat that, in turn, would be transformed into energy. An extremely complex assemblage of tiny mirrors covered the inside surface of each parabolic reflector.

Away from the rocket, perched on the summit of a small crater was a metal tower on top of which was turning the dome of a panoramic radar. The tower stood over 450 feet tall

---

[49] These tanks of reinforced metal are lined with a non-metallic protective coating because fluoride is an incredibly powerful corrosive. (Author's Note)

and therefore well higher than the nose of the vertical space-ship. With this, no false *blip* (echo) caused by radar waves from the ship would be registered.

"According to our predictions, Kariven," Commander Taylor consulted his space watch, "the Selenites won't reach us for around 12 more hours. In one hour and 17 minutes our supply rocket, Mickey, will be arriving from Earth." After a moment of silence full of troubled thoughts he continued, "If Mickey doesn't come, we won't be able to lift anchor. In fact, if we have to face a siege for a while, we'll run out of fluoride and, which is worse, our supply of oxygen and helium, the two elements that the torches gobble up like hogs."

Kariven frowned, "I hate to be the bearer of bad news but if we really have to face a siege, it'll last a long time. These are only the first 'attack squadrons' that will be assailing us. Most of the Selenite forces, if I can call them this, will reach us three or four hours later, and then things will really heat up. The monsters will keep coming non-stop!"

"Charming perspective," the Commander growled into the mic.

"The parabolics are up and running, Commander," Professor Harrington announced.

The astronauts contemplated the six big "mirrors" pointed at the sun to collect its rays. Each of them sparkled with blinding flashes. A watchwork movement kept them following the progress of the sun in the sky.

"In fact, Professor," Kariven asked out of the blue, "what temperature can your reflectors reach?"

"Properly positioned and considering their period of 'acclimation,' in five minutes they'll be able to boil mercury in the thermometers before producing usable energy. So, around 360°C. But if we adjust the angle and direction—by aligning them perpendicular to the sunrays, for example—it could be ten times higher. Really, in a place without an atmosphere, the convergence of rays at its optimal point would be—for this type of reflector—near 4,000°C, or 200 degrees hotter than an atomic hydrogen torch. But our present needs don't call for such temperatures…"

"Super!" Kariven rejoiced. "That's what's going to save us without a hassle!"

All the others looked at him curiously.

"It's very simple," he explained. "Listen up. If we move these six reflectors far enough away from the spaceship, if we point them all, center them all on the sun…"

"We can surround the base with a burning circle of at least 3,500°C," Streiler added feverishly, knowing exactly where his friend was going. "Bravo, Kariven! You've got a really bright idea there!"

"Bright and scorching!" Commander Taylor smiled. "Let's go, Kariven, I'll let you direct the operations. Place the reflectors wherever you want."

Everything else stopped and the Earthlings got to work under the orders of Kariven and Professor Harrington as they chose the best placement for the reflectors. Considering their weight and huge size (each weighed 4.6 tons and measured 30 feet in diameter) it was not possible to move them all at once.

In feverish activity the fragile parabolic reflectors with mirrored facets were lifted up by the mobile jaws and placed on the ground in front of the massive platforms that contained the mechanics for their rotating and tilting movements.

Commander Taylor looked frequently at his watch.

Kariven remarked, "We'll never get them all moved if we leave the motor-blocs intact. How long until *Mickey* gets here?"

"27 minutes."

Then Commander Taylor called Gordon who had stayed in the spaceship to spot the approach of the huge, guided rocket on the radar.

"I've had *Mickey* on the radar for a few minutes," Gordon informed him. "I'm guiding it now with my controls."

"Great. Bring it down as close as possible to *Daisy*. We'll free up some space."

Hurriedly the astronauts took away all the instruments and material for research and observation that they had set up. Everything was brought down to the bottom of the fissure with the Bubble Base.

"There it is! I see the rocket," Clark shouted and pointed at the sky where two blinking lights, red and green among the white stars, indicated the approach of the supply ship.

Automatically programmed to light up at a precise distance from the Moon, *Mickey*'s bright sidelights had just turned on. They seemed to fly back up into outer space before being replaced by a big, red-orange disc. The spaceship had just flipped around to descend and was now perpendicular to the lunar surface, its tail section spitting out torrents of ignition fuel.

All the astronauts bounded away and went to crouch behind a hill to protect themselves from the dangerous exhaust from the tailpipes.

Visible to the naked eye now the body of the rocket grew bigger faster. And the purple glow of its underside grew brighter as it neared.

In *Daisy*'s command post Gordon, the physicist/radar man, was busy on his electronic keyboard adjusting the output of the ship's exhaust, increasing the lateral exhaust to correct the angle of descent and reducing the opposite action while keeping a constant eye on the green blip blinking on the screen.

Mickey was only 500 feet off the ground. It had slowed down considerably and was coming down slowly on a short column of red flames that were quickly absorbed by the lunar air. Its powerful exhaust started kicking up the white lunar dust that spurted out in all directions, sprinkling the reflector mirrors with a thick layer of ash that had to be carefully wiped off to make sure they worked.

The rocket finally landed in a tumultuous cloud of whirling dust and in deathly silence. On Earth, its reactors would have created a deafening din but on the Moon, since sound does not travel in a void, no noise at all could be heard.

The radar man, Gordon, cut the ignition by remote control, closed all contacts and left the cabin to join his friends who were already running toward the newly arrived rocket.

"Let's get to work, boys," Commander Taylor encouraged them. "We've got to get the Weasels[50] out quick. That way we can move the motor-blocs for the reflectors."

The rocket, 90 feet tall and 115 feet wide at the base, looked like a gigantic torpedo, a "well fed" sister of the *Daisy* rocket. An extraordinary diversity of supplies had been stuffed in its sides: six months worth of rations, drinking water, airtight material for a 165-foot diameter permanent base, scientific instruments of all kinds, fuel and combustive, survey and mining equipment, and finally the famous Weasels, four of them, which the Commander had just mentioned.

Already activated by remote control during the landing, a huge panel was open in the rocket's hull. Around 15 by 20 feet it would soon turn into a ramp by adding extensions that could ultimately be used to build the floor of the future base.

The first hold opened 140 feet off the ground. The lower section of the rocket contained the incredibly complex and crowded system of boosters, fuel tanks, pumps, mixers, and of course the tailpipes themselves.

It took more than two hours to assemble the long ramp so they could slide out the important material sent by their home planet.

"The Weasels first!" Commander Taylor ordered, grabbing the ramp to get to one of the machines.

Kariven, Streiler and Lieutenant Clark followed him. 15 minutes later at the opening of the hold, 130 feet up, a kind of yellow mammoth appeared: the first Weasel, a huge tractor mounted on treads, equipped with an airtight cabin with a

---

[50] Giant tractors with an airtight cabin and engine specially designed to be used in areas without an atmosphere. These machines are being studied today in the USA (and probably Russia) for a future manned flight to our satellite first and then later to our planetary neighbors. (Author's Note)

Plexiglas cockpit, and thanks to its two independent engines protected by hermetically sealed armor it could drive in an empty atmosphere.

Looking like a tank and a crane, the first two Weasels rolled out slowly a few minutes apart onto the ramp that led them to the ground. Through the transparent cockpits of the yellow steel monster a man in a spacesuit was waving hello. From this distance Professor Harrington could not see who it was, so he looked for the identification number that every astronaut wore (a black number on a white background) on the front and back of his helmet. He saw the number 3 and knew it was Kariven giving his friendly salute.

Coming next was Commander Taylor followed by two other, different shaped Weasels. On the back of these was a huge, articulated, metal arm with a bucket at the end fitted with steel spikes on the edge to work as an excavator a little like the vibrating picks used by miners. When these giant claws were brought up against a rock wall or rocky ground they would attack it with great violence, able to dislodge the hardest rock. Turning the claws over the machine worked as a very efficient "dredging shovel".

Streiler and Lieutenant Clark were at the helm of these powerful vehicles. With remarkable handling and speed the first two Weasels driven by Taylor and Kariven were steered toward the motor-blocs of the parabolic reflectors. Operating the commands with expertise the two men maneuvered the strong, metal arms of the Weasels over the blocs. The steel jaws clamped down and lifted the blocs with unsettling ease. Like dogs carrying their puppies in their teeth the big vehicles rolled to the locations chosen wisely by Professor Harrington.

In three trips the six motor-blocs were set in place and while three other trips brought over the parabolics the technicians reconnected them—the blocs to the generator—with extension cables. The installation, cleaning and assembly of the reflectors took another couple of hours of feverish activity seeing that time was running out, every minute bringing the Selenites closer to the hustling Earthlings.

"We've still got another hour and a half," Kariven breathed a sigh of relief looking at his watch. "Maybe two hours before the Selenites show up. Everything's OK, Professor?"

Professor Harrington, who was scurrying from one bloc to another checking their working order, answered, "Everything's fine. We can test them out."

"Everyone back to the rocket," Commander Taylor ordered. "Nobody, no matter what, wander off because when the Selenites get here, you won't be able to get through furnace protecting the camp."

In the face of this imminent danger no one had any plans to wander off! The whole team, therefore, was together around the two rockets. The ramp had been sticking out of the safe zone, so it was rapidly dismantled to keep away from the monsters' corrosive attack.

The six reflectors surrounding the camp were all facing the sun, perpendicular to its rays. Professor Harrington stood in front of the control panel next to the generator providing the energy to the motor-blocs. He slowly turned a knob activating the reflectors, which all together swivel slightly on their axis before lowering a few degrees.

Like six blinding maws they became impossible to look at, even from the side where a crescent of light would rip through the retina. A bright conic beam—concentrated solar rays—shot out of their axis. The beam covered a surface of the ground exactly ten feet in diameter. These bright "spots" did not have the same temperature at every point. Their edges were obviously less hot than the center where the convergence of rays reached its optimal point.

The whole set-up, therefore, around the rockets poured out six torrents of thermal rays reaching 3,500°C. However, it did not form a "closed" circle. A blank space of almost 50 feet separated each burning center. To compensate for this serious inconvenience Professor Harrington proposed a "corrective" method:

"I just synchronized the six parabolic reflectors. By turning this knob halfway round to the right, then halfway to the left, the thermal rays will sweep over a 50-foot area from one end to the other where the six beams are now on the ground. This will surround the base with a heat circle. The half-turns from right to left will obviously leave some area open at any given second but the interruption will be so brief that we don't have to worry about it. The Selenites are not fast enough to get through the space in one second anyway. Whatever gets into the area left open by the sweeping beam will be destroyed one second later when the beam comes back."

Lieutenant Clark was lost in thought and spoke probably to himself but the microphone broadcast it to everyone else. "And after?"

"What do you mean, Clark?" Harrington was surprised.

Shaken out of his reverie, the Lieutenant explained, "I'm just wondering what we'll do after the attack, supposing that the Selenites are defeated and driven back. Are we supposed to live on the Moon forever threatened by a new attack from these nasty creatures? In the future we'll have to surround a permanent base with a protective system that is *continually* heated up."

"Unless we discover a radical way to exterminate the Selenites, which is what we'll have to do... as well as whoever comes after us to live in the permanent lunar base that *Mickey* brought to us," Professor Harrington responded.

"Rudy's wise observation leads to another," Kariven wrinkled his forehead. "This high temperature ring will be built with the machines of a permanent base and work constantly thanks to giant reflectors or a separate device that can create its own source of heat rays. But for us this protective ring won't last forever because it depends on the sun. Now, in four Earth hours, *this side of the Moon will turn to night that will last 14 days!*"

His cruel logic literally stunned the astronauts. In fact, when the sun set on the horizon the reflectors would be deprived of its rays and instantly stop shooting their heat beams at the Selenites.

"Once the lunar night is here," Kariven continued, "we won't be able to protect the base with the torches for 336 hours. Long before the next daybreak we'll have run out of fluoride, oxygen and helium for the torches. Therefore, the problem is this: either we find a way to exterminate the monsters completely *within four days* and continue preparations for a future permanent base or we don't, in which case we'll have to gather up all the material already unloaded and leave the Moon to its metallophage inhabitants. And Operation Aphrodite will live on! But how many years will pass before we can come back to our satellite with a squadron of spaceships?

"See, there's no way we can think of coming back with a single rocket followed by the supply rocket 53 hours later. We'll have to land with at least ten giant ships able to transport a base that can be quickly assembled and... permanently defended. We'll have to be able to build a base in less than 14 days, i.e. one lunar day."

The radar man, Gordon, perched on top of the radar antenna, cried out in alarm, waving his binoculars. "They're here! They're here! Good God... It's... It's like the whole planet is rippling! There are thousands, hundreds of thousands of them, everywhere as far as the eye can see... A horrible, brown, moving carpet..."

"Everyone to their post!" Commander Taylor shouted. "Harrington, get ready on your parabala... your parabola... your ray guns!" he muddled.

The crater where the Russians had been unlucky enough to build their base was closer to the libration zone than the American base set up on the plain next to the Kepler crater. Therefore, it was closer on the path of the Selenites crawling to these two rich sources of metal.

Terrified at the sight of the nasty creatures spilling over the rim of the crater, Petrov gave the alarm. With his two men he passed the fluoride tanks through the tear in the spaceship.

Using a cable, 50 of the cylinders were brought down in record time. On the ground six astronauts stood together, torches ready to fire, while the other men carried the rations and water out of the rocket to the base where the center of resistance had been organized.

Zavkom was busy like the others with the preparations. With three men he got the cases of rations safely into the base before they all armed themselves with torches.

The Selenites were only 50 yards from the Russians and were advancing relentlessly, gradually closing in their ranks. Like some menacing flow of brown lava the monsters came closer, surging and swelling. The purple shells of the giant Selenites would sometimes flash a brief luminescence, a kind of rhythmic pulse, mesmerizing in the rough, desolate crater. Now they were less than ten feet from the Earthlings.

"Fire!" Zavkom cried out in a raspy voice and all 11 torches spit their purple flames at the ground.

The first row of Selenites was stopped in its tracks. The next row, trying to advance, pushed the motionless shells but was stopped by this unexpected obstacle. There was a moment of hesitation, then the giant monsters sped up the rhythm of their light pulses and the push continued. The corpses were shoved away and new attackers crawled into the empty spaces. Once again the jets of flame nailed them to the ground.

"Shoot in spurts!" Zavkom ordered. "We have to conserve the Fluoride. Petrov, climb into the rocket and see if the shortwave transmitter is still working. If so, call Kaluga and explain the situation. Our only chance of survival is for them to send us the second rocket... if it's ready with extra torches and tanks. Do it now!"

Petrov gave his torch to Professor Ilyine and a minute later was climbing up the rocket tilted 45° over the base.

While pointing the flame of his torch at the monsters Colonel Zavkom grunted, "We made a fatal mistake coming to this crater. If the astronavigraph weren't damaged we would have had time to explore the region and probably found these weird and dangerous inhabitants of the craters. If we set up on the top of a hill, for example, it'd be a lot easier to defend ourselves."

Petrov was soon bounding back. He grabbed his torch and while shooting at the monsters answered the unasked questions of his comrades whose anxious eyes were staring at him.

"I reached the Kaluga base... Rocket number two won't be ready for... three weeks."

"Three weeks!" Zavkom exploded. "But... we'll be dead before that! Why so late?"

"The factories that were supposed to deliver the radars and the guiding system to Kaluga didn't meet their deadlines."

A string of curses echoed in everyone's helmet thanks to Colonel Zavkom.

"It's unbelievable! We're on the most fantastic conquest in human history and while we're risking our lives on the Moon—for the greater glory of the USSR—these industrialists are late with deliveries! And we see this kind of carelessness, this sloppiness, this waste on every level, social and industrial. The Russian people deserve a new revolution without thinking about the bureaucrats..."

Petrov, bitterly continuing to spit fire, was spurred on, "We're definitely going to leave our corpses on this dirty rock, Colonel, so allow me to say today what I really think about your doctrinal concept of bureaucrats. Don't you see that if a new revolution broke out in Russia, it's the people who would suffer from it? Revolutions have never been made by the bureaucrats. On the contrary, it's against them that they come about, with or without legitimate reason by whoever embraces it. And I am..."

"You're a traitor," Zavkom broke in calmly. "A traitor to the soviet doctrine... but you're a traitor who's going to die with the rest of us and so I'll allow you to talk like this." Zavkom paused before mumbling a conclusion, "Because you're speaking the truth anyway."

The pilot Petrov was taken aback, casting sidelong glances at his chief. He had trouble swallowing and was impressed to find in this brutal, severe man the spirit of justice stripped of prejudice.

He mumbled back, "Thanks, Colonel... For the first time we're in agreement."

A shout of rage suddenly screamed in their helmets. Professor Ilyine's torch had just gone out, without explanation, and the monsters were taking advantage of this "hole" in the ring of flames. They rushed over the corpses. Petrov stepped over and while the physicist was examining the burner he swept over a wider surface with his own to cut off the invaders.

Using a bent steel rod the Professor cleaned off the super-metal burner, thinking this was the cause of the damage.

"The tube must've got blocked when you changed tanks," Petrov suggested, jumping bravely forward to attack the swarming mass of Selenites.

"I think so too," the scientist agreed. "Something got in there and blocked the..." He did not finish because the ground shook beneath him.

The steel tank feeding fluoride to the physicist's torch had exploded! A crack in its interior protective coating had probably done it and the corrosive fluoride had eaten through the reinforced metal that finally snapped under the heavy pressure. Metal fragments flew off in all directions, scattering like grenade fragments, killing Professor Ilyine and smashing the helmets of three men who died immediately with their skulls crushed.

Colonel Zavkom and Petrov, being a little farther away than the others, were thrown up by the suddenly released gas and fell back down on the other side of the base, but they were not hit.

Petrov got up, stumbled a little, dizzily, and picked up his torch that had gone out at the moment of the explosion. He got ready to start firing again but in his daze he saw that Colonel Zavkom was still on the ground, on his back. In one leap he was next to him. The officer's eyes were dilated, his mouth open, trying with difficulty to say something but no sound came through the pilot's helmet. His face suddenly turned purplish-red. Petrov immediately understood what was happening. He picked up his chief and in a few leaps brought him to the decompression chamber. He pushed him into the tube, lay down on him after locking the outside hatch and finally opened the inner hatch. Since the tube was only meant for one person at a time, it seemed like it took forever to do this.

Finally he pulled the Colonel into the first dome and quickly tore off his helmet. Zavkom's face was flushed. It took him 20 minutes to come around while Petrov gave him oxygen and performed artificial respiration.

"Thank you," the Russian officer wheezed.

"Don't talk," Petrov ordered, gladly forgetting that he was addressing his superior.

A faint smile relaxed the latter's face. Petrov examined the helmet closely but found nothing out of the ordinary. However, on the spacesuit's shoulder he found what he was looking for. A metal shard from the exploded tank had hit the thick protective material and made a cut less than an inch long, but enough for the artificial air to escape and suffocate the wearer.

"You almost didn't make it, Colonel," he said.

The officer got slowly to his feet, still feeling light-headed and dizzy. He leaned against the transparent wall and putting his right hand on his rescuer's shoulder told him, "Thank you, Petrov. I was wrong before to treat you like…"

"Bah, you weren't thinking, Colonel."

"It's true, I wasn't thinking. You're a hero."

Colonel Zavkom struggled free of his damaged spacesuit and put on one of the extras. Fitting the helmet onto the collar he spoke through the mic, "Let's go, Petrov. We've still got a few hours to live. Let's not waste it moaning and groaning. Let's kill as many of these damn monsters as we can!"

On the lunar soil the seven survivors reformed their chain and armed with torches threw themselves heroically into the fray, fighting fiercely all the while knowing that they would never escape from the monsters.

When Petrov's fluoride tank ran out he dragged another to his side. His hands shook as he hooked it up and went back to cooking the army of purple creatures now overwhelming them. All of a sudden a cloud of dust surrounded them. Surprised, he turned around. A thick spray of chalky ash hit his helmet. He wiped it off to see where the avalanche of dust was coming from.

An urgent shout told him. "The Selenites have got through to the base! The artificial air is escaping!"

So, that was it! The air was streaming out of the base, whirling up the dust that had surrounded Petrov.

Under the three transparent domes a column of monsters was already wriggling through a crack, sticking to all the metal surfaces, corroding the equipment, the supplies, bursting the water containers and the rectangular armor protecting the generators and air conditioners.

Petrov and Zavkom looked at each other with great sadness, feeling powerless rage and spite. The seven astronauts, torches in hand, picked up the tanks and leaped over to one of the still intact domes. They exchanged looks of resignation, stood close together, and without saying a word, jaws clenched, eyes glinting with hatred for this larval form of life that was destroying their expedition, they shot their flames at the monsters. They would fight until their tanks ran out... or their air supply.

"Goodbye, Zavkom," the pilot muttered through his microphone.

"Goodbye, Petrov," he responded. "I'm sorry we never got to be friends..."

CHAPTER EIGHT

Professor Harrington flipped a switch on his control panel and the six parabolic reflectors, tilted at the desired angle, shot their beams at the dusty ground: six spots of blinding light materialized.

Then the physicist used the dial to direct the reflectors, turning to the right and left. Continually, precisely, he accomplished his task. The six impact zones of concentrated solar rays grazed the first rows of rippling monsters.

"Hurray!" the American astronauts cheered. "It's working beautifully!"

"Look at them squirm!" Lieutenant Clark smiled. "They're quivering a little and will soon be joining their ancestors."

Streiler, first unconsciously then with curiosity, was watching Kariven who looked worried at the initial encouraging results; his mind was elsewhere. He seemed preoccupied, sunk in a well of thoughts that maybe had something to do with their present condition but were nonetheless far different from everybody else's thoughts.

Staring at some imaginary point beyond the zone being swept by the lethal rays Kariven paid no attention to the engineer next to him. When he heard the familiar voice echoing through his helmet he jumped.

"What's cooking, friend?" Streiler asked amiably.

A fleeting expression of annoyance crossed Kariven's face, then looking straight into Streiler's eyes, he turned his mic to "personal" communication and answered, "Your innocent question, Kurt, shows your insight. Something is, in fact, 'cooking,' since the day that Clark saw that light in the Aristarchus crater. My first thought, my suspicion I should say, was confirmed when we witnessed the inexplicable phenomenon on the dark side of the Moon."

"You mean the kind of glowing orb in the crater that disappeared and left behind a huge hole?"

"That's right."

"I don't see what all these mysterious happenings…"

Kariven raised his hand to interrupt. "Listen, old friend, do you trust me?"

"Do you have to ask?" the other shrugged.

"OK, then come with me and let's ask Clark to come with us in the space taxis to the Aristarchus crater."

"No problem seeing that he's wanted to go out there since he got here. But I don't know if the Commander shares his desire… or ours."

"It's absolutely necessary that we get to that crater. Our lives depend on it… I can feel it."

Streiler raised an eyebrow, looked astonished and said, "You… feel it? Hey, Kariven, check to see if your air isn't being blocked. Sometimes that can make you feel funny. Delirium, for example. Joking aside, you don't really believe in omens and all that hocus pocus, do you?"

Kariven held back an angry reaction and forced himself to stay calm. "I was never so serious, Kurt. The base can defend itself without us. As long as the sun is shining, that is, for another 24 hours on this hemisphere. Do you want to go with me and Clark, yes or no?"

"OK, OK. You know very well that we're on the same team," Streiler muttered. "I trust you."

"Good, let's go get Clark."

Ten minutes later the three men stood before the Commander. Kariven spoke with no emotion. "The protection system looks like it's working, Commander."

"Working great… if the waves of attack don't start doing what they just did," he complained.

Streiler was confused and asked what he meant.

"The giant Selenites were trying to dig tunnels under the pile of dwarf corpses. Twice they came out of the ground, unexpectedly, inside the zone of solar rays! We fried them with torches… If they use this tactic more often, we might be invaded sooner or later. There're only nine of us and that's not enough to fight off an attack that could come out of 50 or 100 burrows. Plus, the solar rays can't be used outside or inside the camp where they might fry one of us, not to mention the danger of destroying our equipment."

Kariven realized that *things were not so rosy*. His request was going to be rejected for sure. Nevertheless he tried to voice it. "Commander Taylor, in consideration of our friendship and in memory of our exploration of the past[51], I'm asking you to authorize Streiler, Clark and me to take the space taxis for an hour."

"Take the Space taxis... when the camp is in danger? You're crazy, Kariven! And why do you want to leave the base?"

Kariven answered calmly with another question. "Sorry for insisting without giving you an explanation, Commander, but if we were buried under the shells of these monsters, sure to die, would our presence here save the base and the lives of our comrades?"

Taylor looked at them each in turn, puzzled, without really understanding the question. "I... Our fates are linked, you know that. I'm the head of this expedition and I have the right to know what you want to do outside the base in the space taxis."

"Yes, Commander," Kariven agreed. "You have the right to allow three of your men to try to save the crew. Time is of the essence, Commander. We can do it and when we get back we'll explain the whys, wherefores and howabouts, whatever you want to know."

The officer thought for a second, grumbled something incomprehensible, then decided, "OK, get out of here and go to hell! But be back in an hour!"

The three friends jumped into their space taxis, closed the hatches and took off at exactly the same time. Lieutenant Clark pressed the red button on the control panel in reach of

---

[51] See *The Time Spiral*. (Author's Note)

his left hand and turned up the radio. These very simple maneuvers, however, were somewhat difficult for a pilot lying down on his belly in the rubber-lined "capsule" of the space taxi. To change position was a contortionist act!

"Clark here," he announced. "We made it out but what are we doing in the Aristarchus crater?"

"So, you're not curious to know what that light was, the purple beam that you were the only one to see when we were coming in? That phenomenon, the mysterious footprints and that huge glowing ball that left a crater beyond the libration line have got me thinking that *we're not alone here on the Moon*! Anyway, we'll soon find out. There, straight ahead, the Aristarchus crater."

On the horizon stood a rocky mass, like a fence, smooth but cracked. Soon the outer walls of the lunar crater became clearer, presenting their serrated ridge against the black sky.

"The light beam!" Rudy Clark exploded excitedly.

Coming from a spot that was still invisible behind the top of the crater a weird purple ray was sweeping over the sky. It was searching space, wavered an instant, and then tilted in the direction of the three tiny rockets.

"It... It's coming toward us!" Clark was alarmed, his forehead beading sweat. "Watch out! It's going to touch us! Let's get out of here!"

"Don't panic," Kariven ordered. "Stay behind me in triangular formation. Slow down, only 30 miles an hour. Follow my every move. I don't think we're in any danger since when Clark saw it the first time it didn't do any harm to us."

In fact the cone of purple light was surrounding the three machines but nothing happened.

"Oh, Good God," Lieutenant Clark was stunned when he saw on his periscopic screen the image of the ground they were flying over.

In the Aristarchus crater a gigantic transparent dome rose up, reflecting the rays of the sun. Under the dome, over a mile wide and almost half a mile high on its axis, was a city, a strange city of geometric buildings covered in emerald green metal! At the intersections of the big, rectangular avenues were round gardens with beds of magnificent, multi-colored flowers. On the roofs of the buildings—serving as aero-garages here—spherical vehicles were lined up. The same kind of machines were flying through the air, some cruising slowly only three feet off the wide, uncongested, pink streets.

"Hey, boys, are you... Am I dreaming?" Clark stammered. "Are you seeing what I think I'm seeing, wide awake? God strike me down if I have the slightest idea what this could be!"

"It's unbelievable," Kariven was bewildered. "It looks to me like a base... a base like we Earthlings would build..."

"Look!" Clark cried out, "outside the dome, those disc-shaped machines lined up on the crater floor. They're sitting on some kind of landing field made of three metal hemispheres..."

"Discs... Could they be what some people on Earth call *flying saucers*?"

The three space taxis circled over the fantastic city under the dome. All of a sudden in each of their minds a strange "audible thought" formed, a deep and sometimes warm "voice," a clear and perfectly intelligible telepathic voice:

Welcome, Earthlings, to our lunar base!

"Who... who... who said that?" Clark mumbled uncomfortably.

You are flying over Woonka, our lunar base, the mysterious voice resumed, oddly echoing in the three stupefied astronauts' minds. *We took great interest in your preparations on Earth for the flight of your spaceships to your satellite and we are glad that for your civilization you have finally begun the Astronautical Age. Thus you come a little closer to our stage of evolution.*

"But... who are you?" Streiler asked aloud, wondering if, by this question, he was not encouraging a visual and oral hallucination.

226

We come from Outer Space[52]. *We are men like you, be-*
cause we are morphologically identical to you, even though
we possess various psychic senses that you are not familiar
with. We come from a distant planet in a solar system around
the star you call Polaris. We are, therefore, Polarians. Since
time immemorial, thanks to our tremendous technical possibil-
ities and scientific knowledge that is hard for you to imagine,
we have watched your slow evolution, we have learned your
languages and sometimes we have even made contact with a
few carefully chosen Earthlings. Humans worthy of interest,
both men and women, capable of rising above the petty politi-
cal, religious and racial quarrels, humans with an open mind,
ready to accept the help and teaching of the profound wisdom
that they lack, humans who deep down inside and without be-
ing able to explain why feel like "strangers" on Earth or at
least have seen too much of humanity to wallow in the mire of
its mediocrity and its blindness. These few, selected human
beings bear a mark on their hands, the Mark *of* Knowledge,
though they know not the significance. They are the first of a
new race, the race of the Fourth Cycle, similar to the Dragons
of Wisdom *of the ancient traditions, the remnants of your van-*

---

[52] See *L'Homme de l'Espace* [*The Man from Outer Space*],
winner of the Grand Prize of Science Fiction in 1954. (Author's Note) Once again, Fleuve Noir published the books out
of sequence, and *Operation Aphrodite* which, in many re-
spects, should have preceded *The Man from Outer Space*, was
instead published after it. Again, some confusion may have
arisen, forcing Guieu to duplicate expository materials about
the Polarians and the Denebians in this section. The "Grand
Prix du Roman de Science-Fiction" was something set up by
the publisher in 1954 for marketing purposes and only given
to one of their novels, so it did not carry much credibility. It
was discontinued in 1957. The winners were Guieu's
L'Homme de l'Espace (1954), Jean-Gaston Vandel's *Bureau*
de l'Invisible (1955), Stéfan Wul's *Retour à 0* (1956) and
Max-André Rayjean's *Les Parias de l'Atome* (1957).

ished civilizations. We Polarians are the descendants of these Dragons of Wisdom, *the Instructors of primitive planets or those not yet completing their evolution.*[53]

These special human beings will be of great help to us when we decide to contact the governments on Earth officially... and I'm pleased to tell you that you are included. You all, in fact, bear the Mark of Knowledge on your hands, which our panoptic vision showed us a long time ago. Thanks to you, it will be easier for us to form an Earth-Polarian alliance to confront the threat that looms over this solar system.

"What do you mean?" Streiler asked. "How can a series of planets be threatened except by a natural disaster that's predictable like a solid-nucleus comet, giant meteors and such. And nothing like that seems to have been detected in outer space."

It's not about the end of the world, the telepathic voice continued, *but a threat targeting the human race: the Denebians, green monsters with scaly, shiny skin, hideous creatures from the solar system of the star Deneb, are preparing to conquer Earth and the other planets of this system.*

The revelation of this frightening danger plunged them into stupefied silence. They started nervously when the Man from Outer Space spoke again in their heads.

Now we have to get ready as fast as possible. I know all about the attack that your base is under. Anyway, you set up an excellent defense system and I praise the ingenuity of Earthlings in using their still rudimentary technology. But it's absolutely necessary that you go help your brother Earthlings, the Russians, who are about to cave in under the massive stampede of giant Selenites.

"The Russians! They've reached the Moon too?" Kariven was very surprised.

Soon after you. They're in a crater located about 90 miles to the west of the Kepler crater and your base. Go there immediately to free them with your Weasels. We could easily

---

[53] See *The Time Spiral*. (Author's Note)

help them with our spaceships but we prefer that it be you Earthlings who save your planetary brothers from the clutches of death. The Russians are enemies of Americans only through absurd hegemonic doctrines and will one day become allies. You will be united in brotherhood. The other peoples of the Earth will follow this example and when all are united they will fight next to the Polarians against a real enemy incapable of the slightest humanitarian sentiment and unbelievably more dangerous than the Selenites: the Denebians, those green monsters from the distant star Deneb in the constellation Cygnus. The first alliance that you are going to make now with foreign astronauts in order to fight the Selenites, will, I hope, bind you two people for later. Go, friends, and may the Goddess Kosmos protect you!

The Polarian stopped his telepathic communication leaving the three Earthlings caught in a maze-like web of thoughts riddled with question marks.

Kariven was the first to get hold of himself. "We have to get back to base right away. Let's split up. You two go directly to camp and tell the Commander to ready the Weasels. I'll go to the Russian base and send orders after assessing the situation."

"Great, my brothers!" Clark joked. "The Moon is jam-packed this season."

Following the telepathic instructions given by the Polarian, Kariven steered his rocket west. He sped like lightning over the American base and soon after sent a kind of telegraphic message: "Kariven to Commander Taylor. All's well. Streiler and Clark about to land. Do as they say without delay. Out."

On the ground everyone had received the message. Each of them wondered why he was not landing and what these future orders could be.

After flying 85 miles to the west of the Kepler crater, Kariven slowed down to inspect the craters he was flying over.

In his periscopic viewer he quickly spotted the crater with the Russians.

"Damn! The poor guys had a lot of problems landing. Their rocket is kaput."

On the crater floor the weary survivors had just seen the small rocket that was circling at 600 feet. They could make out the inscription on its side: USSF[54] with the white star of the American armed forces in front.

Colonel Zavkom and his comrades, with their claws on the torches spitting out the last jets of flame, wondered if they were not the victims of a collective hallucination. "A one-person rocket!" he roared.

"It has the white star of the American army," Petrov noted.

The stunned Russians dared not make a move. They watched anxiously as the rocket slowly spiraled toward the ground.

"It's looking for a spot to land that's free of Selenites." Petrov guessed. "Let's clear off a space around 30 feet off to the side by pushing back the monsters."

The seven men climbed on the pile of corpses and started driving the other hideous purple Selenites back with their torches. Under their boots they could feel the death throes of the lunar creatures.

"The pilot understands! He's going to set down!"

Indeed, it had not taken Kariven long to see the Russians' purpose. His space taxi set down gently on a pile of brown and violet corpses, creating a gaping wound or gash that exposed the deep metallic layers where the vital systems worked through endosmosis.

---

[54] United States Space Force as opposed to the USAF, United States Air Force. (Author's Note) Guieu is making this up. During the Cold War, space operations (such as the X-1, etc.) were under the command of NACA (National Advisory Committee for Aeronautics), formed in 1915, which eventually turned into NASA in 1958.

"Keep firing!" Zavkom ordered. "Come with me, Petrov."

The two soviet astronauts approached the rocket whose hatch was starting to open. Petrov helped raise the armored door and stepped back slowly to rejoin his chief while Kariven squirmed out of the capsule. Standing before his rocket he looked around, saw the four corpses still in their torn space-suits and walked toward the two men who had come to welcome him.

"Do you speak English?" he asked into his microphone, certain that the Russians were equipped with a spacesuit similar enough to his.

He heard two "Yes" in his earphones and he shook the claws that served as hands in the soviet spacesuits.

"Kariven, anthropaleontologist and doctor of the American Earth/Moon expedition."

For the Russians, all hatred toward the American Capitalists had vanished. They were filled with an indefinable feeling, a feeling of curiosity, emotion and something like frustration, an inferiority complex maybe, stemming from their present situation. Nevertheless, it was with sincere joy that their claws shook the glove of the newcomer.

"Colonel Zavkom, chief of the Russian expedition," the officer introduced himself. "This is the physicist and pilot of our spaceship, Petrov."

"I wish we were meeting under better circumstances, my friends," Kariven smiled.

Zavkom and Petrov looked at each other. How could a "western capitalist" call two soviet citizens "my friends"?

Kariven smiled at their astonishment. "Does it really surprise you that I call you friends?"

Colonel Zavkom cleared his throat before answering, "Your visit surprises me, in fact. Excuse me but usually Russians and Americans or Westerners in general don't get along so well."

Kariven shook his head. "I'm not a westerner. I'm an Earthling. In truth, if we accept this classification of nationalities, I'm not an American, I'm French. But in the Astronautical Age, being French, Russian or American doesn't mean a thing. We're all Earthlings, brothers of the same planet. Only the selfish minds of tyrannical leaders drunk on power and domination try to pit their peoples against each other. They tell you Russians all day long that in the west there are bigwigs of finance whose only goal is the oppression of the working class. Nothing is more false. There are obviously abuses, everywhere, but the way your leaders blacken us belongs only to the despots of warmongering people."

Taken aback by this rant, Colonel Zavkom suggested, "Dr. Kariven, did you come here to give a lecture on moral rehabilitation and distract us from fighting against the Selenite monsters?"

Kariven smiled again. "No, Colonel Zavkom. It's to tell you to hold out for an hour or two. I'm going to send a message to my chief who will bring two Weasels to your crater here and pull you out of this tight spot. Please excuse me..."

Kariven turned his transmitter to long wave and called the American base.

"Kariven to Commander Taylor... Kariven to Commander Taylor..."

"Commander Taylor here. Talk to me."

"Streiler and Clark have landed?"

"Yes, they just told me your extraordinary adventure. If I didn't know you three, I'd swear you were pulling my leg. But I don't think so."

"And you're right," Kariven said. "Waste no time in sending the two Weasels straight west toward the Marius crater. Just under 100 miles from our base, due west, you'll find a crater about 1.5 miles in diameter where the Russians are holed up... at least what's left of them. The poor guys have lost four of their men. The seven survivors are trying to contain the Selenites with a paltry reserve of fluoride. In an hour their torches will be useless."

"OK, the Weasels are off immediately. Are you coming back?"

"No. I'll stay with the Russians to 'take up the gauntlet.' In an hour I'll send up a space flare so the Weasels can spot us more easily. Over and out."

Turning to the Russians he said, "The Weasels are coming. At 110 miles an hour over bumpy terrain they'll be here in around an hour. In the meantime give me one of those torches."

Colonel Zavkom stared at him a while, then said, "You're a funny man, Dr. Kariven. But you're brave and I like brave men."

The five Russian astronauts who fought on while their chief and Petrov were welcoming the American, had lost ground. They were backing up slowly. Kariven, between Zavkom and Petrov, aimed his torch at the monsters and turned the valve. The jet of purple flames bit deep into the violet shells and stopped them dead in their tracks, quivering on top of the other corpses.

While firing at the metallophage creatures Zavkom, Petrov and Kariven talked about their respective journeys and the adventures of setting up. That was how Kariven learned, in astonishment, that their "seleno-physical" experiment had caused a moonquake that quite accidentally destroyed the soviet spaceship.

"We knew," Colonel Zavkom explained, "that the disaster was an accident. My friend Petrov was the first to come to your defense, arguing that you would certainly have performed experiments by propagating vibrations under the lunar crust. Personally I believed for a moment that you were attacking us. I even suggested awful threats of vengeance against you… and I regret that now after what you are doing for us."

"Well, wouldn't you do the same for us if the roles were reversed?"

"Undoubtedly," the officer admitted, then after a pause he added, "I think your argument concerning people's stupid behavior is correct… *friend*. Brotherly love is not, unfortunately, one of man's dominant virtues."

"I'm glad to hear you say that. It proves that you're evolving. I myself evolved and truly learned to love my fellow man after a brief contact with Men from Outer Space. With them, I learned the magnitude of human stupidity, the bestial blindness that drives men to kill one another when it would be so simple, with a little goodwill, to live as one, happily, on the planet Earth… and even on other planets."

Colonel Zavkom and Petrov looked at each other, not quite understanding.

"What do you mean by 'Men from Outer Space'? Are you referring to your fellow astronauts?"

Kariven tried, not without difficulty in the face of the magnitude of the revelations, to summarize the extraordinary adventure that he and his friends had experienced. When he was finished, it was not surprise that he saw in the eyes of the others, but absolute astonishment.

"So, on the Moon, around 300 miles from this crater, is a huge base, a permanent base established ages ago by the 'men' who come from a solar system that we Earthlings call Polaris?"

"That's the unvarnished truth, Zavkom. And that's why now, using the rational mind of these supra-evolved beings, I think the international disagreements are a little like the bickering of little boys who deserve a good spanking. But before attempting an 'educational crusade' among you, for your own good, the Polarians have to purge the solar system of a ruthless enemy threatening our planet… That's why the Earthlings, above all else, have to be united and think of one another as brothers.

"Don't question me. You'll learn everything you want to know before too long. Now I have to fire the signal flare. The Weasels should be here soon."

CHAPTER NINE

The two steel mammoths mounted on tracks were pushing on through the plain headed for a group of craters. Rolling in a place lacking air, they were kicking up—as happened on Earth—a cloud of dust. The billows of ash spitting out on both sides of the tracks sprinkled down in gentle waves. Soon the bare dust gave way to the Selenites that the Weasels crushed pitilessly. Behind them stretched the long double trail from their tracks filled with brown shells.

Streiler at the wheel of the first Weasel scrutinized the craters and the sky, hoping every second to see the signal flare. Six miles from a crater with gently sloping sides they finally saw a bright red light shoot up into the black sky.

"The flare! They're down there!"

"I saw it too," Lieutenant Clark said as he slowed down. "It came from the crater to the right of that 50-yard wide rift... It won't be easy to climb over the walls covered with Selenites. Look at that mess! I can't see an inch of open ground. The nasty creatures have covered everything."

The Weasels were forced to circle the crater before spotting a part of wall that had collapsed, making a less steep ramp from the plain. Naturally the whole thing was brown and purple with Selenites. The teeming creatures were attacking the walls behind which they knew was the metal food of the rocket and the equipment of the Russian base.

When the Weasels began climbing, Streiler began swearing: the ground seemed to be sinking under the weight of the armored vehicles!

"We're driving on a huge hill of Selenites stacked on top of each other. To form what we thought was a natural slope, these monsters must be piled up 100 feet from the base of the crater. If we want to get through this we're going to have to give it all we've got."

"OK, full speed ahead!"

With the accelerator floored the tracks slid but promptly caught hold and launched the steel mammoths forward. The huge pile of monsters was packed down by the weight of the Weasels that skated over it, sometimes almost tipping over. Speeding up and rearing up, performing one stunt after another, the vehicles continued climbing. Only a few yards from the top Streiler and Clark received a message from the camp:

"Commander Taylor to Patrol S... Commander Taylor to Patrol S..."

"Patrol S here. Go ahead, Commander."

"The Selenites are digging more and more tunnels and coming out in great number beyond the fire zone. We have to use torches more and more often. If the monsters launch more 'sub-lunar' attacks we won't be able to contain them. Get a move on, boys, and come back as quickly as possible. Over."

"Understood, Commander. We'll be back in about two hours. Over."

"Try to make it an hour and a half... *Maximum*. It's bad here. Over and out."

After this message they turned back on their individual transmitters.

"That's all we need!" Clark railed. "There's only six of them at the camp and I bet they're biting their nails."

At the top of the crater they stopped their machines.

"Can we get down the inside slope?" Streiler worried. "I can't see over the front."

Clark's Weasel was leaning farther over to give him a full view. "Everything's OK, Kurt. We can go... and go fast! Look at the Ruskies and Kariven. They're in deep trouble."

In fact, almost all the six fluoride torches were completely run out. The two still working did so in fits and starts, spluttering a weak yellow flame only a few inches long. Petrov and Kariven were handling these two feeble torches, jumping around to face the various fronts. The other astronauts, armed with steel bars, were fighting like they did at first to free the bottom of the rocket covered with the monsters.

The steel bars rose and fell in rhythm on the mounting tide of Selenites that entirely covered the floor several yards thick. In spite of their efforts the men were steadily losing ground. They were gathered in front of Kariven's space taxi. The teeming monsters formed a kind of second crater whose walls were relentlessly closing in.

Kariven's torch went out. In anger he threw it at the monsters and raising the tank over his head threw it as well at the first waves of attack. The heavy tank, though it killed four or five Selenites, was a source of joy to those it did not hit. In seconds its black mass was covered with pink scars. Rolling around under the hungry monsters it crumbled to pieces, cor-roded pieces that finally disappeared under the sacs of the purple metallophages.

From the base that was almost completely destroyed Kariven tore off a section of metal pipe and used it like a club. Backed up against his single-man rocket he defended it against attack, bashing the Selenites like a maniac.

"Hold on, buddy!"

Kariven was startled. These words of encouragement were still echoing in his helmet when he saw the two steel mammoths covered in yellow paint come storming down the southeast slope of the crater. The tractors carved a path by crushing the squirming shells. In five minutes they stopped before the weary survivors. Through their transparent domes Clark and Streiler smiled and waved at the soviet astronauts.

"Climb on, Zavkom," Kariven said. "Split your men be-tween the two vehicles. And make sure they can hold on fast because on the plain the Weasels can reach get up to almost 150 miles an hour. I'll take the lead in the rocket. Good luck!"

Without hearing the Russian officer's thanks, Kariven used the steel pipe to free his space taxi from three giant Sele-nites and after closing the hatch behind him took off. His rear boosters and two side pipes helped the takeoff, pouring a tor-rent of fuel over the monsters.

The seven Russian astronauts lying forward on the back of the Weasels held on tight. With a violent jerk the powerful vehicles skid out of the living "turf" that was already sticking to its tracks.

The inner walls of the crater were scaled at 50 mph. Bouncing from left to right, jolted when a tread hit a stiff pile of purple shells, the Russians did all they could to keep their precarious balance. Once over the top they came down at 100 mph and on the plain they went full speed at almost 150 mph.

Clenching their jaws, trying to keep their helmets from banging against the steel, the Russian astronauts felt worse than during their first test flight in a rocket!

"Well, Kariven, what are the Russians like?" Commander Taylor asked when he landed.

"They've got two arms, two legs, a body and a head, all stuffed unto a spacesuit," Kariven joked. "If you want to talk about their behavior, I think I can assure you that their many mishaps have made them gentle as lambs. They'll be coming here as a consequence... and not as promoters of discord. Events have pacified them."

"And none too soon. We'll welcome them with open arms. But questions remain: What are we going to do? Sharing our rations with them—it'd be inhuman not to—we'll cut in half the length of our stay. That's one! At the end of our shortened stay either we'll all stay here forever or our team will take off and go back to Earth, leaving the Russians to their fate. That's two! And there's no way we can do that either. But since *Daisy* can't take an extra seven men we're stuck in a rut. Plus, *Mickey*, the second spaceship, isn't equipped to transport people. As I said, what are we going to do now?"

Just as Kariven was about to answer, the ground felt like it was shaking under his boots. He jumped to the side and looked down. The lunar dust was moving. It rose up, made a big hump and then erupted as a giant Selenite scrambled through.

"It's starting again!" Commander Taylor was furious as he grabbed his torch. He pointed the flame at the burrow swarming with monsters and told Kariven, "Since they can't get out of the burrows, the moon demons are digging horizontally and coming back up a few yards away. We've been forced to jump all over camp, constantly, to kill the first Selenites coming out of the tunnels. Since they can't break through the ring of fire maintained by the reflectors, they're turning into miners."

Heading at full speed toward the camp, crushing thousands of metallophage creatures in their tracks, the two Weasels appeared on the horizon. The shapes grew bigger to the naked eye.

"Commander Taylor," Professor Harrington called into his mic. "I'm going to stop the reflector beams for ten seconds to let the vehicles through. Cover them and seal off the breach when they're inside the circle. I'll need 17 to 20 seconds of down time to bring the rays back to their optimal performance."

"Got it, Professor. Come with me, Kariven."

The two men, armed with torches, posted themselves 30 feet apart and a few steps back from the zone being continually protected by the heat energy at 3,500°C.

At the edge of the camp the Weasels slowed down. When they were barely 30 feet from the heat zone Professor Harrington abruptly swung away a parabolic reflector: the sweeping spot of light disappeared and the breach was open. The Weasels came through at 50 mph, made a sharp turn and after skidding in the dust stopped near the spaceship *Daisy*.

Following in the wake of the tractors the Selenites crawled surprisingly fast toward the temporary hole in the defense. Commander Taylor and Kariven were up against a massive infiltration. They were attacked from all sides by the insidious slithering of the repulsive creatures.

"Clear the breach!" Professor Harrington shouted into his mic.

The two men jumped back to a respectable distance. Just in time. The reflector was "warmed up" enough to fire its bright 3,500°C cone. Its work of destruction began again. The breach closed up. The Selenites that had infiltrated the circle during the short pause were exterminated with the torches.

A certain unease, a slight coldness followed the arrival of the Russians into the American base. Playing Head of Protocol, Kariven, with Commander Taylor at his side, went to welcome the soviet astronauts as they climbed off the Weasels. After the introductions were made with no formalities Kariven played interpreter for his expedition members to briefly sum up the situation.

"Now we're all here together, not as representatives of opposite sides but as human beings, meaning inhabitants of the same planet in a fight against a common enemy. This enemy is here, facing us, behind us, to the side, everywhere. For now only one thing counts: to close ranks and wait for the final assault. Because we can't fool ourselves, the really big attack hasn't come yet. Look at the horizon just over a mile from here, that gigantic 'wave' of brown and purple coming slowly toward us. That's the bulk of the Selenite troops shuffling along before charging."

"I doubt a massive attack could be stopped by the reflectors heat," Professor Harrington sounded worried.

"At most the stampede will be slowed down," Kariven added.

He had barely finished speaking when a violent shock jolted the ground. The astronauts were thrown off balance, some of them fell into the dust, and the reflectors were shaken out of position, deflecting their rays that went shooting off into other areas inside the camp. Unfortunately, some of the observation and research equipment was in their new line of fire and got liquefied. Kariven's space taxi, whose hatch was still open, was seriously damaged. But by miraculous luck there was no loss of life.

When the moment of surprise had passed the dazed astronauts looked at one another. Then, on the horizon, a column of dust rose up from a crater and came drizzling straight back down.

"That's coming from our crater!" Zavkom grabbed his prismatic binoculars.

"I think I can explain the cause of the moonquake," Petrov declared. "After we left the Selenites must have rushed onto our damaged spaceship, poured in through the gashes and entered all the cabins. They finally reached the holds where our 20 armed missiles were kept... waiting for moonquake experiments."

"That must be it!" Colonel Zavkom agreed. "When the Selenites ate the missiles they must have set off the detonator and caused a missile to explode, which set off all the others. The crazy inferno will pulverize our spaceship and devastate the crater floor."

"Out of every bad some good comes," Kariven philosophized. "And that gives me an idea. Why aren't we attacking the Selenites with our own missiles? The monsters might stop attacking it we bombard them with TNT."

"That's worth a shot," Taylor willingly accepted the proposition on the spot. "Take four men, Kariven, and bring the remaining 25 missiles here. In the meantime I'll set up the mobile launch ramps."

Glad to be of assistance the Russians offered to go with Kariven. He accepted and took Zavkom, Petrov and two other men to *Daisy*. Streiler followed them in his Weasel to carry back the missiles.

Unloading them one by one from the hold using an automatic winch the missiles were grabbed by the strong, telescopic arms of the Weasel and carefully lined up on the rear bed. The Russians' role was simply to guide the explosive cylinders in the claws of the articulated arm. Half an hour later the giant tractor made a tour of the base. Installed in a hurry by the other Russians helping the Americans the five missile launchers each received five missiles.

Now in the international moon camp everyone was working feverishly. The ramps were loaded with their 20-foot long, 3-foot wide missiles. Set up in a circle around the base and aimed to the outside the ramps were ready to go into action.

"Professor Harrington, get ready to cut off your heat rays when we launch the missiles," Kariven advised. "We don't need another incident like what happened with the Russian missiles. As soon as the moonquakes stop, check the reflectors' aim, correct their discrepancies and fire them up again."

"OK. You can start. I'll turn off the rays when the missiles take off."

Kariven talked briefly with Commander Taylor before giving orders in his microphone: "Set the angle of launch for one mile. First salvo, one missile per ramp. Ready?"

"Ready!"

"Fire! Now get down!"

Professor Harrington spun a dial on his control panel to change the angle of the focalizing mirrors and did as the others, throwing himself to the ground.

The five missiles shot into space, their burning rear end flying away, and struck the ground a mile away. Their charge of TNT exploded in absolute silence, throwing up tons of matter and crushing, blasting and pulverizing hundreds of thousands of Selenites. All around the explosion the terrible effects of the shockwave escalated. For almost two minutes the ground trembled violently. One reflector was completely dismantled, its faceted mirrors flying off as the parabolic structure collapsed. A pile of ration crates fell over; a tank of drinking water burst and its contents evaporated. The two spaceships, although huge and sitting solidly on their bases, teetered dangerously, throwing a serious fright into the Earthlings.

At every point of impact, within a range of 500 feet, a new crater was created where the Selenite corpses were piled up. The losses among the monsters were substantial. The bulk of the forces attacking in waves had been dispersed. The massive destruction gave the Earthlings several hours respite while the metallophage creatures regrouped for another attack.

Even at the edge of the base the front ranks were piled up and waiting, motionless, not budging an inch. Professor Harrington used the let-up to once again adjust the parabolic reflectors. Since one of them, however, was out of commission, he took it apart to change the reflecting dome. Once the repairs were finished and the distances corrected the six reflectors went back to work and poured their heat waves over the paralyzed monsters. The Selenites did not even try to move; they just died on the spot. All over the plain they were frozen, petrified with fear of all the moonquakes.

"Take a rest," Commander Taylor ordered his men, "but stay at your post."

Everyone squatted down in the lunar dust, happy to be able to relax a little after the long hours of constant fighting.

"One thing surprises me, Kariven," Taylor confessed. "Why don't your friends the Polarians come to help us? Don't they know that our situation is at the very least... tough, if not desperate?"

"They know, Commander. But they've got other fish to fry right now. They know that we've brought in the crew of the Russian expedition and that with their help we'll organize our defense. What they might not know is that our weapons won't last forever. Our means of defense are, unfortunately, very limited."

"Well, what's so important for them to do?" Colonel Zavkom asked.

"Remember, Zavkom, what I told you about the mission of the Polarians..."

The Russian officer thought for a moment and then remembered an enigmatic statement that Kariven had made. He repeated it as a question. "If I remember correctly, they have to 'purge the solar system of a ruthless enemy threatening our planet'?"

"That's right. And the ruthless enemy..."

He could not finish. Clark's voice was shouting in his helmet, "A flying saucer!"

At these words everyone looked up, scrutinizing the skies. Out of the shimmering constellations in the dark of space a green disc came speeding down, glowing strangely.

Kariven's heart leaped with joy. "The Men from Outer Space are paying us a visit!'

The disc was circling over the base now. It froze for a short while at 1,500 feet altitude, then came straight down.

"It's going to land!"

The captivated astronauts watched the movements of the weird, disc-shaped machine. It landed gently less than 500 feet from their base. Almost 200 feet in diameter it was perfectly circular. An 80-foot high, 30-foot wide tower surmounted it, whose top was rounded into a dome. The spacecraft landed flat, its whole bottom side touching the lunar soil and leaving no free space between it and the Selenites crushed under its colossal weight.

The Earthlings stood agape. No one moved an inch.

"Don't just stand there like statues!" Kariven shouted with joy. "It won't eat you! Professor Harrington, you can turn off the reflectors for a while."

Gladly making the first move Kariven was about to rush through the zone usually swept by the heat rays but he stopped short and hesitated.

In the flying saucer's tower a retractable panel, 15 by 30 feet, was slowly sliding open. The huge doorway opened onto the inside of the craft. Kariven's heart suddenly skipped a beat. An uncontrollable fear choked him. Through the rectangular opening five men in spacesuits had just appeared.

"Get down!" Kariven yelled and he jumped to the closest missile ramp that he maneuvered with surprising skill. "Everyone on the ground, goddamn it!" he roared, aiming the four remaining missiles at the round spaceship.

He pressed the trigger button and in a giant bound fell to the ground 15 feet away. Seeing him do this everyone else, not trying to understand why, did the same, but a layer of dust was already rising up to meet them. A quadruple explosion, terrifying even though silent, had just jolted the lunar surface.

A rain of metal fell upon the base, lifting gusts of chalky ash, digging craters, tearing off rocks and destroying some of the equipment that was still standing after the moonquakes.

When the deluge of metal had let up, the astronauts, half-buried under the ash, risked a glance, at first timidly, then more confidently. The disaster was over. Nothing remained of the flying saucer but a formless mass of metal plates and lumps of machinery among which they could see *hundreds of corpses* in spacesuits horribly mangled.

When Commander Taylor regained his ability to talk he stammered, "Well, Kariven, you, uh… Come on, what got into you to go and blow up the Polarians, the friends of Earthlings?"

No doubt fearing a sudden fit of insanity by Kariven due to edgy nerves after that last 48 hours, he stayed a respectable distance away, his hand on the butt of his Colt, ready to draw and fire at… the madman.

"I didn't have time to explain before acting, Commander," he shook his head. "No, my friends, I'm not crazy. The Space Fever has nothing to do with my apparently disturbing behavior. First of all this flying saucer did not, as I initially thought, have Polarian passengers, those spacemen identical to us. Look, see for yourselves… Come on… Jump over to the wreckage… The Selenites won't attack…"

With the exception of three men staying at the base in case of any mishap, the American and Russian astronauts followed Kariven who started searching through the spaceship debris and dismembered corpses until he found a victim whose suit appeared intact except for a metal shard that had pierced it leaving a one and a half inch hole in the belly.

Kariven squatted down and using a sharp piece of metal split the thick, rubbery material from neck to groin. He ripped it open, tore off the metal helmet that had only a thin horizontal slit at eye level, and in a trembling, angry voice said, "Here's what I mistook for the Polarians!"

The astronauts recoiled in horror on seeing the disgusting corpse: *a body with green skin, covered in horny scales like a lizard!* The green head of the frightening creature had pointy ears and its eyes, opened to death, were red with yellow streaks. Its skull had greenish, fleshy lumps that were glistening like the skin of a toad.

"What is that abomination?"

"It's a Denebian, Commander, an inhabitant of the solar system of the star Deneb, otherwise called Alpha Cygni. These creatures are the staunch enemies of the Men from Space who are constantly hunting them down in our solar system."

"So, that's the monster that the Polarian described to us telepathically when we stumbled upon his base in the Aristarchus crater," Streiler said with a dry throat.

"The Moon," Kariven continued, "is now the site of an interplanetary war... while on Earth men are completely unaware of the danger threatening them and continue their petty quarrelling."

To his companions listening nervously he added, "You Russians and Americans, didn't you just fight side by side, brothers in arms, against a common enemy, the Selenites? In the not too distant future all people of Earth will have to unite, once and for all, to fight against another common enemy, whose corpse you see here all covered with blood... *green blood that is not human!*"

"Watch out!" Clark shouted into his mic. "Another flying saucer!"

A glowing green disc was coming down on the Earthlings at unimaginable speed.

"Get back to camp! It's our only chance!" Kariven shrieked as he bounded forward.

But he stopped right away, imitated by the others who were shaking in the suits, stumbling in the dust. In their heads a strange voice was resounding.

Do not fear, Earthling friends! This is a Polarian talking to you.

Stupefied, all the astronauts listened to this mysterious telepathic voice that just popped up in their minds.

Go back calmly to your camp and I will land.

Without being totally convinced the astronauts obeyed. In spite of the mental reassurance they all wondered if they were not about to fall into clever trap set by the monstrous Denebians. Kariven, however, looked calm and confident.

The flying saucer set down gently on its landing gear made of three metal spheres that rolled around in their electromagnetic housing.

"You see," Kariven explained to his friends, "that landing gear of three spheres is clearly visible, even when the disc is landed. It was, first of all, the absence of this that led me to believe that the other saucer was an enemy. In fact, all the Polarian ships that we saw in the Aristarchus crater had landing gear like this. Secondly, when that other saucer landed no telepathic message come through to us, which was surprising since Clark, Streiler and I got a message right away welcoming us to the base when we went to explore that crater. So, I was surprised not hearing the Polarian thoughts when the disc showed up. And after seeing the ship I knew right away we were in trouble. If I hadn't destroyed that spaceship, the gruesome passengers would certainly have captured us!"

While Kariven explained himself, a platform supported on four telescopic columns descended from the flying saucer. In the middle of the chrome platform stood a Polarian, his legs slightly apart, his thumbs stuck casually in the huge belt of his light green spacesuit fitted with a round, transparent helmet.

With his herculean build the Polarian stood almost six and half feet tall. A lock of his short, brown hair fell over his forehead. His lively face was bronzed, much like the skin of North American Indians. From his belt, on each hip, hung a holster with a kind of big pistol that looked from afar just like a terrestrial gun.

On the shiny platform, at his feet, was a big, cylindrical device, about four feet tall and 15 inches in diameter. Its sides were perforated with countless holes arranged like a checkerboard and it was topped by a kind of control panel with buttons, dials, little screens and blinking lights.

The Man from Outer Space smiled cheerfully, making him look even friendlier. He raised his right hand up to his shoulder as a salute and turned on his tiny, wrist-mounted transmitter.

"I'm glad to meet you, Earthling friends," he spoke in good English. "I bring to you the fraternal greeting of the Polarians. You have proved admirable in fighting against the Selenites. Despite being completely surrounded you didn't give up the fight. Moreover, you Americans open-heartedly saved the Russians from certain death. I followed the event on a televiewer and I congratulate you."

After a brief pause during which he surveyed the monstrous corpses he continued:

"By destroying the Denebian spaceship you showed that you remembered what our enemies look like. What's more, the glowing orb that Kariven, Clark and Streiler saw during their patrol of the dark side was a giant Denebian flying saucer, an enemy astrobase that we had just disintegrated. Its death glow was very interesting to you. But this episode is nothing compared to the epic battle that will break out in your solar system from Mercury to Pluto. So, we need good-hearted Earthlings to fight beside us. But right now, for you, the most important thing is to create an advance guard on Earth… secretly so as not to cause panic among the population. With your help this advance guard or Earth-Polarian Alliance will slowly bring the Earthlings around to admitting the existence of supra-evolved beings from another planet who will defend against the other beings, also more evolved but devoured by their thirst for power. I already know that we can count on you, Kariven…"

Commander Taylor hesitated a moment before speaking. He looked at each of his men, seeing the same determination on their faces. Then he told the Man from Outer Space, "You've got your new allies in us."

Pointing to the survivors of his crew Colonel Zavkom said, "We're also ready to receive orders, Polarian."

"Bravo, friends! I'm proud that I never doubted the Earthlings' open mind. From now on you belong to the Earth-Polarian Alliance that will save your planet. The battle will certainly not take place tomorrow but it is inevitable. And when the Denebians invade your solar system, we'll have organized a huge defense plan."

The Man from Outer Space casually picked up the big cylinder, put it on his shoulder and walked to the center of the American camp, saying, "Just wait a few minutes."

Intrigued, the astronauts watched him bound away and then stop in front of *Daisy* and *Mickey* surrounded by the six parabolic reflectors. The Polarian put the cylinder delicately on the ground, pushed some buttons on the control panel mounted on top of it and after examining the screens pulled down a lever. Satisfied, he glanced one last time at the cylinder before walking calmly back to the Earthlings.

The men suddenly felt their legs tingling, then gradually their entire body. It was not painful, just unpleasant; like pins and needles vibrating inside them, almost like an electric shock but lasting a long time.

"What's that machine do?" Kariven asked. "It's making our bodies tingle."

"Oh that?" the Polarian smiled. "That's a high-frequency 'Radiator' specially designed to work on stars with radical variations in temperature and the total absence of atmosphere magnifies its effect. The waves it constantly emits will kill the Selenites within a half-mile radius. It's not a very powerful one. Our base is equipped with a Radiator that reaches over 60 miles."

The astronauts stood open-mouthed.

"So, all we had to do was simply emit high-frequency waves to keep the Selenites at bay?"

"That's all. Your base is now protected. No Selenite will attack the metal of your spaceships or reflectors. Look around."

Indeed, within half a mile around the camp the brown and purple shells had stopped moving. Beyond this range the monsters were retreating, slowly at first, then faster and faster, leaving pinkish drool between them and the corpses.

But a new phenomenon suddenly captured everyone's attention. Little by little the blinding light of the lunar sun was waning.

"What's going on?" Taylor was astonished to see this weird darkening of the lunar day.

"What do you mean?" the Polarian replied. "Don't you remember that according to your measurement of time May 24, 1956 from 12:55 to 18:27 there's an eclipse of the Moon? At 15:31 it will be total."

"Good grief, that's right!" Professor Harrington exclaimed. "Our astronomical calendars calculated it precisely. The event was put on the back burner in our minds because of all the devastating adventures we just lived through."

"The Selenites didn't forget," the Polarian declared. "They know—through some kind of atavistic memory, I suppose—that in a very short time the Moon will be plunged into total darkness. I won't go so far as to say that they understand this phenomenon of the Moon entering the Earth's shadow, but they were waiting impatiently for your reflectors to lose the sunrays and stop working so they could enter your camp. Under cover of darkness it wouldn't have taken them long to destroy you. Your spaceships and all your equipment would be at their mercy to reduce to metallic dust in a few hours."

At this news the astronauts could not hold back a nervous shiver. Once again they had barely escaped death. Without the arrival of the Polarian, Operation Aphrodite would have seen its last.

"It's time to leave, friends," the Man from Outer Space watched the gradual darkening of the gloomy moonscape. "I'll offer you to stay temporarily in our permanent base. Tomorrow you can come back here to finish your selenographic studies and make your repairs. When you're done you can go back to Earth on board your rockets... carrying Selenites full of platinum! Since the Russian Earthlings have lost their spaceship we'll bring them back home ourselves and then come back to Woonka, our lunar base. But, my Earthling Friends, we won't be separated for long."

A few minutes later, as Earth's shadow eclipsed the Moon, the flying saucer took off. Glowing with a strange green light it headed straight for the Aristarchus crater, the mysterious bowl where astronomers on Earth sometimes see inexplicable flashes of light[55].

In the cockpit with glowing walls, the brave American and Russian astronauts, united in the same battle, thought worriedly about the fantastic, sublime adventure that lay ahead. A future full of unknown dangers and terrifying risks but also of great hope: the total unification of the peoples of Earth and the expansion of Man into the infinite, inhabited worlds of our Universe.

---

[55] True. (Author's Note)

JIMMY GUIEU

L'homme de l'Espace

★★ANTICIPATION★★

Editions
"Fleuve Noir"

THE MAN FROM OUTER SPACE

During a recent scientific assembly held in the USA, a scientist might have produced photographs and documents offering irrefutable concrete proof of the existence, on our planet, of extra-terrestrial visitors.

-- Excerpt from *The Saucerian*, Vol. II, No. 1

CHAPTER ONE

At the wheel of his cream-colored Kaiser,[56] Dr. Jean Kariven was driving slowly. Next to him the geophysicist Michel Dormoy and in the back seat the ethnographer Robert Angelvin were calmly smoking cigarettes. For eight days the three friends had been enjoying a little *chilling out* by visiting all of California, from north to south and east to west.

"This is a nice change from the Antarctic ice[57]," Dormoy said, glancing at the yuccas and palm trees that were starting to line the road leading to Los Angeles.

Kariven nodded and smiled at the remark.

Over the course of these past few years, the three explorers had lived through a great many rather extraordinary adventures. Working for the National Center for Scientific Research, their jobs had earned them a well-deserved celebrity.

The "dean" of the team was Kariven, anthropaleontologist, 33 years-old. His athletic build, his black, well-groomed moustache and his virile, handsome appearance made him look strangely like Clark Gable.

In the back seat, with his legs stretched out casually, Angelvin was humming a tune, smoking a cigarette and contemplating the landscape that the early twilight painted cobalt blue. "Are we still far from Los Angeles?" asked, shifting into a more comfortable position to daydream. "You want to take a look at the map, Michel?"

---

[56] Kaiser Motors (formerly Kaiser-Frazer) Corporation made automobiles at Willow Run, Michigan, United States, from 1945 to 1953. In 1953, Kaiser merged with Willys-Overland to form Willys Motors Incorporated, moving its production operations to the Willys plant at Toledo, Ohio. The company changed its name to Kaiser Jeep Corporation in 1963.

[57] See *The Forgotten World*, q.v. (Author's Note).

After a minute looking at the unfolded map on his knees Dormoy replied, "We left Desert Center at three o'clock. Box Springs is far behind us. If we speed up we can be there around eight."

The anthropologist leaned heavier on the gas pedal and the Kaiser, smooth and silent, reached 55 miles an hour. Its headlights skimmed the straight road with their bright beams.

Six miles outside of Redlands, Kariven suddenly slowed down. A dark Cadillac was in ditch 200 yards up ahead, tilted to one side. The Kaiser parked close to the crashed luxury car. The three friends rushed over but they reached the rear door they stopped, astounded. Coming from the inside the car a groggy voice was torturing a popular song.

Wearing a gray raincoat and a bright-colored shirt a man was singing, slumped in the front seat. His song was peppered with hiccups. Lying at the feet of the crooner was a flask of scotch, stuck between the brake and gas pedals.

"There truly is a God for drunks!" Dormoy laughed with his mind at ease. "This guy must not have been driving too fast because only the Cadillac's left fender is damaged."

With a beaming smile on his lips the man was snoring like a locomotive now. Kariven pushed him over and sat behind the wheel. In spite of all his efforts the car would not budge.

"Ah! Well, let's let him sleep it off and we'll tell the sheriff in Redlands. A ticket won't hurt this…"

The anthropologist broke off when he heard the sound of footsteps.

A young man, at least six feet tall, was walking down the road toward them. Elegantly dressed in a dark gray suit, with brown, wavy hair but cut short, he stopped in front of the travelers and nodded hello. "Anyone hurt?" he asked in a warm, deep voice with a slight accent that was hard to identify.

"No, luckily. The driver of the Cadillac was drunk, that's all."

The stranger leaned through the open window and studied the face of the sleeping drunkard.

"Do you know him?" Angelvin asked.

"No. I don't know anyone around here."

"We're going to tell the Sheriff in Redlands about it. Do you need a ride somewhere?" Kariven offered.

"That'd be great," the drifter said. "I was hoping to catch a bus in Redlands to go to Los Angeles."

"We're going to Los Angeles. Why not come with us?"

Visibly delighted the man accepted and sat in the Kaiser next to Kariven.

When they got to Redlands they stopped the car on Main Street in front of a small, whitewashed building housing the Sheriff and his squad of policemen: five men in all! Kariven had to give his name and address, recount their story and point out in a wall map where the Cadillac had crashed. After all this he got back on the road.

"That drunk made us lose 45 minutes!" Dormoy grumbled.

Kariven drove fast. Without saying anything, he offered a cigarette to his passenger who hesitated to accept.

"Help yourself," the anthropologist finally said. "You can light it yourself," and he held out his lighter in one hand without letting go of the wheel with the other.

The man nodded a thank you and examined the lighter, turning it over in his hands. After a few seconds, he managed to get a flame lit, then he handed it back to Kariven who was surprised by the oddity.

The anthropologist watched him out of the corner of his eye. In the light of the flame his calm, energetic face looked curiously tan. Until now the falling darkness had not allowed the Frenchman to see the stranger clearly. In the flickering light, however, dancing over his face, the anthropologist could see the drifter's bronzed but elegant face.

The cream-colored Kaiser cruised through the suburbs of Pasadena, quickly passed Glendale and crossed the Figueroa bridge over the Los Angeles River before it soon got onto

Sunset Boulevard, the famous street in Hollywood that was lined with rich houses behind wonderful, exotic gardens.

The stranger thanked the three travelers and got dropped off at the corner of Figueroa Street so they could continue on to their hotel at 6811 Hollywood Boulevard.

"That guy wasn't too talkative," Dormoy commented as they entered the sumptuous lobby of the Hollywood Hotel. "He didn't open his mouth the entire trip."

The elevator brought them to the ninth floor where they found their rooms.

"Are you sure you want to go with us tonight, Kariven?" Angelvin asked. "You're really not interested in the *Mocambo*[58]?"

Kariven smiled and shook his head. "I'd rather go to the third Flying Saucers Convention[59] that's being held downstairs later on. You go to the *Mocambo* and I'll meet you there when the meeting's over."

"You could just read the report tomorrow morning in the papers," Angelvin suggested. "Even on vacation you run out on us to investigate this problem of flying saucers."

The anthropologist laughed. "Oh, I know you two. You'd rather investigate the girls in the nightclubs."

More than 1,500 people were in the Hollywood Hotel's convention room. On a stage, sitting behind a long table, six men of different ages were holding the audience breathless by reporting the latest salient facts concerning "unidentified flying objects," otherwise known as "Flying Saucers."

Foreign investigators belonging to various research groups were spread out in the first row. Officers from the US

---

[58] Famous nightclub located on Sunset Boulevard in Hollywood. (Author's Note) 8588 sunset Blvd; it opened in 1941 and closed in 1958.

[59] The first convention was organized by the group Flying Saucers International and took place at he Hollywood Hotel on August 16-18, 1953. (Author's Note)

Air Force and the ATIC[60] were listening attentively to one speaker after another. Although they often showed the greatest skepticism, they were no less interested.

In fact, the US Air Force and the ATIC refused to admit officially the extra-terrestrial origin of the mysterious aircraft. Some rumors to the contrary were running through the public but the officials did indeed stay prudently reserved by refusing openly to admit or deny any hypothesis put forward.

The journalists in the front row were eagerly jotting down notes. Some of them had portable video recorders to tape the proceedings. Sometimes a flash would flood the face of famous speaker with a bright light. Because there was no lack of celebrities at this meeting of specialists, notably George Adamski, Fred Scully, Max B. Miller, Orfeo Angelucci, Williamson, George Van Tassel and others[61].

Wearing a tuxedo because he was going to meet his friends afterward at the *Mocambo*, Kariven had trouble finding a seat in audience that was hanging on the speakers' every word. The last speaker finished his presentation around 12:30 am. In the middle of the crowd slowly trickling toward the exit Kariven suddenly found himself face to face with the stranger

---

[60] Air Technical Intelligence Center, an American governmental organization headquartered at Wright Patterson Air Force Base in Dayton, Ohio, whose purpose is to investigate all phenomena related to flying saucers. (Author's Note). The ATIC was created in May 1951, under the direct command of the Air Materiel Control Department. In 1961 ATIC became the Foreign Technology Division (FTD) which was reassigned to Air Force Systems Command (AFSC). In October 1993, FTD became the National Air Intelligence Center as a component of the Air Intelligence Agency, and was recently renamed the National Air and Space Intelligence Center (NASIC) in 2003.

[61] Famous authors of books about flying saucers and specialists in the study of the phenomena. (Author's Note) Williamson is George Hunt Williamson.

whom he had met a few hours earlier in the deserted road. Just like the anthropologist he was wearing a tuxedo.

An inscrutable smile lit up the tanned man's face. "How do you do?" he held out his hand to Kariven. Then, looking around at the crowd, he added, "Americans seem to be particularly interested in flying saucers, don't you think?"

"Americans in particular but the world in general," Kariven agreed, elbowing through the crowd to stay up with the man. "You're not American, then…?"

Avoiding the question and probably not wanting to give his name, the stranger sidestepped the question. "In fact, I'm not American. But you're not either, if I'm not mistaken?"

"I'm French. My name is Jean Kariven, and I'm an anthropaleontologist."

A surge separated them for a few seconds and when they found each other before the huge Plexiglas doors of the hotel Kariven could not remember if the stranger had introduced himself.

Walking side by side down Hollywood Boulevard they went 100 yards without talking, lost in their thoughts. The tanned man decided to break the silence. "Isn't there somewhere in Los Angeles where people dress up in crazy clothes and cover their faces with masks?" he asked trying to find the appropriate word.

"Do you mean a costume ball?" Kariven was surprised by the long verbiage for such a banal place.

"Costume ball, that's it."

"Certainly. My two friends are at the *Mocambo* right now. It's a club where there's a costume night tonight. Let's go meet them. You're in a tuxedo like me, which isn't breaking the rules that require either formal dress or a costume."

The big, bright dance floor of the *Mocambo* was crowded with dancers, some in tuxedos, others in costumes. There were the customary dukes and duchess, pierrots and harlequins, Tarzans in leopard skins, "Daughters of the Wild" trying to look like Dorothy Lamour, even some funny lads decked out in hobo rags. In a much more modern and trendy style men and women got up in spacesuits complete with plastic helmets—as we sometimes see in comics and science fiction books—playing astronauts escaping from the authorities... or rather from galactic rocket ships.

But the highlight of the costume party was undoubtedly the three bizarre people—one man and two women—like something straight out of science fiction. The man and his companions had covered their bodies with a green, scaly substance that in the spotlights of the dance floor looked like multicolored jasper but mostly green. They all wore orange jackets decorated with expert embroidery and dotted with sparkling gems. A kind of cap covered their heads and ears with flaps coming down over their cheeks and joined under the chin. A black mask hid the top of their faces. Big gloves went up to their elbows and on their feet they wore riding boots. A red and black bodysuit completed their original, very striking costume. The man was dancing with one of the young women, the other being occupied with a spirited Tarzan.

When Kariven and his untalkative companion crossed the dance floor—not without difficulty—full of waving arms and slithering bodies, something unexpected happened.

As if under a spell, the man and the two women with green skin suddenly stopped dancing. They looked furtively at each other, and then smiling together they started spinning round. The anthropologist's companion flinched in surprise. His face, however, quickly resumed its usual calm. But the brief change had not gone unnoticed by Kariven.

Before they reached the far end of the dance floor where Dormoy and Angelvin were sitting, the tanned man put his hand on the explorer's arm. "Excuse me, Mr. Kariven, but I don't feel like sitting down right away. Would you mind ingesting a beverage with me at the bar of this establishment?"

Kariven stared at him, intrigued by his unusual language, then he accepted. They turned to the right, left the dance floor behind, and went to the bar on the air-conditioned terrace.

"Would you like to sit here?" the stranger pointed to a table off to the side of the almost deserted terrace.

The anthropologist noticed that a huge pillar blocked them from the dance floor. When the waiter brought them their cocktails, Kariven offered a cigarette to his strange companion and gave him a light.

"I still haven't got used to these little things that you call lighters."

"That *I call* lighters!" Kariven raised an eyebrow. "What do *you* call these little things?"

The man smiled, was about to answer but said nothing. His smile disappeared, immediately replaced by a weird expression, hard and brutal. His eyes stared at the Plexiglas wall of the air-conditioned terrace.

Kariven looked as well and noticed that the plastic had a mirror effect. They could see the three green-skinned dancers hopping onto the stools at the bar. Their backs were turned to them but the long mirror reflected the image of the table where Kariven and the stranger were sitting. Through the black velvet masks the trio had their six eyes riveted on the reflected image of the tanned-skinned man.

Kariven, slightly taken aback, watched on without understanding. The muscles on the stranger's face tightened up. He gritted his teeth. His eyes, with dilated pupils, *shined like a mirror under a bright spotlight.* Gradually beads of sweat pearled on his forehead creased in concentration. On the table his clenched fists were turning his knuckles white.

"Are you… are you ill?" Kariven asked worriedly.

The man did not answer.

The anthropologist waited a minute, then put his hand on the other's arm. Astonished, he pulled back abruptly. By this simple contact *he had just felt a sting like from an electric charge.*

"What's wrong with you?"

The man stayed mute, his face tense and rigid, his eyes frozen in an expression of dreadful hate.

All of a sudden, at the bar, the sound of broken glass followed by a loud thump made Kariven jump. The three masked dancers, painted green under their orange jackets, were lying motionless at the foot of their stools in a pool of glass from their broken drinks.

Stunned, his mouth hanging open, Kariven wanted to get up and run over but a firm grip held him back. "It's no use, Mr. Kariven. *They're dead...*"

The anthropologist slumped back in his chair and with a trembling hand grabbed his drink. He took a loud, impolite swig and finally managed to blabber, "How do you know that they're... dead?"

Without answering the man stood up. "Let's get out of here, quick!"

"But..." Kariven tried to resist.

Dancers and drinkers were rushing toward the bar. Women screamed, some fainted. Only those who had drunk too much kept singing at their tables, blowing on party favors and clumsily slapping balloons at others unaware of the drama.

"Nobody leaves!" a man in a tuxedo ordered. He stood blocking the door with a Colt 45 in each hand.

Some women screamed again, louder. Other women, preferring to live up to their customary expectations, purposely fainted. A shock wave ran through the crowd of *Mocambo* customers who were upset and offended at being mixed up in God-knows-what scandal. The words "poisoned," "heart attack" and other diagnostics jumped from mouth to mouth. A police siren could be heard, which only aggravated the emotional reactions.

"Come on, Mr. Kariven!" the man dragged him away.

The anthropologist followed, wondering if he might not be incriminating himself by escaping like an accomplice. They dashed around the tables on the deserted terrace and headed for the front door. But before the door was the man in the tuxedo waving his two huge Colts.

"Go back into the room," he barked, pointing with the gun in his right hand.

Undisturbed, Kariven's companion mumbled, "Let me take care of this, Mr. Kariven."

He looked straight into the guard dog's eyes and kept advancing. The menacing tuxedo opened his mouth but did not utter a word. He stepped aside, let the two men pass by and took up his position again, legs apart, ready to push back anyone who got the idea of leaving.

Kariven, more and more astonished, found himself in the garden. The wailing sirens were slowly fading away. The squad cars had stopped in front of the *Mocambo*. Six policemen, guns drawn, were rushing into the nightclub.

Kariven and the stranger crossed the garden, went down a path bordered by sweet-smelling mimosas and magnolias and left unhindered through a door on Loma Vista, a quiet alley.

They walked 100 yards up to Sunset Boulevard where the two men silently climbed into the Kaiser and Kariven started it up. Two police cars sped by them and screeched to a halt in front of the *Mocambo*.

Kariven drove slowly. In the middle of the boulevard a policeman was controlling traffic, yelling out, "Drive on, keep moving..."

The anthropologist was about to do just that when among the customers leaving the nightclub and being put into the squad cars he saw his friends Dormoy and Angelvin. Before he had a chance to call out to the policeman, his companion nudged him with his knee.

Kariven stayed quiet and started gritting his teeth. Then he grumbled, "They're my friends. I can't just sit here and..."

"Yes, of course. But a regular of the *Mocambo* or better yet *a policeman in a tuxedo mingling with the dancers* might recognize us and find it strange that we're driving calmly outside when no one was supposed to leave except to get into those police cars."

264

"You're a funny guy," Kariven said. "You don't call a lighter a lighter, you say 'ingest a beverage' instead of get a drink and... *you murder people just by looking at them!*"

A smile—cynical or simply amused?—crossed the stranger's lips. "And yet I didn't 'murder' the federal agent who was blocking our way out of the establishment... sorry, the *Mocambo*. I just suggested to him mentally to let us leave."

"So, essentially, you admit to having killed those three harmless dancers?" Kariven slammed on the brakes in front of the South Spring office of the FBI. "Get out!" he ordered, grabbing him roughly by the arm. He let go right away. An unpleasant tingling shook his body from head to toe.

"Don't be ridiculous, Mr. Kariven, just kept driving until we get around five miles from Upland[62]. I praise your honesty but I assure you that you did nothing wrong by sneaking out of the *Mocambo* with me. I recognize that I look like an... unusual murderer because it was I, in fact, who killed those three... 'harmless dancers' as you say. But don't you also say 'all's fair in love and war'?"

Kariven frowned and started driving again, taking Colorado Boulevard to get out of Pasadena[63]. "But we're not at war!" the anthropologist complained with a shrug. "Whatever you think, I'm now an accomplice of your triple murder since I'm helping you escape."

The stranger shook his head. "*We* are at war but that's another story. You, however, Mr. Kariven, are not my accomplice. *You're going to become my ally...* Touch my arm, my friend. Touch it," he insisted before his surprised passenger.

Kariven took one hand off the wheel and touched the sleeve of the eerie murderer's tuxedo. He did not feel the awful tingling that he had felt two times before.

---

[62] A town around 25 miles to the east of Los Angeles. (Author's Note)

[63] A suburb to the north-east of Downtown Los Angeles. (Author's Note)

"Well? No reaction?"

"None," Kariven wondered what this was all about.

"Do it again now."

"Damn!" the anthropologist cursed as he pulled back his hand.

"Have you ever heard of 'murderers' who can kill *simply by concentrating their will?* Who can produce electric currents anywhere from a few volts to over 500 volts and electrocute a human?"

"You... You have this power?" Kariven stuttered.

"*We* have this power and many others besides... which is how I chose you."

"We're five or six miles from Upland," Kariven stopped the Kaiser on the shoulder of the road. Suddenly realizing the significance of the stranger's declaration the explorer shuddered. "Chose me? Why?"

"Because you bear *the Mark*, Mr. Kariven... I saw it on your hands."

"But I didn't... What mark? I don't remember you examining my hands."

"I didn't see it with my eyes *but with my mind*. You put this phenomenon among the extra-sensory perceptions and call it 'remote viewing' or 'supravision,' right?"

"Hmm... sure," Kariven agreed. "But what mark are you talking about?"

"Open your hands."

The anthropologist obeyed and held out his hands, palms upward, in the light of the dashboard.

"There's the Mark you have, very prominent," the stranger pointed to *a particular mark formed by a no less particular arrangement of the lines on his hand.* "Don't think that I'm playing fortune teller. This palm reading pseudo-science—Chiromancy—only makes charlatans rich at the expense of the gullible who believe them. No, Mr. Kariven, this has nothing to do with the trickery of any of those dream peddlers. "You have the Mark. Your friends Dormoy and Angelvin also, as well as a few researchers who were talking tonight at the meeting of people interested in what you call Flying Saucers."

"OK, I've got the Mark," Kariven gave in, skeptical. "And you deduce what from it?"

"That you belong to the New Race. To the race being born that will gradually supplant the men of the Ancient Era before the Atomic Age here on Earth. Scientists, researchers, artists, writers, engineers and even a few so-called Average Americans and Average Frenchmen... also have the Mark... without even knowing the profound meaning of it. You belong to the Future Race, Mr. Kariven, the race that one day will wipe out the stupidities of this world, overturn the present dogmas, destroy the inanities and injustices of today in order to establish the Golden Age of Civilization that once preceded yours in the long-forgotten past.

"Think about it, Mr. Kariven. Don't you feel like a stranger in this world, in *your world?* Without sounding like a cliché, don't you feel like a stranger to the pettiness that poisons existence? Are you satisfied with Life, Society, people and things as they are and not as they should be? Don't you aspire to something better, more beautiful, more sublime than the swamp where Humanity is floundering and this in spite of the semblance of evolution and technology it has reached today?"

Kariven looked at his passenger for a long time before responding. "Yes, naturally. You're saying, in fact, what many others and I have always thought. But even if all men and women bearing the Mark get together, how could they change the world? A social revolution on a planetary scale is not a reform that proceeds inevitably from a common decree. 'Moral progress' does not go hand in hand with technical progress, which always precedes it. These asymmetrical progressions—separated by a gulf of trial and error—are, moreover, the cause of slow human evolution. A war advances technology by forcing peoples to search in all fields for a technical way to defeat the enemy. But we can't want a third world war..."

The bronze-skinned man stared at him and spoke slowly and carefully. "The war has been going on, Mr. Kariven, *for centuries*. You saw a little incidence of it at the *Mocambo*."

"The three dancers in costumes?"

The man nodded. "That… man and those two women I killed were not dancers. Nor were they men and women… in the sense you would understand it."

Kariven raised an eyebrow and stammered out, "They… you mean they were… not human?"

"Exactly. What you thought was green paint *was their real skin*. And what you believed to be a costume was nothing other than their usual clothes."

"What! There exists, on Earth, a parallel humanity whose specimens have that awful, scaly skin like a reptile?"

The stranger shook his head, "Not on Earth, Mr. Kariven. I told you that these beings are not human… *They come from another world!*"

CHAPTER TWO

Kariven took a moment to grasp the astonishing magnitude of this revelation. He took a nervous drag off his cigarette, walked the length of the car and looked up into the starry night sky, thoughtfully.

"These beings with green, scaly skin," his odd companion continued, "who look more or less like Earthlings, have come to your planet to study you. They walk around briefly only at night and don't mingle with humans except in the places called 'costume parties,' where they can pass for disguised dancers. During the day they spy on you from the skies on board their spaceships."

"At costume parties? That's unbelievable!"

"Perhaps, but it's the absolute truth. Twice already I've been able to eliminate these extra-terrestrial spies. Tonight, however, it wasn't done discreetly. Their three wills together were focused on mine. I couldn't make them leave the *Mocambo*. Outside it would have been easy to guide them to a deserted place... and eliminate them *completely* without leaving the slightest trace. But their psychic barriers were fused and I had to strike them down right there and it wasn't easy, as you saw by my tense expression, warped by the concentration of my supra-normal abilities."

"Where do they come from? And why are they watching us?"

"These green beings—the *Ptopans*—come from the planet Ptopan in the Omink solar system. For you Earthlings Omink is not a solar system. Your rudimentary astronomical instruments cannot detect the seven planets revolving around the star you call Deneb."

"Deneb!" the anthropologist exclaimed. "The Alpha star in the constellation Cygnus! But this sun is 400 light years[64] away from us!"

"Indeed," the stranger confirmed unemotionally. "These Ptopans—or Denebians if you prefer—are trying to get to know more about you... so they can take over your planet later. Earth, Mars and Venus are targeted. Your three worlds are in what the Denebians think is their *zone of influence*, a zone of space that they intend to colonize."

Kariven flicked his cigarette butt into the grassy ditch, then after lighting another he asked, "Who are you, then, that you know all this? If your story isn't a bunch of hogwash."

His face set in all seriousness, the other responded slowly, "My name is Zimko. I come from the planet Kodha, a world almost exactly like yours but that revolves around the Pole Star."

Kariven's eyes opened wide. "You... You're a *Man from Outer Space* too?"

Zimko the Polarian smiled, "Man from Outer Space? Why, yes."

"But how could a being like you, coming from a planet of the Pole Star—a sun 300 trillion miles away—choose me and not someone else... and why me?"

"The history of our civilization has kept a detailed account of your fabulous adventures when you traveled into the past[65]."

"You're an *Instructor*, a *Dragon of Wisdom*[66]!" the anthropologist exclaimed excitedly. "So, your race has always existed?"

---

[64] The distance traveled by light in one year at 300,000 km/second or around 10 trillion km, i.e. 6 trillion miles. (Author's Note)

[65] See *The Time Spiral*. (Author's Note)

[66] Thus the ancient traditions, notably *The Secret Doctrine* y Mme. H.P. Blavatsky, calls super-evolved beings who, in Earth's distant past, came to our planet to instruct humanity;

"It is indestructible, my friend. It evolves but doesn't disappear. Hundreds of millions of years ago, we spread around the Universe and instructed the worlds with races of thinking beings. Our mission is to educate the primitive species or to guide the advance races on new paths to lead them away from the errors and dangers that threaten them. The Earth and your solar system in general are in danger right now. The Earthlings suspect nothing because they're busy with their usual petty problems: the cold war and quarrelsome demands of the international assemblies that keep them from opening their eyes.

"Those who are on the path of truth are ridiculed and scorned. Didn't you notice the stupid comments by the skeptics and deniers at the conference about flying saucers tonight? The investigators from various research organizations who spoke, professed the existence of UFOs as extraterrestrial vehicles and weren't booed off stage, of course, but like me you felt the audience's lack of belief in what they said."

"So, flying saucers represent a threat to our world?"

Zimko nodded, "For Mars and Venus as well because these two planets each have their own civilization, different from yours, but still targets for the Denebians."

"Except in rare cases, however, flying saucers don't appear to be hostile to Earthlings. They just fly over a city or an area, sometimes exciting the population but doing nothing that

---

see *The Flying Saucers Come from Another World*, q.v. (Author's Note) Helena Blavatsky's (1831-1891) *The Secret Doctrine, the Synthesis of Science, Religion and Philosophy*, was first published as two volumes in 1888; the first named *Cosmogenesis*, the second *Anthropogenesis*. It was an influential example of the revival of interest in esoteric and occult ideas in the modern age, in particular because of its claim to reconcile ancient eastern wisdom with modern science. Blavatsky claimed that its contents had been revealed to her by *mahatmas* who had retained knowledge of humanity's spiritual history, knowledge that it was now possible, in part, to reveal.

could be qualified as an attack. There was indeed that jet of Captain Mantell that was apparently shot down by a flying saucer, as well as four or five fighter jets and bombers that, it might seem, suffered the same fate. However, there's no positive proof that these aerial disasters were actually caused by flying saucers."

"You have to make a distinction, Kariven, because there are really two different kinds of spaceships that you call flying saucers. Some are hostile and spy on you intensively. These are the Denebians who struck down several of your fighter jets and bombers. The other saucers soaring through Earth's skies are totally peaceful: *they are our spaceships*. You Earthlings can't tell the difference between the two similar ships. And this is exactly what will become the most dangerous thing for you... because the Denebians are getting ready to invade the Earth."

"But we have to alert the authorities!" the scientist exploded.

"No, my friend," Zimko shook his head, "the time has not yet come. Besides, it's not strictly necessary since the Special Branch of the Air Technical Intelligence, which investigates the apparitions of flying saucers, has finally faced the facts. The federal agents in this unit have understood that the wild explanations of these phenomena don't stand up to systematic study. Weather balloons, meteors, collective hallucinations, lightning balls, temperature inversions and 'secret weapons' are nonsense that satisfies the ignorant and the usual skeptics who are blinded by an outdated anthropocentrism... or simple hypocrisy.

"The Pentagon *knows* that flying saucers come from another world. An accident in 1952 led them to discover the truth. In the summer of 1952 your scientists were experimenting on a Super V2 in the New Mexico desert. Over 150 miles high, at full speed, the rocket smashed into a flying saucer going almost 5,000 miles an hour. There was a huge explosion—inaudible at that altitude—and the two machines crashed to the ground, demolished and unrecognizable. The technicians at White Sands had seen the blinding flash and the radar men observed the disaster on their radarscope: the V2, a bright spot, hit another bright spot, but bigger, i.e. a flying saucer.

"Among the mangled debris spread over miles of land your scientists found two mutilated corpses, two horrible corpses with green, scaly skin. Nevertheless, a partial reconstruction allowed them to notice their similar morphology to Earthlings. But these green monsters were not Earthlings! The Pentagon reacted. Security measures were taken and strict silence was imposed. Nobody talked about the 'incident' but special agents of the ATIC were doubly vigilant in watching the deserts and isolated areas, setting up 75 observation bases around the world for detecting flying saucers[67], and in the end exchanging information all the time with England and Canada about these mysterious machines. In a word, it was on general alert... but the public knew nothing about it and still knows nothing. Only the independent investigative organizations, long before this incident, had become convinced that flying saucers were not the work of men."

"But why this insistent silence?" the anthropologist spoke up. "It makes no sense to keep the people ignorant of an imminent danger."

"The higher authorities fear a general panic. Imagine the global effect of an announcement of this sensational news if the President of the USA were to sound the alarm? First of all they would have to prepare the public gradually and prudently. They'd have to lead it slowly into accepting the possibility of the existence of intelligent beings on other planets. America, where science fiction is popular, is already inclined to admit this but Europe, the old country, denies these hypotheses that it considers pure fiction.

"When the Earthlings become truly aware of the ships watching them, it will be necessary to propose, by degrees, that other planetary races in the Universe *might* be war-

---

[67] True. (Author's Note)

hungry, *might* be targeting this solar system. Likewise they'll have to understand that there are also races like them, motivated by good intentions toward them and liable to come to Earth some day. This would be our race, Kariven, the Instructors from the Pole Star.

"Therefore, we need allies on this globe. Men like you will be needed by us to save humanity. We prefer to choose first the Earthlings bearing The Mark rather than getting directly in touch with the governments... And you can understand why..."

Kariven, stunned by these revelations, hazarded, "Are you referring to the conflict between the East and West?"

"That's right. The world is divided into two camps. If we Polarians made a pact to help the United States, for example, the Russians would likely accuse us of provocation, of partiality. The opposite is also true. But by only contacting scientists and men of good will who we can trust, men bearing The Mark, in all the countries of the world, in America as well as in Europe and Russia, we have a better chance of getting their governments' cooperation when we reveal ourselves officially. For, the day will come when we will contact all the governments on Earth and appoint all the different men we've made pacts with for man's security. We know that we can trust certain investigators working for the many Commissions in every country studying the still mysterious—for humans—phenomenon of flying saucers."

"You told me just now that the war's been going on for centuries?"

"On the cosmic level, yes. The Denebians are striving by any means possible to conquer the defenseless worlds. Yours is one of them. Because your guns and jet fighters, your ships and atomic warheads won't be much help against the Denebian flying discs capable of unimaginable speeds. We've been fighting for centuries against these space pirates. Our two races hold thousands of planets and solar systems in the Galaxy. But whereas we join with the primitive or under-evolved peoples to help them to develop, the Denebians enslave them by force."

Kariven was thoughtful for a long while before deciding to speak. "What you say disturbs me, Zimko, but I wonder why our detection devices have never spotted the slightest trace of a frequency or the faintest radio or video signal coming from the flying saucers. Because you'd have to communicate between ships, right?"

"Between ships in the same squadron as well as with our astrobases—the 'flying cigars' to you—or even with our planetary bases, we use two means of communication that are both absolutely impossible for you to capture or intercept. Or else we use a viewer that broadcasts on frequencies unknown on Earth, meaning they're based on the gravity/electromagnetic principle, a variation of the energy we use for propulsion, or else we just communicate by mental waves, a kind of super-telepathy... That's how we learned five or six languages on Earth, Mars and Venus."

"But how can you run around in the open on our planet? Aren't you afraid of being rounded up some day? That would force you to..."

"Look at this," Zimko broke in, holding out a passport and ID with the name Ronald Allington, American citizen, traveling salesman, resident of Chandler, a small town in Arizona.

"And this is... fake?"

"My papers are genuine," Zimko informed him. "The civil records in Chandler, Arizona really do have all the information printed on this ID and passport..." He waved the two under his chin casually and smiled slyly, "Hypnosis opens all doors to us. In the presence of a Polarian the civil servants are as gentle as lambs and take pleasure in drawing up any documents we ask for. One simple mental suggestion is enough for a fussy, nitpicking bureaucrat to become our ally and we get a genuine, middle class Earthling past."

A suspicion started tickling Kariven. "But... money? How do you get the money you need for your life here?"

275

The Man from Outer Space shook his head in amusement. "No, Kariven, rest assured. We never use hypnosis except for perfectly honest deals that don't hurt anyone else. We've never robbed a cent or counterfeited the currency on the worlds we visit. On your planet gold is king. We bring gold with us and just sell it to jewelers or anyone else willing to make the transaction. Hypnotic suggestions are helpful to smooth out any difficulties or reticence from the buyer of our precious metals.

"On Venus, for example, gold has no value. The natives, you see, are not evolved enough to extract it from the ground where it lies in abundance in its native state. The Venusians, however, take us for Gods. Therefore, we have no need to worry about cheating them and we've established a permanent observation base there. The same goes for Mars where, on the contrary, the civilization is on its decline."

"Your worlds must be chock full of gold mines and other precious metals."

"Yes and no, Kariven, but it doesn't matter. It's been hundreds of millions of years since we've abandoned minerals, both common and precious. Atomic transmutation is a lot simpler, less tiring and less troublesome in the long run." He smiled, "Your experts in the chemistry of metals will look pretty funny on the day they analyze the gold we sell to live on your planet."

"Isn't it good quality?"

"On the contrary, it's 100% pure! Your 24 carats is only a poor alloy compared to our gold from transmutation. But we don't and never will flood the global market with this gold. We just sell enough to satisfy our needs during our missions. A day will come, my friend…"

In the middle of his sentence the Man from Outer Space howled out inhumanly and collapsed with his hands clutching his head. He writhed on the ground, groaning. He was panting and croaking. In a spasm he flipped over on his back, did the crab—with only his head and feet touching the ground—then fell over on his side, grinding his jaws, covered in sweat.

In a panic Kariven thought that the man was having an epileptic fit but soon he realized that it was something else.

A weird rustling, a kind of swish like the sound of silk gently fluttering, made him look up. 300 feet above him a metal disc, glowing dimly, was slowly swaying overhead. Behind the lighted windows in its upper dome there were shadows milling around.

"A flying saucer!" the anthropologist moaned from his constricted throat.

What to do? What inexplicable seizure brought down the Polarian? Was it purely "natural" or really something caused by this gray disc that was now coming slowly down? And why didn't he, a weak Earthling compared to the Polarian, experience the same thing?

He leaned over Zimko who was shaking uncontrollably, groaning continually but more and more weakly. He clenched his teeth, opened his eyes and seemed to want to make Kariven understand something. His right hand went slowly, with great difficulty, down to his jacket but it fell motionless on the ground.

The mysterious rustling of the flying ship grew louder the closer it got.

All of a sudden the anthropologist understood. The Man from Outer Space wanted to get something from of his jacket or his vest. He quickly felt Zimko's chest and touched a hard, bulky object under his armpit between his tuxedo jacket and his vest. He grabbed it and brought out a flat metal cone furnished with a kind of handle or butt. The explorer held it carefully, knowing that he was wielding a weapon but trying to figure out how it worked. And everything happened quickly, without him being aware of it.

From the cone shot out a bluish, crackling beam of light that rattled the Frenchman's arm violently. Then there was an extraordinary, blinding flash. Kariven's arm was thrown back and the weapon flew in the air, still spraying its bluish radiation before it fell whistling onto the ground. The dazzling beam extinguished.

The explorer found himself sitting in the grass, dazed, in the middle of the ditch on the side of the road. Instinctively he looked up, fearing a counter-attack by the flying saucer. It was gone. He stood up and approached Zimko who was starting to move.

"Lord be praised!" Kariven gasped. "You're OK."

The Polarian stood up and combed his hand through his hair. He winced, "Thanks to you, Kariven. But I really didn't think you'd understand my gesture in time. My mental telepathy faculties were blocked. There was no way I could suggest to you... It was awful! But you found my weapon and... figured out—was it good?—how to use it. Good work," he added, looking around.

Somewhat taken aback, Kariven furrowed his brow and looked to the right and left also. *His Kaiser was sliced diagonally and only half of it remained*, from the right headlight to the left rear fender. A blowtorch could not have done a better job. The other half of the car had disappeared along with the palm tree behind it.

"Don't worry, Kariven, I'll replace it," Zimko promised, giving him a friendly poke.

"But... what happened to my Kaiser? And the palm tree is severed at the base..."

"You must not have had a steady hand on the cone. After disintegrating the flying saucer, the weapon must have got away from you and... wiped out whatever was in its way, that's all."

"That's all," Kariven echoed in a daze. "You... you mean that I'm the one who made half my car disappear?"

"And the palm tree and the spaceship that was shooting its *psychic-lock* waves at me. You could just as easily have disintegrated me," the Polarian joked. "Look at the fanned out groove in the ground and all the plants destroyed. One side of it passed just three feet away from where I was struck down by the waves that were trying to break my will in order to destroy my cerebral neurons. Three feet to the left and I'd be back in space as radiation!"

Kariven wiped his forehead while Zimko went to pick up his formidable weapon.

"So, we were attacked and this simple… pistol was enough to destroy a spaceship and car? That's incredible."

"I was attacked, not you. The Denebians had adjusted their psychic-lock waves to the average Polarian wavelength. The lethal beam went right through you without causing any damage to your brain cells. When I was talking with you I had automatically let down my psychic-repellant barrier that I usually surround myself with. A Denebian spaceship patrolling this area detected me right away. A minor and rather common episode in this cosmic war that we've been fighting for centuries.

"Isn't it strange to think that no Earthling has an inkling of this secret battle—pitting two extraterrestrial races against each other—that happens every day on their planet? How many sudden, inexplicable, mysterious deaths would become so extraordinary if they knew that the corpses didn't belong to earth-bound men?

"The Denebians, for the moment, won't risk staying on your planet. They are perfectly aware that their green, scaly skin would give them away in a split second. So, they're forced to fight with the Polarians while staying on their spaceships. It's very rare for these reptilian lookalikes to take a chance on the ground. With the costume party the ones I killed tonight thought they were safe. We Polarians have the invaluable advantage of passing unnoticed among men. Our bronze skin can easily be mistaken for a natural tan. I've even been with Earthlings who are darker than me. But I wasn't fooled because I didn't detect anything in them like our telepathic manifestations. Our paranormal powers and our extra-sensory perception are unmistakable."

"So, you figure on staying on Earth?" Kariven asked, still troubled by their adventure.

"That is uncertain and depends on the needs of the moment. The first phase of my mission to the USA is finished. I'll be heading off to Europe and then to Asia where another mission is awaiting me. I'll be there to see the Polarians who are looking for men and women with The Mark."

Kariven automatically stared at the palms of his hands. "I feel like I'm living in some crazy novel. But let's stop dreaming. How are you going to get back to Los Angeles? I don't think my half-car will make it there. Furthermore, it's been more than two hours since we've been on this desert highway without seeing a single car pass by. In fact, why did you bring me out here to this deserted spot?"

The Polarian smiled. "For this…" He concentrated hard for ten seconds, his eyes staring off into space, then continued, "In a minute we'll leave for Los Angeles. Look…"

A bright dot appeared in the starry sky, a moving dot, coming down at high speed. It was soon visible as a pale green disc, turning progressively to phosphorescent green. Without a sound, without even a whistle, the green disc slowly dimmed its lights the closer it got to the ground.

The ship was perfectly circular, around 50 feet in diameter. Under its lower part, in the middle, a big window emitted a pale blue light. Three huge spheres encircled this ventral window. On its axis the disc itself was topped by a cylindrical cockpit surrounded by windows and with a round dome on top. Each of the "windows" reflected a yellow, iridescent glow on the upper side of the disc. On the top of the dome a very bright globe lit up the surrounding countryside.

The ship from another world landed or rather hovered silently and perfectly still about one foot off the ground. A strange, very faint, phosphorescent green haloed it.

"Come on!" Zimko ordered.

Kariven could not believe his eyes. He obeyed in spite of everything and followed the Polarian who was walking toward the flying saucer parked 100 yards from them. He had barely covered half the distance when the headlights of a car swept over the road on the horizon.

"Hurry up, Kariven, a car!"

The two men ran as fast as they could. A big oval hatch opened under the disc and an inclined plank came down.

Zimko and Kariven, side by side, ran up. The hatch closed behind them and without even a shudder the ship took off.

"Come on and look out the window," Zimko suggested, dragging his flabbergasted friend down a metal corridor with luminescent walls.

They came into a spacious, circular cabin. In the middle of the floor, which looked like aluminum, was a shiny cylinder. About four feet high with a huge convex window on top made of some transparent material.

Kariven imitated Zimko and leaned on the red metal ramp overlooking the axial window through which he saw the night-shrouded countryside. On the highway, 1,500 feet below them, the car was swerving off the road to park near the remains of the Kaiser. The car doors swung open and two couples jumped out, waving their arms. They looked immediately up into the sky, pointing at where the flying saucer was hovering.

Zimko, amused by their surprise, pressed a bunch of buttons on the edge of the window. The image of the four people zoomed in before the eyes of the two observers, showing four faces frozen in surprise, mouths agape and eyelids fluttering.

What is that? One of the guys asked.

My God, I'm scared! My God, I'm scared! One of the girls kept screaming ludicrously.

A saucer!

A sau... cer? You th... thi... think so? Another girl stuttered, nervously gripping her boyfriend's arm.

Zimko pushed a button and the window was back to a bird's eye view, far above the area.

"You're one of the rare Earthlings to have entered a flying saucer," the Man from Outer Space declared. "Come, I'll give you a quick tour of the spaceship before we drop you at the end of the line," he joked.

"So, you're in contact with other Earthlings here?"

"Here and elsewhere," he answered, following a passageway lit by electroluminescence. "We have one or two trusted men in every country and we visit them on a scheduled date—the 20th of every month—if external conditions allow. By 'external conditions,' I mean the special agents of the Official Investigative Committees. These men, in theory, are chosen from groups of civil and independent investigators but some of them belong to no organization interested in flying saucers."

An oval hatch opened as they approached, revealing a huge, circular cabin. In the middle of it stood a kind of command console, half-moon shaped with a big, rectangular, convex screen overhead.

A blonde girl was busy at the controls that were sparkling with all kinds of bright colors. A short, see-through tunic covered her harmoniously proportioned body and revealed her flawless physique. A tiny, midnight blue bikini emitting a strange phosphorescence completed her minimal outfit. Short, black, shiny boots on her feet. Her legs, arms and bust were bronzed enough to made any film star sunbathing on Manhattan Beach[68] jealous.

She turned around and smiled. Her extraordinarily beautiful face, with very subtle make-up, was perfectly balanced.

"This is Yuln, my sister," Zimko picked the girl up in his arms and planted two loud kisses on her cheeks. "Let me introduce you to my friend Jean Kariven. He saved my life."

"I know," she said when her hardy brother put her back on the metal floor of the command post. "I was just about to intervene..." She stepped forward, still smiling, and raised her right hand with the palm facing the anthropologist. "Hello, Jean."

Kariven raised his hand in response to this new form of greeting, "Hello, Yuln."

The Mark on the palm of the blonde girl's hand was remarkably distinct.

"I observed you, both of you, during the night," she explained, "and I admit that I was scared for my brother. Your

---

[68] A famous beach in Los Angeles. (Author's Note)

carelessness," she reproached him, "almost cost you your life tonight. You should not have let your psychic barrier down."

"You were watching us?" Kariven was astonished.

"With the help of the *tele-projections*," Yuln answered in her melodic voice. "The Polarians on missions on this planet are constantly observed by a spaceship hovering at a very high altitude over their zone of operation. Our tele-projectors are a kind of mix of radar and television. We project a beam of invisible waves at the ground and the portion of the territory we want to appear on this screen with a close-up of the Polarian agent we're supposed to watch or, if need be, protect... It happens sometimes, unfortunately, that we can't act because of the circumstances. Like tonight I hesitated to disintegrate the Denebian spaceship fearing that I might destroy you and my brother. I was finally about to fire the disintegrator when you grabbed Zimko's cone."

"So, thanks to your tele-projections you can see directly through matter?"

"Naturally. I saw you clearly through the walls of the *Mocambo* and through your car's metal. The process is very common; our enemies also have a similar system... regrettably."

"Would you like," Kariven asked after a moment of reflection, "to project your tele-waves at my hotel to check on my friends Dormoy and Angelvin? That is if the police have let them go."

"Certainly. We're flying over Los Angeles right now and I've turned on the invisibility shields. Show me where your hotel is."

On saying this she pressed a blue button on the control panel and the screen lit up, showing a neighborhood of the big Californian city.

"Turn the wheel, Jean," she told him, "and stop when you've spotted the building you want."

The explorer did so and made the different areas of the city scroll by.

"Here it is," he said, pointing to the tall building that towered up on Hollywood Boulevard.

After pressing two different buttons Yuln brought the hotel in close up on the screen. When she turned a kind of selector knob the image scrambled before showing the rooms and their occupants. The images sped by. Sometimes Yuln accelerated even more to avoid any inappropriate peeping.

"There they are!" Kariven cried out but other rooms had already passed by.

Yuln went back through the three previous images and stopped on a room where two men—Dormoy and Angelvin—had just entered. The young woman pressed a red button, adjusted the brightness and then Dormoy's voice boomed out in the cockpit.

The creep! Where could he have got to?

Kariven cleared his throat. "I have the feeling that they're talking about me…"

But I think I saw him on the dance floor with the Sioux, Dormoy added.

Zimko burst out laughing. "That's me now: the Sioux! It's the name of a red-skinned people I believe."

Kariven nodded, without saying a word, and listened carefully with a smile on his face.

Give me a cigarette, Michel. Angelvin said.

I don't have any more. Kariven always keeps an extra pack in his towel.

Angelvin went into the next room and came back with a pack of Lucky Strikes. He offered one to Dormoy and put the pack in his pocket.

"Let's not be shy about it," Kariven laughed.

I won't forget this party at the Mocambo, Dormoy grumbled. *Three clowns disguised as who knows what swallow their birth certificates and the police round us up with the whole lot! I'll never forget your club!*

My club, my club, Angelvin retorted, shrugging his shoulders. *Did I know that a guy and his two girls were going to be poisoned in the middle of a costume party?*

Sure, Dormoy angrily flicked the ash off his cigarette. *But we still ended up in the slammer! And where the devil is he?* He growled, looking around the room as if it was going to tell him that "he"—Jean Kariven—was cruising 1,500 feet above Los Angeles on board a flying saucer.

"It's time that I went to reassure my friends," the anthropologist decided.

Yuln cut the broadcast. "Where do you want us to drop you? Do you know a 100-square foot lot where we can land?

"In the middle of the city?"

"Why not? Our spaceship is protected by an invisibility shield and can land without anyone noticing."

"There's the Country Club, surrounded by palm trees, at the intersection of Wilshire Boulevard and Santa Maria."

Yuln turned on the screen and Kariven, after a brief examination of the aerial view of the city, pointed to the chosen spot.

"I think we can land here."

One minute later the tops of the magnificent palm trees were swaying as if blown by a strong wind. A policeman on patrol looked up and wondered what could be shaking the trees when there was not even a breeze in the city. He took off his hat, perplexed, scratched his head and shrugged his shoulders before continuing on his rounds.

In the axial observation cabin, in front of the exit airlock, Kariven was saying goodbye to his new friends. Yuln and Zimko raised their right hands and the explorer did the same.

"See you soon, Jean," the blonde Polarian girl smiled at him.

"Really?" the explorer suddenly felt an inexplicable nostalgia at the idea of leaving these beings from another planet.

"Really," Yuln assured him, widening her adorable smile. "We'll always know where to reach you even at the ends of the world... which is not very far for us. I registered your wavelength. Lost in the middle of New York, London or Paris, I'll know where and how to contact you."

"See you soon, Yuln, and thank you, Zimko, for revealing the Mark to me. I hope I can prove myself worthy of your trust."

"I'm sure of that, Kariven. The Mark that you bear will be the best letter of introduction to your brothers of the New Race."

CHAPTER THREE

"Ha! There you are!" Dormoy barked when Kariven entered their room in the Hollywood Hotel.

The anthropologist waved a little hello and straightaway turned to Angelvin, "I don't have any more cigarettes, Robert. Can you give me one from the pack you stole out my towel?"

The young ethnographer raised his hand to his pocket, then froze in amazement. Dormoy could not get over it either. Kariven was enjoying every second of his joke. Mimicking Angelvin's angry tone that he had seen on the tele-projector, he repeated the words heard in the spaceship: "The creep! Where could he have got to?... No need to wonder any longer, Robert, I'm going to tell you."

And he told his dumbfounded friends about the extraordinary adventure he had just been through with the Man from Outer Space.

Angelvin poured himself a healthy dose of whiskey and gulped it down before saying, "I have the feeling that our vacation came to an end tonight at the *Mocambo*. What are we going to do?"

"Sleep, boys, things will look better in the morning."

For the third time the telephone rang in Kariven's room. He propped himself up groggily on one elbow, yawned unconsciously and picked up. "Jean Kariven here... Yes, please wait half an hour. Thank you."

He hung up and knocked on the connecting door to his friends' room.

"Hey, wake up! We've got a visitor waiting in the lobby. It's an emergency."

He turned on the television and went to get ready. Half an hour later the three explorers, ready and raring to go, welcomed their morning caller to their richly furnished sitting room.

The man, around 30 years-old, was tall, brown-haired, with a lively, not unfriendly face. He wore a pearl gray gabardine suit with a double-breasted coat, a white shirt and a brightly colored tie. He looked at the three hosts one by one and then turned to the anthropologist.

"Mr. Kariven, no doubt?"

The latter nodded his head and introduced his friends, wondering where he had seen this man before. The stranger smiled kindly and slowly raised his hand, palm open to the three Frenchmen. Kariven, calm but wary, rapidly scrutinized the palm of the weird visitor. The natural lines of the hand clearly formed the Mark. The explorer relaxed and in turn raised his right hand to respond to the greeting that the Polarian had taught him.

"My name's Marlow, John Marlow," the visitor declared. "President of the Flying Saucer Research Organization."

"Glad to meet you, Mr. Marlow. I remember now where I saw you. You spoke last night at the Third International Conference on Flying Saucers."

"That's right, Mr. Kariven. But first can you call the police immediately and ask whether your car has been found?"

"Good Lord!" the anthropologist slapped his forehead.

"Don't be alarmed," the American said. "What was left of your Kaiser was completely disintegrated by Zimko after you came back here to Los Angeles. There was no question of leaving such glaring evidence on the road, as deserted as it was. But to avoid any unpleasant surprise *resulting from the investigation in progress*, we've anticipated what's to come. To cover you in case the four people in the car wrote down your license plate when Yuln's spaceship came to fetch you, I had to inform the police that your car was stolen.

"Yes," he confirmed to the three Frenchmen, "I pretended to be you, Kariven, this morning around 3:30 am and called the police with your license plate number and make of the car. Zimko told me to do it because after the incident at the

Mocambo the special agents of Project Blue Book[69]—the government's 'Flying Saucer Commission'—are on red alert. Read this," he held out a special edition (a rather unusual thing) of the Herald Express, the big evening newspaper.

The bold headline with six columns underneath read:

A FLYING SAUCER HAS LANDED NEAR UPLAND

This morning around 3 am four passengers in a car returning from San Bernardino saw a huge, round contraption on the ground, glowing, some say green, others blue. According to the eyewitnesses—who want to remain anonymous—two men were standing near this thing. When they saw the car coming they ran into the flying saucer that slowly rose up, carrying away its mysterious pilots dressed in dark suits. One of the witnesses even thought these "men" were wearing tuxedos! On the side of the road, not far from the spot where they claim to have seen the flying saucer take off, they found, apparently, a cream-colored Kaiser sliced diagonally but the missing half could not be found.

When our reporter got to the location, after interviewing the four people (still in shock from the experience) he found no evidence of any of this. The mysteriously severed Kaiser was not there, if it ever had been. On the other hand, a palm tree was found cut off approximately three feet from the ground. The tree was not found. The grass, however, in the ditch by the road, as well as the yuccas around the site of the "incident"

---

[69] Name given to the American Commission investigating flying saucers. (Author's Note) Project Blue Book was one of a series of systematic studies of unidentified flying objects (UFOs) conducted by the United States Air Force. It started in 1952, and it was the third study of its kind (the first two were projects Sign (1947) and Grudge (1949)). A termination order was given for the study in December 1969, and all activity under its auspices ceased in January 1970.

were mowed down. The ground, strangely enough, was flat-
tened as smooth as a highway blacktop.

We'll leave the "witnesses" to answer for their allega-
tions and put this away in the always inexplicable file of flying
saucers.

"The article's pretty funny," Marlow commented. "But it doesn't say whether the witnesses got the license number of your car. If they did…"

At this very moment someone knocked on the door. Kariven put a finger to his lips and nodded to Marlow to go into Angelvin's room. The American slipped away silently.

Another knock, louder this time. From the next room where Kariven's two friends had gone, Dormoy tried to play it cool and shouted, "Jean, someone's knocking on your door!"

Kariven muted the television and loosened his tie, calling out, "Come in!"

The door opened and two men entered, wearing dark suits and gray felt hats. "Mr. Jean Kariven?" one of them asked.

Redoing his tie the anthropologist nodded. The two men simultaneously reached for their pocket and pulled out a badge with a number in the middle. Around the edge was engraved Special Branch of the Air Technical Intelligence.

"What can I do for you?" the slightly surprised explorer asked.

"Do you own a cream-colored Kaiser with the California license plate TTX 137 953?"[70]

"Indeed I do. Did you find it?"

"That's police business," one of the agents replied. "Do you mind telling us under what circumstances your car was stolen?"

---

[70] A California license plate from the early 1950s would have had at most 7 characters; the "TT" would indicate Guieu might have used here the plate of an American-made car imported in France.

"Gladly. I'd left it not far from the hotel last night and when I came out of the Flying Saucer Convention that was held here, I was going to take a drive to the countryside with my friend John Marlow, who had invited me to the event. We decided to talk a walk instead and talk together, which we did until 3:30 in the morning."

"Where'd you go?"

Kariven frowned and shrugged his shoulders. "My God, we walked down Sunset Boulevard all the way to Benedict Canyon Road where we wandered around, talking and smoking leisurely. When we got back to Hollywood Boulevard, near the hotel, my car, which I was supposed to take to meet my friends Dormoy and Angelvin at the *Mocambo*, had disappeared. So, I called the police to report it. When I got here, my friends were coming back… very disappointed with their night out," he smiled ambiguously.

Someone else knocked on the door.

"Come in," Kariven raised his voice.

Marlow, who had snuck out of the next room, strolled in. "Hello, Kariven," he said, then pretended to be surprised. "Excuse me, I thought you were alone. I…"

"Come on in, Johnny," the explorer went to shake his hand. "These gentlemen…"

"Hold on," one of the special agents broke in while holding Kariven back politely but firmly. "Where were you, Mr. Marlow, last night between 9 pm and 4 am?"

Marlow put on his surprised face again and repeated exactly what he had heard from his hiding place, thus verifying Kariven's alibi. The agents looked at each other and pursed their lips. They muttered something and left, hoping the anthropologist would find his car soon.

"Just as I feared," Marlow said, "those four people got the license number of your Kaiser, Kariven. Otherwise how can you explain that agents from the Air Technical Intelligence are on the trail? A simple stolen car is a matter for the police, not the government's Saucer Commission attached to the Pentagon. I don't know if they swallowed your little story but we should watch out from now on. These guys are hard-nosed and not easily fooled. All the secret services are on the lookout since that famous November 20, 1952[71]. They're working hard to track down beings that come from another planet but are completely lost at sea, not knowing exactly *who* these beings are or what their intentions are. They know now what some of them look like—the Denebians with green, scaly skin—but they still have no idea that some Polarians, our friends, are already living on Earth.

"However, I strongly suspect that these agents from the ATIC are making a connection 1: between the incident at the *Mocambo* where your friends Dormoy and Angelvin were present, and 2: your stolen car found sliced in two then disappeared, and 3: your own interest in flying saucers. Because it was obviously impossible for us to hide the fact that you attended the Flying Saucer Convention last night at the hotel."

"OK, we have to be careful. But there's no proof that I have anything to do with what happened last night," Kariven remarked.

"And that's good," Marlow concluded. "After Zimko dropped you off at the Country Club, he gave me his orders by metal suggestion. His telepathic communication is extraordinarily clear. When you get one some day you'll think you were really hearing a voice, a clear, distinct voice *talking inside your head*. It's always a surprise, the first time, but you'll get used to it. The weird supernatural powers of the Polarians

---

[71] The day when a flying saucer landed in California and one of its occupants contacted George Adamski. See *The Flying Saucers Come from Another World*, q.v., and *Flying Saucers Have Landed* by Desmond Leslie & George Adamski (1953). (Author's Note) Adamski (1891-1965) was a Polish American citizen who became widely known in UFO circles after he claimed to have photographed alien spaceships met with friendly aliens and flown with them to the Moon. Most investigators have since concluded his claims were a hoax, and he himself was a con artist.

allow them to communicate by telepathy, to talk with others next to them or far away but also to intercept thoughts of another and all this at the same time.

"Now, let's get down to the business at hand. You have to leave the United States within 48 hours and go back to Europe. Zimko's orders. You're going to operate in France where you'll receive instructions soon after you arrive. The American west is my theater of operation," he laughed, "and there are seven of us in the USA that belong to the Earth-Polarian Alliance. You, Kariven, and your friends have to return to France where a member of the Alliance will contact you. An important work is waiting for you. It's up to us to find the representatives of the New Race and reveal to them the profound meaning of the Mark they bear on their hands. You'll have to enroll them in our peaceful, defensive organization. Zimko and the other Polarians on Earth will help us in this just as we have to help them.

"In the interests of the human race we will assist the Polarians... We, the pioneers of the Future Civilization, bearers of the Mark of Knowledge.

"I won't go so far as to say that our mission is dangerous, for the moment at least. However, we have to worry about being spotted some day if the Denebians learn the meaning of the Mark, the stigmata of Homo Superior. But in fact, and paradoxically, it's humans right now that we have to watch out for. The man on the street as well as the scientist, being so self-centered and sometimes obsessed by sacrosanct theories—even though they're old and stale—might spread false ideas to reassure the public about the so-called non-existence of flying saucers.

"When the authorities become aware of the reality of flying saucers, they will quickly see that there are peaceful and hostile sides. Their general appearance is identical and the two types won't be able to be told apart... except in the case of an attack. And in that case the enemy always flees, escaping at terrifying speeds from our jet fighters that can't go so fast. How can we warn the population without throwing them into a panic? A very delicate situation not yet ironed out... and for good reason."

Kariven's ears suddenly pricked up and he turned up the television. On the screen a hand had just passed a piece of paper to the anchorman who announced:

"Dear viewers, here's some breaking news about the Flying Saucer. After a careful investigation by the police it appears that the four people in the car who reported that they saw a flying saucer at dawn were rather... tipsy. The good folks were coming back from a family party and had drunk a lot. Moreover, it's been proven that at 3:30 am—the time when they saw this so-called disc—a weather balloon was in fact in the sky over that area. It was launched by the High Atmosphere Study division of the Mount Wilson observatory and drifted slowly over the highway, causing this very unintentional and unreasonable scare in the passengers from San Bernardino.

"Furthermore, we can say that no trace of any car accident has been found on the road. As for the palm tree that was so 'mysteriously' severed, it was done by a team of road workers who were repairing the highway yesterday. There you have it. Nothing to fear from this new 'gag' that was so hastily called a UFO. It was nothing but a weather balloon, a big, flying bag and not invaders from Mars or Venus.

"And now for some excellent recipes from Aunt Euphrasia..."

Kariven turned the TV off and shrugged. "A weather balloon. And that's the kind of nonsense the authorities in every country have been using to blind the public since 1947. Sensible people who have seen flying saucers are ridiculed if they have the courage to tell the newspapers about the events they witnessed. They turn them into drunks or dreamers if they don't accuse them of hysteria or pranks. The few journalists who haven't hesitated to take a bold position and publish their belief in the extra-terrestrial origins of flying saucers are won over or criticized by the scientists, sincere but ignorant of the facts, or by their narrow-minded colleagues. The Denebians, those space pirates, must be laughing at the incredible extent of human stupidity. Why are they shy about spying on the industrial centers, the atomic laboratories and the war games of Earthlings since officially their existence is denied by the very ones who would sound the alarm?"

Marlow had to force himself to hold back his bitterness. "It's no use ranting against man's blindness. The events that threaten this world will see to it, someday soon unfortunately, that their eyes will be opened. We have a mission to fulfill, the weirdest, most sensitive mission that's ever been. We have to stay in the shadows for the time being and let the Secret Services stumble around every country. Some of their agents bear the Mark but don't know what it means. Because of their specialization they'd refuse to admit what we can reveal to them. The time has not yet come but it will. On that day, the big day, everybody on Earth will have to admit their stupid blindness. Above all they will have to wipe the slate clean of their petty squabbles and join forces to face the invaders coming from outer space... Unless they act before we, men of the Future Race, and the Polarian Agents have set up the Alliance and the first phase of its top-secret plan... The details of this 'operation' under the innocent name of Project Blue Moon will be communicated to you at the appropriate time. Remember this name, Project Blue Moon," he insisted.

"That's easy to remember," Angelvin figured. "Every jazz fan knows the famous song *Blue Moon*."

"This song will also have its role to play," Marlow smiled enigmatically. "And now, my friends, I wish you luck. Get ready to leave. You have to be in France 24 hours from now. Tomorrow morning get on the ionocruiser *Shooting Star* that takes off at 8 am sharp. You'll be in Paris at 10:30 pm[72] and all you have to do is wait. Take the fraternal greeting of the Alliance members to your French friends and any Englishmen you come in contact with. Our countries have to save the world with the potent support of our Polarian brothers."

---

[72] If only!

The American took three tickets out of his wallet with the names of the three explorers.

"Here are your seats reserved on the *Shooting Star* at 8 am. *Bon voyage*, my friends."

He raised his right hand, imitated by his three hosts, and walked out.

"What kind of crazy adventure have we got ourselves mixed up in?" Dormoy wondered aloud. "Now we have to leave California... and its pretty girls. Last night at the *Mocambo* I met one who..."

"Yes, we know," Angelvin cut in. "Go tell your lady love that you've been called back to France by your grandmother and then come back and pack your bags. Unless you'd rather leave us behind," he said with a straight face.

"Don't even think about it! Besides, a little action will do us good. We were starting to get rusty."

The telephone rang. Dormoy picked it up, listened for a few seconds and replied, "I'll get him for you..." Putting his hand over the mouthpiece he whispered, "It's for you, Kariven. The cops want to talk to you."

Kariven blinked slowly to thank him and took the phone. "Hello... yes... that's me... yes... that's right..."

The longer the invisible man on the other end of the line talked, the more his face expressed utter surprise. He answered calmly, forcing himself to sound pleased with what the policeman told him. "Thank you," he ended up saying, "and congratulations to your organization for all the hard work you did. I'll be there shortly."

He hung up and turned to his friends who were impatient to know what it was all about. He told them, "My car... *has been found*."

The two men leaped up at the same time. "Your... They found your car? But if Marlow just told us that its 'half' was disintegrated by Zimko from his flying saucer, I don't get it," Dormoy admitted.

"I said *my car* and not half of it," Kariven smiled. "A cream-colored Kaiser with California license plates TTX 137

953 and registered in my name, Jean Kariven, anthropologist, 11 place Adolphe Chérioux, Paris, 15th arrondissement. Is it my car, yes or no?"

"Hmm, that means… yes," Angelvin said. "It's your license and your address… But since it doesn't exist anymore?"

Kariven shook his head. "The Kaiser I bought 15 days ago doesn't exist, that's a fact. It was disintegrated, half by myself accidentally and half by the Polarians after I got back to Los Angeles. But I understand how they found it… It's a diplomatic ploy, a trick set up by the special agents for me to keep my trap shut if I ever decide to report my adventure. By finding my Kaiser, they automatically destroy the version of the four passengers and everything that happened…"

"So, they didn't believe a word of your story or your alibi?"

"Obviously. But since they have no proof and *they can have absolutely none*, they prefer to play innocent… and buy me a new car identical in every aspect to the one I thought was stolen. It's a lot easier to replace a new car than a car that already has tens of thousands of miles under its belt. The substitution is possible except for a few minor, unimportant details—scratches on the body, maybe a tear in the seat—details that I have to close my eyes to."

Consequently, Kariven went to the headquarters of the Police Department, 200 N. Spring Street,[73] where the chief of police met him in person. This was not a special honor but a sure sign bearing the stamp of the special agents, the same ones who had questioned the "victim" of the theft.

After formally receiving his car in the presence of the chief of police and signing a statement and the release paper presented by a secretary, the chief accompanied the explorer to the door of his office, shook his hand and bid farewell with this advice full of innuendoes:

---

[73] The address of los Angeles' City Hall.

"From now on, Mr. Kariven, don't leave your car for too long to go and talk about Flying Saucers."

"I'll be careful, chief, I'll be careful," the anthropologist promised in the same tone of voice. "And thanks a million for your kind assistance. In fact, be kind enough to congratulate the gentlemen from the ATIC. They work hard and fast when they drop their flying saucers to track down stolen cars."

Behind the wheel of his Kaiser—or rather the one they had just given to him—Kariven smiled. The exchange of phony courtesies was pretty funny. This little game was part of the secret interplanetary war that the Polarians and Denebians were fighting on the ground of the planets being defended by the former and coveted by the latter. A secret war in which Earthlings with the Mark were on one side and on the other were special agents trying to see clearly through the chaos that they could not make heads or tails of. In fact, their confusion and caution were understandable. For them, only one thing was certain: beings from another planet were living on Earth. They looked like Earthlings except for the color and texture of their skin. Three of these beings had just been killed in a mysterious way that could not be connected to humans. Did there exist on our planet other creatures, enemies of the first who were secretly waging a merciless war unbeknownst to the common man? For what purpose? What role, then, did certain Earthlings play in these tangled events that were baffling but somehow connected? Why did these Frenchmen on vacation in Los Angeles, after the incidents of the previous night, just reserve seats on the *Shooting Star* to go back to Europe? What connection was there with John Marlow, the president of the Flying Saucer Research Organization, the private group investigating flying saucers in every state?

This puzzling headache haunted the minds of the special agents of the ATIC. The superior officers of this organization headquartered at Wright Patterson Air Force Base in Dayton, Ohio, followed the inquiry every step of the way but could not get a clear and precise picture to make the information useful. They would have to wait and persevere.

The *Shooting Star* sped into the ionosphere at 2,000 miles an hour, starting to slow down when it was in sight of the French coast, a gray line cutting through the deep blue sea. 75 miles up, the ground was nothing but a brown zone, grayish in places, over which small, white flakes drifted—clouds—sometimes covering a clearer area—a town or city—bathed in sunlight.

Around 10:15 the huge *Shooting Star* started its whistling descent. With its two rows of windows, its delta wings starting at the nose fitted with a radar mast and its gaping jet engines leaving a trail of condensation in its wake, the plane was radiant, like a steel shark seen in profile. It made one round of the capital and then, losing altitude, turned on its decelerating jets to circle back at low speed and finally came down on the long runway reserved for the giants of the ionosphere. The plane landed smoothly at the Paris-Orly airport two and a half hours after its departure from Los Angeles.

While the passengers headed for customs, the "dollies" were busy with the international cargo before leaving for Sydney via Rangoon. Out of the cargo hold and rolling on a tilted conveyor the freight was unloaded: mail, crates and cars boarded as "registered luggage." The splendid Kaiser was picked up by an employee who got it "targeted" by customs before parking it in front of the terminal where its owner and his friends could climb in half an hour later.

The Kaiser was now cruising down Avenue de Paris, an extension of Boulevard Lamouroux and Avenue de Choisy. It was driving smoothly, silently… without its passengers having the least suspicion that a green Frazer [74] had been following 100 yards behind them since Orly.

At 50,000 feet altitude, in what astronomers stubbornly took for a weather balloon or common meteor, Zimko and Yuln were keeping a close watch on the Kaiser through their tele-projection screen. They had spotted Kariven at the Orly

[74] See Note 55.

airport thanks to their wave detector homing in on the young French scientist's frequency. Yuln furrowed her brow and then zoomed in. The Kaiser had just turned left at Place d'Italie to take Boulevard Auguste Blanqui. A second car, a green Frazer, was taking the same route.

"I think I saw that car parked in front of the terminal," Yuln remarked. "Here it is now behind Jean's car. Do you think...?"

"It's possible," Zimko said skeptically. "It wouldn't surprise me that the special agents are already on Kariven's tail."

The Kaiser got off Boulevard Pasteur, turned right and drove down Rue de Vaugirard, still shadowed by the green Frazer.

"I have to warn our friends," Zimko stated.

He stood motionless for a moment and concentrated while his sister piloted the flying disc following the two vehicles on the screen. Inside the Kaiser, Kariven was driving pretty slowly because Rue de Vaugirard at rush hour was full of people crossing the street. All of a sudden he felt weird and slowed down even more. A voice rang out in his head, clear distinct:

Kariven, it's me, Zimko, talking to you...

Troubled at first, the anthropologist suddenly remembered what Marlow had said about the telepathic messages sent across space by the Polarians. Not being able to concentrate on driving, he decided to take the first right turn and pull up to the curb. He waved his friends off so they would not talk to him. Attentive and stressed, he seemed to be listening to a sound or "something" that his stunned and confused friends could not hear.

You're being followed, Kariven. A green car's been with you since Orly. Watch out, it's turning onto your street now... It's passing you... Just take a glance...

Kariven pretended to look out the open window and examine his front fender. Like this he could sneak a peek at the Frazer that was just passing by. Two young men were sitting in the front seat. Their faces betrayed a slight surprise at seeing Kariven leaning out the window. But since he was looking down toward the front of the car, they were not worried. The Frenchmen could not have spotted them.

It's gone, the telepathic voice from the Man from Outer Space resumed. *Did you see who was driving?*

Kariven paused a moment, wondering whether he should answer aloud or mentally but Zimko kept him from lingering over this problem.

I read the answer in your mind, Kariven. You saw them. Stay on your toes and be careful not to be followed from now on. When you have to go to an important appointment or fulfill a mission...

The explorer suddenly felt a strange, emotional shock. It was not the same voice echoing in his head. He was certainly not expecting this voice but its different tone oddly reminded him of Yuln, the blond Polarian girl.

We're with you, Jean, it chanted in his mind. *I told you that we'd find you. Be careful... I don't want anything bad to happen to you.*

Dormoy and Angelvin looked at each other, intrigued by the body language of their companion. Did he just smile?! What was happening? Had he lost his mind?

Why, Yuln, are you so interested in my personal safety? He asked mentally.

I, uh... Oh, men!

And that was all. His mind felt no more telepathic vibrations but his ears heard the surrounding noises. In the sky over the capital three jet fighter planes were soaring up and howling out a shrill sound. Was it a simple exercise or had they spotted the flying saucer?

"Well, Kariven? Are you going to sit there dreaming like that forever?" Angelvin asked impatiently.

"I just got a telepathic message from Zimko. We've been followed since... Hold on, check out that green Frazer that's heading toward us... It's been with us since Orly."

The car slowed down as it passed by the Kaiser again, which, at the very moment, was driving off slowly. They turned around at the end of the block and pulled up at Place Adolphe Chérioux where Kariven lived.

After parking the car in the garage the three friends were about to enter Number 11 when the Frazer passed by the front steps, drove around the Place and off down Rue de Vaugirard. The three of them stood there, puzzled, cooking up all kinds of theories about the stalking without noticing that another car, a black Citroën Traction Avant 15,[75] was crossing Rue de Vaugirard to get on Place Adolphe Chérioux heading for Number 11. The three explorers entered the building and let the glass door close slowly behind them.

In the lobby an old lady was coming toward them with faltering step. They moved out of the way to let her go by. At this very moment a woman screamed out on the street and a weird buzzing or crackling sound filled the lobby. The temperature suddenly become stifling and the old lady slumped over coughing.

"Against the wall!" Kariven yelled, plastering himself against the hallway.

The frosted glass of the big, wrought iron entrance door had melted. A huge hole, three feet in diameter, appeared, bubbled around its irregular edges. The thick metal bars of the entrance door were no longer visible. They had melted!

Kariven hurried out to the front steps and found a young woman passed out, surrounded by passers-by. Her left arm, left hip and the left side of her chest were badly burned. Half of her clothes were missing along with some of her black-fringed underwear that was slipping off to her right side and revealing her body. The material had been burned down a wavy line from the bottom of her skirt up to her left shoulder.

The anthropologist went back to his friends who were squatting around the old lady. They looked at him without saying a word but shaking their head sadly. The poor woman

---

[75] The 15 launched in June 1938 had a 2867 cc (175.0 cu in) six cylinder engine.

was curled up on the floor. Only a blackened sliver of her cane lay on the floor; the rest had evaporated in the hellish heat.

The concierge, turning pale, had came out of his room when the young woman screamed and he kept muttering, "Poor Madame Brun... I saw her fall, Monsieur Kariven, when you stepped aside with your friends to let her by. Poor Madame Brun..."

Kariven looked at his companions and whispered through clenched teeth, "I refuse to believe that the special agents of the ATIC use thermal rays to further their investigations. This innocent old lady got it full in the face what it was meant for us. Zimko was right. We have to be very careful. *Especially now that the green-skinned monsters are out in full daylight and shooting for us!*"

CHAPTER FOUR

When the inspectors from the police investigating the extraordinary attack had left, Kariven offered his friends some whiskey and holding his glass he collapsed into a yellow leather club chair.

"Things are starting to heat up," Angelvin grumbled after gulping down his Black and White scotch.

Kariven stared at him, raising his right eyebrow and wondering if he was making a joke or being dead serious.

"Indeed," Dormoy agreed. "That thermal ray that killed the old lady and melted the metal on the door must have reached at least 2,000°C."

"We barely escaped it. It was a pretty unexpected welcome."

"Do you really think the Denebians were trying to put us out of circulation?"

"I don't see any other possibility, Michel. The pedestrians who heard the woman scream outside saw her collapse right when a black Citroën was passing by. Since they didn't hear any explosions—pistol shots or machine gun fire—they didn't bother to get the car's license. The poor girl got the entire left side of her body licked by the ray right before it stopped firing. That explains why she's still alive, seriously burned but out of harm's way. There's no doubt that this diabolical weapon does not come from Earth. In my opinion, the black Citroën must have followed the Frazer, knowing that they were on our trail and unwittingly leading them to our doorstep."

The anthropologist stood up and took a few nervous steps in the living room, passing by the big window. He looked outside at Place Adolphe Chérioux, the square, the metro station and Rue de Vaugirard. He let his mind wander over the familiar neighborhood that he had always enjoyed. The alleyways off the square were full of the same noisy gangs of young men; the metro entrance had the same flower seller and news stand busy with their customers who were always in a hurry. Wait, there was a second newspaper seller sitting on a folding stool with the dailies spread out on the ground and looking around him with a goofy smile. On the whole nothing had changed; everything was calm. The people were going about their business, unaware of the frightening menace that loomed over the Earth.

"What do you say to some lunch?" Dormoy proposed. "It's 2:30."

"OK. Let's go to the Brasserie Alsacienne. It's right there on Rue de Vaugirard."

Kariven opened the middle drawer of his desk and took out a Colt in its holster. "Forewarned is forearmed," he opened his coat and slipped the weapon under his armpit. "I advise you to do the same when you get home. And to hell with the law if we're breaking it by carrying big guns. This Colt is better than a tiny 7.65…"

On the street Kariven stopped in front of a candy store. "Well, take a look at those chocolates shaped-like discs called Flying Saucers." Then looking in the window's reflection he whispered, "Do you see that newspaper seller behind us at the metro entrance? He pointed at us while talking with that guy who just bought one of his rags…"

Dormoy and Angelvin did indeed see the reflection of the seller talking to his "customer" who was around 40 years old, dressed plainly and wearing a brown felt hat. The guy was casting furtive glances in their direction.

"Come on," Kariven murmured. "Let's eat lunch in peace. We'll see if I'm imagining things or if this guy follows us."

They walked to the *Brasserie Alsacienne* and chose a table in the back of the room. From their table they could see everyone walking by the restaurant. One minute after they were seated, the man in the hat stopped in front of the window and stared at the menu for a long time. Apparently finding it to his taste, he entered and sat close to the door where he could keep the whole restaurant in view.

"Here we go, hooked," Kariven grimaced. "Special agents, the Denebians, and now this spooky guy with a felt hat! I wonder who's he with?"

"Maybe the Denebians have won over some Earthlings to their side?"

"I can't imagine them driving that Citroëns themselves. With their kind of reptilian beauty, there's no way they could show their faces in broad daylight. They've certainly found some accomplices among the local populace. What could they possibly say to win their support? Did the green monsters claim that the Polarians are invaders, or did they just go for the lowlifes and promise them money?"

"Maybe this guy's a flunky of the special agents?"

Kariven shrugged and continued eating. "That's possible too, but he looks pretty seedy to me. Here's what you're going to do, Michel. You go back home and don't leave until six to come back to my place. Robert, do the same, but you'll come at five. Arm yourselves. I'll watch the newspaper guy from my window. Maybe he has other acquaintances in the area. If so, he'll show it in one way or another to his stooge or stooges. Plus, we'll see who of us three will be followed on leaving the restaurant… because we'll leave at different times and take different routes."

At the end of the meal Dormoy shook their hands and left. The man in the hat did not budge but a vagrant outside who had been begging at the door for a while pulled himself together and started walking casually in the footsteps of the geophysician.

"OK, I've got it," Kariven whispered. "It's a cheap trick but it's there. We're going to have personal guardian angels. For Michel it's the bum—*they* could have at least found someone a little less conspicuous—for you it might be a businessman and for me I bet it'll be the rat in the brown hat."

And he was not wrong. On leaving, Angelvin caused a gasman, who had been checking the pipes outside for an hour, to finish up and leave.

Hiding behind his drawn curtains Kariven was spying on the newspaper seller through the window. Angelvin had just passed by him. The man watched him go. One minute later he made a discreet sign with his hand. In the bar on the other side of Rue de Vaugirard a man lowered his head in affirmation and headed toward a telephone booth. The same classic ritual was repeated at six o'clock when Dormoy came by.

"No doubt about it, we're being watch by these creeps," Kariven railed. "We can't go three feet without a chaperon on our heels. Do you have your guns?"

They nodded and patted their left side where their Colts were hidden. Angelvin even had a stiletto in a sheath taped to his forearm with the handle pointing down. One good shake of his arm and the knife would in the hand of the ethnographer, an expert in wielding blades.

Just then the telephone rang.

"Kariven here," he answered.

A woman's voice on the other end of the line hummed. Believing it was a wrong number he was about to hang up when he recognized the first bars of *Blue Moon*, the tune that John Marlow had mentioned.

"We've got your 12-inch record, Monsieur Kariven," the voice broke in, waiting for sign of recognition.

The explorer thought about it and said, "It's the recording of *Blue Moon* that I ordered?"

"Exactly. We got it in this morning. *Your friend and his sister* told us you were back in France. Therefore, I took the liberty of calling you. Would you like to come get it or should we deliver it to you? We can have it there by 7:00."

"That's great. I'll be waiting for your deliveryman and *ask my friends nearby to wait for it*."

"You will have it in half an hour, Monsieur Kariven, and I'm sure that you'd like to listen to it immediately. Too bad for your friends," she laughed. "*They'll have to wait a little long-er. Famous scientists are like film stars: they are always being bothered by bores. That's the price of glory and thank God I'm not one of them.* See you soon."

He hung up, kept his hand on the phone for a minute, lost in thought, then informed his curious friends, "A young wom-an just told me that my *Blue Moon* has arrived. It must be some kind of password. She certainly belongs to the Alliance because she understood right away when I allude to 'my friends waiting outside.' With an equally innocent remark, she let me know that she knew all about them."

A half hour later, the doorbell buzzed. Kariven led in a tall, young lady with long brown hair, very elegant in her black suit and carrying a fake leather briefcase. In the middle of the living room she raised her right hand to greet the three explorers around her. The Mark was very distinct in her palm. They responded in kind. At Kariven's invitation the stranger sat down.

"My name is…"

She stopped abruptly, stared at Angelvin and her face went red.

"Robert!" she cried out. "You… Don't you recognize me?"

Angelvin squinted, searched the depths of his memory and finally exclaimed, "Jenny! Jenny Reynal! We knew each other at the Musée de l'Homme,[76]" he explained to his friends. "We took an ethnography class together and cultural anthro-pology. Oh, how you've changed," he kissed the girl on the cheek. "Really, I didn't recognize you."

"I was blonde then and 17 years old… eight years ago," she admitted, smiling.

"How did you get mixed up in this… adventure?"

---

[76] Anthropology museum in Paris, established in 1937.

"My father was head of the French Institute of Research on OVNIs[77]. We bear the Mark and were contacted by Zimko. It's that simple," she ended by folding her hands on her knees.

"You weren't spotted?" Kariven asked.

"No. Zimko warned me this afternoon that you were being followed by a green American car."

"Followed and even shot at with thermal rays by the Denebians," he filled her in on the adventure of their failed assassination.

Having turned pale she glanced at her old classmate. "These scaly green monsters are unbelievably reckless. I never would have believed that they'd risk such a thing in the middle of the city. We didn't even know there were any of them in France. You said that an old lady was burned in the attack?"

Angelvin bowed his head. "That reminds me of a weird thing that happened in May of 1953 in Drancy, not far from Paris," he said thoughtfully. "A little six-year old girl playing in the street with her friends suddenly went up in flames. Her sister and mother, trying in vain to save her threw a bucket of water on her but couldn't put out the fire consuming her. The mother burned her hands trying to pull her daughter away. No trace of matches or any suspicious object that could have set fire to her dress was found. Her friends were searched, interrogated but to no avail. They had nothing to do with the tragic 'accident' that remained inexplicable and unexplained. The poor girl died 15 days later in the Saint Louis hospital[78]."

---

[77] French acronym for "Objets volants non identifiés", i.e.: Unidentified Flying Object s (UFOs). The term "S.V." for "soucoupe volante" is the equivalent of "F.S." dor flying saucer. (Author's Note)

[78] True story. This strange phenomenon of "spontaneous human combustion" was never explained. The American writer Charles Fort, in his many remarkable books, mentions a number of similarly unexplained cases. (Author's Note) Charles Fort (1874-1932) was an American writer and researcher into

"Do you think there's a connection between this mysterious 'accident' and the fearsome weapon of the Denebians" Dormoy wondered.

"It would be monstrous to attack an innocent little girl!"

"War is a monstrous thing, Robert," Jenny sighed. "How many innocent people have lost their lives? And besides, we're *just Earthlings* to these creatures and therefore potential enemies since they're after our planet… I've got a message for you, Kariven—that's what Zimko calls you—but it concerns Robert and Michel as well. We have to all be at the Guyancourt airport tonight at midnight. It's a deserted place where we won't be disturbed. There's no control tower or administrative buildings and planes never land at night. There's hardly any traffic there except on Sundays when the Aero-Club members fly. Moreover, it was here that for the first time in France a flying saucer—Zimko's—landed in July 1950[79]. Our Polarian friend and one other made contact with my father and other Frenchmen bearing the Mark of the New Race."

"Did Zimko tell you the reason for this nocturnal rendez-vous?"

"He just said that it was very important… for you and for the Alliance."

"We'll be there," Angelvin promised. "But how can we get out of here without being followed?"

"The roofs. It's the only way we can get by them unnoticed," Kariven said. "We'll skip over a whole block and get into a building around the corner."

"I've got a car," Jenny offered. "Tell me where I should wait for you because there's no way we can take your Kaiser since it's known to the special agents and the Denebians."

---

anomalous phenomena. His books include *The Book of the Damned* (1919), *New Lands* (1923) and *Lo!* (1931).

[79] True. In mid-July 1950, *two* flying saucers landed on this airstrip near Paris and two "men" came out and talked with a witness; see *The Flying Saucers Come from Another World*, q.v. (Author's Note)

"Go to the corner of Rue Blomet and Rue du Général Beuret. Make sure you're not followed. You know never know. We'll eat dinner together and then go to Guyancourt."

The young lady left and Kariven hid behind the curtain. At the metro entrance the newspaper seller was sneaking peeks at the window. Jenny walked out of the building and crossed Place Adolphe Chérioux. The news guy barely noticed her, keeping his eyes on the lighted window. So, *they* did not know that she knew Kariven. She was still "off the radar".

"Our man hasn't taken his eyes off the window. He'll keep looking as long as the light's on. When we leave we won't turn it off. The guy will end up going gray before he figures out that we're not here."

The three friends, armed with flashlights and skeleton keys, took the elevator to the sixth floor. They climbed the 15 steps leading to the attic and turned on their flashlights to steer through the maze of old, musty armchairs, picture frames, metal washtubs, a harmonium and a boiler, not to mention all the suitcases... and dust. They clambered up to the roof through a skylight. It was a warm night; the stars were shining in the cloudless sky. Kariven panned around trying to get his bearings in the forest of chimneys.

"We'll get over to that adjoining roof and then cross the next ones diagonally. Rue Blomet is about 250 yards to the right... It won't be easy going," he grinned.

Clinging to the ledges, climbing over chimneys, tripping on the wobbly tiles, every step a risk of breaking bones, the three new-fangled "mountaineers" took 25 minutes to reach a deserted attic where they could slip in silently. The door to the landing, however, was locked. Thanks to the skeleton key Kariven opened the old lock easily. They were on the fifth floor of a posh building. The attic/store room was dusty, as it should be, but the lower floors were gleaming. A thick red carpet absorbed the sound of their footsteps down the stairs.

On the ground floor they passed by an old lady with a bi-focals perched on her nose, eyeing them sourly. Seeing their dusty clothes the old biddy was startled. Wrapping herself in her dignity she stood in the middle of the lobby to watch them come down. Kariven nodded to her shyly and followed his friends walking casually to the front door. Just when they were opening the door a voice called out to them:

"Hey there! I didn't see you go up!"

It was the concierge, a little old man with a wool cap and knit sweater that was desperately trying not to slip off his drooping shoulders.

"Leave," the anthropologist whispered and he turned around, raising his voice, "You didn't see us go up? That doesn't surprise me... We never came in!"

He spun around and jumped out as the good man, after figuring it out, started screaming bloody murder and stop thieves!

Ten yards away Jenny's Vedette [80] was waiting for them. They dove into the car, which took off immediately. The street was empty so no one could get the license number and certainly not the old concierge who was on his hands and knees on the sidewalk searching for the glasses that had fallen off in his heroic chase after the "thieves".

"Where are we going to eat?" Angelvin asked, wiping his forehead.

"At the Eden-Roc," the young lady driving the Vedette did not hesitate. "It's a nice restaurant whose boss I know personally... who's one of us. We have allies in all the trades," she smiled before addressing a mysterious comment to Kariven: "I'm sure you'll appreciate the décor, the excellent cuisine... and the select clientele, you'll see."

The Vedette managed to park between two cars and our friends headed for the corner of Rue Boyon and Rue Villebois-Mareuil. The front room of the Eden-Roc was full.

---

[80] The Simca Vedette was manufactured by French automaker Simca from 1954 to 1961. It had acquired the model from Ford France in 1954 and the car was initially marketed as the Ford Vedette. The Vedette finally evolved into the Esplanada, following Simca's takeover by Chrysler in 1970.

The manager waved discreetly to Jenny and led the newcomers to the second room where only three tables were occupied.

And Kariven saw *her*, delightful and captivating. Her gorgeous mauve dress with gold arabesques revealed her bare shoulders, her perfect shoulders of soft, tanned skin. Just when he was about to pronounce her name, a thought exploded in his head, a commanding although melodic thought, like the sound of her voice: *Call me Betty...*

"Betty!" he called out right away, taking the hands that the young Polarian held out to him. "Jenny didn't tell me I would... see you here."

They sat at her table and ate heartily. Kariven was particularly excited and his flashes of wit would not quit... to the great pleasure of Betty, a.k.a. Yuln. When he looked into her gold-flecked blue yes, she blushed and lowered her eyelids, not because he was looking at her but because *she read what was in his thoughts and in his heart.*

They talked about everything during the dinner except the fear that was tormenting them. All of a sudden, toward the end of the meal, Yuln gripped the edge of the table and her fingernails bit into the tablecloth. Her face was frozen in pain. It lasted only a second or two.

"What happened, Yuln?" Kariven worried.

"The Denebians," the young Polarian huffed out. "They're searching for me. I just felt the pain caused by their psychic detector. They almost *grabbed* my mind but I reacted and pulled free. They can't be far. The pain was strong but brief."

She groaned suddenly, clenched her teeth, then relaxed. "The psychic detector beam brushed by me again. They must be sweeping the city with their invisible projectors. If they get closer they'll find me because I can't resist the psychic detector for long without the protection of a Repeller. I didn't bring it with me since I didn't know the Denebians were already in France."

She concentrated, staring at an imaginary point in front of her, and immediately got in touch with her brother. After a few seconds Zimko's thoughts came back to her:

I can't come right away, Yuln, I'm sorry. Get out of wherever you are and head directly for the rendezvous with our friends. I've located the zone where the Denebian psychic probe is coming from. It's NNE of Paris. Head west and south without delay before going to Guyancourt... I'm finishing up my mission here and will meet you. Courage, little sister. I'm sending out some interference waves to cover your tracks but they won't work too well because our ship is on the other side of the Earth.

Yuln snapped out of her meditation and said, "We have to leave here right now. Zimko is trying to mess up the transmission of the detector waves but his interference won't be very effective. In order for our jamming waves to work at full power they have to be sent at least 3,000 miles from the object."

"3,000 miles!" Kariven was astonished. "But where is Zimko then?"

"He's working in China," is all she would say.

Not wanting to be indiscreet, Kariven changed the subject and joked, "The newspaper seller must be thinking it's been a long time!"

And he explained their strategy to the Girl from Outer Space. She smiled but her face quickly lost its charm and went back to being serious. "You should call the concierge to turn the lights off in your apartment."

"Nah, I'll turn them off tomorrow morning myself," the explorer responded.

"I'm afraid, Jean, that you won't be in Paris tomorrow morning... or in the afternoon or the day after."

"What do you mean?"

"The five of us are leaving tonight on a mission."

The three Frenchmen raised their eyebrows in surprise.

"You see, Betty, we can't just leave like that, with just the clothes on our backs."

"Don't worry, Jean. We've thought of everything and will provide you with whatever you need. Call your concierge so that the light in your apartment being on all night won't attract more attention than not seeing you leave."

Around 11 pm Jenny's Vedette was heading for Guyancourt. Yuln, sitting in back between Kariven and Dormoy, looked nervous. Every time a car came toward them or passed them the anthropologist felt her tense up. All her senses were on alert; she probed the night, trying to detect a hostile presence.

All of a sudden she grabbed Kariven's arm. "I feel it! Their psychic probe just touched me. They're close!"

The three men, without even looking at each other, drew their Colts and flipped the safety off with their thumbs.

"Those aren't going to stop them," Yuln murmured with a weak smile. "When they get in range, it'll be too late."

She opened her handbag and pulled out a small disintegrator cone that she clutched nervously in her hand. "I still don't know if they're looking for us in a car or in the air safe inside their spaceship. They want to kill us, me and Zimko, whatever it takes, in the hope of decapitating the Alliance." She gasped, "They're coming closer!"

The young lady closed her eyes and sent out a flood of psychic waves searching for the green Denebians. Her breath came faster and faster.

"I see them. They're in a car, a black car, around ten miles behind us."

"Speed up, Jenny!" Angelvin ordered. "Take that road on your left. It's not in good shape but it's a short cut to Guyancourt."

The young brunette ethnographer nodded and pulled the wheel sharply, throwing the car onto a rocky road scarred with ruts. After half an hour, when they got in sight of Guyancourt, Yuln felt a horrible pain in her whole body, a weird pain coming from her brain and instantly spreading through every fiber of her nervous system.

"They... they're coming," she pronounced, fighting with all her supra-natural powers to fend off the painful wave that was racking her. "They're on our trail now with the help of a magnetic detector.... The bulk of our car... is their marker..."

"I'm going to skirt along the ditch," Jenny quickly decided, getting a firm grip on the steering wheel. "Everyone jump and I'll let the car roll on by itself onto the airstrip. Chop chop, my darling Robert," she said, finding her collegiate vocabulary return.

Angelvin opened the door and dove out. He jumped up and ran to catch up to the Vedette and pick up his friends. Dormoy and Kariven jumped and were also running next to the car. Yuln threw herself into Kariven's arms. All four of them hurried into the sparse bushes along the road and waited, guns drawn and hearts beating fast. 50 yards on, the brave Jenny jumped out of the moving vehicle. Rolling at only six or seven miles an hour it pretty much kept going straight.

Jenny hiked up her skirt with no false modesty and crawled in the ditch toward her friends. The red lights of the Vedette, which was starting to zigzag now, went slowly into the night. Luckily a cluster of clouds drift over and timidly hid the moon.

"There they are!" Yuln whispered, inching closer to Kariven.

With one elbow on the ground she aimed her disintegrator cone. A black Citroën Traction with its lights off was coming down the road. It was speeding up gradually despite the pits and ditches, going 30 miles an hour only ten yards away from the group lying on the ground. Yuln aimed and pressed the trigger with her index finger. A blue ray shot out, briefly lighting up the countryside, and enveloped the black Citroën. The car turned purple and as bright as molten metal. In a fraction of a second it went from purple to blinding white like a flash of burning magnesium, then everything went black. The car had disappeared, disintegrated, its atoms transformed into free energy.

"Shoo, you didn't miss!" Angelvin breathed a sigh of relief.

Yuln was about to respond but she froze, tense. "Another car is coming... but I don't feel anything..."

"Maybe they're just driving, lovers or something."

No," the young Polarian said. "I see them... they're Denebians! But they don't have a psychic probe. Only the car I disintegrated was carrying the device... I see them very well..."

With a blank expression on her face she seemed to be listening to something that the others could not hear.

"There are three of them," she continued. "Three Denebians and one Earthling behind the wheel. They're all armed with thermal ray rifles. The Denebians won't spot me without a psychic detector until they're 50 yards away. Their paranormal senses are less developed than ours."

After five minutes of anxious waiting a Peugeot 203 arrived, its headlights turned down. When it was in sight of the airfield it stopped and turned off its lights completely.

"They're surprised that they don't see the first car," she whispered, clutching her disintegrator cone. "But they're too far for me to shoot."

The driverless Vedette had stopped almost two miles farther on, running into a runway marker on the airstrip.

"They're not sure and they're going to split up and surround the airport."

Sure enough, the four doors of the Peugeot opened at the same time and three pseudo-men got out, dressed simply in a bodysuit with a big belt from which hung a sheath. Black helmets covered their heads. Each of them held a kind of rifle with a short barrel that ended in a parabolic antenna. Their green, scaly skin glimmered in the moonlight and made them look like living statues, bronze statues but tarnished green. The Earthling who was with them—wearing a dark, felt hat—was also carrying a thermal rifle. They walked toward the Vedette, spreading out and looking around them, intrigued by the absence of the Citroën.

The human accomplice of the Denebians, taking his own way to get to the Vedette from the rear, walked toward the bushes where the explorers and their friends were hiding.

"He's going to find us," the Polarian girl hissed. "We can't hit him with my disintegrator or with your noisy guns or we'll attract the attention of the others."

Angelvin shook his right arm and the stiletto dropped directly into his hand. He got up on his knees, held up the blade and fired it at the man walking ten feet from their hiding place. The stiletto flew off like an arrow and buried itself in the hoodlum's throat. Dropping his rifle the man threw his hands up to his neck. Gasping for air, suffocating, his eyes turned up, he wobbled and then fell into the grass without uttering a sound. Everything happened in total silence. The Denebians did not suspect a thing. Kariven crawled over to the dead man, snatched away the thermal rifle and donned his felt hat, which had rolled off into the grass. He stood up and got on the road the way he was walking. From a distance, in the shadows of the night, the Denebians would not recognize the switch.

Dormoy, Angelvin, Yuln and Jenny started crawling toward the three Denebians. Kariven made a sign to his friends to attack from behind as he got closer to the green monster on his left.

The Denebians slowed down as they converged on the Vedette. When they were than only around 30 yards from each other Kariven made sure that his friends were close enough to fire. He walked another ten yards on the left and pointed the antenna of the rifle at the monsters. Then he pressed the only button on the formidable weapon. A pale yellow ray shot out with a low crackling sound. The light ray hit the first Denebian and charred him in one second. At the same time the Colts fired off a deafening round. The two other green monsters were hit and dropped to the ground. One of them struggled up on one elbow and tried to raise his rifle but the bright flash from Yuln's disintegrator swept over the airfield. The two monstrous corpses looked like they turned into purple puppets before the night once again covered the peaceful terrain. Of the Denebians (the third one had just been disintegrated) nothing remained but a bad memory.

Off in the distance a dog was barking furiously, woken up by the gunshots. The closest house was three miles away so they had no fear of an unexpected visit.

"We got 'em!" Dormoy shouted in joy, as he holstered his pistol.

"Let's get back in the car," Yuln advised, "and leave it at the entrance to the airfield. We can send a message to your father tomorrow, Jenny, so he can come and get it."

The Vedette, whose bumpers were barely dented, was brought back to the entrance on the gravel road, not far from the Peugeot.

Angelvin went back to look at the first corpse. "Come and see this, Kariven!"

Kariven ran over and shined his flashlight on the grimacing face of the dead man. "It's the guy with the brown hat who was spying on us in the restaurant!"

"Exactly," Angelvin retrieved his stiletto from the guy's throat. He wiped the blade on the corpse's clothes and when he was sure there was no trace of blood he put it back into the sheath on his forearm, hidden under his sleeve.

"Get back," the Polarian ordered.

She aimed her disintegrator and made the body disappear in a flash. Then pointing at their hunters' Peugeot, she gave it the same treatment.

"No need to leave any tracks behind us," she said, calmly putting the little cone back into her handbag.

It was no everyday sight, these three men and two young ladies, one in a black suit and the other in a low-cut dress, waiting at a small, empty airport in the middle of the night...

"Zimko at last!" the blond Polarian shouted, looking up.

Her companions raised their eyes but saw nothing but sky and twinkling stars. In a moment, however, one of the stars seemed to be getting bigger, becoming phosphorescent, emerald green and soon turned into a luminous disc spinning around. The flying saucer descended at high speed and stopped on a dime, five feet off the ground. A breath of warm wind rustled the Polarian's dress and lifted Jenny's skirt.

Yuln took Kariven's hand and the two of them hurried toward it, followed by Jenny and Angelvin with Dormoy bringing up the rear. One after another they climbed up the tilted walkway and lowered their heads to enter the hatch of the spaceship.

Zimko, dressed in a Chinese robe of green silk embroidered with black and yellow dragons, burst out laughing at their astonished faces. "I didn't have time to change when I left China."

On his cue they sat in the reclining seats installed around the cockpit. Dormoy and Angelvin could not believe their eyes. They were inside a flying saucer! Inside one of those machines that had been making headlines for years!

Jenny had already visited this spaceship a few years ago.

The disc took off without the slightest vibration and almost straight up into the night sky at 3,000 miles an hour.

"What's the plan for the party and where do we fit in?" Kariven asked, glad to be seeing his extra-terrestrial friend again.

"You're going to take part in a mission as observers, Earthlings and spokesmen. As for our destination... I'll give you three guesses."

Kariven and his companions shrugged their shoulders and frowned.

The Polarian declared calmly, "We're off to Moscow."

CHAPTER FIVE

"To... Moscow?" the anthropologist repeated, dubious and, it must be said, uneasy.

"I know," Zimko smiled, "that Russia is not a very welcoming country. In the present state of international tension it's tough to get in... and especially dangerous to get out, but we have to go there. It's part of our plan to set up the Earth-Polarian Alliance. Your planet, my friends, is split into two hostile blocs. The blows that result could start a war, a stupid war that would profit only our common enemy: the Denebians. Unfortunately, men have not yet reached a high degree of Wisdom. Not the USA and even less so Russia would agree to listen to us calmly without trying to win us over to their side. Now, we refuse categorically to take either side...

"We Polarians whom Earthly Tradition calls the Dragons of Wisdom are in a way the apostles of non-violence. However, we're often forced to use violence. You've witnessed this over the last 48 hours. We hate to kill but we don't hesitate to do so when the security of a planet is at stake. And the Denebians are the very ones putting the future of Earth at risk."

"But what are we going to do in Russia?" Angelvin insisted.

"Kidnap Professor Serge Yegov, the famous atomic physicist, Head of the Atomgrad Factory/Laboratory Center. This very important man is on vacation in Moscow at the moment. It's very unusual and we have to take advantage of it."

"What's the point of kidnapping him?"

"We've done the same with a number of scientists in every country to build up a group of scientific authorities who will, come D-Day, bear witness to our good faith to the countries of Earth."

"The mysterious disappearances of scientists reported over the past few years all over the world are your work?"

"I don't deny it, Kariven. These scientists are neither hostages nor prisoners. We treat them as guests and take them to our Galactic Confederation, meaning the planets that we protect or that we are helping to develop, socially and techno- logically speaking. When we bring them back to Earth at the right time, they'll vouch for our peaceful intentions toward Earthlings. And they will be believed, because of their charac- ter and their arrival all together on Polarian spaceships coming to protect your planet from any eventual attack by the crea- tures from Deneb.

"Right now you will have to excuse me. I'm going to take off this old Chinese rag which was great when getting around China but of little use in the streets of Moscow. Your sport coats and double-breasted jackets," he remarked to the explorers, "and especially the American cut, will make you stand out among the Soviets. We gong to fix all that. Please come with me."

Jenny remained alone with Yuln who had just taken off her dress and put back on her midnight blue bikini with shift- ing colors along with her short, see-through tunic tight at the waist. She swapped her heels for the shiny short boots and went back to her post at the controls, turning off the automatic pilot.

The young French woman contemplated the bronze- skinned Polarian who read everything in her mind like an open book. Then she offered, "Would you like to try on one of these tunics, Jenny? I have a new one that would look radiant on you and match your pale skin perfectly. Go into my cabin," she pointed to an oval hatchway, "and take the protective en- velop marked with a green star out of the metalo-plastic dress- er. You'll find a complete outfit inside. We're pretty much the same size so I think it should fit you fine."

15 minutes later Zimko and the Earthlings came back in- to the cockpit. All four had put on a black uniform, tight at the collar and decorated with stripes on the shoulders. They wore

black boots, black caps with short bills and holstered pistols in their belts. They stopped at the entrance to the cockpit and stared at Jenny.

The young lady, a little confused, had buckled her gold belt around a splendid green, see-through tunic that hid nothing of her graceful curves. Short, green boots with red edges went halfway up her muscular calves. Like Yuln she wore a light helmet the same color as her tunic, from which her brown curls flowed down.

Angelvin purred the usual two-note whistle of admiration and pulled her to him. "A symphony in green! You're ravishing as a Girl from Space, Jenny."

She cuddled his chest for a moment and then gently wriggled free, almost with regret. "What's this costume of yours?" she poked her finger at Angelvin's chest.

"It's not a costume," Zimko corrected her. "These are real uniforms from the MVD[81]... or almost if you consider that they were made in Kodha, the capital planet of the Pole Star. The material is bulletproof and heat resistant up to 2,500°C. With our gloves and attachable hood we can safely walk through 500 yards of inferno. Beyond that the fireproof cloth will still protect us from flames but we'll heat up inside to around 67°C or 150°F, which is not very comfortable."

Where are we? he asked Yuln through telepathy.

The blond girl pressed a button and the screen it up, transformed into a radar display over a map of Central Europe. A red dot was moving east following a path that was roughly east-north-east.

"We're over Warsaw," she announced, slowly turning a small multiplier wheel. On the screen the bright red dot representing the flying saucer suddenly sped up.

---

[81] Special Force of the Ministry of Internal Affairs, *Ministerstvo Vnutrennikh Del*, or MVD, in the USSR. (Author's Note)

Kariven examined the map twice and said, "You just said we were flying over Warsaw and now the red dot just passed Smolensk, around 500 miles away!"

Yuln turned the wheel in the other direction, looked over at a dancing needle and then back to the red dot that slowed down enormously. "But we were only going 30,000 miles an hour," she joked and then mischievously, "Sometimes it's good that they think our ships are just meteors, even though they can go really fast. I brought our speed down to 600 miles an hour and that's nothing compared to what this ship can do in space. For an interstellar voyage our standard of measure is the Parsec and for longer distances the Megaparsec[82]."

"That's mind-boggling," Kariven mumbled, thinking of the immeasurable value of these numbers.

"But at a low speed won't we be detected by the Russian radar?"

"Not to fear, Michel," Zimko assured him. "Our ship is equipped with a special device that absorbs radar waves. The device is working right now. The stations on the ground won't even receive the echo from our passing by, especially since we've been surrounded by an invisibility shield once we entered the Soviet air space."

"We're over the Moscow suburbs now," Yuln announced, reducing speed and turning a micrometric dial."

The map on the screen disappeared and was replaced by a direct video system. Moscow, the powerful capital of the USSR, appeared on the convex surface of the viewer. The dark mass of the Kremlin, surrounded by a wall, stood in the middle of the city in contrast to the brighter Red Square. Everyone seemed to be sleeping in the Bolshevik metropolis

---

[82] Parsec: 19 trillion, 515 billion miles roughly (19,515,000,000,000) or 206,265 times the distance of the Earth from the Sun (around 93 million miles). Megaparsec: 1 million parsecs. Between these two units is the Kiloparsec equal to 1,000 parsecs. (Author's Note)

where only a few lights cut through the night. The big avenues looked like bright ribbons woven around the apartment blocks.

Very slowly the flying saucer set down on a wide lawn bordered by flowers in the middle of Ismailov Park. Hovering five feet off the ground the ship deployed its tilted plank. Yuln and Jenny remained in the cockpit. Zimko and the three explorers opened the hatch underneath after turning off the lighting in the interior corridor, which would have given them away in the dark night.

Walking across the lawn Zimko whispered to his friends, "Don't say a word. Whatever situation we get into, let me do the talking. Besides, our MVD uniforms will be a kind of free pass for us. If I remember correctly from my study of Russian life, the Special Force was pretty fierce and feared by every level of society."

The streets were deserted, lit every step of the way by electric streetlamps. The entrances to the subway were closed. The whole city seemed asleep. Once in a while, in the distance, a motorcycle or car drove by, disturbing the nocturnal silence. Zimko concentrated, standing still amidst his friends at an intersection. The strange, psychic abilities of the Polarian were searching the Soviet capital. In less than a minute his mental projection located the man he sought.

"Professor Yegov is in an apartment provided by the Supreme Soviet, Zimko explained. "But the building is well guarded. We still have a mile to go. The hardest part is yet to come… particularly for us to 'requisition' a car."

When they crossed the intersection they were blinded by the headlights of a big car that was just driving off. It was an aerodynamic, luxury Pobeda.[83] It pulled a quick U-turn and stopped in front of the four men just as they were stepping onto the sidewalk.

"*Stoï!*[84]" shouted one of the passengers inside.

---

[83] The GAZ-M20 Pobeda (Victory) was a passenger car produced in the Soviet Union by GAZ from 1946 until 1958.

[84] Stop! (Author's Note)

Two superior officers of the MVD, hands on the butt of the Nagans[85] on their belts approached the four pseudo-officers.

Zimko snapped to attention, clicking his heels together, right away imitated by the three explorers. The superior officer—blond, square-jawed and with protruding ears—barked something at Zimko. He answered in perfect Russian, still at attention. The Russian eyed the three explorers and their uniforms, then frowned before yelling at Zimko again.

Angelvin received a mental order: *Button your coat!*

The ethnographer realized immediately that he had missed his third button. He corrected his error and went back to his flawless stance of attention.

The officer threw them a nasty look and said, "*Douraki!*[86]"

He shouted a few more curt, stinging remarks. The rare pedestrians crossing the street hurried their step, having little desire to get in trouble with these MVD officers, the terror of the citizens. All of a sudden the superior officer slapped Zimko but in the middle of striking the Polarian a second time the Russian's hand stopped in mid-air and dropped to his side.

The Polarian had just sent into his mind the order to get back in the car and take the wheel himself. The officer slammed the car door before the Pobeda sped off as the four friends saluted it and clicked their heels.

Zimko rubbed his cheek. His eyes, behind his half-closed lids, lit up with a strange, cold glare of rage. "He slapped me because I refused to follow him. We were almost arrested. It seems that the MVD is confined to quarters tonight. Reason: purging the officers."

In the distance they heard a crash, then another, louder, accompanied by the sound of broken glass and smashed metal.

"How careless," Zimko mocked in a tone of false sympathy.

---

[85] Russian automatic pistol. (Author's Note)
[86] Idiots! (Author's Note)

"Do you mean…" Angelvin inquired.

"Yes. The maniac and his three little pigs are now in a better world. Their Pobeda just dove off a bridge over the railroad at 70 miles an hour and smashed 50 yards below into the train tracks. The fast moving Moscow-Voronej will be one and a half hours late tonight. An unfortunate accident," he sighed ironically, massaging his jaw.

Suddenly his expression changed. "The Denebians! I feel them…"

"Here in Russia?" Kariven was surprised. "Have they spotted us?"

"They can't," Zimko answered, concentrating. "I'm protected by the scrambler on board our ship. No, they're searching for someone else. By the Gods! I see them now! The green reptiles are in a Moskvitch[87]… A Russian is driving… They're almost at Professor Yegov's! Not a minute to lose… We have to get a car."

They ran off and got to a big avenue where a few cars were passing by. Zimko stood in the middle of the street and waved his arms over his head. He stopped a Zis [88] that looked like an expensive Packard. The brakes screeched and the big car came to a halt. A young blond was driving, her hair held up by an embroidered silk scarf. With pinched lips she held out her papers frigidly. Zimko made a sign to his friends and threw open the doors. He pushed the young lady aside and sat behind the wheel.

"Keep your papers, I don't care about them," he said, driving off.

The three explorers looked out the rear window to make sure that their "crime" had not attracted attention.

---

[87] Moskvitch was an automobile produced by AZLK from 1946 to 1991.

[88] The Zis was a limousine produced by Zavod Imeni Stalina. It was introduced in 1936 and was equipped with an 5.8 L (354 cu in) straight-8 engine. Production ended in 1941.

The young Russian sat gaping at them, staring at one after another in their MVD uniforms but who were acting in such a weird way. While driving Zimko probed the girl's subconscious. After a minute he turned to her and smiled.

"Don't be afraid, Doniatchka Petrovna. We don't like the MVD any more than you do... even though we're wearing the uniform."

The girl looked at him in fear, then abruptly took something out of her bag. Before she could bring her closed hand to her mouth Zimko grabbed her fist and twisted it. She wailed and opened her hand. A white pill dropped onto her knee and rolled off onto the carpet.

"Cyanide, eh?" Zimko read her mind. "I don't have time to explain to you but I guarantee you that you're not under arrest. We needed your car, Doniatchka. It was just luck that brought you there at that moment, that's all."

The Polarian stopped the Zis just before an intersection and turned to smile at his friends. "Won't she run off and sound the alarm?" Kariven whispered, who had, like his partners, not understood a word of their conversation.

"No. I forced her psychically to wait for us. The poor girl wanted to swallow cyanide, convinced that we belong to the MVD."

"Is that motive enough to commit suicide?"

"Doniatchka's brother recently slipped over into West Germany. So, she's afraid that we heard about why he's disappeared. In which case she would have to suffer the same fate as the relatives of anyone suspected of escaping..."

The Man from Outer Space whispered when they got to modern, eight-story building, "We're here. Behind this door are two soldiers on watch. There are two more in the elevator and another two in the apartment."

Kariven admired the eerie, superhuman abilities that allowed the Polarian to "see" through matter. Zimko concentrated and emitted a flood of mental waves that worked through hypnosis on the soldiers guarding the famous atomic physicist. Then he sent out a psychic order. The door opened. The sentry, like a robot, let them in and quietly closed the door behind them. They climbed up the stairs, careful not to make the steps creak, and on the landing passed between the two guards as still as their colleagues at the entrance. The door of the apartment opened soundlessly and closed behind the intruders. The Russian soldier went back to his place next to his frozen partner.

Stay here. I'll go look for the professor, Zimko told his friends.

In total darkness he headed for a door and entered the room where the Soviet scientist was sleeping. He got around amazingly easily with his paroptic vision compensating for the lack of light. Kariven and his companions held their breath in the dark, under the spell of this weird abduction. Next to them, the regular breathing of the hypnotized guards echoed like snoring in the suffocating silence. A light touch drew their attention and made them shiver.

Open the door, Kariven heard in his head.

The explorer felt around for the doorknob. He stepped forward, bumped into one of the soldiers and jumped back. His heart was beating a thousand miles an hour. Losing his balance the Russian, stiff as a statue, toppled over onto the floor. The noise from his fall was absorbed by the deep-pile carpet. Kariven finally found the knob and opened the door. The faint light from the landing was almost blinding to all of them after the time spent in the dark.

Professor Serge Yegov walked out, staring ahead, unconscious of his guides. Around 50 years old he wore a black suit and dark brown overcoat. He had no tie; his shirt collar was open and his shoes untied. Zimko had to act fast and not worry about the minor details of his clothes.

As they walked downstairs the Polarian worked on Professor Yegov's mind, making him stop. "The Denebians are coming," he whispered to the explorers. "Wait here for me!"

He rushed back up the stairs, ran into the apartment and opened the window looking out on the street. Zimko plucked out what looked like a flashlight from his pocket and pressed a button, holding it out over the car. The door that was opening froze.

The Polarian slipped the device back into his pocket and left. Back with his friends he said, "Quickly! I paralyzed them for 15 minutes."

The hurried down the stairs guiding the professor.

"Take him to the girl's car and don't hesitate to shoot anyone from the MVD if they bother you. I'll meet you there in a minute."

Zimko turned around and cast another dose of hypnotic waves at the sentinels guarding the building. The five Russians, still standing, drooped their heads to sleep for the next eight hours. Then he went to the Moskvitch. On his mental order a Denebian seemed to regain consciousness and got out of the car. Guided by Zimko the green creature walked next to him all the way to the Zis.

"We're taking this Denebian with us, my friends," he said, opening the rear door.

Kariven, Dormoy and Angelvin shuddered at the sight of the monster whose red eyes, striped with yellow, shined brightly in the night. His glistening body gave off a sharp odor. Dormoy sat in the folding seat to the right, Angelvin on the left, leaving the back seat to Kariven, Professor Yegov and the Denebian. Even though unconscious the creature from Deneb still scared the explorers. Angelvin, sitting across from the monster, shrank down and folded his legs under the seat.

Zimko planted himself in front of the Moskvitch and pulled out his disintegrator cone. In the blinding flash the car and its passengers disappeared forever. Back in the Zis he started the car and drove off with a sigh of relief. The trickiest part of their mission was accomplished. Once again, while heading back to Ismailov Park, he probed the girl's mind, which would soon hold no more secrets from him.

Doniatchka Petrovna, a doctor at the Lenin Clinic, was 27 years old. She was living in fear of the day that they would find out that her brother (an engineer) had escaped into West

Berlin two weeks ago. Her distress at the sight of the MVD uniforms was quite understandable.

The Zis finally covered the last 100 yards to the park. Its passengers got out in front of a small door in the monumental gate and hurriedly followed Zimko, who was the only one to "see" the flying saucer protected by its invisibility shield.

"Why did you spare this Denebian and above all what are we going to do with this Russian?"

"I'll explain everything in a minute, Kariven."

Angelvin swore loudly and rubbed his forehead.

"Sorry, pal!" Zimko smiled. "Our ship may be invisible, but it's still very solid. That wasn't empty air you just bumped into, Robert, but the front of the flying saucer."

The ethnographer massaged his forehead and sneered, swearing again as he marched up the plank into the belly of the ship.

On seeing him come in, Jenny threw herself into his arms. "Oh, Robert, I was so worried," she muttered, closing her eyes in relief and rubbing her cheek against his. When she opened her eyes she yelped in fear and jumped back. The Denebian was standing motionless in the middle of the cabin. Its weird uniform hid little of its shiny green, scaly skin. Its red and yellow, expressionless eyes stared straight ahead.

"Don't worry, Jenny, he's hypnotized."

The French girl watched him with the same apprehension. Fighting against these monsters at the Guyancourt airport in the night was one thing but seeing one two feet away another thing entirely! Staying rational, she looked away from the hideous creature and turned curiously to Professor Yegov and the young Russian lady with ash blond hair. She squinted scornfully at Doniatchka's tight-fitting dress, certainly up-to-date in Russia but appalling in the eyes of a French woman, a Parisian to boot.

Yuln was about to press the button for takeoff when her brother stopped her. "Not yet, Yuln. This young lady is not on our program. If she doesn't want to go with us I have no right to keep her. Since she's no celebrity on the Soviet scene, she's different than the professor. I'll question her in English because she speaks it pretty well. The library at her clinic—I saw in her mind—has a number of medical and surgical volumes in English. She's studied them all in detail. For now we should change our clothes," he proposed to the explorers. "After that we can deal with her."

He sent a mental order to the Denebian who crept off and shut himself in Yuln's cabin. When they come back, having traded the MVD uniforms for their usual clothes, the Polarian awoke Doniatchka. The young, blond Russian fluttered her eyelids, turned her head to the right and left, and paid more attention to the room—completely foreign to her—than to the people around her. The circular cabin made of blue metal, lighted mysteriously, with its chrome, half-moon command post, its huge, convex screen, its windows and the two girls wearing such strange clothes... or wearing so little, was all this real or was she dreaming?

Still without saying a word, she looked at Professor Yegov, thought for a minute, then remembered having seen his photo in *Pravda*. What in the world was the greatest Russian atomic physicist doing in her dream? As for the two young beauties in see-through tunics, she recognized them. She had often seen heroines like them in the novels of Yefremov, Belyaev and Bulgakov[89]. It was all very simple: she was subconsciously reliving one of those unlikely adventures she had read about in a science fiction novel. Scraps of memory and some astonishingly precise details were decorating her dream...

"No, Doniatchka," Zimko set her straight, capturing her train of thought. "You're not dreaming. This really is Professor Yegov sitting here and these two young ladies are not heroines out of a science fiction novel. You're on board a ship that we'll discuss later, in Russian, but that you know about

---

[89] Famous Russian science fiction authors. (Author's Note) Ivan Antonovich Yefremov (1908-1972); Alexander Belyaev (1884-1942); Mikhail Bulgakov (1891-1940).

from the American and English radio you often listen to. I'm referring to flying saucers."

Doniatchka, confused, noticed that these men were no longer wearing the MVD uniforms. If she was not dreaming, the man who was talking had lost his mind.

"Don't be stupid!" she exploded. "Where have you taken me and what do you plan to do with me?"

Yuln walked up and put her hand on the girl's shoulder. "My brother isn't joking Doniatchka. You really are inside a spaceship that the Earthlings call a flying saucer. These green tunics that Jenny and I, Yuln, are wearing are the common outfit on the planet that my brother and I come from. But this is an irrelevant detail. You're free, Doniatchka, free to leave. We're not holding you here," and she pointed to the hatch. "However, answer me very honestly and rest assured that we don't belong to the MVD: Do you want to leave Russia? And if so do you want to join your brother in West Berlin?"

Doniatchka had slowly lowered her head. Now her face was buried in hands and she was weeping. "My God! Please, don't let this be a dream!"

Zimko made a sign to his sister. Yuln nodded, went back to the command post and pressed a button. Without the passengers feeling a thing the flying saucer shot straight up into the sky. With a sharp turn to the right it headed west at 1,200 miles an hour.

With Jenny's help, Dormoy tried to calm down the young Russian. Crying with joy, she still hesitated to accept the truth.

When Professor Yegov regained consciousness, the first thing he noticed was the strange outfits of Yuln and Jenny. He could not believe his eyes and let them drop down to the seat he was in. Were these gorgeous beauties nymphs or fairies?

Zimko hurried up to enlighten him and started to explain in detail to him and his blond compatriot the why and wherefore of their presence on board the flying disc. The scientist and young doctor, mouths open, all ears, could not believe the adventure they were on.

"You don't like the war, Professor Yegov," Zimko con-cluded, "any more than the western scientists working like you on atomic weapons. However, on government's orders they have to be produced and you do it. But when will Earthlings be less stupid and join together instead of hating each other? The Earth is threatened! Humanity is facing the greatest dan-ger that it's ever faced. And men are there, in the East on one side and in the West on the other, shaking their fists before slugging each other! It's crazy!"

"The capitalist countries..." the Russian scientist began.

Zimko waved off the objection. "Let go of these ridicu-lous slogans designed to indoctrinate the blind and dumb masses! Are you waiting, you Men of Earth, for millions of Denebians to strike your planet and enslave your race before you finally realize the dreadful danger that's looming over you people?"

Shaken up by this impassioned diatribe Professor Yegov spoke clumsily and without conviction. "Oh! Oh, but there's no immediate danger. You're going to..."

"And *this*?" the Polarian shouted, psychically ordering the Denebian to come out of his hiding place.

Dormoy jumped over and sat next to Doniatchka. "You're going to be scared, very scared, but what you'll see is under the control of Zimko's powerful mental faculties. Try not to be afraid."

Impressed by his words she looked where he did. The door in the blue metal wall slowly opened. The green monster stepped out like a snake-skinned parody of man! Doniatchka screamed and fell against Dormoy. Trembling convulsively she buried her face in the geophysicist's chest.

Professor Yegov jumped up and stumbled back, his legs wobbling before the terrifying Denebian who was walking toward him.

"And *this*, Professor?" Zimko repeated, pointing to the green monster who was now standing still in the middle of the cabin. "Is this proof enough? These horrid creatures are al-ready among the Earthlings... and we were a hair's breadth away from falling into their clutches tonight. In fact," almost as an aside, "it's this prisoner of ours who will tell you why the Denebians wanted to kidnap you. We're lucky that you all understand English otherwise our communication would get pretty complicated."

Turning to the pseudo-human from Deneb, he spoke in English, "Why did you want to kidnap Professor Yegov?"

In a weird, throaty voice the frightful creature answered, "We decided to imitate your tactic, to kidnap scientists and make them serve as witnesses for us later. We treat them with a psychic annihilator and imprint their brains with a film of artificial memories showing life—as Earthlings need to imagine it—on your planets."

"What kind of memories, for example?"

"We insist on our pacifism and our desire to help humans *against the Polarian aggressors*."

"Ah, because you show them that we are the aggressors?" the Polarian emphasized.

"Yes," the blank-eyed monster replied. "17 renowned scientists and 53 specialists in all branches have been captured recently and submitted constantly to this treatment."

"So, where are these Earthlings?"

"Yesterday they were still at our astrobase beyond Pluto's orbit. But while waiting, we decided to bring them to our mobile base stationed in Australia for the moment."

"While waiting for *what*?" the Polarian shouted at these monsters' audacity.

"The order to unleash psychological warfare on Earth."

CHAPTER SIX

Alarmed, the Man from Outer Space demanded details, but to no avail. And searching the Denebian prisoner's brain he found nothing to refute what he had said.

"I don't know exactly what the psychological warfare consists of. I don't know when, how or where it will break out."

"Where in Australia is your base? What role does it play in your plan for domination?"

"Our base is temporarily NNW of the Wyola Lakes in the Great Victoria Desert."

While pursuing his interrogation, Zimko, thanks to his surprising psychic abilities, mentally ordered his sister, "Head for southern Australia and tell me when we're flying over No Man's Land."

"Our base," the green creature went on, "contains a commando unit of 500 Denebian secret agents. They've infiltrated every country on this planet. Working in groups of at least three, they bring the captured scientists back to the base and receive new orders."

"How long have you been operating on Earth?"

"Since the Earth year 1945, basically. Because our attention to this civilization was attracted by the first atomic explosions. Before that we had nothing to do with this solar system."

"It was your first nuclear experiments that also caused us to come to your planet," the Polarian explained to his Earthling friends. "In fact, we're afraid that by manipulating the forces whose power you're still not aware of, you'll cause a disaster, a cataclysm not only fatal to your own world but that could seriously disrupt the orbit of other planets in the solar system."

Zimko put the Denebian in a chair.

"In what countries have you accomplished your missions and what were they about?"

In his hoarse voice the green monster answered calmly, unemotionally because under Zimko's control, "We've operated in the USA, in South America, in Europe and in Asia. Now we're starting to prospect Australia. Our permanent mission is to track down and, as far as possible, eliminate the Polarians. We are also kidnapping scientists and taking stock of the economic and industrial potential of this planet."

"Have you eliminated any Polarians?" Zimko asked, trembling with anger.

"Many, yes. Some were killed. Those we were able to capture killed themselves when we want to interrogate them. Our technicians were forced to create a device to paralyze the bio-electric energy of the Polarians in order to keep them alive until they talked."

The Polarian figured it would be good to enlighten his friends a little: "In a huge release of psychic power, we can gather all our electrostatic energy in our brain. We become, then, a lost cause and short-circuit our cerebral neurons, making our brains explode. Death, of course, is instantaneous. Those of us who fall into Denebian hands do this to avoid betraying our brothers. These monsters' interrogation is useless against us. We're impregnable to hypnosis. You can paralyze us, make us suffer horrible pain by psycho-probes or psychic detectors, but a lengthy incursion into our subconscious is something not possible. If these cursed creatures discover a process to destroy our mental abilities, it would only increase the danger to humans. Our enemies, therefore, have to capture a lot of Polarians and interrogate them on the progress of our operations."

Astounded by everything they had just learned, Professor Yegov and Doniatchka barely flinched only an hour after their departure from Moscow when they heard Yuln announce, "We're flying over the Victoria Desert now."

Covering the distance from Moscow to the Victoria Desert at an average speed of 12,000 miles an hour, the flying saucer was decelerating and spiraling down on the spot over Wyola Lake given by the prisoner. Protected by the invisibility shield, off the radar by its absorber, the saucer hovered 15,000 feet in the air.

It was daytime in this hemisphere of the Earth. Embedded in the vast, ochre sand dunes a group of blue lakes shimmered in the sun. On the screen, a natural map of the area rolled by.

"The Denebian could not have lied," Dormoy figured. "We just can't see very well where or what kind of base is hiding in this desert of sand."

With all his senses on alert, with his eyes fixed on the zoomed-in topography, Zimko probed the captive. In a short time his face relaxed and his eyes lost their weird, purplish glimmer. "I've seen it. It's a giant disc, almost 500 yards in diameter. Its surface has the look of sand, so it's undetectable to naked eye."

Yuln pressed a bunch of buttons on the control panel. The map disappeared from the screen. The image of a huge flying saucer showed up, in relief and in color, to the great surprise of the Earthlings. The gigantic ship, topped by a hemispherical dome with rectangular windows, lay in the yellow desert sand.

All of a sudden on the green radar screen a dot flashed on and off—as the point of reference in the middle of the screen was slowly turning. The dot disappeared and the radar turned off. On the convex screen the natural landscape of the Australian desert was pictured.

"Another flying saucer!" Kariven cried out on seeing the metal disc glimmering in the sunlight.

Yuln zoomed in on the desert. In close-up the ship was shaped more like a horseshoe. In the back, on each side, were installed the jet engines spitting out yellow-purple flames. In the middle was a plexiglas cockpit protecting the pilot who was wearing a stratospheric spacesuit.

"But it's a human!" the Russian girl muttered, her astonished eyes open wide.

Zimko frowned, honestly surprised. He was about to use his paroptic vision and sixth sense but Kariven stopped his psychic inspection. "You have before you, Zimko, the first flying saucer built by men. This ship is nothing other than the Canadian Saucer *Omega*, designed by an English engineer and produced by the Avro Canada factories near Malton[90]. Its being here is perfectly logical. Right now we are over the Woomera Test Facilities[91]. This huge base testing range starts in Pimba, in southern Australia, and ends at Christmas Island in the middle of the Indian Ocean. So, it crosses the whole continent."

At 1,500 miles an hour the Omega shot up into the stratosphere, leaving far behind it the shrill of its multiple jets.

"I was surprised, I admit," Zimko confessed. "We knew of the existence of this ship, still in the experimental stage, but personally I'd never seen it."

---

[90] See *The Flying Saucers Come from Another World*, q.v. (Author's Note) The Avro Canada VZ-9 Avrocar was a VTOL aircraft developed by Avro Aircraft Ltd. (Canada) as part of a secret U.S. military project carried out in the early years of the Cold War. The Avrocar intended to exploit the Coandă effect to provide lift and thrust from a single turborotor blowing exhaust out the rim of the disk-shaped aircraft to provide anticipated VTOL-like performance. In the air, it would have resembled a flying saucer. Originally designed as a fighter-like aircraft capable of very high speeds and altitudes, the project was repeatedly scaled back over time and the U.S. Air Force eventually abandoned it. Development was then taken up by the U.S. Army for a tactical combat aircraft requirement, a sort of high-performance helicopter. In flight testing, the Avrocar proved to have unresolved thrust and stability problems that limited it to a degraded, low-performance flight envelope; subsequently, the project was cancelled in September 1961.

[91] Located in the Gibber Plains, 125 miles NW of Port Augusta. (Author's Note)

"The British technicians," the anthropologist added, "also experimented on cigar-shaped spaceships in this area and maybe even over New Zealand. That would explain the many eyewitness reports from trustworthy Australians and New Zealanders who have seen flying saucers and cigars[92]."

"If Earthlings knew about the features and power of our own spaceships," Zimko smiled, "they would never be able to confuse them with the Omega or other spaceships."

Terribly interested in what he had seen on the screen Professor Yegov, in a slightly pedantic voice, jumped in, "We, too, in Russia, have flying wings and even a nuclear-powered flying cigar. I believe I can say that we're far ahead of the western countries in this."

The Polarian flashed an enigmatic smile. "It's not my job to support or deny you in this opinion. I simply hate, once again, that men are struggling to outdo each other. It would be so simple for you to live together on your planet without trying to build weapons and machines to destroy yourselves. I trust you understand this, my friends? I trust the average Earthling understands this too? But nobody is doing anything in the long run to bring about the Golden Age of peace and brotherhood."

Yuln brought back the tele-projection probes of the Denebian base. The blond Girl from Space suddenly alerted her brother, "Look, Zim, something's going on."

In the lower part of the giant axial dome on top of the disc itself, a metal panel was sliding open, slowly, revealing a rectangular opening about 30 feet high and 80 feet wide. Out of the opening came a small flying saucer, a reconnaissance ship 50 feet in diameter by 20 feet high. The ship wobbled gently in the air of the opening, then reared up and shot into the sky at a terrific speed, quiet as a shadow.

"Follow that ship, Yuln!"

---

[92] See *The Flying Saucers Come from Another World*, q.v. (Author's Note)

The flying saucer went immediately from 0 to 1,200 miles an hour. The passengers in the cockpit had felt nothing. And yet, such an abrupt acceleration—in an airplane, for example—should have crushed them into their seats.

"Our spaceships," the Polarian explained, "are fitted with a totally automatic anti-g device. The atoms in our bodies as well as those of the saucer are electro-magnetically harmonized and *submitted to an individual linear acceleration*: all the molecules move forward at the same time, at the same speed and in the direction of the electro-magnetic field[93] that propels us."

Invisible and undetectable, the Polarian spaceship soon caught up to the enemy disc that was starting to slow down. Beneath the two ships was the vast, deserted zone where rockets were tested from Woomera City.

"But," Angelvin wondered, "don't the saucers of the green monsters have invisibility shields like yours?"

"No, otherwise we wouldn't be able to follow this one. The Denebians have not yet reached our level of culture. Their

---

[93] Much simplified here, this is the hypothesis formulated by Lieutenant Jean Plantier of the French Air Force in September 1953. This hypothesis may be considered highly probable. (Author's Note) In 1953, Plantier's Commanding Officer, Captain Rougier, spotted a flying saucer in Blida, Algeria. This led Plantier to write an article entitled "Une hypothèse sur le fonctionnement des Soucoupes Volantes" published in No. 84 (septembre 1953) of the *Revue Mensuelle de l'Armée de l'Air*, and, in 1955, a book entitled *La Propulsion des Soucoupes Volantes par Action Directe sur l'Atome* (Mame), a work of speculative science concerning the possible atomic propulsion systems of UFOs, which also included dozens of summaries of eye witness reports. Plantier assume that all space is permeated by a form of high-powered energy that is the source of cosmic rays, and that UFOs have found a way to convert that energy into motive force.

technology is very developed compared to you Earthlings, but to us it's a living relic from a distant past."

While keeping the enemy ship under surveillance with his superhuman abilities, he continued, "You should be wondering why such an evolved people as ours is at war with the Denebians? It comes from the fact that we always hesitate to use all our power. We could exterminate the Denebian race in less than an hour but we categorically refuse to commit genocide… at least we have so far. In the past the Denebians were satisfied with annexing lifeless planets—to expand their realm by transplanting their race—or worlds with primitive animals or even just vegetation. But now they're taking a little too much interest in Earth, where the civilization is booming. They know all about the birth of the New Race, those men who will conquer space and rule the Universe some day along with us Polarians, who are also men since our two types of humanity belong to the same *Genus Homo*."

"You mean to say, Zimko, that Earthlings and Polarians are *really related*?" the anthropologist was surprised again.

"Without a doubt, Kariven," Yuln answered with a charming smiled. "Someday we'll tell you the mystery of this relation."

Kariven heard the girl's words even though she had stopped talking and run back to the command post. The sounds had disappeared, replaced by the "mind language." Her calm and peaceful voice came to him telepathically while her fingers ran over the electronic keyboard on the control panel.

You could be a Polarian, Kariven, the inner voice echoed, *and I could be an Earthling. We're physically identical. For us, however, as you know, our mental faculties have reached an unheard of degree of perfection. Our extra senses are "super normal phenomena" for you, extra-sensory perceptions. Independent of its physiological form and function similar to yours, our body is a veritable energy capacitor capable of storing up or letting loose a huge discharge that is normally kept in an electrostatic state.*

While chatting, the young Polarian watched the enemy saucer on the screen. Standing firmly before the control panel, facing the giant screen, she had her back turned to the anthropologist. With precise, deliberate movements she pressed buttons, turned knobs and thus kept the ship on course.

Kariven watched her, delightful and desirable, her see-through tunic floating, gliding with every movement.

Jean, the telepathic voice chanted critically, *are you forgetting that my brother is telepathic too? You shouldn't be thinking such thoughts... with him around*, she added after a pause.

The explorer cleared his throat as if this intimate psychic conversation had been heard by everyone. He looked around at his companions: they were talking among themselves and staring out the windows, paying no attention to him. Zimko was watching the screen and projecting his paroptic vision inside the Denebian disc. The anthropologist was reassured: Zimko had certainly not overheard the thought-conversation.

That's no reason... my dear, Yuln replied to his reflections. *I don't want you to kiss me—again!—in front of everyone... even in thought.*

"That's a good one!" Kariven laughed out loud, then he stopped himself, feeling awkward and confused.

Everyone was looking at him, not understanding what his sudden outburst was about. Was it funny to be chasing a spaceship piloted by green monsters?

Angelvin stared hard at him, "What's gotten into you? Are you losing your marbles?"

"Hmm... I... I suddenly remembered this story," he muttered, trying to wave discreetly to Angelvin to hold his tongue.

Without taking his eyes off the screen Zimko launched a brief collective psychic probe. In less than a second he captured all the thoughts going through everyone's minds.

"That is a good one, indeed!" he broke out laughing, which just added to Kariven's confusion.

Yuln frowned, then smiled shyly and said telepathically, *All in all, Jean, it went over pretty well! You can start over again...*

Scrutinizing the screen she spoke aloud for her brother to hear, "The Denebians are doing something! Their ship's been circling a group of men on the ground around those launching pads."

In fact, at an altitude of 10,000 feet the Denebian flying saucer was slowly turning around the Woomera base. Its occupants had no suspicion that they, too, were being spied on.

15 British and Australian *Rocketeers*[94] were busy at the base of a huge scaffolding of metal girders supporting a three-part super-rocket, as tall as a four-story building. Jeeps and trucks with their engines idling were ready to bring the technicians to the blockhouse a few miles away when the alarm to clear out sounded. Hunkered down in the reinforced bunkers half buried in the ground, the specialist could watch the take-off safe from any accident.

After a quick panoptic check of the enemy spaceship Zimko sounded very satisfied when he declared, "Now we don't have to do anything ourselves. The Denebians are going to kidnap Professors Howard and Morrison, the great British experts in building rockets."

"You can't be serious?"

"But of course, Kariven. Our goal is to free the scientists being held by the Denebians on their base. It's better just to wait for them to kidnap these two men before we attack the giant saucer."

"Isn't that overestimating our forces to think that the four of us can face the 500 Denebians camped in their base?" Dormoy objected.

"Did I ever say that there would be *only* four of us to attack the giant saucer?" he smiled enigmatically without explaining.

---

[94] From Rocket: Technicians and specialists in guided missiles. (Author's Note)

The Denebian spaceship on the screen dropped down, swinging from right to left like a dead leaf blowing in the wind. On the ground the Rocketeers had seen it. Stunned, they looked up, shielding their eyes from the sun with their hands. Were they dreaming or was something really unusual descending on them?

The flying saucer sped up, like it was falling, and plopped down in the desert sand, kicking up a cloud of yellow dust.

The Polarian grinned, "Well, well, their tactic isn't so stupid. Pay attention to everything that happens."

The dumbfounded technicians backed up to the Jeeps and trucks. They gradually slowed down, not sure whether to flee… or to stay and see the results of this strange adventure. Now, in spite of their emotions, a kind of unhealthy curiosity drew them in.

A rectangular door slid open in the flying saucer. The Rocketeers backtracked again, some even climbing onto the sideboards of the trucks. A Denebian had appeared behind the dome's doorway, wearing just a short one-piece covering his hideous, green, scaly body. He scrambled up an inner ladder, waved his arms in the air and fell forward. His body, motionless now, was halfway out the doorway, his legs still inside.

With the moment of surprise passed, the English and Australian engineers were babbling to one another. Three of them ended up stepping away from the group and walking nervously toward the ship and its occupant, who was probably dead, suffocated in the different atmosphere. Because now, in the Rocketeers' minds, this flying saucer and its frightening, green-skinned pilot had to be of extra-terrestrial origin.

"These monsters are real psychologists," Zimko grumbled. "They figured rightly that by putting on this show—very impressive to an Earthling—the two great scientists would be the first to want to approach the spaceship. Indeed, those three men who are cautiously but courageously walking up to the flying saucer are none other than Professors Howard and Morrison and the chief engineer of this secret base, Ronny Kinsington."

The three men, having slowed their pace even more, were now 15 feet away from the flying disc. With their eyebrows raised and mouths open they examined the stunning spectacle and wondered if the ship was real and not just a mirage.

The flying saucer, as a result of its "accidental" fall, was leaning to one side. Part of the ship's edge was buried in the sand. From this (deliberate) position the corpse of the Denebian was clearly visible.

Professors Howard and Morrison whispered together with Kinsington and unanimously decided to climb onto the surface of the disc, which had a bunch of concentric circles carved in whereby they could wedge their feet and grip their hands to help them climb more easily. After a few arduous minutes the three men arrived in front of the rectangular hatchway, five feet high by 7 feet wide. The body of the "unfortunate messenger from another planet" (as Professor Morrison had called him) was not moving. Timidly, fearfully, Professor Howard reached out and touched the shiny arm of the Denebian.

"Extraordinary!" the man of science declared. "Its skin is rough, scaly, like a reptile or a saurian! It's... barely warm, almost cold, and oily like certain crocodiles and alligators. Except for its weird skin, its body is pretty much like ours."

"It's ugly," Morrison observed, shuddering with disgust.

"If the situation were reversed, my friend, imagine how this creature here would react if we landed on his home planet. We'd be just as 'ugly' in its eyes... Are you coming?" and he stepped through the hatch leading inside the spaceship. "If the... this creature had companions they must have suffered the same fate. They can't breathe in our atmosphere."

Professor Morrison was skeptical, not sharing either the enthusiasm or confidence of his colleague. Kinsington was also hesitant.

"If... if there are others like him inside, they would probably be prudent enough to stay shut in their pressured cabin. I'm surprised that a being capable of coming to our planet didn't think of spectrographic analysis. No, really, Howard, we should get down and wait for reinforcements to examine this thing."

Professor Howard considered the wise counsel, waffled for a minute, then stubbornly continued, "Aw, the hell with it! It would be a real pity to miss such an opportunity. I'm going to see what's inside. You're free to wait for me out here... with the corpse," he punctuated his speech by nudging the green body with his toe.

"Professor," Kinsington spoke up. "Please, you're about to do something reckless... maybe even fatal. If this... pseudo-man died by breathing our atmosphere, it means we can't breathe his either. Inside this spaceship will be traces of that polluted air. God knows what it's made of? Methane, ammonia, even cyanide or some unknown component..."

"Howard!" Professor Morrison was upset in the face of his colleague's stubbornness. "I beg you, come back!"

Professor Howard shrugged his shoulders. "Our boys are coming. So, there's our reinforcements. Rest assured, I'm only making a quick tour, then I'll be back."

Under the extra-terrestrial dome everything was dark. Only one corner of the rectangular airlock was lit up by the sun. The rest remained in shadows, hiding even the monsters feet extending hallway inside the cabin.

Feeling around, the bold scientist found the metal ladder and started climbing down cautiously. His feet echoed eerily on the rungs. The English and Australian technicians, somewhat reassured by the motionless "Martian"—because of course that was what they were calling it—were now surrounding the mysterious tilted disc.

Worried about the fate of their boss, some of them shouted, "Professor Howard! Professor Howard! Good God! Come back!"

Affected by the anxiety and hysteria rising in the group, Professor Morrison and Kinsington started to crawl back down. An unpleasant shiver ran down their spine. All of a sudden the Denebian "corpse" shot out its arms and grabbed the physicist and the engineer by their ankles. At that very moment the flying saucer straightened up and soared 300 feet into the sky.

The two scientists were thrown back and lay flat against the dome of the disc. The ship stopped moving and hovered, shimmering, in mid-air. On the ground the terrified Rocketeers ran to the trucks and Jeeps.

The Denebian with its herculean strength snatched up each man with one arm and carried them easily inside the spaceship. In their fall during the sudden acceleration the two Earthlings had passed out. The rectangular hatch closed slowly behind the captives and the flying saucer rose into the sky at fantastic speed.

Struck with terror by the Machiavellian kidnapping the Rocketeers jumped into their vehicles and raced at 60 miles an hour to Woomera City to alert the authorities.

"It's done," Zimko concluded. "Now we have to go back to the Denebian saucer-base. Then we'll come up with a plan to release Morrison, Howard, Kinsington and the other scientists that the monsters captured pretty much everywhere on this planet."

At the commands of the spaceship Yuln headed for Wyola Lake. The ship arrived just as the Denebians were slowly descending to the giant base, apparently covered again with sand and perfectly camouflaged in the desert dunes. The huge rectangular hatch opened in the round dome. The *baby saucer* tilted and went down at an angle, wobbling slightly when it slipped into the gaping hold of the *mother ship*. The hatch closed up, completely hiding the entrance.

For ignorant eyes the Denebian base was nothing but a fat dune of sand with a peculiar form. The wind, however, was sweeping in the sand to assist its weird camouflage.

"Now," the Polarian decided, "it's time to act. But I'm afraid that our 'helping hand' won't come off so easily. Therefore, we're going to have to play it close, very close. We have almost 70 men to save before the green monsters submit them to their psychic treatment."

CHAPTER SEVEN

The Polarian and his Earthling friends cooked up a plan of action to free the scientists being held prisoner in the Denebian base. Yuln suddenly gave the alarm: a spaceship was approaching. The fluorescent radar showed a shiny "beep" that was blinking off and on, coming steadily closer in the visual field. Zimko concentrated, casting his powerful paroptic vision into the detected ship.

"It's a Denebian flying saucer with four occupants. They're coming back to their base after filming the launch pads of the guided missiles built by the Russians in Peenemunde on the Baltic Sea... These monsters are figuring to go back to Europe to kidnap Russian and German specialists in rocket science."

While talking, Zimko had given his telepathic orders to his sister. Without the Earthlings realizing it, the flying saucer under Yuln's command was shooting off to intercept the newcomer. The two discs of almost the same size passed each other over the Gibson Desert, more than 600 miles from Wyola Lake. Yuln read her brother's mind to maneuver the ship. She turned the ship back, keeping an eye on the screen and the Denebian saucer's progress. The blond Girl from Space spun a calibrated knob that moved a needle on the command post. From the top of the dome protecting the cockpit a purple ray shot out, tore through space and enveloped the enemy saucer. It stopped instantly, suspended in mid-air.

Keep it there in the gravito-magnetic interceptor, Zimko ordered psychically, *and bring us up to the ship.*

The spaceship sprang through the air and stopped 50 yards away from the Denebian disc, which was held firm by the strong gravito-magnetic interceptor. With the purple ray flowing out of a bright ball on top of the dome, another ray, pink this time, joined its paralyzing power. Like statues, the four green monsters, confused by the inexplicable freezing of their disc, stood riveted to the spot.

When the Polarian had explained to his companions the nature of these maneuvers, Kariven asked, "But why not just paralyze all the Denebians in the spaceship under the desert sand? It'd be so easy to point this paralyzing ray at the base…"

"No, Kariven. This ray is tuned to Denebian waves. It acts on the nerve centers and paralyzes their movements without stopping the normal functioning of their organs. But it can have disastrous effects on the human organism. We haven't yet figured out the correct wavelength for humans. By projecting this ray on the Denebian base we would risk killing the human prisoners by blocking their body functions and stopping their hearts and lungs."

"Then how are we going to free our fellow men?" Jenny's voice shook, understandably nervous.

Zimko looked like he was thinking deeply. What unsuspected psychic ability was hiding behind this meditative appearance?

"We're going to land," he said after this temporary lull. Then he spoke mentally to his sister, *Guide the Denebian spaceship to the ground.*

The two ships landed gently, 30 feet away from each other.

Yuln left the command post. In her graceful, elegant gait she went up to the metal wall. Her hand skimmed over the luminescent surface and a rectangular panel opened, tilting down horizontally until it was around three feet off the floor. From this unfolded table an extension silently slid out. The young Polarian pressed a series of numbered buttons on the edge of the board. Ten shiny, chrome cylinders emerged from the metal floor, lined up around the long horizontal table.

"I didn't see a restaurant in the area," Yuln smirked. "So, I guess we'll just have to have breakfast 'at home'."

At Zimko's invitation the amazed passengers took their places around this one-of-a-kind table by sitting on the cylinders, which were spongy and very comfortable. Yuln entered another series of numbers on the keyboard before sitting down next to Kariven.

This isn't very intimate, she told him telepathically, *but we owe it to our guests...*

"Indeed, my dear..."

The explorer interrupted himself, cursing under his breath at his scatterbrained forgetfulness. Answering aloud and calling Zimko's sister "my dear"!

Surprised and intrigued, his friends stared at him again. Was he losing his mind? What were all these obscure remarks about?

Kariven mentally heard a kind of guffaw. *Ha, ha, ha. That's a good one!*

His confused and reproachful eyes turned to Zimko, who was casually drumming his fingers on the table.

Trying to change the subject Kariven pointed to the two empty cylinders. "Are you expecting more guests?"

"Two," Zimko was amused at the general astonishment.

All of a sudden he jumped up as if he had heard something. While talking with an invisible other, his face looked excited.

"There they are!" he cried out happily, flipping a switch to open the airlock.

A minute later two Polarians—a man and a young woman—entered the cockpit. The man was wearing short boots, a sky-blue jacket and a dark red bodysuit. The girl with him was a rare beauty, wearing an emerald green, transparent tunic, like Yuln and Jenny. The newcomer threw herself into Zimko's arms and kissed him passionately, not worrying about the human passengers whom she had greeted with a warm smile on entering.

"This is Tlyka, the co-pilot of my good friend Nylak," Zimko introduced them.

The Earthlings saluted with their raised right hands. Somewhat surprised by this strange ceremony Doniatchka hesitated before she herself raised her hand, whispering to Dormoy, "What's this all about, Michel?"

Dormoy took her hand and examined it. "You don't have it but it doesn't matter." He raised the girl's hand to his lips and kissed it.

"What don't I have?" she asked, leaving her hand in the fingers that were squeezing it gently. "Am I missing something?"

While the geophysicist whispered with the young Russian, the new arrivals took their place at the table. Yuln worked the keyboard again. From a recess uncovered by the hidden table ten plastic cubes slid out, each containing four tabs like chocolate bars and a sealed pouch with an iridescent liquid. Yuln handed them out to the guests and started in on hers.

"Don't be fooled by appearance," she said. "These bars have the nutritional value of a gargantuan meal. The liquid is a bacteriolytic tonic that tastes great. Tear off the upper edges of the pouch and drink it with the plastic straw that's on the side."

I've thought a lot about you, dear, Zimko murmured telepathically to Tlyka, the young co-pilot.

I know, my love. Your thoughts have often embraced me when I was far away from you... We were working in Alaska when your call reached us a short time ago. Glancing at Yuln and Kariven, who were munching their bars and speaking volumes with their eyes, she added, *Yuln and this Earthling appear to be consciously practicing the laws of universal love appreciated by our race.*

From the first time they saw each other, Zimko admitted with a tender smile, looking at his sister. *These young lovebirds—especially Kariven—sometimes forget that telepathy is second nature to us.*

Professor Yegov, who had swallowed his bars in no time at all, was sucking the colorful liquid in the clear pouch. He looked around at his neighbors, thought for a minute, then laughed and confessed, "Men really ought to get to know each other better. By the most extraordinary adventures here we are together, my fellow Russian and I with Frenchmen and four charming beings from another planet. And I feel great. I'm even convinced that among English or Americans we'd still be able to eat a friendly breakfast!

"You were right, Zimko. Earthlings are stupid pigs who only hurt one another or bicker like spoiled children. We really need to get to know each other, to tear down borders and make a clean slate of our ridiculous prejudices. That's the solution to the problem of world peace: men of goodwill coming together unconditionally.

"I am glad, Zimko," he concluded without hiding his emotions, "that you and your friends kidnapped me. I will follow your orders and do all I can to support your humanitarian principles."

"We don't give orders to friends, Professor Yegov," the Polarian emphasized. "Earthlings are our friends even though they don't know it. And if, unfortunately, some of them make pacts with the Denebians, they are bad humans, traitors to their own race. Whoever oppresses their brothers are our enemies. We hate to have to fight them like Denebians, but it can't be helped."

To Kariven he added, "You have an expression, I believe, about 'infected sheep'?"

"Black sheep," the anthropologist corrected.

"Yes, they're 'black sheep' when they scorn humanitarian laws and we have to defeat them to protect the ones they persecute."

Changing the subject Zimko asked Nylak, "What's new, Nylak, in your zone of operation?"

"Tlyka and I had to intervene two hours ago to stop an attempted sabotage in Canada. We were headed back to Alaska after observing the American base in Thule, Greenland, when we saw two Denebian ships over Shirley Bay. The wretches were spying on the Canadian observatory of Project

Magnet[95] and getting ready to launch transmutation rays at the buildings. All the specialized machines in the huge laboratory would have been destroyed and the work halted for months on end. We had to disintegrate the two enemy discs."

Tlyka smiled, "The Canadian experts in charge of detecting flying saucers are going to be pretty surprised to see three of these UFOs on the record. And I wonder how they'll explain the sudden disappearance of the two saucers we disintegrated. We'll go back there someday to probe the brains of the scientists and read what thoughts our brief little battle caused."

"Basically you prevented the destruction of an observation post destined to spot your own flying saucers. That's pretty surprising, although I understand your desire to protect the technical advances of humanity."

"In reality, Kariven, it's very simple," the young woman answered familiarly while chatting telepathically of more intimate things with Zimko. "We're not interested in seeing observatories searching for our ships get destroyed for the simple reason that it doesn't do them any good to detect us. They would have to be able to come and catch us and this the Earthlings cannot do.

"Furthermore, since 1952 the American, British and Russian military staffs have known that flying saucers are not hallucinations or weather balloons—simplistic explanations that

---

[95] Name given to the biggest laboratory center for detecting flying saucers that worked in Canada after the summer of 1952. This observatory had the most advanced equipment in the world. (Author's Note) Project Magnet was UFO study programme established by Transport Canada on December 2, 1950, under the direction of Wilbert B. Smith, senior radio engineer for the Transport Canada's Broadcast and Measurements Section. It was formally active until mid-1954, and informally active without government funding until Smith's death in 1962. Smith eventually concluded that UFOs were probably extraterrestrial in origin and likely operated by manipulation of magnetism.

are only satisfactory to thickheaded men. The Governmental Investigation Commissions and especially Project Blue Book[96] know perfectly well that flying saucers come from another planet and that they can't catch one. But that's all they know. The day will come when we Polarians will make contact with the governmental authorities but for now we prefer to deal with just a few, trustworthy Earthlings who want to see peace finally reign on Earth. I'm talking about the growing number of Earthlings who bear the Mark of the New Race."

My dear, she said to Zimko in the meantime, *I can't wait for there to be calm again in this corner of the Universe so we can finally be together. We don't even see each other once a week on this planet. I often think of our wonderful time on Mars at our permanent base there before the Denebians came into this solar system.*

I think of that too, dear Tlyka, but we have to respect the orders of the Galactic Council. On a mission on a planet being threatened with war Polarians bound by an extra-familial emotional tie—the Earthlings call this Love—can't work together and will be assigned to different spaceships. They don't forbid us to see each other or cooperate on missions if necessary...

But they can't live together on the threatened planet, she finished for Zimko, watching him tenderly.

I asked the Council to grant us one earth-day break after this mission we need to accomplish.

Tlyka eyes sparkled with joy. *Let's not lose a second, dear. Tell us your plan.*

"My friends," the Polarian said out loud, "here's how I decided we should free the captive scientists."

Barely 30 feet separated the Zimko's spaceship from the Polarian ship that had just come to join him in Australia. The Denebian flying saucer frozen by the gravito-magnetic rays sat on a sand dune 100 feet farther away. Tlyka and Yuln, along

---

[96] See Note 68. (Author's Note)

with Jenny, Doniatchka and Professor Yegov stayed in their respective ships.

Zimko, Nylak and the three explorers walked over to the intercepted ship. Zimko stood before it and sent out an order to one of the paralyzed Denebians inside. Presently a hatch was opened by the unconscious green monster. The five men entered the spaceship and examined it meticulously. Its four occupants had not escaped the rays. Three were paralyzed at their posts and the fourth was now in the airlock, guarding the closed hatch on Zimko's orders.

"Everything's ready to go. We can take off."

Zimko sent an order to the Denebian pilot under his control and the flying saucer rose up, closely followed by the two ships piloted by Yuln and Tlyka. For this dangerous mission they both remained protected by their invisibility shields. A few minutes later the three discs flying in single file veered down toward the giant saucer camouflaged in the desert sand. By remote control from the reptilian pilot the rectangular panel opened below the dome to receive the expected ship—and the unexpected passengers—so it could park in the vast space inside.

The Polarian fitted around his waist a huge bluish belt with a kind of flat metal box instead of a buckle, with different colored knobs. He gave the explorers the other belts that were provided by his fellow Polarian.

The Earthlings were fairly surprised when they put on their belts, thinking that they were going to "guide" the Denebians by the Polarian's willpower when they got inside the enemy base.

"This box you're wearing around your waist," Zimko explained to them, "is an electronic Multiplex. It's both a weapon and a means of protection with various effects. Six knobs control its six different functions. Give the bright red knob a half turn."

Which he did himself.

"Now we're undetectable. A neutralizing barrier is protecting us and keeping our body waves from being detected by the enemy."

They left the ship that had snuck them into the base and stepped out under a huge metal vault over 250 feet high. The shiny dome contained 50 reconnaissance saucers lined up in rows of ten.

Now we're in the lion's den, the Man from Outer Space used his sixth sense to avoid the easily detectable sound waves. *You have to follow my orders to the letter. Your lives depend on it.*

He probed Yuln and Tlyka in their cockpits and gave them orders before bringing the Denebians out of their spaceship. The two Polarian spaceships, invisible in the garage, were parked as close as possible to the airlock, an empty corridor 60 feet long, 30 high and 60 wide.

The four Denebians left their ship with the Earthling/Polarian commando team still inside and marched like robots toward the big rectangular doorway. Zimko watched them through a window. A few feet from the door they looked like they suddenly became normal and they stepped lively through the opening.

"It looks like they're no longer under hypnosis."

"Don't kid yourself, Kariven. They look normal and can act normal but at the right time they'll do something completely against their will. The motive thought for this act is already implanted in their brain's neural circuit. Now listen…"

A kind of deep hooting echoed endlessly off the silvery, super-metal walls of the giant base.

"What's that?" Dormoy asked.

"One of the Denebians that we let go, the officer of the Space Commandos, just gave the signal for a general assembly. Out of the 500 Denebians making up the detachment on this mobile base, around 480 of them will meet in the central command post. The 20 others will remain at their posts on the second to last floor that houses the energy station and the vital systems. For almost an hour our Denebian will inform his many colleagues about the sensational finds that he thinks he discovered. And I can assure you that his speech will be very exciting!"

It took Zimko ten minutes to visit the whole base thanks to his panoptic vision.

"Come on. Everyone's busy now, some listening to the officer's nonsense and the others keeping an eye on the ship's systems. That's who were going to visit first. The scientists are being held prisoner in the holds but are only being guarded by two monsters."

The five men armed with disintegrator cones went down the endless, twisting, turning corridors in the fantastic space structure lit by wall plates giving off a green electro-luminescence. The eerie light made them look like corpses, pale as a band of ghosts.

An inclined ramp led them up to a bright arch, 30 feet high and around 20 feet wide at the base, framing a reinforced hatch. One of the Denebians released by Zimko was standing at the entrance, frozen, waiting for the psychic order before acting. The Polarian held out the small box with paralyzing rays and gave a very precise order. The green monster suddenly recovered his energy, made the door open and entered the energy station while the Earthlings and Polarians hid on either side of the arch. A few minutes later the Denebian came back. This time he was walking like a robot with jerky movements and handed Zimko his paralyzing ray emitter.

"We can go in," Yuln's brother announced, pushing away the reinforced door.

They saw a huge cylindrical room with a row of chrome stands with wheels, electronic keyboards, switches, dials and blinking lights. 20 Denebians spread around the imposing, gleaming machinery were frozen where the paralyzing ray had just surprised them. When the green monsters saw one of their own entering, they suspected nothing. In a split second the "involuntary traitor" had petrified them in place.

"Perfect," Zimko said. "We're safe as far as this goes. The base has no more pilots or technicians. The next shift should be listening to the officer's speech that I'm keeping under my control. Let's go hear what he's saying."

They followed the spiral corridors again and finally came in front of another giant, luminous archway hatch. Here, too, one of Zimko's Denebians was standing guard. The Polarian once again gave his paralyzing device to the monster and waited. The unconscious creature opened the door. From their hiding place the Earthlings and Polarians heard the officer's harsh voice bellowing sensational "revelations".

The monumental doorway closed behind the hypnotized monster carrying the paralyzing box. When the door reopened an impressive silence covered the assembly of 480 green monsters frozen stiff. Zimko took his device out of the Denebian's claws and peaked inside. In the immense room all the reptilian creatures looked like stone. On an amber sphere over the petrified horde one Denebian was standing up, motionless, his mouth open and his right hand raised, frozen, in mid-speech.

"We can do whatever we want without fear now," the Polarian declared.

He sent a mental message to Yuln and Tlyka to inform them and led off his commando team. A tubular elevator took them to the top floor of the giant disc. They were about to start down a long walkway that led to the holds where the prisoners were held when Zimko stopped short. With his head tilted slightly to the side, his eyes stared straight ahead as if listening to a voice that common mortals could not hear. His face tensed and his fists clenched, obviously under great strain. After a couple of intense minutes he came back to normal and looked at the others, aghast.

"The fourth Denebian we sent out to watch the holds has just been killed by his two compatriots. They found out he was hypnotized... how?... and they executed him in cold blood when he simply stood in front of the doors. The two monsters are protected by a neutralizing field similar to ours. Our mental powers can't do anything. Nylak and I have tried to hypnotize them but it's no use. We'll have to fight it out and risk injuring or killing some of the scientists being held prisoners."

For the first time since they had met the Earthlings saw the Man from Outer Space in the throes of uncertainty, even nervousness.

"Your paralyzing or disintegrating rays have no effect, then, on the neutralizing field?" Angelvin asked.

"The paralyzing rays bounce off, but the neutralizing field doesn't absorb the disintegrator. How can we shoot these monsters with 60 men standing behind them? Disintegrating the guards means killing their prisoners along with them."

After a quick thought Kariven drew his Colt. "This'll do less damage. Do you think these Denebians could deflect a slug with their shield?"

Zimko shook his head and whistled, "In fact, your crude weapon seems to me to be the safest way to kill these creeps."

"Maybe we could knock on the door and ask what time it is," Dormoy joked.

"Why go in through the door?" the anthropologist shrugged. "Taking into the account the huge size of this mobile base, we could imagine that the air ducts in every room are proportionate."

"Brilliant, Kariven!" the Polarian shouted. "You've found the solution. In spite of our super-normal abilities Nylak and I were floundering like wounded birds."

He concentrated for a minute, probed the infrastructure of the giant spaceship and announced, "It's exactly as you guessed, Kariven. The ducts are three feet in diameter carrying the air into the energy station in this hold where the prisoners are held."

Running through the corridors the five men rushed to the station where the Denebian technicians were paralyzed.

"Here's the group of air pumps," Zimko pointed to an impressive machine made of two metal domes from the top of which came the tubular ducts that ran all through the ship. Zimko and Nylak each grabbed a giant tool, a kind of pliers with jointed jaws, and started unbolting a plate on the first tube. Perched on the big, armored dome, after 15 minutes of hard work, they managed to pull off the concave plate. Then they jumped back: a strong gust of air threw the plate onto the metal floor.

Zimko and Kariven slipped through the two-foot wide opening and inside the cylinder. Nylak and the two other explorers put the plate back in place, not without some difficulty, to stop the air from escaping, otherwise several rooms in the base would lose the artificial atmosphere, in particular the hold with the prisoners.

The two men crawled slowly down the narrow duct. Zimko was in the lead, lighting the way with a tiny (but powerful) flashlight. They soon had to get on their bellies to fight against the turbulent flow of air that was constantly pushing them from behind and even lifting them up and tossing them against each other. They reached a fork and Zimko used his panoptic vision to lead them into the duct on the right.

We only communicate by telepathy from now on, Kariven heard in his head. *We're almost there and the airflow could carry our voices into the holds.*

Very soon the Polarian turned off the light. Slithering in the semi-darkness they got to a turn in the duct that was flooded with electroluminescence.

We're at the end of the duct leading to the hold. It comes out in a metal wall six and a half feet off the ground and is covered with a grill with five-inch squares. There's no fan... luckily!

They crawled cautiously up to the grill: in the huge, vaulted hold, 60 men of all ages and nationalities were sitting down in groups of three or four on plastex chairs or on metal crates lined up along the thick walls. Some were sleeping, others thinking quietly or talking among themselves. Standing on either side of the sealed door were the two Denebians protected by their neutralizing field, watching the scientists and the door with thermal rifles in their hands.

With the greatest care Kariven slipped the barrel of his Colt through the grill and lay it on one of the horizontal bars. He took careful aim at the guard on the right of the reinforced door. At the end of the barrel the green monster wavered a little in front of the sight. The anthropologist, sweating profusely, closed his eyes. Breathing fast he opened his eyes again. The arduous trip in the duct had tired his sight. Better to wait a minute before firing. To miss his target could be fatal to all the prisoners. He would only have a split second to hit the second Denebian... after the first was down. One false movement and their whole plan would go up in smoke.

Kariven clenched his teeth, shook his head as if to clear out a nightmare, then he aimed, calmly, and closed his left eye. The Colt's sight was exactly in the middle of the Denebian's chest now. The anthropologist pulled the trigger. The gunfire was terrifying, more like cannon fire.

The green monster collapsed.

Immediately after, the second bullet shot off in a thunder that rolled frightfully around the metal walls.

The scaly head of the nasty creature exploded and the body, almost decapitated, fell forward, spilling pinkish-green blood over the chrome floor.

Watch out!" Zimko shouted. "The first one's not dead!"

CHAPTER EIGHT

Although wounded, the Denebian was crawling along the wall to get out of Kariven's field of vision.

Astonished by this unexpected attack, the captive scientists all jumped to their feet, fretful, not knowing from where or whom the gun shots came. Kept at bay by the surviving guard, they just stood there, looking around the hold. Dribbling a trail of pink-green blood from his lips the Denebian struggled forward. His claws gripped the cushioned butt of the thermal rifle. When he got to the corner of the wall with the air duct opening he stopped, his breath short. He wanted to get up on one elbow to shoot but he slumped back down. His breathing was heavy and his eyes glassy as he finally hoisted himself up on his knees.

In the duct Zimko and Kariven had backed up a few feet, afraid of being hit by a charge of thermal rays. The Polarian, whose panoptic vision saw through matter, watched the struggle of the wounded monster.

He's going to shoot at the air duct. The metal won't melt but it'll get up to 2,000 °C and we'll be roasted!

It was not a pleasant picture for them. In the hold some of the scientists finally figured out where the gunfire had come from. They looked at the air duct, then the dying monster crawling toward it. Three of them whispered anxiously to each other and suddenly, in perfect unison, they picked up their chairs and threw them at the Denebian who was taking aim at the grill in the wall. The three metalo-plastex cube-chairs hit the monster who screamed out in rage, fell flat on the floor and dropped his rifle. A second later a dozen prisoners piled on top of him, swinging their fists. With a final burst of energy the monster fought back, scratching and biting his attackers but with his wound and blood loss he did not last long. A young scientist waved a chair in the air and brought it down hard on the monster's skull. The terrifying, inhuman howls stopped and he lay motionless.

While disintegrating the grill of the air duct Zimko sent a telepathic message to his friends in the energy station: the way was clear. The Polarian and Kariven climbed through the opening and dropped to the floor. All the scientists ran up and bombarded them with questions at the same time as they praised their act of bravery and thanked them warmly. Surrounded by the blabbering scientists Zimko and Kariven opened the entrance door. Their friends came in to join them.

After hurrying back through the luminescent corridors the group came into the huge airlock that led outside, the giant "parking lot" with the 50 reconnaissance saucers and the two Polarian spaceships that were visible now.

Yuln, Tlyka, Jenny, Doniatchka and Professor Yegov were waiting impatiently by the discs. The two Polarians, using their strange super-vision, had watched the various phases of the operation and kept their companions up-to-date. The liberated scientists stared at these young women—so scantily dressed—with some astonishment. However, they were reassured: these pretty girls were "Earthlings." That was where they were wrong, as Zimko's brief speech informed when he welcomed them to the Earth-Polarian Alliance.

"Yegov!" one of the scientists burst out, face beaming. Holding out his arms he threw himself at the Russian physicist, whom he just recognized.

"Nikolai Petchenkov!" the professor thundered back, hugging him. In English to told Zimko, "This is my friend. Petchenkov is the Chief Engineer of the Odobnya plant in the Urals where we built the first artificial satellite."[97]

---

[97] There really was no such plant; Guieu may have been referring to Special Design Bureau No. 1 of R&D Institute No. 88, founded on 16 May 1946, and often known as OKB-1, named after its first chief designer, Sergei Korolev (1946–1966), who was responsible for *Sputnik 1*, the world's first artificial satel-

Among the other scientists two Americans—Professors Wayne and Hammer—exchanged a brief glance. "I think we were really the first ones to build a space station," Wayne whispered in outrage.

Zimko smiled as he read everyone's train of thought. Petchenkov, for example, criticized his friend in Russian after he publicly revealed this USSR military secret: the construction of an artificial satellite along with the location of the factory where it was built.

The Polarian was going to intervene to denounce these ridiculous ideas of "security" and "military secrets" when a thought in Yegov's brain stopped him. The Russian scientist was about to respond to his friend but he held back and instead addressed all his colleagues gathered there. His response concerned them all as much as Petchenkov.

"Gentlemen, or I should say my Brothers," he spoke in English, figuring that most of them would understand, "my old friend Nikolai Petchenkov, whom I've just had the pleasure of seeing again, is Russian like myself. While I headed the labs in Atomgrad where the USSR perfected an H-bomb [98] *whose complete formula I will give to all of you*, Petchenkov was running the secret plant in Odobnya, also in the Urals. In this plant was built an artificial satellite, a space observatory platform that will orbit the Earth to keep surveillance over the different countries. My friend Petchenkov will also give you the secrets of the construction."

Stunned, Petchenkov wondered if Yegov had gone mad. Promising these scientists from capitalist nations to reveal the greatest secrets of the USSR! What treason!

Chinese, French, Argentine, American, English, Italian, all the scientists were astonished. Where was this Russian physicist going—whom they had heard talking so warily on

---

lite launched on October 4, 1957, and the subsequent *Vostok* program.

[98] RDS-6, the first Soviet test of a hydrogen bomb, took place on August 12, 1953.

the radio and in the press—apparently converted to altruism? They understood even less than they understood why the green pseudo-men had kidnapped them?

"My role," Yegov continued, "is not to tell you the whys and wherefores of our unintended meeting in this ship from another planet. Zimko the Polarian will do this. But I'd like to tell you this: I'm Russian; I was kidnapped in Moscow by this man I called Zimko... this man who comes from the solar system around the Pole Star. I'm glad that he kidnapped me because since then I've truly come to believe that all men are my brothers, not only here on Earth, but also in on the infinite worlds of our Galaxy. And no, I am not crazy," he smiled at the skeptical and slightly cynical expressions on some of their faces. "When you know the reason of your kidnapping—because you are going to be kidnapped again but for your benefit and for a admirable goal—if you are men sincerely worthy of the name, you will understand why I call you brothers, you Americans, Frenchmen, Englishmen and others from all over the world. You will understand and join with all your heart this great Earth-Polarian Alliance. Personally, I've already signed up because a horrible danger is threatening our common country: the Earth."

Turning to the Polarian, Professor Yegov, a little shyly, apologize, "I'm sorry, Zimko, I..."

"You did your duty as an Earthling, Professor, by saying exactly what needed to be said."

The Polarian addressed the freed scientists and completed the Russian physicist's explanations but at the same time sent a telepathic message to the astrobase of the Space Legions that was floating around the solar system.

"Now you know the role that you have to play in the new world," he concluded. "You're not our prisoners, rest assured. Moreover, if any of you refuse to participate in our Alliance, you can stay neutral. In any case, we won't force anyone to act against his will or against his own interests. We are ready to leave behind those who express their desire to say here on Earth. They won't be able to betray us because we've taken precautions to wipe their minds clean of everything concerning us. Our Science has reached such a fantastic degree of perfection, a degree that you can't even begin to imagine. We are endowed with psychic abilities that pass the bounds of an Earthling's understanding. All this, one day, will be within your reach. You will be able to use them just like the Polarians, I guarantee it. Don't hesitate to tell me…"

A little commotion started to run through the group of scientists. After talking hurriedly among themselves the oldest of them stepped forward.

"We're with you Polarians," his voice trembled with emotion. "We'll be glad to contribute, as modestly as it might be, to bringing peace to men and thwarting the diabolical plots of the green monsters. We will also revenge our unfortunate colleagues who were murdered before our eyes."

At Zimko's request the spokesman explained to the explorers and his passengers: "Three days ago we decided to try to escape. We waited for our jailors to open the door to bring our evening meal. Then we jumped on the two Denebians on duty while others tackled the ones just coming in. Alas, we were not armed. A green monster arriving alone in the meantime stopped our momentum by shooting at us with a heat wave rifle. Nine of us were burned up."

While the Polarians and their horrified friends listened to the story, back in the cockpit of the enemy base that was now under their control, a giant screen turned on. The green face of a Denebian appeared. His red eyes were popping out of his head from the surprise. In front of the screen the Denebian operator and one of the pilots stood like statues, still under the effect of Zimko's paralyzing ray. The face on the screen went wild. Its lips moved but no sound troubled the silence of the room full of petrified bodies. Paralyzed but conscious the operator could not press the button for audio. Only the video reception was still on at the moment of the attack.

At 30 miles over the Australian desert, in the flying saucer patrol that was calling the base, the pilot abruptly cut the contact. He understood: this paralysis of the team was the work of the Polarians. He had to alert the astrobase orbiting outside Pluto immediately.

The flying saucer shot straight up at lightning speed and flew into space, off to sound the alarm for the green monsters stationed at the ends of the solar system.

Zimko suddenly interrupted the old scientist's speech and raised his voice, "I just felt the brief presence of a Denebian spaceship over the base. It's flying away after it couldn't get in touch with the paralyzed team. Let's get out of here," he ordered, sending a new psychic message to the Polarian astrobase that was already on its way to Earth after his first call.

Yuln and Tlyka rushed back to their ships while Nylak closed the big airlock door. The two flying saucers rose three feet off the metal floor. With the sound of swishing silk they slowly left the base and hovered over the sand 100 yards away.

Led by their rescuers the scientists stepped cautiously over the topside of their former "flying prison" and were soon trudging through the sand. They filled their lungs with the warm, desert air and squinted against the blinding rays of the setting sun. All of a sudden a long shadow stretched over the ground and covered the group. Everyone looked up and uttered their astonishment.

Without a sound of approach an enormous, spindle-shaped ship was coming straight down out of the sky. 3,000 feet long and 500 feet in diameter, the monstrous spaceship, glittering in the dying sunlight, appeared to be red and yellow. The fantastic metal rocket—a torpedo with a double row of windows in the front—landed. Theoretically, a mass of metal like this, weighing hundreds of millions of tons, should have sunk into the sand. Paradoxically, the huge machine looked like it barely touched the surface of the desert, only 100 yards away from the Earthlings.

"That's our astrobase," Zimko explained, pointing proudly at the giant ship where a hatch in the belly was opening. He continued his explanation, "It's what you Earthlings call a 'flying cigar.' There are smaller ones, anywhere from 100 to 600 feet long, that fly over Earth. But generally these space giants, like you see here, don't land very often. Their mission is to patrol from one solar system to another, or one planet to another, transporting the squadrons of flying discs, the Flying Saucers."

"So, these are Saucer-carriers just like we have warships that are aircraft carriers," Dormoy remarked, in awe of the frightening realization of this super-evolved civilization.

"Exactly. The Americans have come up with a term for it: Mother Ship[99]. Our reconnaissance discs being the flying saucers, which are seen pretty much everywhere after leaving the 'Flying Cigar' in the astronomical vicinity of the planet to be observed. They accomplish their reconnaissance or ground missions and go back to the astrobase, the 'Flying Cigar.' We have one or two of these giant spaceships operating in every solar system. The two that today are on Pluto where our technicians set up the latest supply base—the first being put a long time ago on the moon—can't move. Therefore, I called the closest one available from the solar system Alpha Centauri."

"You mean that this ship came here in one hour from a planet in Alpha Centauri?!" the Danish astronomer Nordling exclaimed. "Don't you know that this star system is four light years from Earth and according to Einstein's equation of the speed of light it's impossible for a moving object to..."

"That's one of the many misconceptions of earthly science," the Man from Outer Space broke in, also raising his hand in salute to the Polarians who were walking over from the flying cigar.

Fifteen bronze-skinned men were now surrounding our friends. All of them, like Zimko, were wearing uniforms of the Space Legion: turquoise jacket narrow at the waist with a

---

[99] These stupefying, giant spaceships have been spotted many times on radar when a squadron of flying saucers come back to rejoin them; see *Flying Saucers Come from Another World,* q.v. (Author's Note)

thick belt around it holding the holster for the disintegrator cone on the right side, a dark red bodysuit, short black boots and dark blue insulated gloves.

The superior officer raised his hand in response to Zimko. "Right after receiving your last message we sent a squad after the Denebian disc. We shot it down just as it was sending another message. We don't know if the enemy astrobase got any of that message and if it did, if it was an important part."

Showing his friendly smile to the scientists staring at him and his men, the Polarian officer added, "So, these are our new 'guests'. Welcome to the Alliance, Earthling Friends, and I'm sorry for the cavalier manner in which you were kidnapped. It's obvious that the Denebians who captured you were copying our methods. But where you were prisoners of theirs, with us you are free. These monsters would have stamped your brains with orders making you their agents and accomplices on Earth. You would have become traitors to the human race. We Polarians will tell you everything you don't know about our scientific technology in order to benefit the New World."

Before going back to the scientists who were getting ready (still dazed by their adventure) to enter the monstrous flying cigar, Professor Yegov bid an emotional farewell to the Polarian and the explorers. He kissed the young Russian on the cheek and left, knowing that he would see all these fortuitous friends again someday when he came back to Earth to organize the society on new, peaceful bases after the enemy was conquered.

Doniatchka Petrovna looked on thoughtfully as the professor walked away. She glanced at Zimko, who had his backed turned, watching the Earthlings board the ship. A kind of distress choked her up. She grabbed Dormoy's hand with her own trembling hand and stayed by his side. Wasn't the Polarian going to order her to follow her compatriot into the far-off solar system lost in the frightening depths of the Galaxy?

No, Doniatchka, she identified the telepathic voice of Zimko in her head. *Not for the moment at last. Michel Dormoy would rather keep you near him and I see no problem with that. You'll be the doctor of our team here on Earth.*

She had the weird feeling that she heard a quiet laugh echo through her brain. Looking away, she secretly wiped away her tears of joy. Dormoy caressed her head, feeling the sweet touch of her cheek against his. And he murmured, "Zimko was right."

The Russian girl's big blue eyes watched him, smiling and still leaking tears. She was surprised and confused. "You heard?"

"Our friend figured it best to share his thoughts in my mind. Obviously we need a doctor in our 'commando team' since we've been chosen to participate in the Earth-Polarian missions..."

"So, it's simply for that!" she pushed him away.

"Adorable fool," the geophysician teased, pulling her back into his embrace.

The metal ladder was drawn back into the huge flanks of the space giant and the hatch closed up. The metal mastodon rose up slowly as easily as a common helicopter but perfectly silent. It gained altitude and suddenly the Denebian base in the desert rose up after it. It wobbled gently in the air and then shot off into space.

"But... it's taking off!" Angelvin was surprised by Zimko's indifference.

"Of course," Zimko replied. "You didn't think that we were going to leave the enemy base in the desert did you? It's being taken care of by our giant 'cigar'—thanks to a gravito-magnetic beam—and will be transported back to our planetary capital."

"And the Denebians?"

"They'll suffer the same fate that they would have reserved for us if they had got the upper hand: death by disintegration. But they won't suffer like they made some of ours suffer after falling into their hands."

Tlyka put her hand on Zimko's shoulder. "Since our mission was successful, I think you should have received a confirmation of our requested break?"

"The break has been granted. We've got 24 hours now. But we can't leave Earth. The orders are strict."

"I was hoping to spend our break on the lunar base," Tlyka pouted. "And I'm sure that our Earthling friends would be delighted to visit their satellite."

"I think so too!" Jenny piped up, smiling at Angelvin. "Don't you, Robert?"

"Oh me, you know, I go to the moon all the time," he laughed. "But with you I wouldn't mind at all staying here on Earth."

Yuln and Kariven looked at each other full of tender promises just as Dormoy and Doniatchka did. Someone quietly clearing their throat brought them back to earth.

"Excuse me for interrupting your romantic interlude," Nylak smiled, "but since I also have 24 hours off, please don't forget that a girl with pale blue eyes, Ogny, is waiting for me in Alaska."

"Brrrr!" Zimko shivered and asked his friend, "Don't tell me you want to spend a weekend in the ice?" Seeing his almost heartbroken face he gave him a friendly slap on the shoulder, "Go join your Ogny with pale blue eyes and give her our best. Come back tomorrow at this time to our permanent base. And don't get messed up with the time zones."

A few minutes later the two spaceships shot off into space, each taking a different direction.

In the meantime, crossing the ether at astounding speed the second Denebian base was coming into the solar system, headed for planet Earth. Before being disintegrated by the Polarian squadron chasing after it, the enemy saucer had been able to alert the base, which immediately set off to replace the captured base on Earth.

The colossal spaceship circled the globe once before descending slowly on Australia. It landed silently in the middle of the Victoria Desert, around 300 feet from the where the first base was located. The Polarians would never dream of looking for them in this place. They would never imagine that their enemies would have the audacity to set up a second rally point in the same area.

Their reckoning was simple and not without common sense.

While our friends on board the disc piloted by Yuln were flying toward a secret destination, while the huge Denebian spaceship was setting up in Australia, General Morgan, Commander of the Air Technical Intelligence in Washington DC was in a meeting at the Pentagon with the best agents of the Special Branch created by Project Blue Book.

In the big, concrete room located in the basements of the daunting building, the Saucermen (as they were called in jest) were sitting around a long, metal table covered with a steely gray waterproof varnish. Before them at arm's reach were lying piles of files, questionnaires and reports.

Although General Morgan was around 50 years old, he barely looked 40. He had a thin, black moustache, brown, shifting eyes, a square jaw and black, slightly wavy hair. His impeccable uniform added to his elegance. Though loved by his subordinates he could be, when necessary, firmly authoritative with a loud, cutting voice. And tonight he was proving it.

Standing up at the end of the table the general smashed his fist down on the mountain of files in front of him. "Reports," he growled, "more reports, always reports! We have 18,000 observation reports gathered since 1947. The flying saucers are in pretty much every country and—the height of irony—they've even taunted us over the White House[100] in

---

[100] The airspace over the White House in Washington DC is forbidden to all air traffic. No plane (even of the USAF) has the right to enter it. The jet fighters stationed on the other side of the Potomac River have orders to intercept and shoot down

defiance of the laws that they don't give a damn about. Obviously we've made all the media believe that these UFOs are weather balloons, kites or a mild form of mass hysteria, but these explanations are growing stale. The press is starting to ask uncomfortable questions. Weather balloons and all the other 'hot air' don't satisfy anyone but imbeciles. Yes, I know, you have to think that we, too, at first, during the Kenneth Arnold affair[101], believed that it was just a mirage or a hoax. But now *we know*. Flying saucers come from another world. And their occupants, those hideous green monsters with scaly skin, are walking among us... or almost.

"It didn't take much for the journalists to discover the truth about the *Mocambo* incident in Los Angeles. The three who died mysteriously during the costume party were easily passed off as what they were thought to be: disguised dancers... poisoned by a criminal. However, after the kidnapping of the three Australian scientists last night by a flying saucer piloted by these same green creatures with reptilian skin, the evening press made the connection... embarrassing to say the least. *The Washington Post* and the *New York Herald*," the general berated them, shaking the two newspapers in his hand, "have also made a connection with the many other disappearances of scientists around the world and the spectacular abduction of the three rocketeers in Woomera.

"How much longer can we hide the truth? Soon the people won't be satisfied with our silly press releases. These kill-joys of private investigators of flying saucers have already hit

---

if need be the violators who do not obey their orders. (Author's Note)

[101] Arnold, an amateur pilot, was the first to report a squadron of lenticular spaceships flying at high speed over Mount Rainer in Washington State. (Author's Note) The Kenneth Arnold UFO sighting occurred on June 24, 1947; private pilot Arnold claimed that he saw a string of nine, shiny unidentified flying objects flying past Mount Rainier at speeds that he estimated at a minimum of 1,200 miles an hour

the bull's eye in their publications when they say that the flying saucers are not of earthly origin[102].

"With the help of a few papers and with the ignorant good faith of certain astronomers blinded by outdated dogma, we've tried to destroy the extra-terrestrial hypothesis among the population in general and the 'cult of flying saucers' in particular. But in vain. More and more civilians and, I have to admit, a number of superior officers who don't know everything we know, are openly expressing their belief in the 'outer space' origin of the flying discs. We will soon need to make amends and tell the public that the extravagant claims and flights of fancy of the science fiction magazines and novels fall short of the truth in their flying saucer stories!

"Do you realize the panic that's going to run through the people when we announce the truth? No more innocent reports debunking the eyewitnesses. We'll be forced to admit that the planet is being watched, spied on for years by the green-skinned pseudo-men with yellow-striped red eyes, these monsters from another world, some of whom are already among us, dressing up and going out at night or during the day with their faces covered with bandages so they don't scare the public."

"General, can I say something?" one of the Special Branch agents asked. Around 30 years old he was a civilian, like all his colleagues and had been trying to get a word in for some time.

The Commander looked at him and wiping his forehead, said, "Please, Sullivan, speak up."

"I ask you, General, to consider what I'm going to suggest with the utmost seriousness. It's not a bad joke... Do you

---

[102] See the following journals: *The Saucerian, Flying Saucers Review, Saucers Round Robin* (USA); *Flying Saucers News* (England); *Australian Flying Saucers Magazine* (Australia); *Flying Saucers* (New Zealand); and, in France, *Ouranos*, the publication of the Commission Internationale d'Enquête sur les Soucoupes Volantes. (Author's Note)

really think that these green creatures are the only ones on Earth that come from another planet?"

Special agent Ted Sullivan had asked this calmly. His eyes scrutinized everyone at the meeting. All his colleagues were staring at him, some intrigued, others smiling sarcastically.

"What do you mean, Sullivan?"

"I was at the *Mocambo*, mingling with the dancers in costumes and waiting for the possible appearance of the green monsters. An eyewitness had, in fact, reported to the ATIC about the landing of a flying saucer at Lake Arrowhead about 60 miles from Los Angeles. When this witness said that he had seen 'green men' come out, we were put on alert and prioritized our precautions. As expected three of these creatures went to the only place with a costume party that night: the *Mocambo*."

"I know all this since I gave the orders myself to our agents to attend all costume parties. Cut to the chase, Sullivan."

"I went there, General. And I was watching these three when all of a sudden they stopped in the middle of a dance for a few seconds—surprising their partners—then going back to dancing normally. This sudden, simultaneous halt intrigued me. I informed Holloway, Gardner and Harrison who were in tuxedos like me and mingling with the crowd. They'd noticed it to."

The special agents named by Sullivan nodded in agreement.

"Consequently, when the three monsters were at the bar, I noticed that they froze for no apparent reason. Tense, disturbed, they seemed to be listening to something. Their masks—black velvet wolves—didn't let me see their eyes, but I'm sure they were preoccupied by... by something or other that eluded us. One minute later they collapsed, all three together, dead by something mysterious that our physiologists couldn't explain."

Special agent Gardner spoke up, "I share Sullivan's opinion, General. And I take the liberty to remind you that our agents in France have lost all traces of the three Frenchmen, Kariven, Dormoy and Angelvin who cut short their vacation and left Los Angeles to go back home... right after the incident with the Kaiser.

"McKensie's report we recently received from Paris says that these three men escaped an attack on Kariven's building. A heat ray shot from a Citroën Traction slowing down as it went by was aimed at them. The ray melted the frosted glass and the metal bars of the front door before burning up an old lady who was about to leave. Their trail stops there. They went up to Kariven's apartment, received a visit from the police investigating the attack and didn't come back out. The concierge got a telephone call from this Jean Kariven asking him to turn off his lights that he'd left on by mistake before leaving. Kariven was calling *from outside*. Now, the concierge confirmed that he didn't see Kariven, Dormoy or Angelvin leave. Moreover, the concierge of another building on the next street and an elderly tenant both said they were startled by three individuals leaving their building in quite a hurry... but they'd never seen them come in. We can deduce that these three were our three French vacationers. Why did they use the roofs to leave their apartment? Did they want to throw our agents off their tracks... or were they afraid of *something else*?"

The General passed his hand nervously over his face and sneered, "This story is driving us all crazy! So, you think that these three Frenchmen were afraid of the green monsters or... other beings from outer space? Why?"

"I don't know, General. But I have the feeling that right under our noses some men... Earthlings, have a bone to pick with the monsters or are messing around with them... or with the others."

"It's like trying to square the circle or the triangle in this case!" the General railed. "At the top we have the green monsters, in one corner down below are the Earthlings, certain Earthling connected with the top—how and why?—and in the opposite corner are *the others*. But what *others*? Invisible beings or creatures who would make the green monsters look like beauty queens?

"We're chasing our tails around this triangle. Gentlemen, this cannot last! I need specific information, detailed testimony and not just observation reports telling where and when the grocer on the corner or the farmer picking strawberries in the field saw a bright, round object in the sky. I could care less about that. We need to capture one of these ships whatever it takes and make its occupants talk because these green monsters speak English, that we know since they've got the balls to go costume parties…"

His mouth twisted into a bitter smile. "Costume parties! Beings from another planet are going out dancing in American nightclubs! That takes the cake. It's like some crazy science fiction story. It seems unbelievable. It *is* unbelievable and yet, by God, it's the truth!

"I'm going to give new orders to our Ground Observer Corps. I'll mobilize every fighter jet on all the American bases around the globe if I have to and I'll order them to shoot down the first flying saucer that even looks like it's charging at one of our planes. In this case the fighter could call it 'legitimate defense' and down the disc. From now on the DX 97 ionospheric planes are going to take off from secret hangars with their 6,000 miles an hour[103]. I really hope they'll blast one these damned ships!"

All of a sudden a deep voice, as if coming out of nowhere, echoed gloomily through the huge, underground room: *Don't do that, General Morgan!*

---

[103] One can reasonably imagine that the USA today has planes capable of such speeds. The Douglas X3, a.k.a. the "Flying Stiletto", could (at the end of 1953) reach almost 2,000 miles an hour and almost 200,000 feet altitude. The performance of the latest experimental prototypes can certainly triple this. Let's point out that the US Air Force has strictly forbidden its pilots to "shoot at flying saucers." (Author's Note)

The general and the special agents jumped out of their seats. Stunned, all of them looked at one another. Were they suffering a collective hallucination?

The "Voice" set them straight: *Don't try to shoot down the flying saucers. It's a friend of the Earth talking to you. Agent Ted Sullivan is right. The Denebians are not the only ones operating on your planet. In your present state of technological knowledge you couldn't do a thing against the flying discs. You'd have to reach... The "Others" are keeping watch and will reveal themselves to you at the right time.*

When these mystifying words had faded away the silence was crushing. General Morgan fiddled with his thin moustache, completely flabbergasted, eyes bulging out. Ted Sullivan had turned white.

"Gentlemen," the General whispered after sitting back down, knowing perfectly well the underground set-up of the Pentagon and its sound system, "I can assure you that this *voice* did not come from any of our broadcasting systems. Plus, the Electronic Eye on the speaker never turned on. Our transmission, therefore, is out of the question. Besides, you must have noticed that the *voice* seemed to be coming out of thin air, in the middle of the room. It's extraordinary but we've just received a message from an extra-terrestrial being!"

"He... or rather his voice said *Denebian* when speaking of the green monsters," one of the agents said, looking around as if searching for the mysterious *He*.

"I presume that *He* meant *coming from Deneb* or more precisely from a planet orbiting this star... It's absolutely extraordinary! In fact, everything about this adventure is extraordinary! Deneb... This sun is 400 light years away from Earth. It's unimaginable that spaceships could travel such a distance. And yet, I believe it."

"But what's awaiting us? And where did that voice come from?"

CHAPTER NINE

In the flying saucer piloted by Yuln whipping through space at 22 miles altitude, Zimko turned off the tele-projection sound. All his friends looked at him in surprise. For what reason and to whom was he giving advice?

"When flying over Washington on his way to Alaska," he explained, "Nylak pointed his tele-projector at the Pentagon, thereby catching a meeting presided over by General Morgan with the best special agents of Project Saucer. Nylak immediately reported their discussion to me and I figured it best to send them a message."

The Polarian told them briefly about the meeting and concluded, "Since they're not ready, the Earthlings should in no way fight the saucers... whose friendly or hostile origins they can't judge. Their entrance on the scene of the secret war we are waging against the Denebians would be premature and hobble our actions. For, despite their good intentions, the Earthlings could shoot down our ships and our enemies' indistinctly. Therefore, I hope that General Morgan takes my advice in consideration and that he'll wait..."

"Wait for what exactly?" Kariven asked.

"The decision of the *Brahytma*, the King of the World," the Man from Outer Space answered slowly. "We Polarians reign over an infinite number of planets spread throughout the Galaxy. But each of these planets has a King, unknown to its inhabitants, a King whom only the very rare initiates know and contact. Thus, on Earth, we have a secret permanent base that was built millions of years ago. Civilizations come and go, reach the apex of knowledge or fall into the abyss of bestiality just as the progressive planetary cycles require. But during all these manifestations of intelligent life, during these hundreds of thousands of centuries, there are astounding beings who reign in secret over the Earth, coming and going as well, one after another on the throne of the King of the World."

"So, when there were the now lost continents of Lemuria, Gondwana, Mu and Atlantis, a King of the World was living on Earth? A King they sometimes called the Grand Instructor?" Kariven asked, remembering the adventures during his time travel[104].

"Yes, Kariven, just like today there reigns another King of the World, Brahytma, who Himself, on His death, will be replaced by another Genie and so on until the end of ages. But the leaders or governments of nations have never known about His presence. The King of the World doesn't literally reign but just watches over and watches out for the world. He watches over the slow evolution of man and regularly communicates to us the results of his observations. When an *entire* civilization is in danger—I'm not talking about the kind of wars that have happened so far—the King of the World alerts us to act, because His role is not to act. He is, if you want, the Guardian Angel of humanity… of its *Destiny*.

"In your year 1945, Brahytma alerted us: the Earthlings had unleashed a pretty rudimentary form of the forces of nature, nuclear energy. The first experimental bomb had been tested in Alamogordo in the New Mexico desert. Two other bombs, no longer experimental, soon hit Japan. This atomic power is a danger to humanity in its present state, which is borderline barbarian. After the A bomb you developed the H-bomb, which will inevitably be followed by another weapon capable of annihilating all life on the planet!

"Therefore, in 1945 the Space Legion contacted by the King of the World left Kodha, the capital planet of the Pole Star, and came to reoccupy their original bases in your solar system on Mars and Venus and now on the Moon.[105] I was named Chief of Operations of Sector Earth. Since that date the flying saucers have been patrolling the skies to the utter

---

[104] See *The Time Spiral*. (Author's Note)

[105] See *Operation Aphrodite*. (Author's Note)

amazement of those who see them. Naturally we've watched the Earth all the time on board our disc-shaped spacecraft, but it's only since that time that our visits became more frequent[106]."

"That's incredible," Doniatchka gasped. "I think I'm dreaming. But where is your permanent base and how could it escape the curiosity of Earthlings?"

"Our base, which is called Agharti[107] and is where Brahytma the King of the World has his palace, has always escaped explorers and other travelers because it was built inside a mountain. Agharti is an underground base buried deep in the unexplored mountains of Eastern Tibet, somewhere between Djogar-Tong and Barka-Tala. Let's just say that it's in the province of Khan in the Eastern Trans-Himalaya. That's as precise as I can get."

"Tibet…" Kariven looked thoughtfully at his two partners in adventure. "Does that remind you of anything?"

"And how!" Angelvin uttered. "That reminds me of Bakrahna, the Buddhist citadel where we almost lost our lives[108]."

---

[106] Indeed, the first flying discs of our Atomic Age made their ever more frequent appearances starting in 1945. However, the legends and traditions of all peoples on Earth make allusion to mysterious "flying chariots" (Vimanas) and other "aerial vehicles occupied by "beings from the heavens". We find their trace among the Hindus millennia ago and long before that among the Atlantans; see *The Flying Saucers Come from Another World*, q.v. (Author's Note)

[107] The oldest traditions in Asia mention this fantastic secret city; see *Beasts, Men and Gods* by Ferdinand Ossendowski (1925). (Author's Note)

[108] See *La Dimension X* [*Dimension X*] by Jimmy Guieu. (Author's Note) A 1953 novel by Guieu in which Kariven locates the lost city of Bakrahna in Tibet where seven old men and their army of Yeti plot to take over the world.

"The King of the World knows all about your exploits," the Polarian said. "Glad to know that you're by my side he authorized me *just this very instant* to bring you to Agharti."

Indeed, while the Man from Outer Space was talking he had communicated psychically with Brahytma. Dumbstruck to say the least, Kariven, Dormoy and Angelvin all had a look on their face that betrayed their surprise.

"So, we're going to... Agharti?"

"We are there," Zimko pronounced slowly, amused by their quizzical expressions.

"We... We're under the Earth? I mean in the underground Polarian base?" Jenny stammered skeptically.

"We haven't landed yet, though," Dormoy observed, sticking his nose against the window of the cockpit.

Through the translucent material he saw them diving down a kind of gray wall glinting with metal.

"We're in a giant pit 150 feet in diameter," Yuln informed them as she watched the dials on her instrument panel. "We haven't landed yet because we're going down over 3,000 feet in the heart of the mountain. Only the Polarians who belong to the Space Legions know the location of this access pit to the Forbidden Realm. The rocky mass that covers it on top swings open at the psychic command of the pilots wanting to get into the underground base. Your radars and other locating devise will never be able to detect our mental waves operating the mechanism to open it. And since there are always thick clouds blanketing the mobile rock that serves as a lid, we have no fear of being seen by a plane or a wandering Sherpa."

"We can get out. The disc has landed."

No noise or bump, however, had signaled their landing.

When they left the flying saucer, an unexpected and paradoxical sight filled them with wonder. The material on the ground could have passed for concrete, but strangely elastic concrete. The Earthlings and their Polarian friends were under a huge, vaulted ceiling of blue metal, at least 5,000 feet in diameter, irradiating a light as bright as the day. In the middle of the gigantic "bell" stood Agharti, the secret Polarian base on Earth. The extraordinary Forbidden Realm—a harmonious assembly of cubes and rhomboids in polished metal—reflected the dazzling light of the dome and shimmered in a weird blue with yellow sparkles. An incalculable number of big windows pierced the terraced facades. The buildings, connected by interlacing, aerial paths, rose up from their wide base to over 1,500 feet tall. On the whole, Agharti looked like a gigantic cone formed of different sized buildings, arranged in tiers and pointing toward the summit. At the top of the terraced base was an imposing palace, as clear as glass and glimmering with multicolored fires. Its domes and turrets, also transparent, made it the jewel of an architectural style unknown on Earth.

1,300 feet above the base, in the blue vault, a giant chimney led up to the surface. Overwhelmed by the majesty and impressive silence of the place, Kariven and his companions did not dare say a word. Fascinated, they contemplated this Polarian masterpiece that had defied centuries and millennia in the heart of our planet, all the while watching over the maintenance of our civilization.

Zimko slipped his arm around Tlyka waist and turning his eyes to the wonderful city he spoke to the Earthlings, "You're the first humans to enter Agharti. The transparent palace on top of the base belongs to Brahytma, the King of the World. We're expected…"

Walking behind the Polarian, they headed toward a raised path with a very shiny metal surface, a kind of wide, purple ribbon. With a wave of his hand Zimko invited them to get on the ribbon, which seemed to be vibrating gently. Kariven took Yuln's arm and both of them climbed onto the path that went up to the city. They felt themselves becoming light and instantly lost all awareness of their weight. Just like their friends they were floating, gradually rising off the ground.

Zimko reassured them psychically, *We've entered the gravito-magnetic field of the lifting path. It makes you feel like you're losing your weight. In fact, the field inverses the polarity of our atomic structure and transforms us into a "pole" of the same polarity as the Earth. By varying the intensity of our "energy charge", the field lifts us up through progressive impulses.*

In spite of the total absence of danger Doniatchka clung fearfully to Dormoy. Angelvin, holding Jenny's hand, tried to "stay in place" by wiggling back and forth against the invisible, propulsive coils of the gravito-magnetic field.

The lifting path wound around the Polarian city over broad streets. Seen from on high, the few oval vehicles floating around could have passed for cars. Scantily dressed Polarian men and women were walking around, mostly in couples, and all of them gave a friendly salute to Zimko and his group.

At the intersection of two aerial paths the Polarian stopped abruptly. He'd just seen one of his old friends and called out to him in English, "Kn'toog! It's been ten years since we've seen each other... but Vrin'ha!" he added on recognizing the pretty girl on the bronze man's arm.

The two of them were wearing a kind of mauve sweater and spotless white bodysuit. On their chests was embroidered a big badge in the form of a spindle-shaped rocket ship intersected by a zigzagging lightning bolt.

"We were working in the Cygnus sector," Kn'toog also spoke in English. "After a long mission Vrin'ha and I got a break from our respective units and decided to meet on this planet." He gave him a tender look and added, "When there's two, the Agharti base always has lots of nice things to do."

"Is it calm in your sector?" Yuln asked after introducing her Earthling friends.

"Nah," Kn'toog frowned in disappointment, "we had some run-ins with those damned Denebians on and around planet 17 of the star Cygnus 61. Routine missions, really, but generally the situation is calm, too calm in my opinion. These green demons must be cooking something up in another corner of the galactic zone."

"You know it," Zimko agreed. "They're focusing on this solar system. It wouldn't surprise me if open war broke out on

Earth... before too long. But let's forget about our duties for the time being. Where are you staying?"

"In the Iltug block. Come and spend the night in our *Dream Synthesizer*."

The two young Polarians bid them farewell and continued on their romantic way in the heart of the mysterious, underground city. Kariven was puzzled and wondered what Kn'toog meant by "spend the night in our Dream Synthesizer.

The Dream Synthesizer is a wonderful thing, my dear, Yuln whispered in his mind. *You'd never want to "leave". You'll experience it for yourself... if you want.*

They arrived in front of the gigantic, transparent palace. But the façade, richly decorated with multicolored, geometric designs, had no door! A stairway with huge steps brought them up to a clear wall whose decorations seemed to sink into the mass, disappearing in endless relief and a profusion of bright colors.

"Go on in," Zimko invited.

Doniatchka tilted her head to one side, baffled. "Go in? But where?"

"Follow me," is all he said.

He walked calmly toward the wall and... melted into it, vanished. Yuln dragged Kariven after her and they vanished only to come out in a grand hall with emerald green walls that looked like they were gently rippling.

"You know," Zimko explained, "that between the atoms in matter—whether it's the human body or anything else—there's an empty space, a comparatively endless void at the atomic level. Thanks to variations in the gravito-magnetic field that pervades the palace, the energy charges of our atoms are modified and, in a way, tuned to a compatible polarity with respect to the atomic structure of the walls. We can, therefore, pass through walls, our atoms 'passing' between its atoms, a little like a bunch of ball bearings passing through a big sieve. Only here there's no friction. It's very simple."

"Quite," Doniatchka poked fun and grinned clownishly.

In the same way they entered a purplish-blue wall that appeared to be the end of the hall and come out in a semi-circular room about 100 feet in diameter and 65 feet high.

Jenny and the young Russian stared at the center of the room, unblinking. Under a huge, transparent globe a bronzed man was sitting on a kind of blue, opalescent throne, watching them approach. He was dressed in a leotard with flashes of gold and looked around 30 years old. On his head was a big, red helmet with a dozen electrodes sticking out, connected to multicolored cables that ran into a control panel within arm's reach of the weird creature.

Brahytma, the King of the World, was over six and a half feet tall. His impassive face, titanic shoulders, black leotard and strange helmet added to the inexplicable feeling of awkwardness that oppressed his visitors.

Zimko, Yuln and Tlyka bowed their heads respectfully and raised their right hand. Gravely impressed the Earthlings did the same. An indefinable smile crossed the hermetic face of Brahytma and his telepathic, neutral voice vibrated in their minds:

Welcome to Agharti, Earth-Polarian Brothers. My different appearance and my strange get-up under this psycho-planetary receptor are shocking to you Earthlings, I see in your minds. You weren't expecting to find the King of the World as an ANDROID... since I am an android, a biological robot, half-human and half-artificial. The enormous psychic work of the King of the World—capturing the thoughts of hundreds of thousands of Earthlings at the same time—is beyond the abilities, however unimaginable, of the Polarians who designed me. Only an Android endowed with an electronic super-brain can survey the leading human brains: scientists, politicians, religious leaders and other personalities of earth's civilization.

During the ten centuries of my reign, three of which are still to come, I have watched over the security of the world, meaning external security because the "little" wars of men up until the Atomic Age were not serious enough to warrant my intervention. But in freeing nuclear energy Man, who is not yet evolved on the path of Wisdom, has forced me to sound the alarm. In his foolhardy tests on forces that he knows little about, Man risks exterminating the human race. Furthermore, his atomic explosions have drawn the Denebians, hungry for conquest, into the solar system. Obviously the scientists could never accept that their atomic explosions were detected IN-STANTLY by the Denebians. They would deny the fact, arguing that the light from the bombs takes 400 years to reach the Deneb system at 186,000 miles per second. They don't know that the Denebians—and Polarians as well, fortunately!—have spaceships and interstellar viewers that work at absolute speed. Such means render it possible to communicate and travel from one end of the Galaxy to the other... at the speed of thought!

These same scientists refuse to accept that extra-terrestrial beings might be living comfortably on this planet. They imagine that other planets must be surrounded by a toxic, unbreathable atmosphere. This is true for some but one must not make generalizations. The Polarians, for example, live on several planets with an atmosphere absolutely identical to Earth's. It's not the same for the original world of the Denebians, but these cursed creatures don't care because they're sympodic and can adapt automatically to almost any place. They are as comfortable in ammoniac-cyanogens as they are in Earth's oxygen.

What you have to keep in mind and communicate later, Earth Friends, is that your planet is threatened on two sides: first by the invaders from space, then by man himself playing mindlessly with the forces imprisoned in matter. But the Polarians are watching over you now with me. Our mission is to deter the Denebian threat.

I'm glad to have seen you, Earthlings, and I wish you a peaceful stay in Agharti with your Polarian brothers and sisters.

The inner voice went quiet in each of their heads. The visitors bowed and left, shaken up by this Android King who secretly controlled the thoughts of the leading Earthlings and played an important role for mankind.

Leaning on the guardrail of a spiral path they contemplated the base of Agharti, dreamily, savoring the extraordinary peace of mind.

"The whole city is washed in an atmosphere and in patches of regenerative radiation," the Polarian explained. "That's why those who come here feel a physical and mental euphoria making them more relaxed than ever. Agharti, contrary to what you might believe, is not a strategic base. It's a place of rest and distractions or of everything that a man or woman from the Space Legion could ask for. Of course there's this squadron of flying saucers that we saw parked on the edge of the city, but they're only reconnaissance ships. Most of the Polarian force is stationed off Earth.

"We come here especially to spend a nice and completely safe break, or as you would say 'a leave'. You must have noticed that the aerial paths and roads on the ground are not generally taken except by couples. After successive separations on space or planetary missions, the Polarian couples who are romantically involved meet here in Agharti or in another base on Mars, Venus or the Moon, or even in another solar system if they want."

Imperceptibly the bright blue light of the dome darkened into an electric blue of night. Like a giant planetarium with stars twinkling and forming constellations. They could even see there on a phosphorescent band going from one side of the horizon to the other the powdery stretch of the eternal Milky Way.

After strolling through the wide streets of Agharti for a while, Zimko and his companions stopped in front of an octagonal building, very tall with hundreds of big windows of different colors.

"We're here in the Iltung block," he said, entering a lighted porch. "This building is exclusively dedicated to rooms with Dream Synthesizers."

The Polarian stepped up to a sliding door and put his hand flat against a chrome plate embedded in the wall. The door slid open silently. Zimko and Tlyka went in, followed by Yuln, Kariven and the other Earthlings. Lighted metal walls formed a cube. Automatically on entering the cube they lowered their heads to avoid hitting a staircase and looked down... which made them cry out in terror. Kariven felt a horrendous fear twist his guts. Under their feet was empty space, bottomless space and yet without any support they were standing up and not falling! Zimko turned on the lifting gravito-magnetic field. In a few seconds this shocking "floorless elevator" took them up to the 97th floor.

Kn'toog and his friend Vrin'ha welcomed them into their sumptuous apartment—oh, how different it was from the beautiful terrestrial apartments! Pictures in relief whose figures moved and acted naturally were hung on the walls. In one frame was a splendid, 3D, Polarian "Eve," lascivious and smiling her *animated* smile. The realism of these bio-dioramas was striking. Movements, 3D, sounds and colors, everything was a startling reflection of life! The furniture, although very similar to the ultra-modern furniture of Earthlings, changed color and form constantly depending on what angle it was seen from.

While the young hostess in a ravishing, multi-colored two-piece bikini was chatting with Yuln and her friends, Kn'toog circulated among the guests with a rectangular box full of small, colorful cylinders. The explorers took one each and like a cigarette put it to their lips, imitating Zimko.

Angelvin was about to offer Jenny a light when the Polarian stopped him. "You don't smoke it, Robert! It's solid liquid. You tasted it a little while ago..."

Rather disappointed the ethnographer put away his lighter. But he cheered up right away when the solid liqueur melted very slowly between his lips—it was exquisite.

Kn'toog went over to a small control panel on the wall and pushed a red button. Without knowing what happened our Earthling friends along with the Polarians found themselves in a jungle, standing in the middle of a clearing! Heady odors and the humid heat of the green forest mingled with the cries of monkeys, the warbling of birds and, in the distance, the muffled rhythm of a tom-tom.

"Oh no, dear!" Vrin'ha complained, "Not the Earth jungle, we were just there."

Kn'toog shrugged his shoulders, smiled, and kept enjoying the liqueur stick. Vrin'ha went to a huge, perfumed flower, parted the foliage and found the keypad of the geo-stereogenic selector, where she firmly pressed the blue button. Before the Earthlings could get over their first surprise, still as if by magic, they were transported to a sandy beach on the Pacific Ocean! Palm trees swayed on the shore, gently caressed by an evening breeze. Soft music and Hawaiian chanting floated through the scented air.

"Oh, Vrin'ha! The Pacific Islands again!" Nylak teased. "I think our friends will prefer the Dream Synthesizer."

That said, he pressed another button on the keypad that was hidden behind a rock this time, being washed by the iridescent waves. The charming landscape disappeared, covered by thick darkness. As if born out nothingness the still blurry walls of a phosphorescent grotto took shape.

"Yuln, have you thought this through?" Zimko put his hand on his sister's shoulder.

Thought through *what*? Kariven thought, intrigued.

"Yes, Zim," she whispered, nodding her head twice.

"Be happy, little sister," he smiled and tapped her cheek.

"What's with all this mystery?" Kariven asked, looking around.

His friends had just melted into the darkness. Holding the Earth girls in their arms. The Polarian couples of Zimko and Tlyka, Kn'toog and Vrin'ha also faded into the expanding darkness of the phosphorescent cave.

"It's only a mystery to you and your compatriots, Kariven. The Dream Synthesizer, as it name implies, has the ability to materialize dreams, all thought-dreams. If you and I go farther into the Enchanted Grotto—that's the poetic name of the Dream Synthesizer—our dreams will become real."

"But," he pulled her to him, "isn't that wonderful? Isn't that what we both desire... without having admitted it?"

"Yes, I desire it as much as you... But for both of us to enter the Synthesizer means... a kind of pyscho-physical union..."

"You mean a marriage?"

"Not a marriage, not as you Earthlings understand it, but something more solid than a scrap of paper with administrative scribbles written on it. For us Polarians to enter the Dream Synthesizer means that we are forever bound to each other by 'emotional ties'."

"That's what I said," Kariven kissed the girl. "It's wonderful!"

And hugging each other, inflamed by delight in a torrent of subtle radiations, they walked into the magical maze of the Enchanted Grotto. Forgetting the world and the Universe they advanced toward the Dream, which tenaciously took hold of their minds, of their hearts, of their bodies...

Kariven, wake up! The Denebians have started the psychological war!

It was hard for Kariven to open his eyes. He closed and opened them again several times wondering where he was. Something silky was caressing his cheek. He looked to his side, without moving his head, and all the memories came flooding back to him. Yuln's sleeping face was lying in the hollow of his arm. They were in a golden room, unbelievably luxurious, where wisps of evanescent gas, multi-colored and delightfully scented, were floating in the air. How did they get here? Was this the "end" of the Enchanted Grotto? Of the Dream Synthesizer grotto where he and the adorable Girl from Space had spent unforgettable moments?

Kariven, we're taking off in 15 minutes, the telepathic voice of Zimko rang out his head for a second time.

The other Earthlings were as astonished as the anthropologist. One after another, they woke up in an unfamiliar place with their partners next to them. Each floundered in semi-consciousness, drowsy from the ineffable delight that, thanks to the Dream Synthesizer, would never leave them for the rest of their life.

Still, Zimko's psychic call brought them promptly back to reality. *The Denebians have started the psychological war! Departure in 15 minutes!*

When they were all together in the "transformation room" of their hosts, Zimko said, "I just received a message from the King of the World. The Denebian monsters have shot down a few airplanes over the United States and Russia."

"That's no psychological war!" Kariven fumed.

"It is, and you'll find out why. These wretches managed to intercept and capture a squadron of Polarian saucers between Mars and Jupiter! Then they used a diabolical trick. When the Air Force jet fighters were in sight, they sent one of these flying saucers, with its pilots paralyzed, after them. Guided by remote control the disc disintegrated one of the planes. The green monsters have obviously perfected a new technology to accomplish this exploit.

"Seeing that they were under attack the fighters shot back at the saucer, which was just drifting now, and downed it. Of course the Denebians were cruising quietly at a very high altitude and were practically undetectable. The fighter pilots, therefore, thought they had shot down a hostile saucer. In the wreckage of the ship they found the mangled bodies of the Polarians and logically concluded that they had finally unmasked the real enemies of Earth!

"This Machiavellian set-up was also orchestrated in Russia. The fact that two hostile nations, Eastern and Western, are both convinced that a common enemy attacked them, will end the cold war. They'll even end up joining forces, without misgivings, and fall into the hands of the Denebians, whom they will take for allies come to their rescue from a distant planet! The situation is serious. We have to act quickly. Come…"

They hurried to the first aerial road and jumped on the gravito-magnetic pathway. Five seconds later they were running full speed across the underground airfield. Some Polarians, alerted by the Android who watched over the security of the world, were also running to the flying saucers parked in the base. One after another, the spaceships took off, shooting up the huge chimney out of Agharti. The squadron flew out of the giant pit and soared into the sky at terrifying speeds. The pilots had their instructions and steered their ships to specific destinations.

"We've been played!" Zimko raged, pacing the floor of the cockpit. "The King of the World found the location of the new Denebian base on Earth. If we had time for 20 questions, I'd let you guess... The giant disc Number 2 landed in exactly the same place as the enemy base we captured. It was so simple! While our probes and detectors were searching other continents, the new base, after being informed by the saucer that was destroyed by our giant cigar, just strolled into Australia and landed in Victoria Desert."

General Morgan was again with his special agents called to an emergency meeting in the basements of the Pentagon. He was reviewing the situation before organizing the defense.

"Ted Sullivan was right!" he announced, pale and haggard. "Our jet fighters just shot down a flying saucer that had attacked them. Our technicians found three mangled corpse in the wreckage of the disc. Three corpses of beings that are physically identical to us but whose skin is copper or bronze. Your fears were well founded, Sullivan. There really are beings other than the reptilian pseudo-men on Earth. But contrary to what we feared, it wasn't the green monsters who attacked us, it was the... the *others, the bronze men!* We have to act quickly and strike back with every weapon we have at our disposal. We have to track down these bronze men..."

"But, General," an agent broke in, "we can't arrest every person on the street who is really tan."

"No, but I'm going to order a general mobilization with the support of all the police and armed forces. We're going to put the entire territory under surveillance so that not even a doghouse will escape our search. We have to find these men from space at any cost since they must be hiding somewhere in the United States or elsewhere. With the cooperation of other countries we'll find them and destroy them!"

Zimko's flying saucer along with Kn'toog's was flying over the Australian continent at 300 miles altitude. Yuln adjusted her viewer and got a close-up of the site of the Denebian base. In the heart of the desert a dot, made bright by the tele-projector, appeared on the screen. The young Polarian pressed three keys on the electronic keyboard. On the screen of a ballistic calculator a parabola of bright points lit up: the dot marking the enemy base was exactly under the curve of this parabola. Yuln pressed a button and waited.

The two flying saucers, at 30,000 miles an hour, dove toward the ground and in a fraction of a second followed the parabola drawn by the electronic calculator. Just as they were speeding like lightning over the spaceship camouflaged in the sand dune, a ghastly, purple flash lit up the desert. The Denebian base with its 500 occupants had been disintegrated. In its place was nothing but a huge crate with walls of vitrified sand.

At pretty much the same time in Alaska, France, Russia, the USA, China and Argentina, the Polarian flying saucers tracked down and disintegrated the spaceships of the green monsters that were chasing military aircraft so they could shoot them down and crash one of their captured Polarian discs.

The spaceships of the Polarians were able to save their brothers paralyzed in their own ships and freefalling after the destruction of the enemy. Grabbed by the gravito-magnetic beams they were brought back to Agharti, the permanent Polarian base under the Tibetan mountains.

Zimko stood staring, breathing calmly, and concentrating for a moment in the middle of the cockpit. After 30 seconds his face came alive again.

"All the Denebian flying saucers have been disintegrated. The Polarian pilots engaged over the various continents just sent me their reports."

"The nightmare is over," Doniatchka sighed, wrapping her arms around Dormoy's neck. "We're finally going to be able to live happily."

"Don't kid yourself," the Polarian burst her bubble. "We've simply won the first round. It's a fact: there are no more Denebians on Earth… at least I hope not. But in the distant galactic zone of Deneb, 400 light years away from this solar system, they still exist and are a constant threat to your planet. If their saucers were able to capture some of our ships, we can be sure that the green monsters have recently perfected some secret weapons that we know nothing about. Faced with this new factor I sent a message to the King of the World. Within an hour the Earth will be protected at 32,000 feet altitude by a neutralizing field, a protective envelope, that the Denebian flying saucers won't be able to break through."

Kariven took Yuln's hands and exclaimed, "But then the world is saved! We can go back to France and, like Doniatchka said, live in peace and quiet."

Zimko hesitated, looking at all his Earthling companions, his faithful friends who had risked their lives so many times at his side. He smiled warmly at his sister Yuln, glad to see her happy with his friend Kariven. He also watched Dormoy and Doniatchka, Angelvin and Jenny, standing together, waiting, hoping for some hopeful words from him that would seal their happiness.

Zimko took Tlyka in his arms, kissed her tenderly and turned to his companions, "Yes, Friends, we can live happily. We're heading for France and we can set up there and hope that Fate will smile on us."

While he was saying this, expressing a certainty that he was far from truly feeling, the Man from Outer Space sent a psychic message to General Morgan and all his special agents in the Pentagon.

Kariven and the others had not even noticed Zimko's subtle movement to press the button of the psychophonic tele-projector. However, the message was not sent only to the US. General Gorochenko with his general staff in the Kremlin also received it, to the great astonishment of all of them.

"No, General Morgan! No, General Gorochenko!" Zimko's voice shouted, echoing strangely in Washington and Moscow in the ears of the highest leaders of the two hostile nations.

"The bronze men are not the enemies of the Earth. My previous order remains valid. Don't shoot at the flying saucers. The bronze men whose corpses you recovered from the disc wreckage and examined, these men, I guarantee you, are your friends. Don't trust the green monsters. The Earth, by a miracle, barely escaped their attacks aimed at throwing your minds into confusion. We won the first stage of this interplanetary war, but God alone knows the twists and turns of Fate.

"Peace has returned… Forget your quarrels and your hatred between nations. Love each other and be united. The threat is gone for the time being, but *the Earth is not permanently safe from an invasion from outer space…* Don't ever forget this, Generals. All men are brothers and should be united.

"One day you will understand why you should be…"